Winter's Maiden 1

Winter's Magic Part 1

L. STARLA

To request permission, contact the author:
laelia@starlaarts.com

Cover illustration © Jana Hoffmann
Graphics & book design by L. Starla
Editing by Felix Staica

First edition 2021.

ISBN-13 978-0-6488424-3-9

Self-published.

Author's Note

This book contains coarse language and explicit scenes, including depictions of sexual violence that may trigger some people. Reader discretion is advised.

Dedication

—This one is for Mum, the woman who brought magic into my world.

Epigraph

"This is why magic is worse even than quantum physics. Because, while both spit in the eye of common sense, I've never yet had a Higgs bosun turn up and try to have a conversation with me."
—Ben Aaronovitch

Playlist

"So Say We All" by Landroid

"Run" by Dan White

"Stay" by The Score

"Believer" by Imagine Dragons

"The Hype" by Twenty One Pilots

"Night Time" by The Birthday Massacre

"Evoke" by Grey Hearts Red

"Art of Doubt" by Metric

"Legends are Made" by Sam Tinnesz

"Only Bones" by RedHook

"Wonderful Life" by Bring Me the Horizon

"Hallelujah (So Low)" by Editors

"Blood Like Lemonade" by Sneaker Pimps

"In This Moment" by Reside

"Born for This" by The Score

"The Hunter" by Adam Jensen

"Deceiver" by The Beautiful Monument

"Despicable" by grandson

"Alligator" by Of Monsters and Men

Playlist available on Spotify.

Prologue

Nine Years Ago

'So, I will be a knight of Camelot, Lana will be the princess,' Liam lunged forward with his plastic sword pointed at his brother, 'and Brendan, you can be the roguish bandit. It will be my mission to rescue Lana from you.'

Brendan crossed his arms, scowling. 'Why can't I be the knight for a change?'

Stepping back, Liam frowned. 'Because I'm the older brother. Besides, I'm the one with the warrior's name.'

Alannah looked at both cousins hoping they were not about to start fighting again.

'That's a stupid reason. I wanna turn at being the hero.' Brendan stamped his foot and maintained his stance.

Liam shook his head. 'You make a much better rogue than I do. I don't know how to be a bad guy.'

Brendan looked at Alannah. 'What do you think? Who do you want to rescue you?'

She sighed. 'You know I love you both, but you do make a better rogue, Brendan.'

Liam beamed. 'Well, that settles it. Lana, you can go hide now.'

Turning to face the house, Brendan huffed, closed his eyes, and started counting.

Alannah took off, running across the lawn, into the scrubland bordering her family's rural property on the Fleurieu Peninsula. She passed gum trees, wattles, grevilleas, and bottlebrushes until she reached another manicured section of garden with lawn, flower beds, and a fenced enclosure full of smelly plants Mum called herbs. She ducked behind the giant weeping willow forming a centrepiece and provided ample concealment.

'Ready or not, here I come,' Brendan's faint voice cried out in the distance.

Her heart was pounding as she leaned back against the rough bark of the tree trunk. *I should have a few minutes to catch my breath before needing to leave this refuge.* She thanked the Goddess for the cool breeze and comforting shade. Despite the recent break in the weather, Alannah's pale skin was already blistering from an hour of playing in the sun.

Liam sped past her hideout and took cover behind the Moreton Bay Fig several metres away. He looked at her, bringing a finger to his lips to keep her quiet and turned his attention to the front of the yard.

Wondering how far away Brendan was, Alannah chanced a peek around the tree. *Oh Gods!* He was coming straight for her.

'*Run, Princess!* I will protect you!' Liam cried.

She surged on, approaching the rear boundary, and running out of ground to put between herself and Brendan. Stopping behind the Mulberry tree, she watched as Liam jumped out, sword in hand.

He took a fighting stance. 'En garde!'

Brendan drew his own plastic blade, and the battle began. Alannah waited with bated breath. Brendan's technique was improving, and he was forcing Liam back. Her knight was losing this battle. Knowing it was only a matter of time before the rogue reached her, she decided to take advantage of his distracted state to circle back, so she flew past them.

It did not take long for Brendan to realise what she was doing, and his own footsteps were rapidly gaining on her. In no time, he caught up, wrapping his arms around her. Tackling her to the ground, he laughed. 'Gotcha! Now you're mine, Princess.' Rolling Alannah onto her back, he straddled her, pressing a kiss on her lips, and winking.

Alannah's cheeks flushed as she squealed. '*Help me!* Sir Liam, where are you?'

'*Fear not, Princess, I'm coming!*' With that, Liam grappled the rogue away from her, pinning him to the ground. 'Run back to the castle!'

She did not hesitate to sprint back to the house, where she wrapped her arms around one of the steel pillars on the porch.

Liam was not far behind and he rushed to hug her. 'Are you okay, Princess? Did that rogue hurt you?'

Returning the embrace, she smiled, looking up into his beautiful blue eyes. 'I am fine, thank you, oh brave and honourable knight.' She planted a kiss on his cheek.

Blushing, he returned the favour with a quick peck on the lips and cried out as he thrust his sword in the air, 'Victory for Camelot once again!'

With the game over, the three of them sat around the outdoor table to enjoy a cool softdrink.

'I want to marry you one day, Lana,' Liam declared, grinning at her.

She smiled warmly. 'I would be honoured.'

'But *I* want to marry Lana!' Brendan protested.

'Don't be silly, brother, I'm the one she wants. Right Lana?' They both looked at her with unwavering focus.

Oh hell! She loved them both. *How can I choose?* 'Well…'

'*Alannah! Come here please sweetie. Daddy and I need to talk to you.*' Her mother Aileen's voice called from inside.

Answering her summons, she found her parents sitting in the family room. 'Yes, Mummy?'

Aileen smiled. 'Take a seat, honey. We have some important news to share.'

She sat between them.

'Hey beautiful girl,' Dennis, her father, kissed her on the forehead. 'I received a really good job offer, which I have decided to accept. This will mean a lot more money for toys and outings.'

'That's great Daddy! Congratulations.'

'Thanks sweetheart. There's one catch though…' He paused a moment and Alannah's stomach twisted into knots. 'The job is in Melbourne, so we are going to have to move.'

Tears brimmed in her eyes. 'But why, Daddy? I love living here with the boys.'

Mummy put her arm around Alannah. 'I know you do, darling, but this is an important opportunity for Daddy.'

'Well I don't want to go!' Storming off to her room, she slammed the door. She flung herself on her bed and cried her heart out.

Chapter One
The Present

Alannah jumped out of her dad's Mercedes and marched across the freshly cut lawn in front of her Melbourne high school. She stopped at a picnic table to meet her two best friends, Emma and Melissa. The three of them, dressed head to toe in black, wore matching pale foundation, thick black eyeliner, and blood red lipstick. The trio had adopted the look after a sudden aneurysm had ended Alannah's mother's life three years ago. Not that Alannah's porcelain complexion required any cosmetics to achieve the pallor she wanted.

As they made their entrance, fellow students stepped aside and gawked at them.

Zac, a rugby player who also happened to be the hottest guy in year eleven (according to an official poll), moved to block their path. 'Oh look, it's the Graveyard Girls!' Gesturing toward his groin with a lewd grin, he continued, 'Hey vamp tramps, you wanna suck my blood?' He high fived his mate Bryce and they bent over laughing.

Rolling her eyes, Alannah pushed past them and continued walking along the corridor.

Emma followed suit, turning to her, and pretending to stick her fingers down her throat. 'Zac is so gross!'

'Yeah, but you'd bone him given the chance,' Melissa added.

When they reached their lockers, Alannah dumped her bag inside. She was about to retrieve her books when she felt a hand on her backside. Grabbing the offending limb, she spun around and pushed its owner against the neighbouring lockers. Her breathing eased when she saw who he was.

'Jumpy much?' Cole grinned at her beneath his long, choppy fringe.

'Sorry.' She smiled coyly, following up on her apology with a heated kiss on her boyfriend's mouth, savouring the cool mint taste on his breath and the smell of his earthy fragrance.

'Ick, get a room you two!' Emma complained.

Alannah broke away from the kiss, pressed her head against Cole's chest, and turned to face her friend. 'You're just jealous you're not getting any.'

'Damn straight! I'm…' A loud horn cut her off. 'Hey, I've been saved by the bell. Come on, let's get moving.' Emma closed her locker and took off.

After planting one more kiss on Cole's lips, Alannah took her books and chased after Emma. She made it to homeroom in the nick of time, yawning her way through the roll call and morning announcements. Her first period was Ancient History, the only subject she had any interest in at school. Given her Irish heritage, she was eager to learn about the Celts. As part of her research assignment, she had decided to raid the attic and dig out some of her mother's old books and papers. Casting her mind back to the previous night…

> *She was rifling through a pile of musty papers containing crests and pedigree diagrams. When she put them aside, she found a large ornate trunk made from polished wood, with brass filigree designs embellishing the corners of the locked lid. Brass medallions shaped in Celtic knots, adorned the chest and a moonstone sat in the middle of each one. When she attempted to unfasten the clasps, they did not budge.*

There must be a trick to this. *Studying the box for some time, the intricate patterns in the knotwork entranced her. Almost without thinking, she ran a finger beneath the central fastening and drew it back with a start when she pricked herself. A small drop of blood fell upon the moonstone adorning it and she heard the catch mechanism release. When she tried each of the other closures with her bloodied finger, they opened. 'How strange. They must be in a state of disrepair. Simply needed a bit more work to open.'*

Alannah gasped as she lifted the lid, discovering several tarnished, silver trinkets, including a small dagger, a carved wooden stick, a mirror, and a chalice. There were also various crystals and gems. One item caught her attention: a book bound in black leather and embossed with a silver symbol depicting two crescent moons either side of a circular design.

Before she had much time to investigate further, she heard Dad

*calling her, so she tucked the book and
the family history papers in her bag,
closed the box and ran downstairs.*

Sitting at her desk in History, she retrieved the mysterious black volume from her bookbag and read the title page: '*Leabhar Scáthanna an Clan Gheimhridh*'. *Is that Gaelic?* Alannah recognised *Gheimhridh* as the original form of her surname, Winters. After starting up her laptop, she plugged the words into a translator. 'The Winters Clan's Book of Shadows.'

'Cool book. What is it?' Emma asked from the seat next to her.

'I don't know exactly, but it was my mum's. I think it might be a family heirloom or something. It's all in Gaelic, so I need to work on translating it.'

'Neat. I wish I had some family history stuff that was relevant.' Emma ran her finger over the symbol on the cover. 'What's this mean?'

'No idea. I'm gonna Google it now.' Alannah looked for 'Celtic knot with crescent moons and circle.' The references to witchcraft did not surprise Alannah. Her mum had been interested in all that wiccan stuff and owned a shop that had sold crystals and new age music. Alannah's search results suggested the knot was probably a Triple

Moon, also known as the Triple Goddess symbol, although she could not find an exact match for the central dendriform motif.

As she delved deeper into her research on Celtic knots, she came across a familiar design known as the 'Shield'. The symbol, commonly used for protection, resembled the medallions on the old chest in the attic. She started taking down notes on symbology, deciding this would be her focus for the assignment.

She was engrossed in her work when Emma nudged her. 'You gonna respond to that?'

Alannah blinked at her friend. 'What?'

'You got called to the front office.'

'Really?' Alannah stood up. Before she left, she decided to put her mum's book in her bag. She did not want to take any chances leaving something so valuable lying around. When she reached the reception desk, her heart stopped at the sight of two uniformed police officers.

'Step into my office, please Alannah.' Principal Daniels gestured with his gnarled hand.

'But I haven't done anything wrong, I swear,' Alannah protested.

'No one is accusing you of anything, Alannah. Now please come in and take a seat.' He stepped through the door and moved behind his black particle board desk.

Alannah sat in one of the visitor's chairs, and the police officers followed. She noticed Cathy White, the school counsellor, sitting within. When the second officer—a woman with a permanent scowl on her face and upright, rigid posture—closed the door, Alannah's heart rate quickened. Directing her gaze at Mr. Daniels, she asked, 'What's this about?'

'I'm afraid these officers have some bad news for you. I'm terribly sorry, Alannah,' replied Mr. Daniels.

'Are you Alannah Winters, daughter of Dennis Wagner?' The other officer asked. She adopted a more casual pose than her partner and the delicate features of her face focused on Alannah.

'Yes. Why, what's wrong?'

'There was an incident at your home this morning. I'm sorry, Miss Winters, but your father's injuries were fatal,' the kind one replied.

Tears threatened to rain down Alannah's face for the first time in three years. Her jaw was too slack to speak, so she stared at the ladies in blue with wide eyes.

'We understand this can be a very difficult time and would like to offer a free counselling service for victims of crime in addition to the support I'm sure you will get from Mrs. White here.'

One word stood out to Alannah. 'Crime?' Her voice was barely more than a whisper.

'Yes. I'm afraid your dad stumbled upon a robbery in progress when he returned home this morning. The thief must have been armed. I'm so sorry, Miss. We have organised a safe place for you to stay until more permanent living arrangements can be made. When you are ready, we will drive you there. Take your time, we will wait outside.' She stood and left the room, along with her colleague.

Cathy put her arm around Alannah. 'Would you like me to call your friends up here to support you?'

Still unable to speak, Alannah simply nodded.

The rest of the day passed in a haze of tears and Alannah, vaguely moving from one set of arms to another until she arrived at a foster home.

Luna, the fluffy white Siberian cat, meowed and rubbed up against Alannah, who sat on the window seat of the living room. Over the last few days, she had come to share the feline's favourite pastime of watching the world go by. They had also developed a special bond, which Alannah knew was dangerous because her foster home was only temporary, but Luna, the cat, had been a great comfort to her.

Alannah was grateful the school had excused her for the time being. It would be impossible to focus on her studies in her state of mind. She sighed, gathering the fluffball up into her lap. After a little patting, Luna drifted off to sleep and Alannah returned to her trance. Memories of happier times with both of her parents filled her thoughts.

The doorbell rang, breaking Alannah from her reverie. She heard Marjorie rushing from the backyard with an infant attached to her hip. Her foster carer had been kind and considerate, but as a family day-care worker, she always had her hands full with the tiny tots and Alannah did not want to impose. At sixteen, she was generally capable of looking after herself during the day.

Marjorie ushered in the visitor and Alannah recognised the kind policewoman's voice. 'Alannah dear, Officer Smith is here to see you.' Her voice preceded her as they both walked into the room before returning to her duties with the kids outside.

'Hi Alannah. How are you holding up?' Smith asked.

Alannah shrugged. 'Surviving.'

'I see you've made a new friend here.' She looked at the cat in Alannah's lap.

This brought a slight smile to Alannah's face. 'Yeah. Luna's a sweetie.'

'I have some news for you, Alannah. Social Services have arranged a permanent home for you. I know this is likely to be a big change, but we all believe this is the best option.'

'Oh?' Alannah's heart started pounding *What sort of home am I going to?*

'It is policy to place minors with family wherever possible, so long as those family members are capable of course. The only family we have been able to track down for you are your South Australian Uncle and Aunt. I understand you lived with them as a child?'

'Yeah, that's right.' Alannah's heart quickened. *Moving interstate means leaving all my friends behind.* Her lip trembled as she turned her attention to the cat in her lap. But memories of her time in Gaeilge Shores surfaced. When she thought about living with her cousins again, her frown morphed into a smile.

'Right, well your Uncle and Aunt will be coming over for the funeral tomorrow. They will take you home with them.'

Shit! Tomorrow is too soon. Once Officer Smith left, Alannah updated Marjorie. Returning to her spot by the window, she sent Cole and her friends a message: **Please come over 2nite. We need to talk.**

Alannah's friends entered the lounge room and Marjorie gave them some privacy. After a round of hugs, Alannah slumped on the couch beside her boyfriend.

Cole drew Alannah into his arms. 'So, what's going on? Have the police caught the bastard yet?'

She sighed. 'I haven't heard any more about that.' Taking a deep breath, Alannah continued, 'But they made a more permanent living arrangement for me. I move tomorrow.'

'What?' Emma sat up. 'Move to where?'

Alannah felt Cole's grip around her tighten. She looked at him with tears in her eyes. 'I'm moving back to South Australia, to live with my Uncle Ross and his family.'

'Oh, fuck!' Cole closed his eyes and pressed his forehead against hers.

'That totally sucks balls!' Melissa cried. 'Why can't they find you somewhere in Melbourne?'

Alannah sat back and looked at her friends. 'Because these people are my only remaining family,' she conceded. 'We can still keep in touch and visit during school holidays and whatnot.'

'Yeah, but it won't be the same. School is gonna stink without you!' Emma sought Melissa's embrace and they sobbed into each other's arms.

'I'm sorry guys. It's not like I have a choice in the matter.' Alannah's own tears broke free and Cole pulled her closer.

'It's okay babe, we know. It's just, being separated from you will hurt like hell.' Cole hugged her tight.

His arms feel so good. Why do I have to leave them?

After several minutes, Melissa spoke up. 'Well, I don't fancy crying away our last night with Alannah. We should make the most of our time together. I say we watch some tacky movies and stuff ourselves with pizza for old times' sake.'

Emma wiped her eyes. 'I second that.'

'Good idea. Thanks guys.' Alannah settled in to enjoy the B-grade entertainment.

As *Sharknado*, their second film, finished, Emma stretched her arms. 'I think we need to change things up a bit before I fall asleep. How about we all share our favourite Alannah moments?'

'Brilliant,' Melissa agreed.

Alannah snorted. 'Oh gawd, guys. Please don't embarrass me!'

'Hey, this'll be good. I promise.' Emma smiled.

'Fine.' Alannah directed her gaze to Cole. 'But nothing too personal, please.'

He gave them an impish grin. 'I'll try my best.'

'Right, well I'm gonna start,' Emma declared. 'I remember the first time Alannah got drunk.'

Shaking her head, Alannah face palmed. 'Oh God, no!'

Emma giggled. 'It was at Hayley's party last year. She started touching everyone's hair and telling us how nice it felt.'

'Yes! I remember. That was hilarious.' Melissa laughed.

'Right up until she started on the other guys anyway. That's when I had to drag her away before they got any ideas,' Cole added. 'But since we're on funny moments, let's not forget the time Alannah got us to glitter bomb Zac and his buddies.' He kissed her on the cheek. 'Their reactions were priceless. I was so proud of you that day.'

'Yeah, I'm pretty sure those guys are still sparkling,' Alannah agreed.

'Hey, what about the time Alannah was giving that oral presentation where she accidentally said sex instead of six?' Melissa chuckled.

Emma bent over in hysterics.

Alannah grinned. 'That was pretty funny.'

Once Emma had recovered from her fit, she sat up. 'Okay, now for our most treasured moments. Mine was the day Alannah bought me this best friend charm.' She held up her half of the broken silver heart a small tear escaped her eye.

Melissa started to sniffle too. 'I will never forget the day I started at our school and Alannah found me sitting alone at lunch, so she dragged my arse over to sit with you guys.'

Alannah felt her eyes watering.

'Well since I probably can't mention any of the amazing sex, I guess I'll have to be soppy too.' Cole squeezed Alannah's hand before continuing, 'For me it was *my* first day of High School, which was also when Alannah started.' He looked directly into her eyes. 'The moment I saw you walk through our homeroom door; I knew I was in love. You were and still are the most beautiful girl I have ever seen.'

'Jesus, Cole.' Alannah's lips collapsed against his in a desperate kiss.

'On that note, we'll leave you lovebirds to it. See you tomorrow chickadee.' Emma stood and walked out with Melissa in tow.

Alannah stealthily led Cole to her bedroom where they spent the next few hours making love as if their lives depended upon it.

At about three in the morning, he looked at her with tearful eyes and whispered, 'Where do we go from here?'

Alannah sighed. 'I'd like to think we could make things work long-distance, but that wouldn't really be fair on either of us. We both need to move on.'

'I was worried you'd say that.' He closed his eyes as a tear trickled down his cheek. 'Can we still be friends and stay in touch?'

'Yes, of course. But please don't hold onto any hopes. Let's take life as it comes, okay?' She kissed his forehead.

''Kay.'

With that, they fell asleep in each other's arms.

It was the day of the funeral and Alannah would soon be leaving Melbourne. She had chosen to wear her favourite black lace dress and one of her mum's Celtic pendants. After running a brush through her long, black hair, she grabbed the last of her bags and dawdled to the front door.

She gave her foster parents a civil goodbye and stepped outside. Dark clouds filled the sky. They resembled her eyes; heavy with tears aching for release. She needed to hold it together a little longer, at least until she reached her father's coffin.

As soon as she spotted Aunt Nora, Alannah rushed to embrace the tall woman with brown hair and blue eyes. Her aunt's arms were warm, easing some of the tension in Alannah's muscles. 'Hi sweetheart. I'm so sorry about your dad.'

When Alannah stepped back, Uncle Ross came forward. 'Hey kiddo.' He hugged her briefly, took her bags and put them in the rental car. The family resemblance was so obvious with Ross that she looked more like him than her actual dad. She knew it was because they shared the Winters colouring: pale skin, black hair, and green eyes.

The three of them walked silently into the funeral home together and took their seats. Alannah was the last of her dad's surviving family, so the only other people in attendance were Emma and Melissa along with a few of her dad's friends and business associates. Cole had agreed it would make things harder for them both if he made an appearance, so he gave her the space she had asked for.

Once the service concluded, Alannah said her final farewells to her two best friends.

Nora turned to Alannah. 'We ought to get moving if we're gonna get our flight in time. Have you packed all of your essentials, sweetie?'

'Yeah, but what about everything else?'

'The police will box up the rest of the house and send it across. They said it isn't safe for us to go back there.' Nora placed a hand on the small of Alannah's back and led her to the car.

Ross took the driver's seat. 'Having you back home will be good, Alannah. The boys are looking forward to seeing you again.'

'Yeah, I'm excited to see them,' Alannah replied in a lack-lustre tone. It was a shame they could not be there to pay their last respects to her dad, but she understood they were busy with school. She had not seen her cousins since her mother's funeral when she was thirteen and wondered what sort of men they had grown into.

Chapter Two

The journey only took a few hours overall, but it was tiring after such an emotional day. Alannah was glad to be stepping through the familiar doors of the Federation house at the heart of Cailleach Estate. She walked along the hallway, letting the warm glow of the vintage filament globes on the timber interior soothe her.

When she reached the living room, she dumped her handbag on the table and took a moment to regard the two young men who stood to attention the moment she entered. *Christ! How much have they grown?*

Liam was easily six feet tall with arm muscles bulging from beneath the short sleeves of his Quicksilver shirt. He wore his brown hair short on the sides and spiked on top, a style that flattered him almost as much as the gorgeous smile radiating from his blue eyes and full lips. *When did he become so hot?* She could not stop looking at him, despite the smug grin taking over his visage.

Closing the distance between them, Liam caught her in a bear hug, speaking gently into her ear. 'It's good to see you again, Lana. Although I'm sorry for the circumstances that brought you here.'

Alannah's chest fluttered when Liam used the diminutive of her name, something she only liked her cousins doing. She breathed in his fresh scent, which reminded her of the ocean. 'Thanks. It's good to see you and to be home again.'

They released each other hesitantly when Brendan cleared his throat. 'Bring it Cuz.' He held his arms out and grinned.

She moved into Brendan's firm hold and the first thing she noticed was his musky cologne. He was slightly shorter than his older brother, but still taller than Alannah by at least five inches. Slimmer than Liam too, but still toned and strong enough to lift her off the ground and spin her around, prompting her to laugh for the first time all day. His black hair was medium length with an angled fringe almost covering his right eye but exposed the eyebrow ring on his left, along with a matching sleeper through his left ear.

Brendan resembled Uncle Ross the most, right down to the green eyes and porcelain skin, while Liam took after his mother more. After releasing his hold on her, Brendan led Alannah to a couch and sat beside her. Liam took a seat in one of the armchairs and kept his gaze pinned on Alannah, compelling her to do likewise.

'Would you like a cup of tea, Alannah dear?' Nora asked.

Wrenching her eyes away from Liam, Alannah faced her aunt. 'Yes please. White and one, thanks.' She watched as Nora and Ross walked into the kitchen.

'Whadda ya know, Liam, our little Lana's all grown up.' Brendan's gruff voice brought Alannah's attention back to her cousins.

Liam smiled. 'Yes, I can see that.'

'Hey, I'm not little. I'm only one week younger than you, Brendan.' It was her usual comeback.

'But you've always been shorter than us. The goth look suits you, by the way.'

She raised an eyebrow. 'Are you being facetious?'

Brendan raised his hands in supplication. 'Nope, all genuine here. Seriously, you look good.'

'Thanks, I guess.' Alannah was glad she took the time to touch up her makeup after all the crying.

Nora returned and handed Alannah her tea. 'Right, I'll leave you kids to it. I'm going to prepare dinner.'

Liam waited for his mum to leave the room before questioning his cousin. 'So, Lana, tell us about yourself. What are you into these days?'

'Come on man, she must be exhausted after the day she had. Surely the twenty questions can wait?' Brendan rebuked Liam.

'It's okay, Brendan, I don't mind. I'd rather focus my thoughts elsewhere anyway.' Alannah returned her gorgeous green eyes in Liam's direction and smiled.

It was enough to jolt his heart into overdrive. Liam could not believe how stunning Alannah had become. She had always been a pretty girl, but in the years since he had seen her last, she had grown into a woman with thick, glossy hair, high-cheekbones, plump heart-shaped lips, and a curvaceous, hourglass figure. Even though he did not usually find goths attractive, Alannah was exceptional.

'I like listening to alternative rock music and going to parties.' Her voice was deep and husky.

Brendan leaned back and stretched his arms across the back of the couch. 'Awesome, a party girl. You're looking at your ticket into the best parties in town.'

Liam frowned. *Brendan sure isn't holding back. He must be loving how much more Alannah has in common with himself than me.* If she were anyone else, he would have left them to their own devices. But Liam was not about to give up on Alannah.

'What about sport?' Liam continued.

'Can't say I'm a fan. You're clearly athletic though, Liam. What do you play?' She glanced at his chest and arms briefly.

Liam's blood superheated as it rushed throughout his body. He shifted uncomfortably in his chair, fighting the growing bulge in his pants. 'I like water sports, especially surfing.'

'That explains the tan. You're lucky you didn't inherit the Geimhreadh complexion, otherwise you'd look like a lobster.'

He laughed. 'I guess so. I take it you don't spend a lot of time in the sun?'

'Too right. I gotta lather on the sunblock if I get more than a few minutes of exposure. I tend to be pretty nocturnal though.'

'Ah, a woman after my own heart,' Brendan chimed in, bringing his arm down to her shoulders, grinning at Liam in the process.

She glanced at Brendan. 'Oh? And what keeps you up at night?'

'Wouldn't you like to know?' The filthy little flirt winked at her.

Alannah laughed. 'I'm sure I'll find out soon enough.'

Liam coughed. 'So, Lana, what do you channel the most?'

When she looked at him again, her brow furrowed. 'What do you mean?'

'You know, what's your favourite power source?'

She blinked a few times. 'Um, that's an odd question. I suppose any form of renewable energy is fine by me. The environment could use a break.'

Brendan shot him a wide-eyed look. *Has he drawn the same conclusion as me? Alannah's parents raised her ignorant of her heritage.* When Brendan began to open his mouth, Liam jumped up and smiled at Alannah. 'Well, I think we have probably overwhelmed you enough with our interrogation.' He turned to Brendan. 'I think we should let Lana rest for a bit. Let's see if Mum needs a hand.'

'But—' Brendan started to protest.

'Come on, brother.' He grabbed Brendan's arm, dragging him into the kitchen and out into the backyard.

As soon as they were outside, Brendan broke free of Liam's grip. 'What the fuck, man? That hurt.' He peered down at the red finger marks on his arm and glared at Liam.

'I could see you were about to open a seriously big can of worms on her. Obviously, she doesn't know anything about what we are, so we need to tread carefully.'

Brendan sighed. 'I guess you're right. *Shit!* I can't believe Aunt Aileen would hide the truth from her.'

'She must have had her reasons.'

'I suppose. So how do you want to handle this? It's not fair to keep her in the dark anymore.'

'I know.' Liam closed his eyes to think. As much as he hated to admit it, Brendan was the best equipped to tell her. 'I think you should break it to her gently, but not tonight.'

He shook his head. 'Nuh, uh! Why me?'

'You have a better chance of getting through to her with your attunements.'

'Wait, are you admitting I'm better than you at something?' He grinned.

Liam shrugged. 'Just this once, yes. Don't get used to it though.'

Brendan punched him lightly in the arm. 'Excuse me while I savour this feeling.' He closed his eyes and took a few deep breaths. When he opened them, he was beaming. 'Don't worry bro, Lana will be in safe hands.' He started walking toward the house.

Liam called after him, 'So long as you keep your actual hands off her.'

Brendan waved his arm in a dismissive gesture before disappearing inside.

Brendan made a point of sitting next to Alannah at dinner so he could breathe in her sweet musky perfume and admire her beauty at close range. He did not even care that their proximity meant her emotional state was playing havoc with his senses. 'What's your fave band, Lana?'

'Hmm. If I had to narrow it down, I'd say both The Score and Metric rate pretty high for me.' She faced him as she replied, and this was when he first noticed the sexy little diamond stud in the right-hand side of her nose.

I wonder if she has any other piercings. 'No shit? They are up there with my faves too.'

'They're okay, I guess,' Liam interjected, 'although my preference is for punk and grunge bands.' Unfortunately, he chose the seat on Alannah's other side and kept drawing her attention. This time he locked her gaze.

'So, Alannah, I can probably get tomorrow off work if you'd like some company.' His mum interrupted them from their visual disrobing of each other and Brendan could have kissed her for it.

'Oh, I was hoping to start school tomorrow.'

Brendan snorted. 'Seriously? Mum's offering you time off school and you're not taking it? No offence, but I didn't have you pegged for the academic type.'

'Brendan!' Dad scolded him, piercing him with his green eyes.

'It's okay, Uncle Ross. He's right. I'm not very studious, but I miss being around people and I'm looking forward to meeting Liam and Brendan's friends.'

Brendan smiled. 'Well, I'm not sure about Liam's mates, but you'll love mine.' He placed his hand on her shoulder. 'Stick with me and mine, Cuz, and we'll look after you.'

Alannah gave him a lascivious glance that made his pulse race. 'Thanks, *Cuz*.'

'Are you not hungry, Alannah?' Mum asked.

Alannah had barely touched her dinner and was pushing the remains around her plate. 'Uh, not really. Sorry. It was nice, but I haven't had much appetite with everything that's happened.'

'Understandable.' Mum took Alannah's plate. 'Here, I'll pop it in the fridge, and you can reheat it if you get peckish later.'

'Thanks. Let me help with the dishes.' Alannah stood up and started to follow Mum.

'Don't be silly. This is your first night here and you've had such a hard day. Relax. Besides, it's Liam's turn anyway.'

'That's right, go and make yourself comfortable. I'll be with you shortly.' Liam grinned as he cleared the plates.

Alannah was drooling as she watched Liam leave the room carrying a stack of dishes.

Brendan grabbed her hand. 'Come on, I'll show you how to work the entertainment system.' He led her into the family room. 'What sort of TV shows and movies do you like?'

'Anything occult, horror, or thriller.' She took a seat on one end of the couch.

He zeroed in on the spot next to her. 'Gods damn, woman, you keep makin' me hard.'

She laughed. 'You sure know how to make a girl feel special.'

He nudged her side before reaching for the remote controls. 'Believe me, "special" doesn't even begin to cover it.'

After showing her how to connect to the various streaming services, they settled on watching *A Quiet Place*.

When Liam entered the room and observed the seating arrangements, he scowled at Brendan, who gave him a smug grin in response.

Alannah was fast asleep by the time the movie ended, so Brendan took in the sight of her precious face resting peacefully. The view was such a contrast to the spark that existed when she was awake. 'I'll carry her up to bed.' He moved in, preparing to gather her into his arms.

'Get your smutty paws away from her.' Liam pulled him back by his t-shirt neckline. 'I'll put her to bed. At least then I know her slumber won't be disturbed.'

'Bah! I'm not that disturbing, and I haven't received any complaints yet.'

Liam's eyes blazed as he bared his teeth. 'I mean it when I say, "keep your hands off." This is Lana, not some random slut. If you hurt her, you *will* face my wrath.'

'Oh wow, you've got it bad for her, don't you?'

'You of all people shouldn't need to ask.' Liam scooped Alannah into his arms and carried her out the room.

Shit! Brendan knew what Liam was capable of and he did not fancy going head-to-head with such power.

Chapter Three

Alannah beelined for the coffee machine and guzzled half her cup before she even registered someone else's presence in the kitchen.

When she looked up, Brendan was grinning as he watched her with twinkling green eyes. 'You know, with Dad being a doctor, we could probably get our hands on an I.V. drip so you can mainline that coffee and be done with it.'

A hearty laugh spilled out of Alannah. *God it feels good to laugh so much.* 'Morning, Brendan.' Grabbing a banana, she headed back to her room to get ready. She decided on an off-the-shoulder black tank-top with a whiskey logo, short black skirt, fishnet stockings, Dr. Martin boots and her usual goth makeup. Once she was ready, she raced back to an empty kitchen. Her heart thumped loudly against her ribs. *I hope I don't need to find my own way to school.*

'Ready?' Brendan's voice startled her.

She spun around to look at him in his black skinny jeans and an Imagine Dragons hoodie. 'Where's everyone else?'

He gasped at the sight of her, scanning her attire. Nodding with approval, he licked his lips and gave her a lop-sided grin. 'The folks both had early shifts. Liam is doing his morning workout at the gym. So, it's just us.'

Alannah ignored the way his expression stirred tingles through her body. 'How do we get to school?'

'The bus, of course. Come on. We'd better get going or we'll miss it.' Brendan moved toward the front door.

'Oh.' Alannah had never caught a bus to school.

After she followed Brendan out the door, he locked up and gave her a set of house keys. 'These are yours.' They walked a few kilometres to a roadside rest stop, enough to leave Alannah breathless, yet Brendan did not show signs of tiring. He dumped his bag on the picnic table and sat next to it, with his feet on the bench seat.

Alannah looked around. Big old gum trees and a few wattles surrounded their gravel-covered island. There was no bus signage of any sort. 'This is a bus stop?'

'Yup.' Brendan's eyes narrowed as he studied her, then a smile dawned. 'Oh right, you've turned into a city chick. We don't have metro buses out here, but this is a school bus route. Don't worry, it'll be here soon.'

She breathed out a sigh. 'So, you mentioned Liam is at the gym. When do you work out?'

He smirked. 'Good of you to notice, Lana.' Brendan gazed upon her intensely for a silent moment and her pulse raced. He leaned forward, elbows on his knees and chin in his hands. 'Like you, I'm not a morning person, so, I exercise after school.' In that moment, a large yellow bus drove up beside them. Brendan jumped up, bag in hand. 'Follow close behind me—we sit up the back.'

After climbing the steps, she peered down the aisle of seats, most of them filled with teenagers. With all eyes on her, she gulped. Alannah had grown used to drawing attention to herself, but this crowd was a lot rougher than that of her Melbourne school. *I may not have made the best choice of attire.* She was going for a 'don't mess with me' vibe, but she may as well have stamped the word 'whore' on her forehead for the leering looks she was getting.

To begin with, she passed a few loners before reaching a small group of nerds. The middle of the bus was full of bogans and rednecks, dressed in flannelette shirts or footy guernseys, who offered several lewd remarks as she passed. Finally, they reached the back of the bus. Numerous counterculture kids mingled in the rear seats, including goths, emos, punks, hipsters, and metalheads. The scene surprised Alannah. She had not ever seen so many piercings and tattoos in one place. The clique that had been an outcast minority in her Melbourne school was clearly the majority here. This was where Brendan greeted a bunch of his friends with fist bumps and other odd handshakes, before taking the very back seat and pulling her down beside him.

He put his arm across her shoulders. 'This here is my cousin, Alannah.'

Everyone had turned to stare at her, but she tried to ignore most of them, instead focusing on Brendan's friends.

Brendan smacked a hand on one guy's shoulder. 'This is my mate, Jacob.'

Jacob had dark red hair, chubby cheeks and a build that implied a love of food rather than exercise. 'Hi, Alannah. It's good to meet you.' He offered her a mischievous grin.

She smiled at him. 'Hi Jacob.'

Brendan gestured to the girl next to Jacob. 'And this is Cara.'

Cara beamed. 'Hi Alannah. It's so good to finally meet you.' This girl had the most incredible dye job. The ombre effect ran from dark red on top to yellow at the tips resembling flames.

'Thanks, Cara.'

The introductions continued. 'Locky, Ben, Bianca, Nick, Amy, Connor, Bailey, Caleb…' Too many names washed over her in quick succession.

Alannah breathed easily again when they reached their destination.

'I'll take you to the front office so you can enrol in your classes.' Brendan blew the long, black strands of his fringe out of his eyes as he threw his protective arm across her shoulder and led them away from the hordes.

The school was smaller than her last one, but unfamiliarity gave the impression of increased size. When they reached the reception desk, a woman with orange-red hair and a flowing, floral dress looked up and smiled at them.

Brendan puffed his chest out as he spoke. 'Hi Miss O'Leary. This is my cousin, Alannah Winters. She's starting school today.'

'Thanks Brendan. Hi Alannah. Welcome to Gaeilge High.' She reached for a bunch of paperwork and handed it to Alannah. 'Take a seat and Mrs. Burke will see you shortly. She will help with your subject selection and enrolment papers.'

'Is it okay if I wait with Alannah and help her find her classes?' Brendan asked.

'Yes, that should be fine. Thank you, Brendan.' She filled out a slip of paper and handed it to him. 'Here's a hall pass.'

Mrs. Burke, the Careers Counsellor, called Alannah into an office a minute later. 'I received your transfer papers from Melbourne. You can probably take the equivalent subjects here, although you might like to have a look at our other courses to see if you'd like to try any of those instead.' She opened one of the booklets sitting in front of Alannah and pointed to the social sciences syllabus. 'It might interest you to know that a number of our students have chosen to learn Irish Gaelic with Language & Culture. Could tie in well with your project on The Celts.'

'That would be good actually. I've been wanting to learn the language anyway. The Women's Studies course also intrigues me.'

Mrs. Burke smiled. 'I thought it might.'

That's presumptive of her. 'Why do you say that?'

'Let's just say, your family's reputation precedes you.'

Who is this woman referring to? I can't imagine my cousins having feminist tendencies. 'Right, well I'll take it, along with the Gaelic subject. I want to stick with Ancient Studies and obviously I have to continue with English and Maths.'

'Certainly. Please fill out those forms while I arrange your classes.' She moved to her computer.

Brendan jumped up from his chair the moment Alannah emerged from the office. 'Give us a look at your schedule.'

She handed the page to him.

'Sweet! We're in the same Language class. You wanna learn Gaelic with me?'

'That was the plan. Do we have any other classes together?'

'Yup. Homegroup and English. Oh, and I'm pretty sure you'll find Cara in your next two lessons. Speaking of which, I should probably get you there, although I'd rather play hooky with you.' Brendan's face lit up and he fluttered his extraordinary lashes.

She grabbed her timetable back from him. 'Sorry to disappoint, but I'm not wagging on my first day.'

He pouted a moment before exhaling dramatically. 'Fine.' When he started striding away, Alannah struggled to keep up.

'What about textbooks?'

'I'll take you to the library at morning break.' He did not even slow down when replying. His abrupt mood change turned Alannah's stomach upside down.

Did I say or do something wrong?

'We've already missed Homegroup, so here's your classroom for first period. I'll meet you back here after.' He walked off.

What the hell? Brendan's behaviour could be the topic of a mystery novel. She shrugged, deciding to focus on more pressing issues.

'Hey Alannah! Are you in this class too?' Cara entered the empty room and took the desk next to her, lighting up the room with her blazing hair. The girl had pale skin too, but aside from mascara, she didn't appear to be wearing much makeup.

'Yeah. I don't have any books yet though. Mind if we share?'

'No probs, hun. I'd be happy to catch you up on stuff too. We've been working on a text using this gender analysis framework.' She handed Alannah her notebook.

'Thanks.' She took the book and started making her own notes as the room filled with the buzz of other students. The din ceased, and Alannah looked up to see her teacher and the rest of the class staring at her.

'Hello Alannah. I'm Irene Dempsey.' She smiled. 'It is so good to have a Winters woman in my class. Perhaps we can start to have some more intelligent group discussions.'

Alannah returned the smile. 'Um, thanks, Ms. Dempsey.'

During the personal study time, Alannah turned to Cara and whispered, 'Why do people keep staring at me?'

'They're in awe of you. You have a powerful presence and you're the first Winters woman they have met in person.'

'Oh. But what about my Aunt Nora?'

Cara's brow shot up as her head jerked back. 'Doesn't count. She married into the family. You're the one with Winters blood coursing through your veins.'

I am going to have to ask my cousins to fill me in on some family history.

By the time lunch started, Alannah had seen most of the campus thanks to Cara who had established herself as Alannah's new best friend.

When they reached the lunch tables, Brendan gave Alannah a huge grin. 'I see Cara has taken you under her wing. Thank you, Cara.'

Cara beamed and her fiery hair practically glowed as she sat down. 'It's been an absolute pleasure.' She gestured for Alannah to sit between herself and Brendan.

Brendan leaned in, tickling her neck with his breath. 'So, Lana, are you surviving your first day okay?'

She looked at Brendan and returned his smile. 'So far, so good.'

'Oh great, it's the fuckin' townies,' one of Brendan's mates complained. He was the one with scruffy brown hair and lots of stubble. *Was his name Connor?*

'Townies?' Alannah asked.

'The rich and famous. Most of them live in town, but there are a few from rural estates who think they're better than the rest of us,' Connor replied.

45

When she faced the direction of his gaze, Alannah saw a group of attractive people in brand-name clothes approaching. Her heart stopped when she realised who led the group.

'There you are. How are you today, Lana?' Liam's blue eyes pierced her with their intensity.

Alannah's heart leaped out of her chest, making way for the butterfly invasion. 'I'm okay, thanks.'

'Glad to hear it. Would you like to join me for lunch?'

She glanced at Liam's friends, catching a few glares. The tanned blonde girl standing next to him gave Alannah an icy stare, sending chills down her spine. Alannah gulped.

Cara cleared her throat. 'Listen, jerk. Alannah is fine with us, so you can all take your fancy threads elsewhere.'

Liam scowled at her, turning back to Alannah. 'You don't really want to sit with this riff-raff, do you?'

Alannah sensed Brendan stiffen beside her. *Oh God!* She hated being in the middle of conflict. Part of her desperately wanted to go with Liam, but his friends were not exactly welcoming. And she did not want to hurt the friends she had already made. 'Actually, I think I'm good where I am, but thanks for the invite, Liam. I'll see you after school.'

Liam's eyes bugged out before he adopted a cold, detached mask. 'Very well. Later then.' He turned and strode away, posse in tow.

Cara flipped them off as soon as they turned their backs. 'Ugh. Elitist pricks.'

Brendan laughed. 'Nice burn, Lana. I could kiss you right now.'

In any other circumstances Alannah might have felt good about sticking up for herself and her friends but refusing Liam left her nauseous. As she watched him leave, she kept picturing that awful mask going up. 'I can't believe Liam would associate with people like that.'

'Sorry to burst your bubble, Lana, but Liam's a bit of a golden boy.'

'You must be Alannah.' A tall guy with a buff build drew her attention back to the group. Standing across the table from her, he must have arrived recently. He was stunning: long black hair framing a chiselled face with a sexy five o'clock shadow. 'Is everything okay? You look as though someone ate your puppy.' A pair of large, bright blue, luminescent eyes were peering down at her.

How could this man be young enough for school?

Brendan answered for her, 'She just discovered what my brother dearest is really like. Alannah, this is Austin.'

Austin sat down and looked directly into her eyes. 'I'm sorry Liam's upset you, Alannah. I know it's not much consolation, but at least you learned the truth sooner rather than later.'

He makes a good point. Alannah's stomach fluttered under Austin's scrutiny. *By God, those eyes were incredible!*

'So, what subjects are you studying Austin? Am I likely to see you in any of my classes?'

His smile dropped. 'Unlikely, I'm afraid.'

'Austin's a senior and a prodigy to boot. Loves all that friggin maths and science crap,' Brendan explained.

'Really? It's a pity we won't be studying together.' Licking her lips, she grinned at Austin.

He glanced at her mouth before returning his intense gaze to her eyes. 'Yes, that is a shame.'

Liam's chest ached. It was an unfamiliar feeling, and he could not stand it. *I can't believe Alannah rejected me.*

'I don't see what's so great about her anyway.' Monique was still walking alongside him, her long blonde hair flowing in the breeze. 'So what if she's a Winters chick. I bet she'll end up on the left-hand path anyway.'

Liam turned to confront his ex. 'Shut your damn mouth, Monique. You don't know what you're talking about.'

'Hey, I'm just calling it as I see it. Besides, what hope does she have with company like that?' She threw her hand back in the direction of Brendan's friends.

As much as he hated to admit it, Monique had a point. Brendan's friends would be a bad influence. *But what else can I do? I hope I get enough time with her to set her on the right path.* He sighed. 'I'm sorry for snapping at you, Monique, but you should know I don't take kindly to anyone hurting or insulting Lana. She means a lot to me.'

Monique huffed. 'Fine, whatever.' She stormed off to join the rest of the girls in their crew.

'Hey bro, I wouldn't worry about her.' Blake, his best mate and cousin from Mum's side, stood close by with his usual can of cola in hand. He took a sip of the drink, adding, 'She's jealous.'

'That's what worries me. Envy can be a dangerous emotion.'

Blake's blue eyes dipped as he furrowed his brow. 'Right. You want me to watch her? Distract her a little? I bet Steve could help.'

'Good idea. Thanks man.' Liam released some tension as he exhaled. Not having to deal with Monique would ease his burdens considerably. He had broken up with Monique the moment news of Alannah's return reached his ears, but Monique was still behaving like she had a claim.

'You still wanna hit the boats after school?' Blake asked as his fingers combed through his mid-length brown hair.

Liam almost confirmed with an affirmative out of habit, but hesitated. 'I dunno. It depends on what Lana's plans are.'

'Right. Of course. I hope you don't miss too much training because of her.'

'If things go according to plan, I'll be practising with her. Problem is, I think I need a new plan.'

Blake snorted. 'You think? The way things look right now, your brother has more hope of becoming her training partner, among other things.'

Liam growled. 'Don't remind me. I never thought I'd see the day Lana chooses him over me.' *That little twerp is becoming a huge thorn in my side.*

'So how much Gaelic do you know, Lana?' Brendan asked as he sat at the desk next to Alannah.

'Not much.' Alannah flicked through her textbook, feeling herself grow cross-eyed. 'Wow, this grammar stuff looks complicated.'

Brendan grinned at her. '*Is é*[1].'

'Jesus, what have I gotten myself into?' Alannah shook her head.

'Don't worry. This is like the one school subject I'm good at. I'll help you out.'

'Thanks. I'm kinda hoping for some help with translating this.' She pulled her mum's old book from the bottom of the pile.

The moment it hit the desk, Brendan's eyes and mouth opened wide. He lowered his voice to ask, 'Where the hell did ya find that?'

She tried to match his volume. 'In a box of Mum's stuff, hidden away in the Melbourne attic, along with a bunch of old artefacts and jewellery. Unfortunately, this was the only treasure I was able to retrieve before Dad…' She paused to choke back the threatening tears. 'I hope the burglar didn't get to the rest of that trunk.'

'*Oh shit!*' Brendan whispered. He glanced around the room. 'You better put that book away for now. I'll help you with it at home.'

---

[1] It is

51

'Why? What is it?' Alannah's heart started racing.

'Just put it away. I'll tell you everything later,' Brendan hissed at her.

'Oh-kay.' She slid it beneath the stack on her desk and glowered at Brendan. The whole situation puzzled her. *Is the leather-bound volume forbidden? Why would Mum have anything illicit or scandalous in her possession? She had always been an upstanding citizen with a caring heart.*

Brendan leaned in to whisper. 'Look, there's nothing wrong with the book per se, but it's not the sort of thing to show in public. You shouldn't advertise having it either. Please trust me on this.'

She forced a smile. 'Yeah, okay. So, what are you working on?'

'An analysis of a film called *The Guard*. You need to watch an Irish movie and write a report on it. I recommend using the same as me. It's not bad, plus the lead actor has a pretty good name.' He smirked as he handed her the details.

Alannah giggled.

'Do I need to find you a new seat, Miss Winters?' Mr. Dougherty frowned.

She bit her lip. 'Sorry, Sir.' Opening her textbook again, she tried to focus on reading the first chapter. A few minutes later she glanced at

Brendan and caught him still looking at her. 'What?' she mouthed silently.

He shook his head and returned to his work.

After school, Alannah walked through the library, the sound of papers shuffling and computers humming filling the air. She had agreed to stick around and wait for both of her cousins to get a lift with them. Given the amount of study she needed to catch up on, she figured this was an opportune time to do so. A familiar face was sitting at a table beneath the flickering of the bright fluoro lights. Her heart was racing as she approached him. 'Hi, Austin. Mind if I join you?'

He gave her an alluring smile when he looked up from his work. 'Please, by all means.' His soft, husky voice and glowing blue eyes were enough to make her weak at the knees.

She took the seat across the table to avoid disturbing the ordered mess of books surrounding him. 'Do you always study here after school?'

'Most afternoons, yes. I find this place more peaceful than home, where I have three younger siblings.'

'Fair call. I hope my presence isn't too disruptive. I can find another table if—'

'Please,' Austin cut in, 'you are a welcome distraction from the monotony of these calculus equations. My eyes were starting to blur anyway.' He glanced at the book about the Celts she had placed on the table. 'Reading up on a bit of family history, I see.'

'How did you know?'

'That you're Irish? Come on, this is an Irish settlement, and everyone knows the Winters clan was one of the founding families.'

'Oh, I didn't realise.' *Explains some of my family's reputation.*

The trace of a frown fled his face almost as soon as it had appeared. 'You really don't know much about your heritage, do you?'

'No, unfortunately. I'd like to learn more though. Especially given the apparent significance of my surname.'

'I'd be happy to help. I know a local expert on the families here.' He paused for a moment, locking in her gaze. 'It might interest you to know that the first Winters woman to set foot in this town was an Alannah. I'm guessing you were named after her.'

'That is curious.' Lowering her gaze, Alannah tapped her pen on the table as she became lost in thought. *It is a little disturbing that this guy I only just met knows more about my family history than I do, but apparently most of the town is more clued in than me.* Pushing those thoughts aside, she looked up into his eyes again. 'What about your family? How long have they been in Gaeilge Shores?'

'Almost as long as yours. The Pearce family arrived in 1865, twenty years after settlement. We have a couple of properties in town.'

'Did they come from Ireland too?'

'No. They were from Somerset, England. Wait there a second.' He stood up and moved into the reference shelves. When he emerged a few minutes later, he was carrying a book about their town. 'Here, this has some of the basics.'

A brief inspection of the contents revealed a compilation of names, dates, and family crests. 'Wow, this is awesome. Thanks, Austin.'

'Anytime.'

She became so absorbed in reading about the town's history that she lost track of time.

'Hey Lana, it's time to go.' Brendan's voice startled her.

When she looked up, she caught a glimpse of the clock on the wall behind him. It was nearly half past five. 'Okay. I gotta return this first.' She closed the book and stood.

'Here, allow me.' Austin held his hand out.

She gave him a warm smile. 'Thanks. See you tomorrow.'

'No worries.' Austin raised his hand for a fist bump with Brendan.

'Laters man.' Brendan threw his arm over Alannah's shoulder and led her out to the car park.

Liam watched as Brendan escorted Alannah out of the library toward his SUV. Seeing Brendan's possessive arm draped across her made Liam's blood boil. As they drew closer, Liam moved to the front passenger door, holding it open for Alannah. 'Hey Lana.'

The moment she looked at him, her smile disappeared, and she averted her gaze. 'Thanks, Liam,' she whispered as she lowered herself into the car.

Is she sensing my mood? Once Alannah took her seat, Liam closed the door, glaring at Brendan before returning to the driver's side.

They travelled for a few kilometres before Brendan spoke up. 'You can drop me at Bianca's.'

What an unexpected turn of events. Liam looked at Brendan in the rear-view mirror with a cocked brow. 'Are you sure?'

'Of course I'm bloody sure. What's it to you, anyway?'

Liam sneered into the mirror. 'I'm not complaining, just surprised.' *Have I misjudged Brendan's feelings for Alannah?* He looked across to gauge her reaction, but her expression was blank.

Brendan snorted. 'Right, whatever.' When they pulled into Bianca's drive, he leaned forward. 'Don't wait up for me.' He jumped out, pausing to stick his head back in the door. 'Night, Lana.'

She turned and smiled at him. 'Night.'

As they were driving away, Alannah turned to Liam. 'So, what's the deal with Bianca?'

Liam kept his face forward to hide his smug grin. 'She's been Brendan's main squeeze for years.'

'I didn't know he had a girl.' Her neutral tone did not betray disappointment.

Maybe Lana doesn't fancy Brendan after all, Liam thought. 'I probably shouldn't tell you this, but…'

'But what?'

'I guess you'll probably find out eventually… Brendan sleeps around, and I mean a lot.'

'Oh.' She fell quiet for the rest of the journey.

Liam's shoulder's hunched. *Then again. Perhaps Lana was hiding her feelings initially.*

As they entered the living room together, Alannah broke the silence. 'Hey Liam…'

His muscles tensed as he looked at her. 'Yeah?' *Please quit talking about Brendan*, he silently pleaded.

'Why is it being a Winters woman has people staring at me?'

He jolted. *Talk about left field.* After a deep breath he faced her head on. 'You should ask Brendan about that.'

Alannah collapsed on the couch. 'Well he's not here, so I'm asking you. Do you know the reason?'

Liam bit his lip. 'Yes, but I don't want to talk about it with you.'

Crinkling her nose, Alannah crossed her arms, her eyes glistening with unshed tears. 'Why? What's the problem? Did my choice of lunch companions offend you so much that you don't even want to talk to me now?'

He sighed as he settled into one of the armchairs. 'No, it's nothing like that. Look, I'm sorry Lana, but it's difficult for me to explain. I really think you should wait for Brendan on this one.'

The moment Brendan stepped into Bianca's bedroom, she launched herself at him and kissed him deeply.

A few minutes later, Brendan pulled back from her. 'I want to try something different tonight.'

Pressing her hands against his chest, Bianca's darkly lined eyes became sultry. 'Is it kinky? I like kinky.'

He laughed. 'That's not what I had in mind.'

Bianca stepped back and pouted. 'What? You don't want to have fun tonight?'

She looks fucking adorable pouting at me like that with those long, turquoise pigtails. After pulling her back into his arms, Brendan smiled. 'Okay, maybe we can still have a little fun, but only after I've had a chance to try my new party trick.'

She yelped and clapped her hands. 'Oh? And what does that involve?'

Brendan pressed a finger to her forehead. 'I want you to let me in here.'

'That's pretty ambitious. Are you sure about this?'

'Absolutely positive. I'm sick of living in my brother's shadow, so it's about time I upped my game. But this stays between us, okay? You can't tell a soul.'

Bianca offered him a sly grin. 'Ooh, you are a sneaky one. I promise you my lips are sealed.'

'Good. Now let's get comfortable because this is gonna be a long night.'

Chapter Four

When Alannah entered the party, she recognised The Score's "Stay" blaring from the stereo. Being one of her favourite songs, it did wonders to calm her racing heart as she took in the sights. The rich, earthy aroma of beer wafted across the front lounge room, where bodies crowded together, filling the space with the din of chatter.

Apparently, 'gatherings' like this were a regular occurrence on Friday nights. Brendan had explained their size could vary depending on the host, who on this occasion was a Senior named Lucas who floated between groups. His home was a huge country estate, comparable to Cailleach.

Brendan had brought Alannah to the party, entering with his protective arm over her shoulder. 'Hey Lana, let's do shots.'

She smiled. 'Sounds great.'

Brendan grabbed her hand and dragged her into the kitchen. 'Greetings my lads and ladies. It's time to get this party started.' He set the box he had been carrying with his other arm on the bench. Reaching inside, he retrieved a bunch of plastic shot cups and a bottle of Jose Cuervo tequila.

Jacob stepped forward, with dimples showing in his chubby cheeks as he grinned. 'You're an absolute champ, Brendo.'

Alannah knew the drill. She spied the bowl of lemons near the sink, so she set about slicing them into wedges.

'Let me help with that.'

Glancing up, Alannah spied Nick's smiling eyes. 'Um, sure.'

The massively muscular punk, with a bright pink sidecut, wore a plain black t-shirt stretching tight across heavily inked arms. Picking up the sharp knife, he looked ready to step onto the set of a crime show, but the impression eased with such a domestic task. Nick smiled at Alannah as he chopped the lemons. 'You settling in okay?'

'I guess so. You guys have all been great.' Alannah finished slicing the last of the lemons and threw them in a bowl.

'Glad to hear it.'

She grabbed a saltshaker and placed it on the central counter with everything else.

Brendan grinned at her. 'I love a girl who knows how to drink.'

Cara snorted. 'I pegged you more for liking the cheap drunks.'

'Lowered inhibitions certainly don't hurt,' Brendan agreed.

'Ugh.' Cara flicked back her flaming red hair as she rolled her eyes.

Caleb and Locky, the two goth guys in the group, sniggered. They made an interesting pair standing together. Caleb's locks were long and black, while Locky kept his bright green hair short and messy. Both were skinny with soft, delicate facial features that were almost feminine. Given their proximity to one another, she wondered if they were a gay couple.

'Right, let's line 'em up.' Bailey—the guy with two-tone spiky hair—poured the drinks like a pro. He handed Alannah the salt, indicating she should start.

'Wow, where'd you learn to do that?' she inquired.

'My folks own the only pub in town,' Bailey explained.

After seasoning her wrist, she handed the salt to Brendan, who had been watching her closely, only looking away to apply the salt to his own wrist and pass it on. Once everyone else had followed suit and grabbed their drink, Brendan raised his cup and drew her attention again. 'I toast to Lana's return. Welcome home, Cuz.'

'To Alannah!' The rest of the group cried.

Brendan kept his gaze locked with hers as he licked his wrist slowly. Alannah remembered their old game of Sleazy Chicken and felt compelled to imitate him. He did not back down. Her attempt only sparked a salacious gleam in his eyes. The moment was intense, and Alannah realised Brendan was probably leagues ahead of her in this game. She felt her cheeks flush, breaking their trance when she threw back her shot, welcoming the burn of the liquor down her throat.

She heard Brendan laughing beside her before he whispered in her ear, 'Making you blush has become too easy.'

Alannah could not turn down a challenge like that. She turned so her lips were touching his ear. 'Don't get used to it, I'm just out of practice.'

'Right, next round!' Brendan poured more tequila for everyone. As Alannah went to lick the salt from her wrist, Brendan grabbed her hand. 'Uh, uh. Here.' He presented her with his own salted wrist.

Narrowing her eyes at him, she drew his arm toward her mouth and whispered close to his ear. 'Game on.' When she licked Brendan's wrist, Alannah sensed his body stiffen. Her pulse quickened at the thought of possible victory. *I got a reaction out of him. Perhaps he did not expect me to rise to his challenge.* But when she looked up, he kept a straight face, no hint of colour. *Dammit!*

After sculling her drink, she picked up a wedge of lemon, but Brendan plucked it from her hand and placed it between his teeth for her. *By God! He is relentless.* She looked around to see who was watching. Only a few friends remained in the kitchen and they preoccupied themselves with their own conversations. She took a deep breath and started moving closer to him. His eyes lit up when he saw her approach. *Crap! What does he plan to do when I retrieve my piece of fruit?*

'Hey gorgeous, guess who!' A curvy brunette walked up behind Brendan and clamped her hands over his eyes.

After withdrawing the citrus wedge, Brendan grinned. 'Hi Chelsea.' He spun around and drew the girl into his arms, kissing her passionately.

When Chelsea wrapped her legs around his waist and Brendan's hand climbed beneath the girl's skirt, Alannah wondered if they were about to start fucking then and there. It was fortunate Brendan could not see Alannah's face, because the display reddened her cheeks.

'Come on, let's find the beer kegs.' Cara was standing beside her with a hand on Alannah's left shoulder.

'Good plan,' Alannah agreed, as she followed Cara into the rear living room.

'Thanks.' Alannah took the cup of beer from Cara. 'Is it true, Brendan's a womaniser?'

Cara bit her lip. 'Is that what Liam told you?'

'Yeah. Is it wrong?'

After sipping her drink, Cara sighed. 'No. It's true, although womaniser is a pretty harsh term. It's not like he promises any form of commitment. The girls know what they're getting. Are you disappointed in him?'

'Not really. It's not like it's any of my business really, I was merely curious. Have you ever—'

'Oh, Gods no! That's a line I've never wanted to cross in our friendship, not that it stops him trying every so often. I kinda pride myself on being one of the few girls in our year who hasn't succumbed to his charms.'

Alannah shook her head. 'Is he really that promiscuous?'

''Fraid so. But hey, at least in you, I now have a friend in the minority, right?' Tilting her head forward, Cara's brows rose as she looked at Alannah with wide, unblinking eyes.

Alannah laughed. 'Trust me, Brendan's not the cousin I'm interested in.'

Cara's jaw dropped. 'What the hell? Wait, are you and Liam…?'

She shook her head. 'No, not yet. I'm not entirely sure if he likes me in that way. Besides, I'm still getting over my ex.'

'Oh, what happened with your ex?' Cara led her to a couch and sat down.

'It was a mutual agreement to split when I had to move here. We decided it would be too hard to maintain a long-distance relationship.'

Solemn clouds marred Cara's features. 'Oh man, that's tough. How long were you guys together?'

Alannah looked down into her beer. 'About eighteen months. Although Cole was one of my best friends before we hooked up. He'd had a crush on me since we first met in Year Seven.'

'I'm so sorry, Alannah. It sounds like you guys had something special.'

'Yeah, I suppose we did. But I need to move on with my life and Liam's always been pretty special to me too.'

'I get your need to move on, but Liam? Seriously? He is such a douche.' She clapped a hand to her mouth. 'Sorry, I don't mean to offend.'

'It's okay. I get you don't see eye to eye with him. But I've always known a different side of Liam.'

'Speaking of the devil,' Cara gestured toward the front door.

When Alannah looked up, she saw Liam enter with his townie friends who strode in like they owned the place. The moment Liam's baby blue eyes locked with hers, he smiled and moved toward her.

Cara whispered in her ear, 'I can see he has a soft spot for you.'

Liam reached her in a matter of seconds. 'Hi Lana. Can I get you a drink?'

After finishing the last of her ale, she handed him the cup and smiled. 'Yeah sure. I'll have a beer, thanks.'

His hand brushed against hers as he took the cup, sending sparks through her nerves. His smile turned into a wide grin. 'Great. I'll be right back.'

Once he moved away, Alannah's eyes landed on the fierce glare of a tall blonde. 'Cara, who's that tanned Barbie doll sending me the deadly daggers?'

'That's Queen Bee Monique, Liam's girl…' The moment Cara caught the pain in Alannah's eyes, she realised what she'd said. 'Oh, shit! Sorry, hun. I forgot to mention… fuck!'

Alannah's heart sunk. 'Of course he has a girlfriend. I was stupid to think otherwise.'

Liam returned a moment later and handed Alannah another beer. His own drink was a can of cola.

'Thanks.' Alannah accepted the drink. Squeezing onto the sofa, Liam surprised her. She chanced another glance at Monique and saw the girl huff and turn away. Alannah turned back to Liam. 'Monique doesn't look very happy.'

He shrugged. 'She'll get over it.'

She gaped at him. 'Isn't she your girlfriend, though?'

Liam's head jerked back as his eyes narrowed. 'Not anymore.'

'Oh.' *Oh. A recent breakup coinciding with my arrival. Could she feel threatened?*

'Wow—did you finally dump her bony arse? When did that happen?' Cara laughed.

Liam scowled at Cara. 'I broke up with her on Monday. Looks like you're out of the loop, Hughes.'

Cara returned the scowl. 'Forgive me for not showing an interest in the rumour mill, Winters.' She stood. 'Excuse me Alannah, I'm gonna mingle some more.' She walked away.

Liam sighed. 'I'm sorry, Lana, I know she's your friend. It's just…'

Raising her hand, Alannah cut him off. 'I get it, okay. Please leave me out of it. How about we change the subject?'

That made him smile. 'Sure. How are you?'

'Okay, I suppose… all things considered. The last week's been pretty rough.'

He placed a comforting hand on her shoulder blades. 'You've been through a lot. I'm impressed by how well you're holding up.'

'It probably has more to do with my ability to ignore my emotions. I got good at it when Mum died.'

A frown formed on his face. 'That doesn't sound healthy. You know you can talk to me about anything at any time, right?'

'Yeah, thanks.' Alannah forced a smile as she looked into Liam's eyes. A buzzing noise in her bag drew her attention. She pulled her phone out and exhaled sharply when she saw who was calling: Cole. 'Excuse me a minute, Liam.'

He glanced briefly at her phone and frowned.

'Hi Cole. Give me a sec.' Alannah walked upstairs in pursuit of some peace and quiet. She found a storage room and shut herself inside. 'Sorry about that. I'm at a party.'

'No probs. How are you?'

'I'm coping. My family here have been a great comfort. How about you?'

'Bored and missing you like crazy. But otherwise, I've been great.'

'The sarcasm is still strong with you,' Alannah replied with an amused tone before sighing. 'But yeah, I miss you too.'

'You sure you don't wanna try and make things work between us?'

Alannah closed her eyes, and an image of Liam came to her mind. 'I'm sorry, Cole. I don't think it's a good idea.'

'I s'pose you're right.' The pain in his voice was evident. 'So, how's your new school?'

'It's pretty crazy. The kids here make your school look tame. There's a lot of schoolyard fights and the detention room's often full.'

'Damn. Now I really wish I could move there. That party you're at sounded pretty wild too.'

'It's alright.'

'I guess I'd better let you get back to it. I'll catch you later.'

'Yeah, sure. See ya.' After signing off, Alannah made her way back down the corridor.

Before she reached the stairs, Monique and three other girls cornered her. 'Hey Winters, I was hoping to get a moment alone with you.'

Alannah glanced at the other girls. 'Well in that case, you might want to send your minions away.' If they were hoping to intimidate her, they were not doing a very good job. Alannah had dealt with her fair share of bitches at her last school and she never took crap from anyone.

Monique's friends tittered.

'Not what I meant, Winters. I wanted to warn you to stay away from Liam. He's mine and if you touch him, I will end you.'

The empty threat made Alannah laugh hysterically. 'Oh my God, you're so funny.' She paused to regain her composure. 'Listen, Monique,

Liam doesn't want you anymore, so get over yourself and suck it up.'

A chorus of knuckle cracking came from the four girls. 'You have no idea who you're dealing with. Mess with us and we will break you so hard, your dear Uncle won't be able to put you back together.'

'Alannah?' A familiar voice broke through the group.

Alannah looked up and the other girls spun around to face Austin.

Pursing his lips, Austin focused his eyes on Alannah. 'Everything okay here?'

Monique grinned. 'Fine, thanks Pearce. We were simply becoming more acquainted with Alannah here.'

Austin furrowed his brow, studying Monique a moment before returning his attention to Alannah. Pushing past Monique, he placed an arm around Alannah's shoulders and glowered at the bullies. 'I apologise for interrupting, but I'd like a word with Alannah.' He drew her away from them and out on a balcony down the hall.

'Are you okay?' Austin's stunning blue eyes locked with hers.

'I'm fine, but thanks for the intercept.'

He smiled. 'Anytime. Be careful of those girls, though; they're trouble.'

Breaking from his gaze, she placed her hands on the railing and looked out over the immaculate cottage gardens. 'I'll be fine. I've dealt with their sort before.'

'Oh, and what sort do you think they are?'

'Pretentious snobs who get their kicks from pushing their weight around.'

He laughed. 'I can see why you get along better with your younger cousin. It's rare for anyone in the founding families to be so down to earth, but you and Brendan are definitely the exceptions.'

'Is that what those girls are? Members of the founding families?'

'Yes, they are. Which is why you need to watch your back around them. They're very… powerful.'

'I'm sure I can handle myself with the likes of them, but thanks for the warning.' Alannah remembered what she had wanted to ask him earlier. 'I missed you at lunch today, So I'm glad I caught you tonight 'cause I have a favour to ask.'

'Oh?'

'I was hoping for some help with maths. I've fallen seriously behind, with everything that's happened, and I'm struggling to catch up. Would you mind tutoring me?' Alannah was starting to feel the cold.

'I'd love to. Anytime you need help, seek me out in the library after school.' He turned to face her, removing his coat. 'Here, looks like you need this more than me.' As he stepped up to drape it over her shoulders, a door slammed behind them.

'That won't be necessary. It's much warmer inside anyway.' Liam stood at the door, glaring at Austin, who was equally unimpressed.

Did Austin growl at Liam?

Liam turned his attention to Alannah. 'I've been looking everywhere for you, Lana. You've been gone a while.'

Shit. She forgot she had left him hanging when she took that call from Cole. Alannah's eyes lowered as she brought her hand up to cover her mouth. 'Sorry Liam. I had a run in with Monique, but Austin came to my rescue.' She turned back to Austin. 'Thanks again. I'll see you on Monday, okay?'

'No worries. See you then.'

Liam led her back inside. They were walking through the downstairs crowd when Liam stopped and put his hand on her shoulder. 'Are you okay?

You mentioned an altercation with Monique. Did she hurt you?'

'I'm fine. Nothing really happened. They merely expelled a bunch of hot air.'

'Oh look, isn't that precious? A touching family moment for the Winters clan.' A deep, gruff voice behind Alannah startled her and she spun around to find one of the flannel-clad red necks staring down at her, a lewd grin on his face. 'Not that I'd mind touching a piece of that arse.'

A few loud sniggers came from the four blokes standing behind him.

'Back off, Chad, and keep your hands to your filthy selves.' Liam's tone was serious.

'Or you'll what? You don't scare us, Winters. None of your kind do.' Chad—the muscular behemoth—stepped a sizeable stride forward, closing the gap between himself and Alannah, his mates filing in around her.

'I'm warning you, Chad. Get away from her.' Liam's body pressed into her back, his hand still on her shoulder.

Chad reached out to grab Alannah and the next moment became a blur as Liam pulled her out of the way and dived at the guy.

'Liam!' She screamed as the five burly blokes piled in and started pummelling Liam.

A series of shouts and crashing noises followed and a few seconds later some of Liam's friends were pulling the brutes off him and throwing their own punches.

Alannah felt hands grab her, trying to pull her away from the fray, but she resisted. She could not see Liam and her mind raced through all the horrid possibilities.

Brendan was fastening the belt on his pants when he heard the ruckus coming from downstairs. He shot Chelsea a look. 'Stay here.' Without further ado, he sped off toward the racket. As he approached the stairs, he heard Alannah's shrieking. Drawing closer, he felt her panic, prompting him to pick up the pace.

Shit! It's the fucking ogres. He noticed Blake trying to restrain Alannah, who was protesting and shouting something about Liam. *Where is Liam?* A bright flash from the middle of the skirmish answered his question a second later. *Fuck!* Things were about to get ugly. He needed to step in and do something.

When Blake spotted him, he cried out, 'Brendan! Get Alannah out of here.'

'But I…'

'*No! Get her to safety*. We can't fight properly with her here.' Blake pushed Alannah into his arms, before jumping into the scuffle.

Alannah was frantic. '*Liam's in there*. He's been hurt!'

Brendan pinned her flailing arms to her sides with his own. 'He'll be fine. Now let's get you home.'

'*No, Brendan*, you've got to help him!' She tried to push away from him.

But Brendan picked her up and threw her over his shoulder. 'He has enough backup, and he will fight better knowing you're safe. Now come on.'

She continued to thrash at him, even gouged at the bare skin on his back as he walked her out to the carpark.

Brendan was relieved to find Austin outside, standing by his car. 'Need a lift?'

'Yup. Thanks man.'

Austin opened one of the back doors and Brendan piled in with Alannah, grappling her to prevent her escape.

Once the car was moving, Austin laughed. 'Your cousin's pretty feisty, Brendan.'

He looked at Alannah, still struggling in his arms, and grinned. 'Yeah, she's a Winters alright.'

Once away from the fight, Brendan was able to focus on calming her, stroking her arms as he whispered, 'Hush. It's okay, Lana. Liam will be okay, I promise.'

She went limp in his arms, curling up and resting her head against his naked chest.

The skin-to-skin contact was thrilling. Brendan pulled her into a tighter embrace and stuffed his face in her strawberry scented hair. *Gods, it smells good!* Brendan started imagining those locks wrapped around his hands as he kissed her, as he fucked her. He knew he should not be having these thoughts about her, especially with her in this condition. But she pressed her sexy body up against him, rendering him powerless to resist. Feeling her trembling and the faint sound of sobbing switched his thoughts back to concern for her wellbeing.

'Hey, everything will be okay. I promise.' He continued to whisper soothing words for the rest of the drive home.

Chapter Five

Alannah jumped out of bed with a thumping heartbeat. First her sleeping mind then her waking thoughts fixated on the fight the night before and she teared up when she thought about Liam. She had to find him and make sure he was okay. A quick check of her alarm clock told her it was only 6AM. She put on her white silk dressing gown and grey slippers, before making her way down the hall.

There was a good chance the boys were still asleep, so she found Liam's room and knocked lightly on the door. No response. She tried the door handle: unlocked. After gently opening the door, Alannah peeked inside. Liam was sleeping soundly in his bed. Wanting to see the extent of his injuries, she stepped inside.

As soon as Liam's form came into full view, Alannah gasped. He had pushed his quilt down to his hips, revealing a chest of sun-kissed skin. *Wow, that looks like an eight pack!* She could also see most of his happy trail. *He sleeps naked!* It was tempting to tug the quilt a little lower, but she remembered why she was invading his privacy. This was the second reason for her gasping. There was not a single scratch on his perfect body, not even a bruise on his face. *How did he escape so unscathed? Did I imagine last night?*

She slipped out of the room and crept back toward her own. But she paused outside Brendan's. Waking him at such an ungodly hour was tempting fate, but she needed to ask him some questions. She sighed. The questions would have to wait. But she could not move away. Perhaps it was perverse curiosity leading her to open his door.

Apparently both guys overheated in their sleep. Brendan, unlike his big brother, was lying on his side, with the quilt tangled around his legs. He also slept naked. Some marks on his back drew Alannah's attention, so she moved closer to inspect them. There were a series of deep gouges, likely from a girl's finger nails. She grinned. *Kinky fucker!* But a flashback from the party smacked her in the face. Brendan had picked her up and carried her away from the fight. Those marks were her doing. *Shit!*

Brendan moaned and rolled onto his back. Alannah jumped back and stumbled when her feet landed on a pile of clothes. She righted her balance and started for the door.

'Mm, Lana.'

Alannah froze. *I'm so busted! How do I explain this?* She slowly turned around to face the music.

But Brendan's eyes remained closed. *Is he dreaming about me?* That was when she noticed the impressive tent he made with the quilt. *Geeezuuus!* She stood there gobsmacked. *No wonder he is so popular with the girls.* His quilt started moving down and she bolted.

After Ross and Nora joined Alannah for breakfast, they both left for work and the house fell silent again because the boys were still in bed. She decided to take the opportunity to video call her two best friends in Melbourne.

'Alannah! It's so good to see you,' Emma cried.

'We've missed you so much,' Melissa added.

'Hi guys. I've missed you too.'

Emma frowned. 'How have you been? Are they treating you okay over there?'

'My family here have been very supportive. Aunt Nora's an absolute gem.'

'Oh good,' Emma replied. 'And what about school? Cole mentioned you thought it was crazy there.'

'It is, but I haven't had any real problems other than falling behind with my studies. The worst thing that's really happened was a run in with the popular girls at a party last night. You know the type, like Olivia's group. Of course, I put them in their place.'

'You go girl.' Emma clapped her hands with delight.

'So, have you made friends with any hot guys?' Melissa asked.

'A few.'

Emma's eyes lit up. 'Oooh. Are any of them viable hook-ups or boyfriend material?'

'I suppose a couple are.'

'Alannah, you dirty minx,' Melissa giggled.

Alannah rolled her eyes. 'Please don't tell Cole though, in case the news hurts him. I'm not ready to start dating any of the guys here, but still. I miss Cole heaps and I know it'd kill me to think he'd moved on already.'

Emma nodded. 'Yeah, yeah. We get it. So, what are your dreamboat cousins like these days?'

Alannah let out a sigh. 'Well let's just say Liam is one of those hot prospects who I mentioned before. Like seriously out of this world hot.'

Emma laughed as Melissa replied, 'O. M. G. Seriously?'

Beaming, she nodded. 'Yeah, seriously. That said, he's also the most popular guy at school and hangs out with a bunch of A-holes, so I don't like my chances. I'm not really his type.'

Emma shrugged. 'Hm, pity. What about the younger cousin? The totally fuckable one. His name was Brendan, right?' Emma had met both the guys at Alannah's mum's funeral and Brendan left the biggest impression on her friend.

'He's cool. A lot like me, except funnier and a hell of a lot sluttier. I hang with his friends at school.'

'Do you agree with Emma? Is he totally fuckable?' Melissa asked with an impish grin.

Alannah blushed again, remembering the eyeful she had copped earlier that day. 'Yeah. He's slept with most of the girls in our year level; so, they clearly think so too.'

Melissa furrowed her brow. 'So, is he one of your choices?'

Alannah sighed. 'Brendan and I are too close, like best friends. Always have been. It's different with Liam, though. I grew up crushing on him and now…' She fanned her face for effect.

'Makes sense to me,' Emma admitted with a giggle, but Melissa shook her head.

The conversation shifted to gossiping about her old school for a while, which was followed by the tear-jerking farewells with promises to meet up in the winter break.

The scent of fried food drew Alannah to the kitchen at midday. When she entered, she found Liam and Brendan both stuffing their faces with the makings of a full Irish breakfast. It smelled incredible.

Liam looked up at her, smiling once he finished his mouthful. 'Morning, Lana. Did you pull up okay?'

'Yeah. I've been up for hours, so good afternoon to both of you.'

Brendan laughed and scoffed another mouthful.

'I guess I overslept a bit,' Liam agreed. 'Help yourself to the leftovers.'

She filled her plate with bacon, sausages, hash browns, mushrooms, and beans. Sitting at the table across from Liam, she cast her eyes over him again, looking for battle scars.

When he looked up, his eyes focused on her. 'You didn't get hurt from the fight last night, did you?'

'No. Not a scratch.' Alannah blushed at her choice of words and glanced at Brendan.

Of course, Brendan noticed. He narrowed his eyes at her.

She turned her attention back to Liam. 'I'm surprised you don't have any bruises. I hope you didn't end up with any internal injuries.'

'I'm fine. Don't worry about me. I can hold my own in a fight. I'm glad you're okay.' After finishing his food, he stood and put his plate and cutlery in the dishwasher. He turned back to her. 'Sorry, but I gotta fly. I need to get to a study session at Blake's. I'll see you tonight.'

Alannah tried to hide her disappointment, instead focussing on her meal. It was her first weekend with the boys in years and Liam was already bailing. After swallowing her mouthful, she looked at him. 'Sure, no probs. See ya.' She watched him go with a sigh and continued eating.

'Hey, Lana… have any good dreams lately?' Brendan inquired after dropping his plate in the dishwasher.

She shot him a sidelong glance.

He sat down again, this time directly across from her. 'I had a great dream this morning.'

Alannah felt the colour in her cheeks rise. 'Oh? What was it about?'

Brendan leaned forward. 'A girl with long black hair, dressed in white entered my room while I slept.'

Her eyes grew wider. 'You knew?'

'I sensed you enter my room. It woke me up. What were you doing there, Lana?'

'I uh… um, I… just wanted to check on you after last night, to make sure you weren't badly injured.'

'Right. You do realise, I didn't get involved with the fighting?' Brendan paused to gather a moment of awkward silence. 'So, did you like what you saw?'

Alannah's cheeks turned crimson.

He smirked. 'I got you good, this time.'

'Yeah, I guess you did.' She burst into laughter and Brendan joined in. Alannah felt weeks of tension releasing from her muscles. Regaining her composure, Alannah realised she had not been the subject of one of his twisted wet dreams. *At least not this morning anyway. Am I relieved or disappointed?* She finished eating and headed into the living room.

Brendan followed her. 'You wanna know how I detected your presence when I was asleep?'

Alannah slumped down on the couch. 'I suppose.'

'I used magic.'

'Ha ha. Very funny. You gonna give me the real answer?' Alannah replied playfully.

'I'm serious. I'm a mage. So is Liam and every other member of our bloodline. That includes you. You're not initiated, so you can't use your powers yet.'

Alannah's brow furrowed as she glanced at him askew. In a rare serious moment, intense focus replaced the usual impish glint in his eyes.

'You still don't believe me? Go grab that book of your mum's.'

'Fine.' Alannah retrieved the black leather binder. When she returned to the sofa, she sat next to Brendan and placed the book on the coffee table in front of them.

'This was your mum's Book of Shadows. It's both a spell book and reference guide for our practices. All mages have one, but this one is special because our ancestors handed it down the line from the original Winters woman. See this page?' He flicked to the second leaf which had a long list of names and signatures. 'These are the dedications of each mage who has used this book. They were all women, and they signed this page on the day of their initiation.'

'Wow, this is an incredible piece of family history.'

'Yes, it is. My own Book of Shadows is not an impressive heirloom.' He stood and found his own leather-bound volume. It was much thinner and the symbol on the front was different, but otherwise it looked similar. The title on the front page was in English: *Brendan's Book of Shadows*. 'Most mages need to create their own from scratch. The women of the Winters clan, however, wanted to hand down their knowledge to the first-born daughter of each generation. What you have there is a collection of very powerful spells and rituals from centuries of mage craft.'

Alannah was gobsmacked. She took another look at the list of names. 'So, who was the first Winters woman? This list of names goes on for pages.'

'Yup. That's because the first Winters mage was the daughter of the Goddess Cailleach. She was born in the Bronze Age.'

She stared at Brendan, completely dumbfounded. *Is he pulling my leg? How can that be true?* 'I didn't think the Celts had any written records. How could this book be from that time? not to mention the pages couldn't have survived for so long.'

'I understand your scepticism. It took me a while to believe some of our history when I started training. From what I understand, our ancestors created most of the book much later, when a written form of the Gaelic language emerged. They passed the knowledge down orally at first. But the dedication pages start with Bébinn Gheimhridh, our first Ancestor. Look here.' He pointed to a name. 'This was an archaic form of writing created by mages. All of the pages in this book have been magically treated to preserve them.' Brendan paused a moment. 'I'll get you a drink and give you a moment to process things. I imagine you will have some questions for me when I get back.'

Alannah was still unsure about the whole magic side of things, but the family history she was learning was fascinating. She wanted to know more.

When Brendan returned, he handed her a cup of tea.

'Thanks.' She took a few sips in silence before questioning him. 'So, are the Winters clan the only mages? Is that why Winters women have a reputation for being powerful?'

'No. There are millions of mage families around the world, all dating back to around Eight Hundred B.C. Mages are essentially demigods, the result of powerful beings from the celestial realms coupling with humans. We have come to call these beings Gods and Goddesses and they were worshipped by various pagan cultures.' He took a sip of his own tea.

Enthralled by his explanation, Alannah waited silently for him to continue.

'The Creator God, Lugh, fathered most Irish mage families. But Cailleach, the creator Goddess, gave rise to the Winters clan. This is why we are the only matriarchal clan of Celtic origin. Being matriarchal is the reason we carry the surname of our Grandmother rather than our Grandfather, and why your mum didn't change her name when she married your dad.'

'Wait. Does that mean I'm like the head of the family now?'

'Not yet. Get initiated and became a full magus. Then you'd own me.' Brendan waggled his brows.

Alannah grinned. 'Sweet. So, what's the deal with magic? How does it work?'

'Mages channel different sources of mana, or magic power. Most of us focus on attuning ourselves to a couple of power sources, which we refer to as our attunements. It allows us to specialise so we can graduate to full magus status when we turn eighteen. These days, most mages use their attunements to guide their career choices. The spells we cast make use of our own attunements. Rituals, on the other hand, tend to be a joint effort. They involve a group of mages and are either a more powerful version of a spell, or they are a form of worship. We still pay homage to the Celtic Gods and Goddesses in this town.'

Alannah nodded. She was beginning to understand all the references to the Goddess Cailleach. 'So, are there any other mages at our school?'

He sat back and put his feet up on the ottoman. 'Yup. There's a bunch of 'em. In fact, mages make up about thirty-five percent of the town's population.'

Wide eyed, Alannah gaped at him. 'So, who are the mages I know at school?'

'Well, there's Cara for one, plus Connor and Bailey. Most of Liam's friends too.'

She sipped her tea as she digested this information. 'And each of you have different power source thingies?'

Brendan smiled. 'Attunements, yup. They are the main mana sources we can channel. As initiates, we spend a lot of time learning what mana we are most attuned to. Once we have identified our two primary sources, we hone our skills by practising basic spells and rituals that use them.'

'So, what are your attunements?'

Brendan stiffened and hesitated for a moment. 'Emotions and the five senses, which means I will most likely become an enchanter when I reach full magus status.'

Alannah wondered why he became uncomfortable with the conversation. 'Why do I get the feeling you're not happy about being an enchanter?'

He sighed. 'It's not that I mind being one, we just get a bad rap these days. There have been some notorious enchanters throughout history.'

'Really? Like whom?'

'Well Hitler's the first who comes to mind. I swear a few bad eggs and the rest of us are in the doghouse.'

'Oh wow.' Alannah started thinking about all the historical figures she knew about and wondered how many of them were mages. 'Can you demonstrate your powers?'

Relaxing, Brendan gave her a wicked grin. 'I'd love to, but Liam would totally kick my arse if he caught me.'

Her curiosity piqued. 'Why? What can you do?'

He leaned closer and held her gaze. 'I can read and manipulate emotions and enhance the senses. Makes for some pretty wild times in the sack.'

She blushed. 'Oh. So, uh… what can, uh… Liam do?'

Brendan laughed. 'Well, he is attuned to the elements and energy forces, which he uses for offensive magic like fireballs and lightning bolts. He is training to become a warlock.'

'What about your parents? What are they?'

He sat back again. 'Dad's an abjurer, like your mum was. They do healing and protective magic. Mum's a shaman who can channel elemental and emotional mana. She mostly uses it to help animals, which is why she's such a damn good vet. Cara's training to be a shaman too, although she's more interested in working with plants.' He paused and studied her. 'I'm sorry, I've overwhelmed you. I think we should leave all further talk of magic for another day.'

'Not a bad idea. Thanks.'

'You wanna watch a movie?'

Alannah picked up the DVD of *The Guard*. 'Actually, I do need to start studying this.'

The moment Liam walked into the living room late that afternoon, Alannah accosted him. She leaped up from the couch and blocked his path. *What the hell?*

'So, is it true?' she asked.

Feeling completely bewildered, he bit. 'Is what true?'

'That you can lob lightning bolts and shit.' She used an odd hand gesture to demonstrate her idea of a lightning bolt.

Liam let out a sigh of relief. 'So, he finally told you.'

'Yeah, Brendan told me what we are and all about what you can do. I'm still not sure I believe it though.'

He raised his eyebrows in surprise. 'So, he didn't give you a demonstration of his own powers?'

Alannah shook her head. 'No. That would've been inappropriate, and he said you'd kick his arse if he did.'

'Well he's not wrong. Come on.' He started walking out.

'Where are you going?' she asked, trailing him.

'The training room. It's safer to demonstrate in there.'

Liam led her into the cellar that had been built especially for training and group rituals. She gasped as she took in the sights. He had forgotten how awe inspiring the room had been for him the first time he entered. The most obvious feature was the enormous pentagram painted on the stone floor, each point marked with the symbols of the five elements of ritual magic: earth, air, fire, water, and Aether.

As her eyes shifted from the decorated floor, they scanned the bookshelves, lining the North wall, and locked behind bulletproof glass. Next, her attention wandered to the East where a series of shadow boards held various magic tools and weapons. She turned to him. 'How did I not know about this room before? Has it always been down here?'

'The house was built around this room. Our parents kept it locked tight and hidden from us until our initiation. I probably shouldn't be bringing you down here yet, but you deserve to learn the truth.'

She ran her hands along Liam's ritual robe.

'Oh, I should ask you to refrain from touching anything at this stage. We have consecrated most of our tools for individual use.'

Alannah snapped her hand back and offered him an apologetic smile. 'Sorry.'

He moved further into the room and picked up his staurolite elemental talisman ring. 'This ring has been charged with the four physical elements.' After giving Alannah a glimpse, he slipped it on his right index finger. He stood back from the target on the South wall, pulling Alannah back with him by a gentle tug of her arm. Taking aim, he fired a bolt of electricity from his pointed finger straight at the bullseye of the grounded target.

'*Fucking hell!*' Alannah cried. Her mouth gaped open when he looked at her.

Liam smiled. 'Are you okay? I hope that wasn't too *shocking* for you.'

Clenching her mouth shut, she slapped him lightly on the arm. 'The only thing that was too shocking for me was your terrible attempt at humour.'

'Right, well I hope you are okay because things are about to heat up in here.' This time when he aimed at the target, he shot a fireball about the size of a golf ball at a heatproof target. It sizzled out as soon as it hit the bullseye.

'Wow. That's incredible. So, it is true! Magic is fucking real.' Alannah gasped, her eyes wide like a kid in a toy store.

'Yes, it is most definitely real.' Liam smiled at her amazement.

Chapter Six

Alannah decided there was no time like the present to broach the topic with Ross and Nora. They sat at the dining table for a family meal and she both boys would back her up. 'So, I've been thinking, I'd like to be initiated.'

Nora's fork fell to her plate as she gawked at Alannah.

Liam and Brendan both shot her reassuring smiles.

Ross clenched his jaw as he purposefully placed his cutlery along the side of his plate. 'No.'

'*What, why not?*' Brendan jumped to her defence. 'She has the r—'

'Because it is too dangerous,' Ross interjected.

Alannah could see Brendan was about to speak on her behalf again, but she put a hand up to silence him. 'With all due respect, Uncle Ross, don't you think I'd be more equipped to defend myself from said dangers if I trained properly?'

'Alannah makes a very valid point, Dad.' This time it was Liam who had her back.

'Becoming initiated would expose Alannah to a greater set of risks. Things none of you could even begin to fathom.' He sighed and drank a large mouthful of his wine. 'Listen, Alannah. Your mother removed you from the magic world for a good reason and I'm not willing to disrespect her wishes after all the sacrifices she made to protect you.'

The room fell silent for a moment.

Liam cleared his throat. 'Look, Dad. Aunt Aileen might have been able to hide her safely in Melbourne, but Alannah is now living in a predominantly magical town and she can't even see what she's up against. How is ignorance going to protect her here?'

'I expect the four of us should be able to handle that for her. With your abilities and proximity, Liam, you are well positioned to defend her should the need arise.'

Alannah could see the fierce intensity in Brendan's glare, and she expected to see smoke billowing out of his nostrils any moment. 'But she's a Winters woman, for Christ's sake! And the first-born of her generation at that. She's entitled to her birthright. Shouldn't this be her decision?'

Ross turned to Brendan, scowling. 'Being a Winters woman is exactly why she shouldn't be initiated. I will not have any more shame brought upon this family.' He stormed out of the room.

Blinking from her uncle's outburst, Alannah turned her attention to Nora.

Nora shook her head. 'I'm sorry dear. It's a touchy subject for him.'

'But why? What happened?' Alannah asked.

After a pregnant pause, Nora sighed. 'Your grandmother and great aunt grew power-hungry and tried to overthrow the Arch Mage. They were both outlawed for practising forbidden magic.'

'Oh.' Alannah did not know what else to say. *Is that what Ross fears will happen to me?* She did not think she was a bad person, nor was she ambitious. Perhaps she could convince him things would be different for her.

They all finished their dinner in silence. After cleaning up, Brendan approached her. 'Hey, Lana. Connor's having a few friends over tonight. Wanna join me?'

'Sounds great, but…' Alannah looked toward Liam, wondering what his plans were.

Shrugging, Liam forced a smile. 'I've got a heap of study to do this weekend, so I won't be much company. Sorry.'

'Right. I'm gonna change. Our ride will be here in half an hour.' Brendan walked out of the kitchen.

As Alannah was about to head to her own room, Liam stopped her. 'Wait a sec, Lana.'

She turned to find Liam biting his lip. 'What's up?'

'Please be careful. Brendan has some pretty shady friends. I don't trust them, and I hate not being there to protect you tonight. Do me a favour and either stick with Brendan or Cara, okay?'

This surprised her. 'I thought you hated Cara?'

'There's some bad blood between us, but that has more to do with our relationship history. She's still a good person and one of the few people in that group I trust.'

'I'll be careful. I promise.'

'Good.' He relaxed and smiled slightly. Walking up, he hugged her, taking her by surprise.

She returned the embrace, savouring the contact. Pressing up against his rock-hard abs felt incredible and the ocean-fresh scent surrounding her was intoxicating.

He whispered in her ear, 'Have a good night.' Releasing her, he swiftly left the room.

'Good evening, Alannah. You look stunning tonight.' Austin was holding the front passenger door of his car open for her.

Alannah wondered who said chivalry was dead. She took the opportunity to look at his wheels properly for the first time. Austin drove a black Lexus with heavily tinted windows that blocked any view of the occupants from the outside. The vehicle was sleek and sexy, much like the driver. 'Hey, Austin. Thanks.' She climbed in and noticed the heavy music playing through the stereo.

'Ah man, I love these guys!' Brendan declared as he jumped into the back.

When she glanced at the streaming display on Austin's phone, Alannah saw the band was Grey Hearts Red. 'They sound good. Who are they?'

'A local hard rock band. They put on a great live show too,' Austin replied as he sat behind the wheel.

'Nice.' Once the car was moving, Alannah gazed out the window and let her mind wander. After the unbelievable day she'd had, chilling out and having some fun was exactly what she needed.

Five minutes later, they stopped, and Cara burst into the back of the car. 'Hi guys! Oh my God, Alannah, I'm so glad Brendan finally told you about magic!'

So much for an easy night, Alannah thought. She spun around and focussed on Cara. 'Wait, you knew about me being in the dark?'

Cara looked sheepish. 'Yeah, Brendan wanted us all to keep our mouths shut until he'd had a chance to explain things. It's been a hard secret to keep, believe me.'

Alannah turned to Austin, then back to Cara and whispered, 'Does Austin know about this stuff?'

'Yes, Alannah, I know that you are all mages.' Austin's raspy voice startled her.

'But you're not a mage, are you?'

He laughed softly. 'No, I'm not.'

When they arrived at Connor's house, Alannah discovered 'a few friends over' was not an accurate description for the gathering. It was a full-fledged party, though smaller than the one on Friday night.

As they approached the door, Cara linked arms with Alannah. 'Come on girl, let's get tanked!'

They filed into the hallway when Brendan walked up behind Alannah and Cara. 'Excuse me ladies, this house is full of lusty hotties just waiting for me.' He put his arms around them both. 'That is unless either or both of you want to learn first-hand how magical I am.'

'*Ugh, gross!*' Cara cried, pushing him away. 'You are such a man-slut. Why don't you try using your powers for good occasionally?'

Directing his gaze at Alannah, Brendan grinned. 'What can I say? Once a rogue, always a rogue.' He took off and threw his arm around some redhead standing by the beer keg.

Alannah leaned in to whisper to Cara, 'The way he uses his powers to seduce girls; isn't that wrong?'

'It's one of those moral grey areas. He doesn't make them do anything they don't want to, so it's not like rape or anything, but it is a more selfish use of his powers. He isn't hurting anyone, so it's not outlawed behaviour,' Cara explained. She poured a beer and handed it to Alannah before getting herself one.

They found their host surrounded by a few other friends. The short, spunky red-headed Amy engaged Connor in conversation. Alannah recognised the signs well enough to know Amy would not appreciate any disruptions.

The other couple in the room was Ben and Bianca. Ben's long, golden locks had fallen forward, blocking his face, but his body language was enough to suggest his intentions and Bianca was every bit as complicit in the flirting.

Everyone was pairing off and Alannah's thoughts shifted to Austin. *Where did he disappear to? Is he hooking up with someone?* A pang of jealousy pinched at her gut, startling her. *Why should I care, especially when Liam is still a prospect?*

After finding a couch away from the crowds, Alannah needed to ask, 'Um, Cara…'

Cara sighed. 'Ugh, Brendan warned me you might try to bombard me with mage questions. What would you like to know?'

'No, this isn't about magic. It's about Liam.'

This time, Cara rolled her eyes, but Alannah also noticed her stiffen a little. 'Go on.'

She put on her best pleading face as she addressed Cara. 'He briefly mentioned your ill feelings were the result of something that happened between the two of you. I was hoping you could fill me in.'

'Oh, that.' Cara sipped her drink. 'We used to be good friends when I moved here in Year Seven.' She paused a moment, taking another swig of beer before elaborating. 'I developed a pretty big crush on him during that time. Then one night, he kissed me.' She let out a derisive laugh. 'The next day he acted like nothing happened and when I questioned him, he told me we could never be more than friends, that I needed to get over him.'

'Shit, Cara, I'm so sorry. I had no idea Liam could be like that. That's a horrid thing to do.' Alannah's opinion of Liam had taken a bit of a plunge on her first day at Gaeilge High, but Cara's story was sending it to rock bottom. 'He was such a sweet kid when we were younger. What the hell happened to him?'

Cara's head drooped. 'Truth is, he was still sweet then too, but he let his need for social status and the approval of his parents get the better of him.'

'What do you mean?'

She looked back up at Alannah. 'I'm not a pure mage, so his parents would not have approved of me dating him. Your family, along with several other clans, are pretty strict about only coupling with full mages, to keep the bloodline pure.'

Alannah's jaw hit the floor. 'That's so archaic!'

'You're telling me. I'm kinda thankful in a way, that I'm not a pure mage. I can't imagine being forced into an arranged marriage. At least in your case, the guy you like is on the pre-approved list, so your Uncle probably won't need to organise a spouse for either of you.' She clapped her hand over her mouth for a moment. 'Oh shit! That probably sounded really rude.'

Still reeling from the revelation, Alannah barely took notice of Cara's tone. 'It's okay. Don't worry about it. But hey, what about Brendan? He doesn't seem to care about how pure a girl's bloodline is.'

'That's true and I respect him for it. He doesn't care for status. That said, I doubt your Uncle would let him openly date a non-pure. I'm guessing that's part of the reason Brendan doesn't commit to one girl. When the time comes, I bet he'll elope to spite his folks.'

Alannah laughed. 'You're probably right.'

'Hey Cara, Alannah.' Jacob approached them with Austin in tow. 'You wanna join us for a game of beer pong?'

'Sounds great,' Alannah agreed. It was exactly what she needed.

Cara jumped up. 'Absolutely!' She pulled Alannah up from the sofa and they headed outside.

Ugh! Damn hangovers. Alannah dragged her sorry arse out of bed and glanced at the clock: 11AM.

Wondering if it was too late to join the others for breakfast, she threw some warm clothes on and made her way downstairs.

Liam stood at the island bench drinking a smoothie. He raised a single eyebrow and gave her an amused grin when she entered the kitchen. 'Morning sunshine. Drink a bit, did you?'

Her splitting headache had her in a foul mood, so she replied by flipping him off.

Laughing, he grabbed a green concoction in a clear glass bottle, along with a shot glass and handed them to her. 'Here, have some of this.'

Alannah eyed the elixir in the fancy flask doubtfully.

'It's Dad's magically enhanced hangover cure. Perfectly safe, trust me.'

Thankfully, she did trust Liam, so she poured some of the potion into the glass and sculled it. '*Yuck!*' It tasted like a disgusting mix of wheatgrass and bitter herbs. She handed the bottle back to Liam, sitting down to wait for it to kick in. Amazingly, it only took a couple of minutes for the fog to clear and her stomach to settle. She smiled. 'Wow, that stuff's incredible. Your dad ought to sell it.'

'He does, but only to magic folk. Like most potions, it's toxic for humans.'

'Oh.' It was going to take a long time to wrap her head around the magic world. 'Must be handy having a father with magical healing abilities.'

'More than you'd realise,' Liam agreed. 'He fixes me up good whenever I get in fights.'

'Oh my God! That's why you looked unharmed after the fight on Friday night!'

Liam nodded.

She wondered how bad his injuries were before Ross healed him. Another thought struck: *Why didn't Brendan get his dad to tend to the scratches I left on his back? Did he enjoy that?* Pushing those questions to the back of her mind, she grabbed some toast and made her way to the table.

A few minutes later, Brendan sauntered in with messy hair, wearing a stupid grin and the same clothes from last night. *Trust Brendan to make the walk of shame look so hot.*

Wait, what? Alannah blinked away the ridiculous thought. *Casual, I mean* casual!

Liam glared at Brendan. 'Did you just get home?'

'Yup. Morning Lana.' He shot her a wicked grin before raiding the fridge.

'You were meant to keep an eye on Lana last night.' Liam clenched his jaw.

After grabbing the milk, he shut the fridge. 'I did, right Cuz?' He winked at her. 'I made sure she got home safe before heading over to Bianca's.'

Liam gave her a sidelong glance. 'Lana?'

'It's true. I stuck with Cara all night and Brendan was never far.'

As he exhaled, Liam's shoulders relaxed. 'You've been spending a lot of time with that nymph lately. Be careful Brendan, people might start thinking something serious is going on.'

'People can think what they like. Bianca's only a friend… with a lot of benefits.' Brendan poured a huge bowl of cereal and a coffee. He sat across from Alannah at the table. 'Where are the folks?'

Liam sat next to her. 'Council meeting. Which reminds me, Lana, we need to talk about getting you initiated.'

Brendan sprayed the remnants of his mouthful of coffee across the table, staring at Liam. 'This is a first! Liam defying Dad's orders. Never thought I'd see the day.'

'Well, this is the first time I've disagreed with him so adamantly. I really do think Lana needs to be initiated.' Turning to Alannah, he continued, 'That is, of course, if you want to do it.'

She did not know what to think. Uncle Ross' downright refusal to discuss the issue had infuriated her, but it also got her thinking about the reasons her mum had for hiding her. 'I dunno, to be honest. I don't know what the risks are.'

Liam sighed. 'I think staying in the dark is a bigger risk, especially in this town. You can't see past glamour, so you don't know who you're dealing with when you're out in public. Plus, it could be good to learn some protective spells.'

'Wait, what do you mean see "past glamour?"' Alannah inquired.

Liam shot Brendan a stern glance. 'You didn't tell her about other magicals?'

'Not yet. You told me to break things to her slowly. She was already reeling from the little I covered yesterday.'

Alannah raised a hand. 'Hang on a minute, guys. Firstly—Liam—you told Brendan to tell me about magic? Why couldn't you do it?'

Liam groaned. 'Because Brendan would be able to read your emotions and gauge when it was appropriate to tell you. Plus, if you got hysterical, he would have been able to calm you down.'

Alannah directed a piercing gaze at Brendan. 'You've been reading my emotions?'

He nodded.

'All of them?'

He lowered his gaze and nodded again.

She felt so violated. *How many private feelings has he witnessed me experience?*

Liam hung his head. 'If it's any consolation, half the time he can't switch it off. Besides, I was the one who asked him to read you.'

Narrowing her eyes, she spoke in a deadly serious tone. 'Brendan, have you told anyone about my feelings?'

He sat upright, shaking his head. 'Gods no! I keep that shit to myself. I do have a moral code, fuzzy as it may seem.'

'Well I still don't like it. Please refrain from reading me where possible in future.'

'Duly noted.' Curling his top lip, Brendan wrinkled the bridge of his nose.

Why is he taking offence when he wronged me? Alannah sighed. 'Now tell me, what are these other magicals?'

'Other supernatural creatures. They hide behind magic known as glamour to disguise their true form from humans and the uninitiated. Fairies, or fae as we tend to call them, are the most common,' Liam explained.

She was utterly gobsmacked. 'Uh, so… what else is there?'

'Almost anything you can recall from myth or legend is likely to be real to some extent, although humans tended to twist the truth in their versions of the stories,' replied Liam.

'But if these creatures are hiding with… what's that magic called?'

Brendan returned to the conversation. 'Glamour.'

Alannah nodded. 'Right, if they use glamour, how did these so-called myths come about?'

After a nod from Liam, Brendan answered, 'We used to all coexist openly with humans, but they started to hunt us like monsters when they developed monotheistic religions.'

'So, if fairies are real, what about elves and dwarves?'

'They exist,' Brendan confirmed. 'You familiar with *The Lord of the Rings*?'

'Yeah, of course.' Alannah knew the books and movies inside out.

'Tolkien was a mage, so he described them pretty accurately.'

'Orcs and goblins?' Alannah asked.

Brendan nodded. 'Yup, both real.'

'Wow,' she whispered. Then raising her voice, 'What about unicorns?'

Brendan smiled. 'You still got a thing for them, huh? You'll be pleased to know they are real, although rare. Apparently only virgin mages can see them though.'

Alannah felt a wave of disappointment and tried her hardest to keep a neutral face.

Brendan snorted. 'Kidding. About the virgin thing anyway. They are rare though. I had you there for a moment.' He gave her a knowing grin.

Shit! Brendan must have been reading her. 'Yeah, you got me good.'

Liam cleared his throat. 'It would take a long time to explain everything to you, so I think you would benefit from a structured training plan, much like what Brendan and I have undergone. You would start with the theory. When you are ready, you can be initiated and begin the practical lessons.'

Alannah sighed. 'You mean if I want to? I'm still not sure about learning magic.'

'Think about it. But remember, there are some real monsters out there, Lana, and you are safer seeing people for what they are.'

Chapter Seven

Austin looked up at Alannah from his homework and smiled. His eyes were almost glowing, and the effect was incredibly alluring. 'Did you need some help with maths today?'

Sitting down next to him at the library table, Alannah became overwhelmed by his strong, spicy fragrance. Everything about this man's appearance was such a contrast to Liam's beauty, yet she still found him insanely sexy. 'Yeah, I do, if that's okay?'

'Of course. What topic is stumping you?'

She laughed. 'All of them. But let's start with angle geometry.' After opening her textbook, she found the section that had been frustrating her the most.

Austin was a brilliant teacher, so patient and clear in his explanations. Within an hour, she had the concepts down pat.

'Wow! I totally get it now. Thank you, Austin, you're amazing.'

He was beaming from her praise. 'No problem. You should try some more practice questions to consolidate your understanding.'

Alannah attempted to do that, but after a couple of questions, her mind started to wander. She dropped her pen and gazed upon the gorgeous guy sitting next to her. He had gone back to his own maths, which looked beyond complicated. 'Austin?'

His focus returned to her. 'Yes?'

'Are you some kind of magical person? I get the sense you are super-human somehow.'

A soft laugh escaped his luscious lips. 'I'll take that as a compliment.' Leaning closer, he dropped his voice to a whisper. 'But, yes, you are right. I am not human. If you can detect that before initiation, I imagine you'll be a very powerful mage one day.'

Alannah frowned, remembering what she learned of her grandmother. 'Not too powerful, I hope.'

The comment earned her a sidelong glance. 'Would you like to know what I am?'

Curiosity dangled a length of twine in front of her, and like an impulsive kitten, Alannah almost reached out to grab it. But this world was still too new to her. 'No, not yet. I want to learn more about the true nature of magical people first. That way I won't let pop culture influence me with prejudice.'

He gave her a nod. 'That's a very noble approach. Perhaps you could try teaching the word "tolerance" to your cousin, Liam.'

The thought of Liam's attitudes made her sigh. 'I wish I could. Why does he behave like such an arse around you guys?'

'Most pure mages do. You and Brendan are the exceptions, I'm afraid.'

Interesting. Why did Brendan turn out different? Alannah grew up in the human world, ignorant of her heritage, so that explained her position. *But Brendan?* She made a mental note to question him later. 'So, why does having a higher concentration of mage blood make them such pompous pricks?'

Austin laughed heartily, prompting a scowl and shush from the librarian. 'Your colourful language is delightful, Alannah.'

She grinned.

'Pure mages take their position as magic law keepers very seriously.'

'Law keepers?'

'The Gods created mages for the purpose of bringing order to the magic world and ensuring our peaceful coexistence with humans. It is literally your God-given right to rule over us. It is why they make a point of keeping the bloodlines pure, to maintain their power. That's also why it is so common for mage cousins to marry one another.' Austin's tone was verging on bitter.

'Well shit. No wonder you're jumping to help me with my maths.'

His expression softened. 'You think I don't want to do this? I'll take any opportunity to spend time with you, Alannah.'

Those words alone knocked the air out of her, but his gleaming eyes also enchanted her. Alannah could not breathe, let alone speak or move. It was like his gaze trapped her and she savoured every second of it.

'Alannah? Are you okay? You look like you're about to faint.' Austin's voice broke her trance.

Her lungs remembered they needed oxygen and she sucked in a huge breath. 'Yeah, I'm fine.' She gave him a coy smile as she extracted some strands of hair from the side of her face and tucked them behind her ear.

'Hey Lana, time to go.' Brendan appeared out of nowhere, with Liam at his side.

Did Austin use magic? She looked up at her cousins.

Liam was glaring at Austin.

'Give me a sec.' While packing her books away, she took a moment to contemplate Liam's behaviour. *Is he jealous of Austin? But if he really wants me, why hasn't he made his move yet?* 'Okay, I'm ready. Thanks for your help, Austin.'

Another award-winning smile. 'It was a pleasure.'

'I'd like to begin my training tonight,' Alannah announced, breaking the uncomfortable silence that had set in on the drive home.

'That's great, Lana!' Brendan shifted forward on the back seat. 'I'm sure we'll have you initiated in no time. I can't wait to see what your attunements will be.'

She laughed. 'Easy, tiger. I haven't even started with the theory yet. I was hoping to begin with reading up on the different magical people.'

'Let me guess, you want to learn all about Austin's filthy race.' Liam's tone cut to the bone.

Turning to face him, Alannah tried to read his expression, but his attention was still on the road. *How dare he talk to me like that!* 'I don't know what Austin is yet and I don't want to know until I've read up on all the magic races. Same goes for the rest of my friends. I want to learn the facts first before I let the myths cloud my judgement. Besides, I thought *you* were the one who wanted me to know about the *monsters* out there.'

Liam scoffed. 'I wanted you to learn who the *monsters* are so you'd avoid them, not run into their arms.'

'I don't know what your problem is, Liam, and frankly I don't give a crap.' She huffed and crossed her arms, wishing she wasn't sitting next to him in a moving vehicle.

Brendan whistled through his teeth. 'Man, you two are already acting like an old married couple and you haven't even…'

'Shut up, Brendan!' They both snapped at him.

The car fell silent again. Alannah kept her focus fixed on the lush green hills and bushland passing them by as they approached Cailleach Estate. It was such a beautiful part of the world.

When they got home, Liam stormed off to his room and slammed the door.

Brendan laughed at his brother's temper, putting his arm around Alannah's shoulders. 'Come on, Lana, let's get some food, then start on your training.'

There was a remarkable number of books in the cellar. They were organised by subject matter, with one full shelf devoted to the magical races. There were also books dedicated to each of the magus specialisations, others on paganism and spirituality, and an extensive history collection of the Irish mage clans. And all the books sat behind locked, durable glass doors.

Brendan unlocked one of the bookcases and picked out a few volumes for her. 'These are all the beginner guides.'

Alannah flicked through each of the large, hard-cover reference books as he placed them on the reading desk next to her. *Preparing for Initiation, A Compendium of Magical People and Beasts, The Celtic Pantheon,* and *Celtic Traditions in the Modern Age.* She looked up at Brendan with a wry smile. 'So just a little light reading then.'

'Fear not, Lana. I'm sure you'll power through them. And if nothing else, they'll help you build muscle tone in your arms.' He grinned as he pushed the pile of books toward her.

Her weedy arms sank under their weight and she almost dropped a couple, but Brendan caught them. 'Bloody hell, Brendan, are you trying to kill me, or destroy the books?'

'You're gonna have to start working out, too. Mages need to be physically fit and strong.'

Alannah groaned. 'Seriously?'

Brendan gestured for her to head back upstairs. 'Yup. When we channel mana, we become a conduit for that power, and it can put a lot of stress on the body. Physical and mental endurance are essential. It also pays to prepare for all manner of challenges.'

'I'm not so sure I wanna be a mage anymore,' she complained. Alannah had always hated P.E.

When they returned to the living room, he turned to her and flashed a wicked smile. 'Hey, on the plus side, you could exercise with me and check out this glorious body in action.' He flexed his biceps as he spoke.

She rolled her eyes and continued making her way to her room, where she planned to conduct her research away from her uncle's prying eyes.

'There you go.' Brendan dropped the two books he had carried on her desk. 'Enjoy.'

Alannah looked up at him. 'So, you're not gonna guide me through any of my reading?'

He raised his eyebrows, sat on the edge of her bed and held his hands out to her. 'You want me to hold your hand through the process?'

She moved forward and gripped his hands in hers, digging her nails into his palms. 'I probably need my hands to hold those damn books.'

Wincing a little, he pulled her onto his lap such that she was straddling him. 'I could spoon you while you read in bed.'

Alannah narrowed her eyes on him. 'Oh sure, then when I fall asleep from boredom, you can wake me up by poking me in the arse.'

Brendan sucked in a breath, flipping her onto the mattress, he pinned her down. His expression was ferocious and wild. 'Don't fucking tempt me, Lana.'

Her face went bright red.

Standing up, Brendan clapped his hands together victoriously. 'My win streak continues.' He made his way to her door, pausing with a hand pressed against the frame, speaking without turning, 'I'll be here to answer any questions you have from your studies.'

Alannah's skin blazed, so she pulled off her jumper and grabbed the compendium to commence her reading.

Chapter One: The Origin of Magical Races.

Little is known of the time before the first mages. There were no written records and most magical people were secretive about their own histories, but over time many of them assimilated with humanity and came to trust their new overseers.

Most accounts agree dragons were the first of the demigods, created from the primordial by the God of Wisdom and Knowledge, and they took to the skies. Elves—the offspring of Sun, Moon, and nature Gods and Goddesses—soon followed and they claimed the forests. Then came the giants of the plains, the dwarves of the mountains, the orcs of the hills and pastures, mermaid/mermen of the seas, and the gorgons of the deep, dark places of the world.

Magical people's souls leaving the mortal plane either ascended to the Celestial realm as spirits, or the Gods cursed and banished them to the underworld as demons.

Each of these races ruled in their own domains and rarely strayed from *their homes, until humans began to populate the world. Trade and commerce became the means through which these people mingled and interbred, learning to live in harmony. But some of them also sought to increase their power and wealth.*

A new generation of magical people arose. The most common hybrids were the faeries, or fae, the result of prolific mating between elves and other races. The other hybrids that came about during this time were the gnomes, and nāga.

In the Ninth Century B.C. the first mages were created to bring order to the magic world and establish peace among magical people and humans. With the mages came a new range of hybrids, including endarkened fae, enlightened fae, and were-creatures.

Not all mages were content to carry out the will of the Gods, however. Some went dark, disregarding the laws of society entirely and becoming obsessed with power. But the worst perpetrators were those who practised forbidden magic, bringing a curse upon themselves and their descendants: the ghouls, the liches, the succubi/incubi, and the vampires.

Liam found Brendan watching television in the living room. Knowing Alannah was busy studying, he approached his younger brother. 'Should the time Lana spends with Austin worry me? He hangs with your group; do you know if something's going on between them?'

Brendan looked up from his viewing. 'Austin's definitely hot for her, that much is obvious to everyone; but I haven't seen them kiss or anything.' He returned to watching his show, some dumb occult rubbish.

After collapsing on the sofa next to Brendan, Liam grabbed the remote and muted the volume.

'Hey, I was watching that.' He tried to grab it back, but Liam was too quick.

Holding the controller behind his back, he pressed on. 'What sort of a read have you got on her feelings?'

Brendan glared at him. 'I can't tell you that. You know it goes against my code.'

'Come on man. It's not like I'm asking how she feels about *me*.'

He shook his head, but Brendan's resolve was slipping at the sight of Liam's pleading eyes. 'Okay, fine, but you owe me one if this bites me in the arse.'

'Answer the bloody question.'

'Yes, she likes him.' Brendan's own pain was evident in his eyes.

Jumping up, Liam threw the remote control at one of the armchairs. '*Shit!*' He began pacing the room. 'Do you think her interest in him will wane when she learns the truth?'

'Probably. I get the sense she has a thing for bad boys. If you don't watch out, she might come after me next.'

Liam could not think of anything worse. 'Yeah right. Seriously though, I don't trust Austin. Beside his race or history—I still get a bad vibe from him.'

'Since when are you attuned to emotions? That's *my* specialty.'

Liam laughed. 'It's not like you ever use your powers constructively.'

'Touché.' Brendan put his feet up and stretched out.

'You know Mum channels emotions for the greater good. Wouldn't hurt you to give it a go sometime.'

'My approach is more fun though.' He slapped Liam on the leg. 'You know fun? You should try it sometime. It can't be good for you to keep walkin' around with that stick up your arse.'

'Please keep an eye on Austin, for Lana's sake,' Liam snarled.

Brendan adopted one of his rare serious expressions. 'Fine. Not that I've ever seen or read anything to give me cause for concern, not since he reformed. But if you're worried about Lana, so am I.'

Chapter Eight

'Alannah Winters and Brendan Winters to reception.'

Alannah was in second period English on Friday when the call came over the P.A. She froze in a panic. Her last summons over loud speaker was because of her dad. Images of the whole incident flashed through her mind.

'Lana, it's okay. I got you. Lana?' Brendan's hand on hers brought her back to the present. 'Come on.' He helped her up and led her down the hall.

Alannah continued holding onto his hand for dear life. When they reached the front office, Aunt Nora was there, talking to Liam, and they were both in good spirits. When they turned to face Alannah and Brendan, both of their gazes shot to the vice grip between them.

Nora appeared curious, but Liam's countenance darkened, so Alannah quickly released

Brendan. She did not want Liam to get the wrong idea. Things had been tense enough between them since her study session with Austin at the start of the week. At least they started talking again on Tuesday.

'Mum? What are you doing here?' Brendan asked.

Facing Alannah, she smiled. 'I thought you might like to help me with the boxes that arrived from Melbourne. The Principal has agreed to let me take you home early.'

Relief washed over her. There was no bad news. 'That sounds great. Thanks.'

'And you boys are coming to help with the heavy lifting.'

Brendan's passive expression lifted, and he grinned. 'Any excuse to get off school's fine with me.'

As the four of them walked out to the car park, Alannah overheard the boys talking in hushed voices behind her.

'What the hell was *that* about?' Liam growled.

'Don't get your jocks in a knot. She freaked out when Miss O'Leary called her name over the P.A. Lana needed my support.'

'I don't need to warn you again, do I?' Liam's tone was serious.

'Fuck you, bro. I'm the least of your concerns right now.' Brendan shot forward to walk alongside Nora.

So, Liam *was* jealous. It gave Alannah a perverse sense of satisfaction.

Liam appeared to her left. 'You okay, Lana? Brendan told me you had a scare.'

'Yeah, I'm fine now. It's just… the last time someone beckoned me to the office like that… it was the day Dad…'

'Oh, shit, I'm sorry Lana.' He drew her into his arms.

They reached Nora's Mazda SUV and Liam pulled Alannah into the back seat with him.

'What about your car?' she asked him.

'I left it at home and rode with Mum today.' After fastening both of their seatbelts, he drew her back into his arms.

Alannah had not realised how much she missed Liam holding her. He used to hug her all the time when they were kids, but their physical contact had been less frequent since her return. Being this close to his warmth was one of her favourite feelings.

They spent the rest of the day moving and unpacking boxes. Nora stored most of the household items in the shed for Alannah to retrieve when she established her own home later. But there were a few items, like photos and ornaments, she put around the place.

When they reached the boxes marked 'attic', Alannah called it: 'I'm exhausted. Let's leave these for later.'

'Okay, sweetheart. Let's order some takeaway for dinner.' Nora sounded relieved to finish.

After their meal, Alannah retired to the living room with the boys to watch movies.

Liam beelined for the couch and looked up at Alannah in anticipation. When she sat next to him, she curled up in his arms and fell asleep during the first film.

Nora and Ross were busy with work the next day, but Alannah was keen to get stuck into the rest of the boxes and both of her cousins were happy to help. They had been sorting for hours and only a handful of cartons remained.

'I expect the last of these boxes to contain my parents' magic gear,' Alannah explained.

'Sweet.' Brendan rubbed his hands together in anticipation.

The first two were full of old family photos. She avoided the temptation to linger along memory lane. Yet she still paused and smiled when she came across a framed picture of her with the boys on her seventh birthday. That had occurred nine months before she left South Australia. Both boys draped their arms around Alannah and they were looking at her while she smiled for the camera.

'I remember that day.' Liam kneeled close to her, his chin on her shoulder. 'They were good times.'

'Yeah, they were,' she agreed. Much simpler, too.

'Give us a look,' Brendan stuck his hand out.

Alannah handed him the photo.

'Oh Gods, I was such a weed back then. No wonder Liam was always kicking my arse.'

Liam laughed. 'I can still kick your arse, bro.'

'Not if it's a fair fight, without magic,' Brendan grinned.

Alannah moved on, leaving them to their pointless debate. When she opened the next carton, she gasped. The strange, decorated trunk. It was too heavy to lift, so she cut the cardboard from around it.

'*Wowsers!*' Brendan drew closer and exhaled sharply. 'Is that a mystic chest?'

'A what?'

Liam joined them. 'Yes, it is. A mystic chest is a magically sealed box used to protect powerful artefacts. The trick will be working out how to open it.'

'I managed to open it back in Melbourne. This was where I found the Winters Clan Book of Shadows.'

'You what?' Liam's head jerked back as his jaw gaped open. 'You have the family's Book of Shadows?'

'Uh, yeah. I told you I had my mum's book.'

'I assumed it was one of Aunt Aileen's notebooks. I didn't realise you meant *that* book. I thought our grandmother took it.' Liam shook his head. 'We should probably lock it up in the Cellar, along with the contents of this trunk, especially now you've broken the seal on it.'

Brendan tried to lift the lid of the chest, but it did not budge. 'Um, I don't think Lana broke the seal.'

After his own attempt, Liam's eyes narrowed on Alannah. 'But how?'

'I dunno. I fiddled with these Celtic knot thingies. Like this.' She ran her fingers under the medallions as she had done before, pricking her finger like last time. '*Ouch!* Damn thing got me again.' Drawing her injured hand up, she looked at the cut on her finger and it dawned on her. 'After doing that, I touched this moonstone.' Which she did with her bloody finger and the catch released.

'A blood seal,' Brendan pointed out. 'Only the person who made the seal, or a direct descendent, can open one of those.'

Liam frowned. 'A gamble though: Aunt Aileen risked bringing down the vampiric curse on herself and Alannah by using it.'

'I'm guessing you aren't cursed, Lana, although you are pale enough to be a vampire.' He bumped her with his shoulder. 'You don't get cravings to drink blood, do you Cuz?'

Giggling, she returned the shove. 'Not yet, but I'll be sure to bite you first if I do.'

A huge grin formed on Brendan's face. 'Have you read the chapter on vampires yet?'

'No, why?'

He leaned in to whisper in her ear. 'Because vampire bites feel orgasmic.'

Alannah would have pushed Brendan further, but she looked at Liam, whose fists clenched while his face reddened, so she decided against it. Clearing her throat, she returned her attention to the mystical box. Everything was still there.

'Looks like a full set of magic tools,' Liam observed. 'You could have them consecrated for your own use when you're initiated.'

'They seem pretty old,' Alannah replied.

Brendan peeked inside the chest and whistled. 'That's 'cause they are. I read about these in one of our clan's history books. Our ancestors forged them in the Middle Ages.'

Too astonished for words, Alannah closed the trunk and moved on to the next carton. It was full of files and folded papers. She pulled out a sheet.

'An updated family tree. Nice.' Liam was behind her.

'It's in Gaelic, though. Can you read it?'

'Yes, of course,' Liam replied. 'That's you, 'Alannah Geimhreadh, born thirtieth of July 2002, not yet tested.' He pointed to her name. 'And your parents.' His finger slid up the page. He froze. When Alannah looked at him, his face had gone almost as white as hers and he dropped the page.

'Liam? What's wrong?' she asked in a small voice.

Brendan grabbed the chart and finished translating it for her. 'Daughter of Aileen

Geimhreadh, born sixth of June 1980, one hundred percent mage; and Dennis Wagner, born seventeenth of April 1978, one hundred percent human… Well shit! Your old man was human. We always assumed he was one of the German pure mages.'

Remembering what Cara had told her, Alannah understood Liam's reaction and her heart sank. Her blood was not pure. Liam stood and left the room without a word. It was enough to break her. Tears burst from her eyes as she collapsed on the floor.

'*Oh shit!*' Brendan sat beside her and pulled her into his arms. 'I guess you know about the whole stupid bloodline crap.' He tried stroking her back and mumbling soothing words, but he sounded too distraught to be calming her. '*Fuck!* Dammit, I'm sorry Lana.'

An hour later, Brendan was still embracing Alannah. Her tears had dried and she felt ready to stand, desperately needing a drink of water.

When she moved into the kitchen, Brendan followed her. 'My parents won't be back until well after midnight, apparently. Did you want to order pizza and watch stupid movies?'

Three guzzled glasses of water later, Alannah replied, 'Pizza sounds great.' She slumped into one of the dining chairs and dropped her head onto the table, supporting it with her folded arms. Moving on from Cole had been hard enough. *How am I going to get over a lifetime's worth of feelings?*

'Right, well dinner is on its way.' Brendan had rung through the order without her even noticing.

'Thanks.'

He sat beside her. 'You wanna talk about it?'

'Not really.' She sighed, turning her head to face him.

Brendan was watching her intently, concern plastered to his face. 'Okay…'

'I always imagined ending up with Liam and it really fucking hurts to know that can never be a reality.' She shot up from the table. 'Where do your folks stash their booze? I need to get shit-faced.'

He grinned. 'That's the spirit. Follow me.' Brendan led her out to the guest house, situated about two-hundred metres back from the main house on the left side of the block. After opening the antique cupboard behind the bar, he stepped aside. 'Help yourself.'

'Oh good, there's whiskey. Grab us some glasses, will you?' She retrieved the bottle of liquid gold and took it to the lounge area of the guest house. When Brendan placed the glasses in front of her, she poured them both a drink.

'What, no shot measure?'

'Too much effort.' She held her glass out to clink with Brendan's before throwing it back in synchronisation with him. The sudden burn in her throat was just the ticket. But, requiring more, she poured another round.

'Gods, that stuff is good,' Brendan declared after his second shot.

The doorbell sounded through the guest house intercom speaker.

'Pizza!' His voice was verging on melodic. 'I'll be right back.' He jumped up and dashed out the room.

Alannah downed two more shots and finally welcomed the first signs of alcohol numbing her emotions. She was working on another when Brendan returned.

'Jesus, woman, save some for me.' He sank into the seat next to her with two pizza boxes in hand.

She shot him a rueful smile and dived for the food. 'Thanks for the grub.'

After shovelling a few slices into her mouth, she looked up to see Brendan grinning as he watched her. 'What?' she asked.

'Are you inhaling that food?'

'This is how I eat when I've been drinking. Does the sight disgust you?'

'Hell no! If anything, it turns me on.' He gave a lewd grin.

Alannah punched him in the arm, but she hit solid muscle and it only made him laugh.

Once they finished the pizza, the drinking continued.

'How's the reading going?' Brendan asked after a few more shots each.

'Smashish...smashging...great.' She giggled as she bumbled about with words. *'Words' is such a funny word. Words, words, words.* 'I'm halfway through the one about magical people.'

'That's good. Is it all making sense?'

'Mostly. Although I don't get how gorgons could mate to create those snake people if their gaze always turns humans to stone.'

'Blindfolds. Where do you think BDSM originates from?'

'BD what now?'

Brendan's jaw dropped. 'You don't know what BDSM is? I figured you for someone with an extensive sex vocab. It means bondage/discipline, domination/submission, and sadomasochism. It's how gorgons have sex with humans and make baby nāga.'

This time Alannah was gobsmacked. 'Are you for real?'

'Yup. No way I'd lie about shit like that.'

'Well there was the unicorn thing.'

'Hey that was one time, and I came clean *almost* straight away. Besides, it was a very *educational* experience.'

Alannah snorted. 'How was it eduma...educational?'

'Well, you learned the whole virgin thing is a myth and I learned you're not a virgin.' He beamed, apparently pleased with himself for such a deduction.

She burst into laughter and Brendan joined a moment later. After several minutes, they calmed down and had another drink.

'Have you read anything in the other books yet?' he asked her.

'I read a bit about the different types of mages and channelling stuff, but it looks pretty complicated. I haven't gotten to the other books yet. There's so-o much to get through. Why do I have to read about paganism to learn magic, anyway?'

'Imagine it like this, yeah?' Brendan was up out of his seat, clearly enthused by the topic. 'You've got this guy, so he's a dude, but he's not all that well-endowed physically, right? He's barely six inches on his own—'

'Does it always have to be a sex analogy?' Attempting to appear wearied, Alannah secretly praised herself for pronouncing analogy right in one go.

'Yup, it does. Also, shoosh. So, you've got this poor guy—let's call him Liam for argument's sake—*but* he's an illusionist. So well attuned in fact, that not only can he make himself look nine inches, but he can also make it *feel* like nine. So, for all intents and purposes, what is he actually packing? Is it barely-six or a nine?'

Pausing only a couple of times to giggle and burp, Alannah answered, 'Oh, I know where this is going. This is about how reality is subjectsh...subjunc...how it is what we see it as, right? So, the answer is nine.'

'Well sure, but the point of the question is, magic is not its own self-contained thing. It's all bound up in science and religion and philosophy.' Brendan gave Alannah the most unsteady bedroom eyes she had ever seen, before saying, 'Really. Philosophically. Deep.'

She glared at him levelly. 'You're such a slut.'

'I am a lover…' Brendan countered quickly, before misjudging the position of his seat and falling to the floor: 'Of knowledge.'

They fell silent a moment. Brendan sighed and looked at Alannah with a furrowed brow and pursed lips. 'Ya know what? I reckon you ought to say, "to hell with Liam." You're a beautiful woman and there's plenty more fishes in the sea.'

'Thanks, Brendan, you're tha best. What would I do without ya?'

'W-e-l-l, luckily for you, I aint goin' anywhere, so you'll never have to know.' He tried to stand, but staggered and fell again. 'Nope, nowhere.'

Alannah giggled. 'I don't think I should even try getting up. My arms and legs feel glued to this couch.'

'Well in that case, I'm joining you.' Brendan crawled around behind the sofa. Suddenly, the backrest collapsed, prompting a squeal from Alannah. He followed this up by climbing onto the futon bed and collapsing beside her.

A blanket and two pillows appeared out of nowhere and before she knew it, Brendan had tucked her in. She snuggled up alongside him and promptly fell asleep.

A morning run and workout left Liam soaked through to the bone with sweat and rain. He walked into the kitchen to grab a bottle of water for his parched throat and found Alannah knocking back a shot of Dad's hangover cure. 'I didn't know you went out last night.'

She gave him an irritated glance, moving over to the coffee machine. 'I didn't go anywhere. Brendan and I raided the liquor cabinet.'

Images of Brendan taking advantage of a drunk Alannah started flashing through his mind and he had to work hard at shaking them off. 'Lana?'

'What?' Her tone was curt as she poured her espresso.

'I'm sorry about how I reacted yesterday. It's just…'

Alannah cut him off. 'Enough, okay? I get it. My blood is tainted. Let's move on.'

Liam gasped at her dismissal. 'But…'

'I mean it, Liam, please drop the subject.' She stormed off as quickly as she could without risking a spill of her hot beverage.

Brendan strolled into the room as soon as she left, his scruffy hair suggesting he'd recently gotten out of bed. 'So, the moment you find out she's not pure, you drop her like a sack of potatoes. Nice… real nice.'

Liam filled his tone with equal contempt. 'Like you can talk. When have you ever done more than use girls?'

'At least I know when I'm on to a good thing, and I'd never let anything petty, like rules, get in the way of going after what I want.'

'Oh, is that why you string Bianca along?'

'Bianca's only a friend and she knows it.' He poured himself a shot of the hangover cure and sculled it before smirking at Liam. 'It sure is good that Lana has *my* shoulder to cry on.'

Liam had him up against the wall a second later, clutching the neckline of his top. 'Stay the *fuck* away from her.'

'Or you'll what, stretch my favourite shirt out of shape? What's it to you, anyway? You don't even want her anymore.' Brendan pushed him back and straightened his Bring-Me-The-Horizon t-shirt.

'I *do* still care about her.'

'Newsflash, Brother: you can't have everything your way. Either grow a pair and get the girl or let her go. But don't take too long to decide, else you might find she's moved on.' Brendan took a few steps toward the door. He paused, still facing away. 'By the way, it might interest you to know she didn't sleep alone last night.' As if anticipating the chase, he took off at a sprint.

Liam tried to chase him along the hall, but Dad stepped out of the study in time to catch him.

'By the Gods. What's gotten into you? Aren't you a bit old to be playing chasey in the house?' Ross stood firm, crossing his arms over his chest.

After letting out a huge sigh, Liam stepped back. 'Sorry, Dad. That brat's really pissing me off today.'

'I can see that. Listen, I need your help with some Council business. Come on.' He stepped back in the study, gesturing for Liam to follow.

Chapter Nine

'Mm, something smells divine,' Alannah commented as she walked through the front door, the smell of roasting food filling her nose. It was Friday and she had managed to avoid Liam for most of the week thanks to a busy study schedule and by opting to have Austin drive her home. Things were developing well with him, but she had not had a chance to make a move. Brendan always showed up whenever she attempted to get a moment alone with Austin.

Shadowing her into the house, Brendan placed a hand on her shoulder. 'It's the Winter Solstice early tomorrow morning, so Mum's cooking up a feast for us to enjoy tonight.'

'Nice. I better go see if I can help with anything.'

'No, don't go in there!' Brendan almost yanked her arm off when he pulled her back from her approach toward the kitchen. 'She's turned the kitchen into a sacred space. Mum treats the food preparation for such occasions as a ritual process.'

'Oh. Is the eating a ritual too?'

He dragged her into the front lounge area so they could take the long way around the house. 'There are some ritual elements, like prayer, but it's mostly a feast. A lot like Christmas for Christians. We celebrate the Triple Goddess tonight.'

Alannah simply nodded as she took in the ambience. She noticed a fire was burning in the hearth, and there were decorations all about the place, putting her in mind of the Christmas in July celebrations Emma's family had invited her to. There were fairy lights strung up around the room, along with boughs of greenery. They walked through the formal dining room next, which only added to her impressions. The table display included a Yule log as the centrepiece, surrounded by candles. A scattering of fruits, berries, and pinecones completed the look.

'Mum and Dad are going to one of their friend's houses after dinner to perform a group ritual.' They had reached the living room and Brendan slumped onto the couch. 'Liam and I are both inviting a few mage friends over tonight to perform our own ritual. You should join us; would be a great opportunity to see what the spiritual aspect of mage life is like.'

'Really? I didn't think I could attend rituals before initiation.' She sat beside Brendan.

'It's only for worship, not to perform magic, so you don't need access to powers to participate,' Brendan explained.

'Would Liam mind my being there?'

'Would I mind you being where?' Liam entered from the backyard, dripping with sweat from one of his many workouts, which had become more frequent of late.

Alannah gulped, trying to quell the tingle she felt between her thighs at the sight of him. 'At your ritual gathering tonight.'

He smiled. 'Of course you're welcome. I planned on asking you myself, but you've been a hard woman to catch this week.'

When Alannah gazed upon the curve of his full lips, her disposition toward him softened. 'Great, count me in.'

'Excellent. I'm gonna hit the shower, but I'll see you at dinner.' Liam strode out with a renewed pep in his step.

Alannah was waiting with Brendan in the ritual space of the cellar. She was thankful Cara and

Connor had also joined them because she was anxious about Liam's friends coming.

'What's *she* doing here?' As if on cue, Monique entered the room, took one look at Alannah and spun around to challenge Liam.

'Hey bitch, I'm right here. If you have a problem, take it up with me directly,' Alannah spat. 'And to answer your question, I *live* here, or did you forget that little detail?'

Monique turned her glaring eyes on Alannah. 'You don't belong down here though. You're not even initiated yet.'

Stepping beside her, Liam put a hand on her shoulder. 'Give it a rest, Monique. Brendan and I both invited her. She is family after all, and she has started her training.' The physical contact appeared to ease Monique's mood, but it did little for Alannah's.

Brendan must have read her apprehension because he put his arm across her shoulders and pulled her deeper into the room. 'Come on Lana.' He stood back from the pentagram marked on the floor, leaving a space for her between him and Cara.

'Here, take this.' Brendan handed her a small dagger with a jewelled hilt. 'It's an athame. Once the circle has been cast, you may only leave it by cutting yourself away. Do this by drawing the blade across the line on each side of your position.'

'Thanks. This was my mother's, wasn't it?'

He nodded.

With everyone standing in place, Monique directed proceedings. She walked around the perimeter of the circle with her own athame before lighting the red candle positioned at a pentagram point. 'I call upon the Guardians of the North to watch over us and grant us the blessing of fire. We invoke the name of Belenus. May your energy and willpower guide us.'

At this point everyone except Alannah responded with, 'Belenus, we invoke thee.'

Monique moved to the yellow candle. 'I call upon the Guardians of the East to watch over us and grant us the blessing of air. We invoke the name of Ecne. May your knowledge and wisdom guide us.'

'Ecne, we invoke thee.'

Lighting a green candle, she continued, 'I call upon the Guardians of the South to watch over us and grant us the blessing of earth. We invoke the name of The Dagda. May your endurance and strength guide us.'

Alannah knew the drill by this point and joined the chorus. 'The Dagda, we invoke thee.'

She lit a blue candle. 'I call upon the Guardians of the West to watch over us and grant us the blessing of water. We invoke the name of Cliodhna. May your passion and emotion guide us.'

'Cliodhna, we invoke thee.'

Finally, she stood before the silver candle at the apex of the star. 'I call upon Lugh, the father of mages, to watch over us and to grant us the blessings of Aether. We invoke you and pray that you guide us on the right path.'

'Lugh, we invoke thee.'

Monique moved to each participant and asked, 'How do you enter the circle?'.

Each person responded, 'With love and peace.'

To which Monique replied, 'Blessed be.' She hesitated slightly when she reached Alannah, but she put her grievances aside.

Once inside the circle, Alannah joined her companions on the floor, grateful for the small cushion protecting her backside from the cold stone.

Their ritual leader knelt at the altar in the centre where she crossed her arms and looked to the ceiling, a gesture copied by everyone else. 'Cailleach, Goddess of Winter, we praise you in all of your forms. You are the Beautiful Maiden, the Blessed Mother, and the Divine Crone. The vessel from which all life springs forth. We ask you to honour us and allow us to feel your presence in our hearts.'

She lifted her arms and began chanting. 'I am the Maiden, the Mother and the Crone, and I live within you.'

The girls in the group, including Alannah, followed suit, repeating the mantra several times. As she spoke, Alannah felt a tingling sensation followed by an almost orgasmic rush of power flow through her. It was intoxicating. She looked around her and found everyone staring at her in amazement. When she drew her hands down, she noticed a faint glow emanating from her skin. *What the hell?* Overcome by the inexplicable need to touch something, she placed her fingers on her athame and a jolt of energy shot through her and into the knife.

Cara gasped. 'Alannah, did you just perform magic?'

Monique concluded the ritual and closed the circle in a rushed manner. She walked over to Alannah. 'How did you do that?'

Alannah shook her head, still reeling from the high she was on. 'I don't know. I don't even understand what I did.'

'My guess is, you imbued your athame with the power of the Goddess. May I examine it a moment?' Monique's attitude toward her had done a one-eighty-degree turn.

'Um, sure.' Alannah handed her the blade that had become luminescent.

'Wow, that's incredible. You made yourself a very potent magic tool.' She handed it back to Alannah. 'I've never seen or heard of an uninitiated mage being able to do this. It normally takes years of practice to infuse an object with the most basic of powers.'

Alannah smiled. If magic felt this good, she wanted more. 'I guess that settles it then. I better get myself initiated.'

Brendan headed toward the living room. Most of their guests had left by this stage, but Cara had remained and was chatting animatedly with Alannah on the couch. He stood in the doorway to admire the woman who had not only drawn down the moon without an inkling of how to do it but invoked the full power of the Goddess and transferred it to a Medieval dagger.

'She's remarkable, isn't she?' Liam had moved up behind Brendan and spoke quietly.

'That's a fucking understatement,' he whispered back.

Alannah looked up at them, beaming, probably still buzzing from the rush.

Witnessing her channel that power had been a huge turn-on, and Brendan still felt stirrings at the sight of her. 'She's definitely a Winters woman, pure blood or not.' He walked into the room and sat on one of the armchairs facing the sofa.

Liam took a seat too. 'So how are we going to do this without involving The Council of Mages? Because getting Alannah initiated without Mum and Dad knowing will mean going behind the backs of the whole Council.'

'We simply need to find experienced specialists in each field, right?' Cara pointed out.

'And a High Magus. Although, in theory an ex-High Magus would do.' Brendan was beginning to formulate a plan. 'I think I have the answer. I know a guy who can get us some specialists to help on a no questions asked basis, for the right price, of course.'

'I dunno,' Liam countered. 'They sound like shady people if they would work like that.'

'That's kinda the point, Brother. We're not looking to invite these folks into our home for tea and scones. We only need them to perform their part of the ritual, then they will bugger off.'

'But what if they try to harm Lana?'

Brendan should have figured Liam would not like his plan. 'That's unlikely, but we will protect her. You could even call on your goon squad. Monique seems to have changed her tune. Did you see the look of awe in her eyes tonight? With her on board, I imagine the rest of them would be happy to help Lana. Just don't tell those girls about Lana's human parentage.'

'Wait, what?' Cara broke in.

Brendan glanced at Alannah. 'You didn't tell Cara?'

The smile vanished from Alannah's face as she shook her head and Brendan could have kicked himself for being such a mood killer.

'Tell me what?' Cara demanded.

'My dad was human, so I'm not a pureblood.' Alannah's tone sounded so defeated it tore at Brendan's heart.

'Oh.' Cara's lips pulled back in a sympathetic grimace.

Liam huffed. 'I'm not planning on telling anyone, and I suggest the rest of you keep it under wraps too. The fewer people who know, the better.'

He heaved a sigh. 'I don't like your proposal, Brendan, but it's probably our only option.'

Brendan shot up from his seat. 'Right then. Lana, continue reading those prep books. Liam and Cara: you guys can work out the venue. Leave the rest to me.'

'Hey, Austin. You got a minute?' Alannah had found the guy hiding in the library at lunch on the Monday following the Solstice.

Grinning, he spoke in a hushed tone. 'For you, Alannah, I have all day.'

His admission sent a thrill through her blood stream. She sat down next to him and whispered. 'The most awesome thing happened on Saturday night at the Solstice ritual. I performed magic! I'm not even initiated yet and I channelled power.' Alannah explained what had happened.

Austin's beautiful blue eyes were wide and his jaw agape by the time she finished. 'That's amazing.'

'I know, right. So now the guys are gonna setup a covert initiation ritual for me.' She had already told him about her uncle's stubborn attitude, and he'd agreed it was ridiculous. 'I still need to finish reading all my prep books though.'

'That's great news. Have you finished that book on magical people yet?'

'Yes, I have. Only three other huge volumes to get through.'

'Come on, there's something I want to show you.' He grabbed her hand and led her into a secluded spot behind the shelves where he pushed one of the bricks in the wall. A hidden passageway opened in the floor.

Alannah gasped. 'What's this for?'

'Safe travel between buildings. Because of this…' Austin walked along the wall until he reached a window where he held his hand out into a beam of sunlight. He withdrew his limb quickly as it started to burn.

'By the Gods.' Alannah kept her voice to a whisper as she took his burned hand and looked at the speed with which it healed. When she stared into his eyes, she understood their appeal. 'You're a vampire.'

'Yes,' he agreed. 'Does that scare you?'

'No. It fascinates me.'

Austin gave her a sly smile. 'Good. Now come with me.'

They entered the secret passage and Alannah found herself becoming thrilled by a rush of uncertainty and a sense of being somewhere dangerous and forbidden. The entranceway closed over, leaving them in complete darkness and making her jump.

Austin pulled her nearer, surrounding her in a cloud of his strong, spicy fragrance. 'Now you're afraid. I can smell it. Sorry, it's easy to forget others can't see in the dark. I take my vision for granted. Here.' A small light emanating from his smartphone lit the subterranean corridor. It was not much, but it was enough to calm her nerves.

'Thank you.' She looked up at him with wide eyes. 'Were you born this way, or did you…'

'The curse has been in my family for hundreds of years,' he explained.

Nodding, she pressed herself against him, brushing her fingertips along the side of his face. His eyes flickered at her touch. 'I know vampires can hypnotise people with their gaze. Is that what you've been doing to me?'

'No, at least not intentionally. Like an initiate mage, I'm not in full control of my powers, but I have tried hard to avoid impressing my will on you.'

Her eyes felt locked to his in that moment. 'Is your hypnotism power active now?'

'No.' He pressed his lips to hers, gripping the nape of her neck with a firm hand to draw her closer.

Alannah yielded without hesitation. His full lips were strong and demanding and the kiss soon heated, becoming full of need. When he opened his mouth to her probing tongue, she was grateful he had used breath mints to disguise the taste of his liquid lunch.

His other arm encircled her waist and just like that, his phone was forgotten, dropping to the ground and sending them back into pitch black. Only this time, Alannah did not mind at all.

The bell sounding the end of lunch brought an end to their moment of passion.

'Wow,' Austin whispered.

'Yeah.' Alannah's vision had adjusted slightly to the dark, enough to make out the gorgeous features on Austin's face by the light of his glowing eyes. She pressed her lips to his chiselled jawline. 'I guess we should get to class, huh? Not that I want to. It's only Mindfulness anyway.'

'You make a good point. Kissing you is much more therapeutic than meditation.' Austin stooped to pick up and pocket his phone. He grabbed her hand. 'I still want to show you something though.' After walking a few metres, they reached a door opening into a plush living area and neat dining space, illuminated by a few warm light globes. 'The vampire common room. Don't open the fridges if you get faint at the sight of blood.'

'Nice. So, is this where you hide most lunch times?'

'I try to join our friends when the sky is overcast, but yes, this is where I come when the sun is out. Unless I have study to do in the library, of course.' He moved into the room and pulled her down onto a couch.

'Does anyone else use this room much?'

'Only my cousins, but they don't come here often. My brother doesn't start high school until next year and there are no other vampires attending the school.'

Alannah climbed across his lap to straddle him. 'Are you telling me we have this place to ourselves?' She fluttered her lashes.

His hands pressed across her hips and he grinned. 'Pretty much. Please don't tell anyone else about it.'

They made out for the rest of fifth period.

Austin walked Alannah to her locker so she could collect her books for Ancient Studies.

'There you are. I missed you in Mindfulness.' Brendan was waiting at her locker. He nodded to Austin. 'Hey man.'

'Hi Brendan. I better get going, Alannah, but I'll see you after school.' He embraced her and they kissed briefly.

Her body was humming as she watched Austin's shapely backside moving away.

When she turned to Brendan, his eyes were wide. 'Did you guys skip class for a nooner?'

She laughed. 'Things were pretty heated, but they didn't go *that* far.'

'Geez, woman.' He shook his head. 'Why didn't you tell me about hooking up with Austin?' His brow creased.

'Relax, Brendan. It only just happened at lunch today. As if you didn't see this coming anyway.'

'Okay, fine.' Smiling, Brendan added, 'You're right though, I totally called it. Congrats, Lana.' He threw his arms around her, pulling her into a hug and whispered in her ear, 'I can't wait to see the look on Liam's face when he finds out.'

She pushed him back and slapped his arm. 'You're a horrible brother.'

'Yup. But I'm an awesome cousin.' He winked as he took a few backward steps before spinning around and walking away.

Liam was waiting for Alannah when she left her classroom at the end of the day and there was no sign of Austin. *Shit.*

He grabbed her arm, hauling her into an empty classroom and slammed the door. 'Is it true?'

Annoyed that he manhandled her roughly, she shook her arm loose from his grip. 'Is what true?'

'Don't play dumb with me, Lana. Did you kiss Austin?' His eyes blazed as he pursed his lips.

'Who told you?' *Had Brendan been that eager to rub it in Liam's face?*

'Does it matter? Word travels fast in these halls and several people claim to have seen the two of you. But I'm still not inclined to believe them over you. So, tell me the truth, Lana.'

'Yeah, it's true. I really like him, okay. I don't see what the big deal is.'

Unshed tears glistened in Liam's eyes a moment before his face reddened. 'You wouldn't say that if you knew what he was.'

Alannah crossed her arms in defiance. 'I know he's a vampire. That doesn't worry me.'

'It fucking well should, Lana. He's dangerous. How do you know he isn't coercing you with hypnotism?'

'Because he told me he isn't.'

Liam shook his head in disbelief. 'And you're gonna take his word for it?'

'Yeah, I am. I trust him. He hasn't done anything to hurt me even though he's had multiple opportunities to do so.' Alannah walked to the door, pausing as she gripped the handle. 'And he doesn't seem to mind how tainted my blood is.'

He moved at lighting speed, pulling Alannah back from the door and spinning her around with a hand on her shoulder. 'Has he fed on you?' Fear had overtaken his countenance.

This was getting ridiculous. 'You're overreacting, Liam. If I were to let Austin bite me, that would be my prerogative and it wouldn't be any of your business. Now let me go.'

His hand slipped away from her shoulder, but his brow remained creased.

Alannah turned and stormed out the room. It was time to move on and put Liam behind her.

Chapter Ten

It was a frosty August night when Alannah followed her cousins into the middle of a forest, carrying a velvet bag full of her mother's magic tools. She wore a long, white ritual dress, looking forward to the presentation of her ceremonial robe to help combat her shivers. Butterflies were having a dance party inside her stomach, but she also wore a smile a mile wide. Months of study had brought her to this point, and she was about to experience one of the most important rites of passage in her life. There would be no turning back once she opened herself up to the magic world.

She wished Austin could be there to support her. Their relationship had progressed well, and she felt herself finally letting go of the pain of an unrequited love. Liam had been cold and distant around her for a few weeks when she started seeing Austin, but things had returned to some form of normality between them in the last month. He even put in considerable effort to be civil around Austin at her seventeenth birthday party.

'Here we are.' Liam stopped beside the makings of a bonfire in the middle of a clearing. He looked toward a line of trees and called out, '*Táimid an Geimhreadh*[2]. You can show yourselves.'

Eleven mages in robes of various colours stepped forward. They ranged in age from late twenties to approximately eighty. One elderly man with long white hair walked right up to them and addressed her. 'You must be Alannah. I am Magus Ciardha. It is an honour to direct proceedings for you tonight.' He took her hand and pressed a chaste kiss to her knuckles.

'Thank you, Magus,' Alannah replied softly as her spare hand twisted in the folds of her dress.

'Do you have your magic tools ready for me?' He took the bag she offered him, turning to the boys to discuss logistics. The man wore black robes with a gold Celtic trinity knot emblem on the back.

Liam and Brendan both shook his hand. Liam ushered Magus Ciardha to the altar next to the wood pile. The magus busied himself with

---

[2] We are Winter

preparations while Liam lit a fire with the click of his fingers.

'How are you feeling, Lana?' Brendan stood beside her as she watched Liam perform his magic. She knew Brendan did not need to ask, but since he had learned to control his powers more, he had been respectful enough to avoid reading her without permission.

'Seriously fucking nervous. But I'm hyped too. I really want this, Brendan. I know there are risks, but I'm sure I'll handle them with you and Liam alongside me.'

'That's my Lana.' He smiled and threw an arm across her shoulders and pulled her in close to him.

Alannah savoured the warmth emanating from his body as they waited.

Before long, a ritual circle was cast and Ciardha consecrated her tools. He beckoned them forward. 'Who seeks to enter this sacred space?'

Brendan, who Alannah had chosen as her guide, presented her. 'I bring the daughter of a mage who wishes to know the wonders of the magic world and to honour the Gods and Goddesses of the Celtic faith.'

'What is your name, daughter of mages?' Ciardha asked her.

'Alannah,' she replied.

'Please kneel before the Gods and Goddesses.'

Brendan helped her to her knees, standing behind her.

Ciardha continued, 'Are you ready to be purified?'

'Yes, I am.'

The magus placed a candle in her hand, encircled her with a cloud of incense, drew a line of dirt across her forehead, and sprinkled her with water. 'As a mage you will join a spiritual society. Do you vow to honour all the Gods and Goddesses by observing the Sabbats and the Esbats?'

'Yes, I do.'

'As a mage you will contribute to a peaceful magic community. Do you vow to uphold the laws of the magic world and do your best to protect the human world from the forces of magic?'

'Yes, I do.'

'We accept you as a member of our society.' He handed her a feather quill and inkwell.

She used them to sign the dedication page of her mother's book of shadows, claiming it for herself.

'It is time to open yourself up to the mysteries of the world.' Ciardha stepped back to form a circle with the other mages.

Alannah blew out the candle she was holding and set it aside. Closing her eyes, she reclined back against her calves and sank into a meditative state. The chanting began. It was an eerie sound, and she could feel a warm breeze circle about her as the voices rose in a crescendo.

Austin watched the ritual from the vantage of an elevated gum tree branch nearby. While he had seen numerous mage ceremonies, he had never witnessed an initiation before. It was a fascinating sight to behold and Alannah looked gorgeous in her white dress. She wore her long black hair in a partial braid, leaving strands cascading down her back in loose curls. He wished he could pull her into his arms and run his fingers through those locks, breathing in their strawberry scent.

She sank back against her bent legs and the assorted group of outcast mages began reciting various mantras. Supposedly, the man in the role of High Magus was lifting the veil, allowing her to see past glamour, while the other ten mages would open her up to the different mana sources. There was a twelfth mage in black robes a short distance beyond the tree line who was also chanting, but none of the other ritual participants were aware of her presence, nor did they know the woman's intentions.

As the chanting ended, the mysterious woman left her position among the trees. The head magus presented Alannah with her dark blue robe, adorned with the Winters matriarchal emblem: The Tree of Life flanked by the Triple Goddess. He returned Alannah's consecrated tools and concluded the ritual.

Austin jumped down from his hiding spot and made his way out of the forest. When he reached the roadside, the strange woman who had gate-crashed Alannah's party approached him. 'Hello Austin.'

He stopped abruptly, startled by her forward manner. 'How do you know my name?'

She slipped her hood back. 'Because I know all my subjects by name.'

Gasping, he dropped to one knee as a sign of proper respect for royalty. 'I'm sorry My Lady, I did not recognise you.'

'You may stand. I wish to speak with you in my car.' She gestured to the limousine parked a few metres down the road.

Austin followed her promptly. After opening the door for her, he made his way around to the other rear passenger seat.

They had moved several kilometres away when the Duchess spoke again. 'It would appear you have become close to the Winters girl, yes?'

'Yes, my Lady. We are… extremely close.'

'This will indeed please her Majesty. Our Queen will join us soon. She has an important job for you, relying on your relationship with this girl. I assume I do not need to remind you that your loyalty to your sovereign comes before all other alliances.'

'Of course, my Lady.'

'Very well. Expect contact from one of Her Majesty's messengers shortly.' She fell silent, dismissing him when they reached his parked car.

The first change Alannah noticed was the fields of different coloured light surrounding everyone. She blinked several times to be sure she was not hallucinating, but they remained even after she arrived home.

'Are you sure you're okay, Lana?' Liam asked again when they entered the living room.

She had been quiet and withdrawn since the ritual ended, insisting she was fine when the boys

171

asked after her. 'What are those colours surrounding everyone?'

Brendan and Liam exchanged wide-eyed looks. They turned back to her.

'You can already see coloured auras?' Brendan asked.

'Is that what they are?'

'Yup. What colours can you see surrounding us?'

'Liam's aura is mostly deep red with a hint of bright pink, while yours is yellow and bright pink.'

Brendan smiled and the pink light around him pulsed a bright red. 'Damn girl, you're channelling *and* reading emotions. Now you know what it's like for me most of the time.'

'Most mages can only see people's auras as a bright white light, and they can tell how powerful another mage is by the size of their aura,' Liam explained. 'Colour reading is an enchanter's power.'

'So, Lana, you want to tell us whose is bigger?' Brendan smirked.

She rolled her eyes, directing her question at Liam. 'Does that mean I'm going to be an enchanter?'

Liam shook his head. 'It's too early to tell. You need to spend time channelling other mana sources to find what you are most attuned to.' He yawned. 'It's been a long day and we have school tomorrow, so I think we should call it a night.'

'Yeah, I guess. I don't know if I'll manage sleep though.' Alannah stood and followed her cousins up the stairs.

After Liam wished them goodnight and disappeared in his room, Alannah stopped at Brendan's room. 'Hey Brendan, can I ask you something?'

He smiled. 'You wanna know what the colours mean, don't you?'

'Yeah.'

'The main colour represents a person's personality, while the outer part of the aura indicates their current emotions. Liam's deep red aura shows he is strong-willed and stubborn, but also honest and loyal.' He paused for a moment to think. 'No one else ever told me the colour of my aura. I was a little surprised to learn my personality is yellow. That usually means someone is intelligent, but also easy-going, optimistic and friendly.'

'Sounds about right. You are smart when you apply yourself, Brendan.'

'I suppose.'

'What's my main colour?'

'Orange, meaning you are bold, courageous and creative. Definitely all true.'

Alannah snorted. 'Right. So, what does the bright pink emotion aura mean?'

'Feelings of love and affection, although the nature of the love can be difficult to read and generally requires more advanced insights. For example, it can be hard to distinguish between the love felt for a friend or relative and romantic love merely by looking at the colour. With practice, an enchanter can *feel* the emotions of the person they are reading, or they can read a person's thoughts.'

'I see. Well, thanks for explaining that. Good night, Brendan.'

'Night, Lana.' Brendan opened his door.

Before she moved away, she popped her head into his room before the door closed. 'One last question.'

After pulling off his shirt, he looked up at her. 'What's that?'

The sight of his bare, muscular chest momentarily distracted Alannah. Heat pulsed between her thighs and she clenched them. Biting her lip, she glanced up. 'What about the bright red emotion?' The colour had continued pulsing around Brendan most of the time they had been speaking and she was curious.

He closed in on her with an impish grin. 'Why don't you tell me, Lana? It just flashed in your aura too.'

Blushing, she made a quick exit.

Alannah's stomach did backflips when she thought of Brendan, so she decided to avoid him the next morning. Getting up early, she was able to catch a ride to school with Liam after leaving a brief note with some excuse about needing to study at the library before school.

'Are you still seeing coloured auras?' Liam asked her on the drive.

'No. Yours is only bright white now. It's kind of a relief to be honest. I don't know how Brendan can stand it. There are some things I'd rather not know about people's feelings.'

Liam laughed. 'When you put it that way, and knowing what blokes can be like, I can appreciate it might be a bit much. But it could also be useful for gaining insight into people you don't know well.'

'I suppose. Like most powers, it's probably better when you can control it. Did you have problems controlling your fireballs in the beginning? I imagine a power like that could be dangerous.'

'Not exactly. Offensive magics like that are what we call activated spells. I always trained under controlled conditions, so I didn't set the house on fire. It's the passive powers most mages struggle with in the beginning. The biggest issue I had was in controlling my passive channelling of physical forces. It was a little awkward when I turned myself into a magnet in year eight.'

Alannah laughed. 'I bet. Oh crap, what's it gonna be like when I start passive channelling?'

'You'll be fine. The trick is to use mindfulness to switch it off. Not so easy for a thirteen-year-old, of course, but I'm sure you will manage fine, especially now we have classes in it at school.'

'Speaking of controlling powers, you have your eighteenth birthday coming up later this month. Doesn't that mean you'll be sitting the magus test soon?'

He sighed. 'Yes, preparations start next week. It's annoying that they can't wait until I've finished my high school studies. Graduating to full magus, makes me a deployable warlock.'

'Shit. Is that like compulsory enlistment?'

'More like being in the Reserves. Signing on as a registered warlock in the first place is optional and it won't be a full-time job, but they will call me up if the need arises.'

'That's kinda scary.'

'That's life as a mage. It's what we all sign up for in some form. Although, warlocks and conjurers are more likely to see active combat than other specialists. Deployment of Abjurers is just as likely in the event of magic war, but they work behind the scenes. Thankfully, outright war is rare. We usually only have law enforcement issues in our own backyards.'

Alannah realised Liam had been referring to her as part of his world. The fact that she was an active mage was going to take some getting used to.

When they arrived at school, Liam looked at her a moment. 'Today is going to be a challenge for you. Go easy on yourself, okay? If you need timeout, take it.'

'Thanks.'

They both headed straight for the gym. Alannah had started working out on the advice of both her cousins. Fitness was essential for all mages and more so for those who ended up doing combat training. Thankfully the only other people using the gym that morning were a couple of humans, so Alannah was able to work out in relative peace.

It was when she made her way down the corridor, heading to homeroom, she became overwhelmed with what she saw. There were so many non-humans! Nothing could have prepared her for what they looked like with the veil lifted. She thought fairies would be pretty (and sure some of them were) but there were so many sharp teeth and claws, some with skin in shades of green, grey, silver, or gold and all of them with pointed ears. Then there were the orcs with their horns and olive-green skin.

But the most horrifying of the lot were the ogres: they were grotesque, with mammoth-sized muscles, droopy skin like a Shar-Pei puppy (without the cute), and protruding fangs that leered at her. The moment she spotted them, she yelped and ducked into an empty classroom, locking the door behind her.

There was a knock.

'Go away,' she shouted.

'Alannah, it's me,' Austin's voice called from beyond the door.

Gods, she had forgotten about seeing his true form for the first time. She was not ready. Could not deal with it yet. 'Leave me alone, Austin.'

'Alannah, please. It's only me. Let me help you.'

'No, Austin. I'm not ready.' Slumping to the floor, she leaned her back against the wall next to the door. *Why did I decide it was a good idea to attempt this without Brendan to calm me down?* Remembering last night, she blushed again. *Oh, that's right! Fuck, fuck, fuck!*

'I promise, I'm not that scary to look at. Please let me in so I can help you.'

She heard muffled voices talking beyond the door. Another knock.

'Lana, it's Liam. I've sent Austin away to cool down. Can I come in?'

She flicked the lock, opening the door for him.

Liam fastened it again after walking into the room. 'Come here.' He opened his arms for her.

She entered his embrace. 'Is there a way to turn the glamour back on?'

'Yes, with practice, you can learn to distinguish between someone's true form and glamoured appearance. You wanna tell me what happened with Austin?'

Alannah sighed. 'Nothing really. I freaked out when I saw so many magical people and the ogres were the last straw. I haven't even seen Austin yet and I'm afraid of what he will look like.

I'm worried it will alter my feelings and I'm not ready for that.'

Liam took her hand and drew her over to a desk. After pulling a chair out for her, he sat on the table. 'I'll probably come to regret saying this, but in this instance, you don't have anything to worry about with Austin. Vampires don't show their true form unless they are feeding. Most of the time you only see their glowing eyes and pale skin. Even their true form isn't as disturbing as an orc or ogre's face.'

'Really?'

'Yes, really.'

'Lana, are you in there?' Brendan tapped gently on the door.

'*Shit*,' she cursed under her breath.

Liam raised an eyebrow in response. 'Are you avoiding Brendan?'

She bit her lip and nodded.

'You gonna tell me why?'

'No,' she replied promptly as her cheeks flushed.

'I see…. Do you want me to send him away too?'

'No.' She sighed again. 'Facing him is inevitable. Leaving it longer will make things more awkward. Besides, I could use his help with facing the horrors out there.'

'Okay.' He walked over to the door and let Brendan in the room. 'Go easy on her. She's struggling with seeing people's true forms.'

'No shit, bro. I can sense her emotions a mile away.' Brendan crossed the room and pulled a chair up alongside her. 'Do you want me to help?' he asked in a soft tone.

Avoiding eye contact, she nodded.

Brendan began rubbing her back and she could feel a sense of calm pouring through from where his finger touched her. It was incredible how easily he soothed her. 'Do you feel ready to brave the crowds again?'

'Yeah, but can you stay with me in case I freak out again?'

'Of course.'

Alannah stood, ready to leave, but hesitated a moment. 'Can you get Austin for me first?'

'Sure, no probs.' Brendan left the room.

Liam locked the door again and walked up to her. 'Hey, I know I don't have Brendan's magic calming powers, and we are in different groups at school, but if you ever need anything, please don't hesitate to call on me, okay? I'll always be here for you.'

'Thanks, Liam.' She hugged him, holding on until she heard the door.

Liam left the room for her to have a few minutes alone with Austin.

Alannah chose to await his entrance with her back to him. She wanted him to come to her first. He did, placing his hands on her shoulders.

'I'm sorry, Alannah,' he whispered.

She turned around slowly and looked at him. To her surprise, he appeared exactly the same. 'No, I'm sorry. I shouldn't have shut you out.' She ran her fingers along his face, marvelling at how she had always seen him for what he is. 'You're the same.'

'Well I'm not about to feed, so I'm not showing you my true form. But aren't my eyes different?'

'They've always been a striking luminescent blue to me. And your skin has always been pale, but I never thought your complexion was strange considering my own pallor.'

He smiled. 'That means you've been able to see me through the glamour even before your initiation. I knew you were special.' Pulling her close, he pressed his lips to hers.

After kissing for a few minutes, a knock at the door interrupted them. Alannah looked up and saw Brendan through the window where he mimed being sick. 'Come on guys, I'd tell you to get a room, but since you're already in one, I figured that would be asking for trouble.'

Laughing, Alannah unlocked the door. She was ready to face the world.

To make things easier on Alannah, her friends had agreed to join the lunch table one at a time, while Brendan continued to soothe her with his magic touch. The mages came first. The only significant change she observed were the large white auras surrounding them, which varied in size to indicate their relative power levels. Bailey was the strongest—though nothing compared to a pure mage like Brendan or Liam. Connor was next, followed by Cara who also used cosmetic glamour to achieve her flaming red 'dye job'. Her natural hair colour was an orange red.

Amy was a dwarf, so the main feature she hid was her muscular bulk, something considered less desirable among human girls. Amazingly, her dark red hair was a true colour, as was Bianca's turquoise hair. But the nymph's skin colour was interesting: where she chose a pallor like Alannah's, piercing the veil showed a tan with a green vine pattern running along her arms and legs. Being fae, she also had pointy ears.

Bianca smiled at Alannah's gaping mouth and wide eyes. 'You should see my brother if you think I look interesting. We call the males of my race satyrs and they have stag horns.'

'I recall reading about you guys, but words on a page did little to prepare me for the reality of seeing you in the flesh.'

Bianca nodded her understanding.

Caleb sat in front of her next, with a smirk on his face. 'Hey Alannah. Top marks if you can pick what I am.'

'Hm, pointy ears and silvery grey skin, so probably fae?' *And such a pretty face, but I'm not about to say that out loud.*

'So far so good. Go on.'

'Your teeth and nails aren't especially sharp, so you aren't a boggart. That leaves sídhe or endarkened, right?'

'Yes, but one's seelie, the other unseelie. So, which am I?'

'The dark tint in your skin makes me think endarkened.'

He leaned forward with an intense gaze. 'You aced the test. Does my being unseelie scare you?'

'No. Why would it? My boyfriend is a vampire, remember?' She glanced at Austin, who sat to her left, offering him a warm smile. Fortunately, the wintry weather was doing a great job of blocking out the sun.

Caleb sat back smiling. 'Good point. That said, unseelie fae get a bad rap because we are usually prone to corruption. I'm not a part of any criminal syndicates, but most unseelie are.'

'Gee thanks for spilling those beans,' Jacob added as he sat beside Caleb.

Sucking in a sharp breath, Alannah took a moment to process the revelation that aside from his chubby build, Jacob was nothing like his glamoured form. Grey skin, short black hair, pointy ears, sharp teeth and claws. 'Boggart?'

'Yeah. For the record, I only do petty theft for the family.'

She laughed. 'Good to know.'

When Locky sat down she understood his choice of hair dye. It was a good match to his green skin tone. Aside from that, he looked similar to Jacob. He grinned. 'Yeah, so I'm a goblin. For the record I don't know who my dad is, and I hate all ogres.' The subtext she took from that was Locky's ogre father had raped his elven mother. That was generally how ogres bred with folk outside their own cursed race.

'It's all good, Locky. I'm not one to judge, but thanks for clarifying.'

Alannah laughed when Ben approached. 'Are you even magical?'

Aside from his faint aura, that could have been on a human, Ben was exactly the same. 'Way to wound a guy's ego, Alannah.' He grinned to show he was jesting. 'I bet my true form would terrify you though. I prefer to avoid the shape shifting if I'm not hunting.'

'Werecreature?' she asked with wide eyes.

'Yep, weredingo to be precise.'

Nick was the last of her friends to join the table and Alannah understood why he went to the back of the queue. She could feel a strong wave of calming magic pour into her from Brendan's hand as the orc sat down. The most obvious feature was his stag horns which made him look especially scary when combined with his olive green, leathery skin. Still, he was generally more attractive than those nasty ogres.

'Thanks for being patient with me, guys. It's been a big day.'

'I think I speak for all of us here,' Austin explained, 'in saying we totally understand, and we are glad you are willing to look past our monstrous features and focus on what lies beneath the skin.'

There was a chorus of consensus around the table.

With an arm across her shoulder, Brendan pulled her into his side. 'I'm so damn proud of you, Lana.'

The following night Alannah snuck Austin into her room, a feat made easier by his ability to levitate. She had managed to get through a full day without freaking out much and felt pleased with herself. With that in mind, she had invited her boyfriend over for a late-night rendezvous, although she had kept her intentions to herself, in case she lost her nerve.

Grinning at the sight of her in a skimpy black silk negligee, he pulled her into a firm hold the moment her window closed. 'You are full of surprises, Alannah.'

'You ain't seen nothing yet,' she whispered, offering him a cheeky smile. Alannah lured Austin down to her bed, where she straddled and kissed him deeply. A few minutes later, she came up for air and took a deep breath. 'I want to see your true form.'

'What? Are you sure? After everything you went through these last two days?' Stroking her hair gently, Austin focused on her with unwavering eyes and pursed lips.

'I'm sure, but I don't want you to simply show me. I want you to bite me. I want you to taste me as you make love to me.'

Austin was completely gobsmacked. 'I... I can't, Alannah. I mean, I'll absolutely make love to you tonight if that's what you want, but not the feeding. I don't want to hurt you and I'm afraid of draining too much of your blood.'

She put a finger to his lips. 'Shh. It's okay. I'll stop you if I start to feel faint. I want this, Austin. I want all of you.'

'Do you promise to stop me?'

'Yes, I promise.'

That was all the convincing Austin needed. He flipped Alannah onto her back and stood up to undress, removing everything except his silk boxers. Her breathing quickened at the sight of his arousal. *I'll never get over how sexy Austin is. I can't believe I've held out this long.*

They kissed more before he removed her satin slip; at which point he sat back to take in the view of her naked body. 'You are absolutely gorgeous, Alannah.' Clutching her breasts, he brought his mouth down on her nipples.

Arching her back, Alannah moaned softly. It felt like years since she had last had sex, even though it was only months. Her body was more than ready, even before he slipped his fingers inside her. She came after two thrusts of his hand, colours dancing across her closed lids.

'Gods, I love how responsive your body is to me, Alannah.' A moment later, Austin sat back, and she heard the unmistakable sound of foil ripping. When he shifted back atop her, he looked into her eyes a moment before pushing into her. As soon as Alannah felt Austin inside her, she groaned.

They moved together, slowly at first to continue kissing. As Alannah's core clenched around him, Austin pulled back. 'Are you sure about this?'

'Yes. Show me who you are, Austin.'

He thrust hard into her and buried his face against her neck. When he looked at her again, his visage had changed. His forehead creased, red rings surrounded his eyes, and his canines protruded into sharp fangs. After giving her a moment to register his true form, Austin sank his teeth into her jugular.

After a brief sting, Alannah felt nothing but pure ecstasy coursing through her blood: blood that was slowly draining from her body and nourishing the man who was also bringing her countless orgasms.

Brendan drank his coffee and waited in anticipation of Alannah's entrance into the kitchen. 'Good Morning, Lana.'

'Morning,' she replied blearily.

After waiting for Alannah to pour her own caffeinated beverage and join him at the table, he added, 'And what a fine morning it is after having such a good night.' He winked at her.

She cursed under her breath. 'Could you stop reading me for like one day at least?'

'Come on, Lana, any numpty could read that afterglow radiating on your face.'

Alannah simply glared at him.

But Brendan was not going to let something like the evil eye deter him. 'But it was pretty good, right? Let me guess: you let him bite you?'

'What, how?'

He grinned in satisfaction. 'With orgasms so intense, they woke me up, they'd either have to be from sex with an enchanter or a feeding vampire. And since I was alone in my own bed last night and your boyfriend *is* a vampire, I'm going to guess it was the second option.'

Alannah's eyes were wide. '*Shit!* You felt that?'

'Yup.' He took a sip of his coffee for effect before continuing: 'It's a good thing Mum sleeps at the other end of the house and not two doors down from your room, else you might have rocked her world too.' The sight of her face turning bright red gave him a thrilling sense of victory even though he was not trying to get a Sleazy Chicken win.

'I guess I'll have to do it elsewhere in future,' she conceded.

'By all means, let me live vicariously.'

Alannah scoffed. 'You get enough of your own action; you don't need to share mine.' She sighed. 'Please don't tell Liam.'

'Don't tell him what? That you're sleeping with Austin? Because we all saw that coming, pun totally intended. Or do you mean the fact that it was kinky vampire sex?'

That earned him a famous Alannah eyeroll. 'Both, but especially the fact that I let Austin feed on me. Liam would totally freak out.'

'And for once I wouldn't blame him for overreacting. I'm a little surprised Austin agreed to your request, to be honest.' He could see Alannah was about to cut him off, but he held a hand up to hush her. 'I know you asked because he never would have instigated something like that. Not after working so hard on his rehab. You ought to know you're playing with fire, Lana. Your lover hasn't always been a boy scout.'

'What? Why are you only telling me this now?' Fear oozed from her and it was about damn time.

'Because until now, I didn't think you would have been stupid enough to ask a vampire to bite you. I had intended to leave Austin's past where it belongs and let him fill you in if he so desired. Besides, his story interweaves with mine and it's not something I'm proud of either. They were very dark times for both of us.'

Alannah blinked at him. 'So, what was it you guys did?'

'Nuh, uh. I'm not going there. Ask Austin if you want the sordid details.'

'Please, Brendan? You can't drop a bombshell like that and leave me hanging.' Her pouting was almost enough to do him in.

'I can't, Lana. It's not my place to tell you.'

'But it's your story, too.'

'If it was only about me, I'd tell you in a heartbeat. But I'm not going to betray Austin.' Having finished his coffee, Brendan rose from the table and left the room.

Emma and Melissa's beaming faces appeared on Alannah's laptop screen. 'Hi Alannah.'

'Hi guys. Has it really been a month?' Their video calls had declined in frequency from weekly at first to monthly. They had all agreed it would be easier that way.

'I know, right. How's that tall, dark, and handsome hunk of yours?' Emma asked.

'Have you fucked him yet?' Trust one-track-mind Melissa to ask.

'Things have been good with Austin and yes, we've had sex.' Alannah sighed, remembering what Brendan had warned her about. *Why did he have to go and throw a wet blanket on my mood? I was looking forward to telling the girls about my phenomenal night.*

Melissa frowned. 'Oh, so he's not much of a performer?'

'Actually, he's incredible. It was the best sex of my life.'

'But?' Emma prompted.

'But I just learned that Austin has some skeletons in his closet. Brendan warned me to be careful. It pisses me off that he waited this long to tell me because Austin hasn't even hinted at having a troubled past. So, now I'm worried about trusting

Austin and I don't know if I should ask him to fess up.'

'Oh wow. That's heavy. Do you have any suspicions about what Austin might have done in the past?' Emma's brow furrowed.

'I have an inkling, but it doesn't gel with the man I know. Austin is so kind and gentle.'

'Well maybe he is a changed man, and he didn't tell you about his past because he has moved on and put it behind him,' Melissa suggested. 'Do you think knowing what he did in a past life will make you feel better?'

'I don't know. Probably not if it is really as bad as Brendan implied.'

'Then don't ask him about it. Heed whatever caution Brendan has given you and let Austin open up when he's ready,' Emma advised.

'I suppose you're right. So, any word on how Cole is doing? I haven't heard from him for a couple of months now.'

The girls looked at each other and Emma's shoulders hunched.

'Come on guys, what's going on?'

'I'm sorry, hun, I wanted to wait until I knew you had moved on before telling you.'

'Well clearly, I have moved on, so tell me. Who has he hooked up with?'

'It was only one night, and he felt super guilty for betraying your memory. I'm sorry, Alannah. We were drunk and it just happened.' Emma blurted out her confession at lightning speed.

'Woah, Emma, relax. It's okay. If you like each other, go for it. I want him to be happy and I'd rather see him with one of you girls than some slag.'

'Really? Are you sure?' Emma's eyes lit up.

'Yeah, I'm sure.'

Chapter Eleven

Brendan stepped into the training room and closed the door. Given that Liam had already grabbed his supplies for the graduation ceremony that night, he figured he should have the room to himself for a few hours.

After donning his robe, he cast the circle, sat at the altar, and began with a few minutes of meditation to clear his mind. He opened himself up to the emotions in the house, a process that had become second nature. Liam's heightened state came to him straight away: a mix of excitement and pride. Brendan reached out for Alannah next and felt her cheerful mood laced with an underlying anxiety that had been with her for a couple of weeks, ever since he had told her about Austin's dark past.

Liam's parents were both happy and pleased with their eldest son. *Of course they are. Liam has never screwed up or disappointed them.* But he was not going to be the only one to make them proud. Brendan gradually extended the range of his awareness, picking up on the people living in the country estates first. Most of their dispositions were pleasant, with the occasional frustrated child. Brendan let each of their emotions fill him with power.

He pushed himself further than ever before. This was the real test. *Can I reach into town?* The outskirts hit him first and he felt a rush of energy surge through his body. One last push. *By the Gods! So much emotion! It's… too much.* All the fear, the sadness, the greed, the anger. Brendan felt overwhelmed by the rush. '*Fuck!*' The pain became unbearable. Suddenly, he went numb and darkness took him.

'Have you seen Brendan?' Liam asked Alannah as she joined him in the living room.

'No. You want me to go check his room?'

He shook his head. 'I did that. Come on, let's go. He can catch a ride with Mum and Dad. I'm not letting that wretch ruin my night by making me late.'

'Yeah, okay.' She made her way to the front door, a breathtaking vision in her new dress of blue and white velvet: a perfect match for the robes she had draped over her arm.

Liam wore a basic suit that he would cover in robes at the ceremony. They jumped in the car and took off toward the estate of the High Magus.

'Are you excited?' Alannah asked him.

A huge smile filled his face. 'Hell yeah. I aced those tests, Lana. After tonight, I'm gonna be a full magus. It kind of makes high school graduation an anti-climax.'

'Yeah, it's pretty awesome. I'm so proud of you, Liam.'

'Thanks. How have you been getting on with your training? I'm sorry I've been too caught up with the tests to check-in before now.'

She sighed. 'Quite slow. So far I've only been able to consistently connect with one source.'

'It's early days yet, Lana. Don't lose hope. The fact that you have a consistent attunement already is impressive. It took me a full year to get to that stage. What source have you attuned to?'

'The invocation of names.'

'Curious. Makes sense though, considering what happened at the Winter Solstice ritual. It'd be pretty cool if you ended up becoming a conjurer.' The thought filled him with hope. It'd be great to work closely with Alannah.

'Yeah, I guess it would. Honestly, though, I'd be happy with almost any specialisation, except necromancy. The thought of talking to ghosts scares me.'

Liam laughed. 'Of all the aspects of necromancy to freak you out.'

'Well, it's pretty much the only useful thing a registered necromancer is allowed to do.'

'I suppose.' Liam pulled into the driveway of the Lane family estate.

They made their way to the ritual grounds behind the grand Georgian style manor where High Magus Kieran greeted them personally. 'Good evening Initiate Winters.' The man gave Liam a firm handshake.

Liam gestured to Alannah. 'High Magus Kieran, this is my cousin, Alannah Winters.'

Kieran took Alannah's hand and kissed her knuckles. 'It's good to finally meet you, Miss Winters.' The smile he wore did not suit his hard features.

'Thank you, Your Honour,' she replied awkwardly, clearly unimpressed by Kieran's charms.

Liam noticed Monique approaching, having stepped out from the house during the introductions.

Kieran continued addressing Alannah, 'It is not customary for the uninitiated to attend official ceremonies, but I think we can make an exception for a Winters lady.'

'That won't be necessary, Dad, because Alannah *is* an initiate.'

'Monique!' Liam hissed.

'Oh, I'm sorry. Was that meant to be a secret still? Oops.' Monique's tone was facetious.

Alannah glared at her.

Fucking great! What's with Monique? I thought she'd put her pettiness behind her at the Winter Solstice.

'Is that so?' Kieran inquired. 'And how did such an event escape my notice?'

'I'm sorry, Your Honour, but Alannah went elsewhere because my father thought it unsafe to initiate her. A covert ceremony was necessary for her protection.'

Kieran frowned. 'This is most irregular. Alannah, I do hope you will register through the proper channels when you come of age.'

'That is my intention, Your Honour.' Alannah's knees wobbled as she toyed with a strand of her hair.

'Good. I do not abide maverick mages in my town.'

'Nor can we tolerate rogues, right Daddy?' Monique piped up, still looking at Alannah.

'That's right, sweetheart. We adhere to all magic laws here. Now Liam, we need to prepare for your graduation. Please come with me.'

Liam hesitated, not wanting to leave Alannah alone with Monique, but it was not like he had a choice. He followed the High Magus to the sacred circle.

'What's your problem, Monique?' Alannah snapped the moment Kieran and Liam were out of earshot.

'You are, Winters. I can't stand you and all that your line of bitches stand for. You think you're so good. You might think you're powerful, but I have a theory your bloodline has reached saturation. You'll probably go rogue like the others, and when you do, I'll be here to put you down.' Monique turned and strode away.

Alannah shook her head. *The bitch must be jealous still.* She looked around the crowd of gathering guests, spotting Ross and Nora, but caught no sight of Brendan. She approached her Aunt and Uncle. 'Hi.'

'Hi Sweetie,' Nora replied with a brief hug.

'Where's Brendan?' Alannah asked.

Nora frowned. 'We were hoping you'd tell us. Didn't he come with you and Liam?'

'No, we couldn't find him, and Liam was in a rush, so we assumed he would catch a ride with you.'

Ross grumbled. 'I'm getting fed up with that boy's insolent attitude. I know he and Liam aren't exactly best friends, but to miss his brother's graduation is extremely disrespectful.'

Nora sighed. 'I hope he's late and getting a lift with a friend.'

The three of them found seats in the front ring of chairs surrounding the sacred circle. It was time to watch Liam advance to full magus.

Liam was still buzzing when they arrived home. *I am a magus!* And it was the dawn of his eighteenth birthday to boot.

'I'm going to make some coffee,' Mum declared. 'I don't think I'll be able to sleep now anyway.' She walked up to Liam and hugged him. 'I'm so thrilled for you, sweetheart.'

Dad slapped his shoulder. 'You have made us both proud, son.'

When his parents disappeared into the kitchen, Alannah approached him with a big smile.

She threw her arms around him. 'Congratulations and happy birthday, Liam.'

'Thanks, Lana.' Their embrace was probably longer and closer than appropriate, but Liam was not going to complain. 'I'm gonna put my stuff away, then I'll join you all in the kitchen.' He pulled away from her arms hesitantly, making his way down to the cellar.

The illumination beneath the door was the first clue something was wrong. *Is someone in our ritual space?* Liam readied a lightning bolt before bursting into the room, stopping dead in his tracks. *Oh Gods!* 'Brendan!' he cried as he ran to his brother's collapsed form. He checked the boy's pulse. *Fuck!* It was there, but too faint. He ran back upstairs in a panic. *'Dad! Come quick! It's Brendan!'*

Three sets of eyes doubled in size when they stared at him. They followed promptly.

Mum and Alannah both yelped at the sight of Brendan on the floor. Alannah even threw herself at him and started sobbing hysterically.

'I need you to move aside, Alannah,' Dad instructed. 'I can't heal him with you in the way. Please.'

But she would not budge.

Liam had to remove her by force, but he did so as gently as possible, pulling her into his arms.

She continued to sob, and he wished he could comfort her, but he felt helpless. Brendan would have been able to soothe her nerves. *Shit!* All this time he assumed his brother had shirked out on Liam. *How long has he been lying here unconscious?* It made him feel like such an arsehole.

'He's suffered from some sort of magic overload,' Dad announced. 'I'm going to take him to bed and continue working on him there. Mind out.'

Liam drew Alannah aside so his father could carry Brendan through. They followed him upstairs.

After several torturous moments, Dad sat back on the edge of the bed. 'I've done all I can. His body needs to rest, but he's stable. It should only be a matter of time before he comes 'round.'

A chorus of relieved sighs filled the room.

Dad walked to the door, pausing to speak. 'I'm completely drained of magic and energy, so I'm going to bed. I suggest all of you get some rest too.'

Liam shook his head. 'I'm not going anywhere until Brendan wakes up.'

'Me neither,' Alannah chimed in.

'Suit yourselves. Nora?'

Mum, who had been quiet the whole time, stood and accepted Dad's hand with a yawn. They closed the door behind them.

Liam and Alannah sat on either side of Brendan and settled into their vigil.

When Brendan awoke, he needed to blink a few times. 'Lana?'

She was in bed, lying beside him and staring straight at his face. A smile tugged at her lips. 'Hi.'

He reached out a hand to touch the side of her face. 'Am I still dreaming?' But he heard someone clear their throat behind him. Rolling over, he found Liam sitting up against the bedhead. 'What the fuck? Please tell me I'm not dreaming because if I am, my subconscious is far more disturbed than I realised.'

Liam laughed. 'Oh, you're plenty disturbed, but you're not dreaming. You gave us one hell of a fright there, Brother.'

'Why? What happened?'

'We found you unconscious on the practice room floor. You wanna tell us what you were doing in there?'

Memories of his training exercise came back to him. '*Shit!* I guess I overextended myself. I was trying to increase the reach of my emotional channelling. When I tapped into everyone in town, all the negativity overwhelmed me.'

Liam's eyes bugged out. 'By the Gods, Brendan! How did you even reach that far? That's insane, especially for a mage of your age.' Squinting, he huffed. 'You could have killed yourself tapping into so much power at once. That was really fucking stupid.'

'Gee, thanks for the brief moment of sympathy there, bro. So how long was I out cold for? I hope we aren't gonna be too late for your graduation.'

Liam's demeanour changed in a flash as he averted his eyes. 'I'm sorry, Brendan. I didn't know where you were.'

'What do you mean, why are you sorry?'

Liam fell silent.

He felt Alannah's hand on his shoulder. 'Liam graduated already.'

'Wait, did you leave me passed out on the floor all that time? For what… five hours at least?' He could feel his muscles tensing and heartbeat rising. *That selfish bastard!*

'I'm sorry, okay. I had no idea where you were and assumed you weren't coming.' Liam sounded genuine, but Brendan's blood was too hot to back down.

'Christ, Liam! Of course, you wouldn't think to check I was okay. Your head is too far up your arse to worry about little ol' me.'

Alannah's grip tightened on him. 'Brendan, please. Liam already apologised. You need to calm down and rest.'

'He's right, Lana. And I feel like shit because of it,' Liam conceded.

Holy crap! Liam never admitted to his faults. At least not to him.

Liam stood up. 'I should let you rest.' He hesitated before adding, 'Brendan, please don't take risks like that without someone else present.'

Once Liam had gone, Brendan turned to face Alannah. He noticed her eyes were blood-shot and puffy. 'Hey, are you okay, Lana?' he whispered as his thumb skimmed under one of her eyes.

'I'm fine. You're the one I'm worried about.'

Her level of concern touched his heart, deep. It made him want to kiss away all her fears. *Fuck! I'm falling for her again, falling hard.* He pushed that thought aside to reassure her. 'I feel perfectly healthy. I promise.'

'Good. I'll let you get some sleep. Night.' She pressed her lips to his forehead.

The intimate touch caused stirrings that were not only physical. *God damn!* It took all his willpower to refrain from dragging her back to his bed as she stood and left his room.

Chapter Twelve

A familiar tapping sound had Alannah out of bed and rushing to her window. She still got such a thrill from sneaking around with her boyfriend and their late-night escapades had only intensified since Brendan's warning. She wondered if it was possible to become addicted to feeding a vampire. 'Hey, you.'

'Hi beautiful.' Austin wrapped his arms around her and drew her into a deep kiss. After stepping back to look at her more closely, his eyes narrowed. 'Hey, what's wrong?'

'Brendan had a near-death experience tonight. He overreached with his channelling and blacked out. It took everything Uncle Ross had to bring him back from the brink.'

'Oh Gods, is he okay?' Austin's concern warmed her heart. *Who would have thought vampires were loving, caring people?* Mythology and pop-culture had a lot to answer for. They were not even undead. Austin's body was as warm and living as Alannah's. The main difference: he was immortal and would stop ageing at twenty-one, that and he had heightened senses, an aversion to sunlight, and a need to drink blood. Most of his other powers were much like those of mages.

'Brendan is fine now, thank the Gods.'

Visibly relaxing, he let out a sigh of relief. 'Good. I'll understand if you're not in the mood tonight. We can just—'

She hushed him with a finger on his lips before kissing him.

Austin responded avidly, lifting her so he could carry her to bed. Before long, clothes flew across the room in a frenzy between their impassioned touches, scratches, and bites.

Gods did Alannah love those bites!

Dawn approached as Austin carefully extricated himself from Alannah's bed, making a stealthy exit through her window. He would have to hurry back to his car if he was going to avoid the sun.

As he stepped onto the roadside, the faint sound of a twig snapping alerted him to someone else's presence. Human hearing would not have picked up on the sound. His pulse started racing and he let his hunting instincts take over.

He scouted the perimeter and found a woman leaning against a large wattle, facing the road with her back to him. She wore floral perfume and a long red velvet cape with a hood covering her face.

A few more silent steps forward. He froze.

The woman laughed. 'Stand down, vampire.' She turned and revealed her face.

Austin gasped and dropped to his knees. 'Pardon me, Your Majesty.'

The Queen of the Cursed. She was both as beautiful and terrifying as the rumours had suggested. Her once black hair had turned as white as the colourless eyes staring back at him, with only the tiniest slits of black for pupils. But her skin was perfect and her features well defined. She did not appear a day over twenty, even though she had been closer to thirty when she stopped ageing.

'Please, get up.' She looked him over a moment once he was standing. 'You have performed your part exceptionally well, Austin Pearce. A little too well perhaps.'

Mystified, he blinked silently.

'My sister instructed you to win Alannah's trust so you could feed on her. That did not mean falling in love with the girl.'

'What? How did you know?'

'I am attuned to all emotions, remember? I felt the two of you together tonight.' She grinned and glanced up to the house. 'And I am not the only one.'

Cursing silently, Austin staggered and fell against a nearby tree. 'I'm sorry, Your Majesty. I didn't mean to.' The sun started to touch the southern hemisphere with its first rays, so he moved into the shade of the canopy.

The Queen had no reason to fear the dawning light. She was not a vampire or ghoul. 'It matters not. I think we can work this new angle to my advantage. I imagine you will not fancy an eternity alone. Few of us do. Win her heart over and invite her to join our ranks. That is your new mission.'

Austin felt relieved. The thought of having Alannah killed—or worse, having to do so himself—would have broken him. This way, he would always have her by his side. 'I am most grateful, Your Majesty. Shall I turn her into a vampire? Or will you want to make her one of the undead, such as you are?'

'The nature of her curse matters little to me. If you want a vampire lover, make her yourself. If you have not the guts, send her to me. Now get out of here before you burst into flames.'

'Yes, Your Majesty.'

'I think we ought to all train together. Now my magus exams are over with, I should be able to devote more time to helping you both.' Liam's declaration, along with his sudden appearance in the kitchen, startled Brendan.

He had just taken his first sip of coffee and the jolt caused him to spray it all over the table. Brendan glared at Liam. 'Hold up there, Brother, do you want to train *with* us? Or do you want to supervise *my* training?'

Liam slapped his hand on Brendan's shoulder. 'I want to train *with* you both. I think it would be advantageous to work as a group. And I'm sure Lana would benefit from the process too.' The guy was dripping with perspiration, clearly back from a recent workout. He smelled like the boys' change room at school. *Ick!*

Alannah looked up from her breakfast and smiled. 'Sure, sounds good.' Aside from her initial greeting, it was the first thing she had said that morning.

Brendan knew what she had spent the rest of her night doing and much like any other morning following such activities, she was avoiding eye contact and any conversation that might earn her a reprimand or further embarrassment. The fact that she continued the kinky sex in such proximity to Brendan was curious, however. *Is she doing it for safety reasons? Or did she enjoy sharing the experience with me?* In either case, he was glad she kept him close and not simply because it gave him a thrill.

'Brendan?' Liam fixed unwavering eyes upon him.

'Sure. Fine. Whatever.' He kept his tone indifferent; secretly pleased Liam cared enough to watch out for him.

'Great. I'll meet you both in the ritual room after you've finished breakfast.' He walked off, hopefully to shower.

Sliding off her chair, Alannah took her dishes to the sink. 'This is going to be fun. The three of us working together.'

'Are you a masochist, Lana? Because if not, you clearly have a different interpretation of fun than I do.'

She was faux pouting. 'What? You don't want to work with me?'

He could not help but laugh as he rinsed his own dishes. 'Nice duck lips. For the record, I am going to love working with you. It's just, Liam is an Antarctica-sized wet blanket.'

Alannah stood close behind him and whispered in his ear, 'To answer your question, of course I'm a masochist. But I'm also a sadist, so Liam won't be the only one whipping you into shape.' She slapped his arse with a loud *smack* before taking off toward the cellar at breakneck speed.

The brutal slap stung like hell and Brendan's dick was rock hard because of it. Taking a few minutes to breathe deeply, he calmed himself before following her. He found Alannah alone and kneeling before the altar. 'I wonder if you enjoyed that as much as I did.'

She laughed. 'You're losing your touch if you think that'll turn me red.'

'Who said I was playing?'

'Playing what?' Liam asked as he appeared in the doorway.

'Nothing.' Brendan grabbed his practice robes and got ready for their training session.

'Right. So, Lana, would you like to draw the circle today? It is traditionally your role as matriarch.'

Alannah began to tremble. 'Um. I'll give it a go. I've only ever done it for my own private training, so I don't know if I'm any good at it.'

Liam placed a hand on her shoulder. 'It's okay, we will help you if you need any prompting.'

They began the ritual and Brendan gaped at her with wide eyes. Alannah's recitation was perfect. The three of them converged at the altar to meditate for several minutes.

Liam broke the silence. 'Lana, what mana source did you want to open up to today?'

'I'd like to try matter again.'

Brendan knew she was pushing herself to become a conjurer and her success with invocation had suggested this as her most likely direction, but she had been struggling with matter.

After retrieving several rings from their locked box beneath the altar, Liam handed one to Alannah. The gold band with a bright orange citrine crystal contained the power of matter. He placed three rings in front of Brendan. The usual two: Botswana agate for channelling emotions, and blue lace agate for attunement with the senses. Brendan picked up the third ring, which he did not recognise, and examined it. The crystal, set in a thick metal band, was a swirl of blue, purple and green.

'Fluorite. It should help you work with large doses of power,' Liam explained.

'Thanks.' Brendan did not know what else to say.

Liam chose the peridot for himself. That could mean only one thing: he was opening himself to all mana and would channel the first source he connected with. It was the type of ring they had all used as new initiates. As a registered warlock, Liam was attuned to all the mana sources he needed. Expanding his repertoire was not necessary, not unless he had ambitions of becoming High Magus. He must have noticed Brendan's scrutiny. 'I'm testing the waters. It was Dad's suggestion.'

'Figures.' Pushing envy aside, he chose to work with the Botswana agate and put the fluorite on his other hand.

They sank back into their meditative states, but this time the three of them focused on their respective sources. Brendan pushed his reach into town again. It was painful at first, but this time he found himself able to control the flow of power. He used it to manipulate his own emotions, switching between each one (except for the forbidden:

gluttony, greed, and pride) and finishing in a state of calm.

When he opened his eyes, Alannah and Liam were both looking at him.

Smiling, he nodded. 'It worked.'

'That's awesome!' Alannah threw her arms around him.

Breathing in the scent of her hair, he tried to draw in deep breaths to maintain his tranquillity, but that was never going to happen in Alannah's arms. 'So, uh, how did you go, Lana?'

'I did it. I was able to stay attuned to matter. I guess the next step is to work with my attunements, right?'

'Right,' he replied, releasing her reluctantly.

Liam was eyeing him warily a moment. He turned his attention to Alannah. 'Normally an initiate conjurer would start with basic summoning, but given your experience at the Winter Solstice, you could skip straight to imbuing items. Up to you, really.'

'I'd like to try summoning. How did you go, Liam?'

'Nothing new for me today,' Liam shrugged. 'No big deal. It's early days yet.'

Brendan removed his rings and placed them in the trinket box. 'I'd like to start practising something new next week.'

'Oh?' Liam looked at him with wide, unblinking eyes.

'Yup. I think it's time to try my hand at telepathic communication.'

Alannah grinned. 'Sounds like fun.'

'With you, I'm sure it's gonna be.' He winked at her.

A few days after their group training session, Liam sat at the dining table with Brendan, books on magic spread out in front of them. Learning any new power required a lot of theory study to start with. While Brendan was reading up on telepathy, Liam was learning about defensive energy circles.

When he looked up at the clock, the passing of hours surprised him. Alannah should have been back from her date by now. The sound of the front door slamming halted his hammering heart. That was until his father stepped into the room.

Steam was billowing out of Dad's ears, and his face resembled the tomatoes on the kitchen bench. 'I just had an interesting chat with High Magus Kieran. Can you guess what he told me, Liam?'

Brendan looked up at the sound of Dad's voice. He turned to Liam and the twerp started to grin.

Liam had not yet told Brendan what Kieran knew about Alannah. He shook his head, returning his attention to their father. 'It was her choice, Dad.'

'*Shit, Liam!* You told the High Magus about Lana?' Brendan roared.

'Of course not. Monique tattled.'

Dad stepped closer and fixed Liam with an icy gaze. 'And when were you going to enlighten your parents, who also happen to be Alannah's guardians?'

'Whenever Alannah was ready.' Liam refused to stand down on this issue.

'All three of you have been very foolish and insolent.' Dad leaned against the wall and crossed his arms. 'By initiating her into the magic world, you have made her presence known to someone her mother and I were trying to hide her from.'

Standing to face Dad square on, Liam also crossed his own arms. 'How does initiation make her presence known? And who are you hiding her from?'

A smooth, deep voice spoke from the doorway. 'The Queen of the Cursed.'

They all spun to face the vampire.

'Austin?' Dad asked. 'Where did you appear from? And what do you know about the Queen?'

Austin stepped into the room. 'I was dropping Alannah home after our date and heard you talking.' When Dad glanced around, Austin added, 'Don't worry, she went straight upstairs. As for the Queen, I know plenty about her because she married the Vampire King. I also know she's in town now and wants Alannah. Word travels fast among the cursed.'

Brendan finally stood up to join the conversation. 'Hold up. Who is this Queen? And what the hell does she want with Lana?'

'The Queen wants to eliminate Alannah's magic potential because she is the last female mage in her line and the only real threat to the Queen's power. Knowing that, who do you think the Queen is?' Austin replied.

Brendan shot Dad an alarmed look. 'No way! Dad, you said she was dead and gone.'

'Technically both true statements. She's undead and she left the country.' Dad's tone was cold, and bitter.

Liam shook his head. 'So, does that mean she succeeded in the most forbidden of all magic rituals? Is she a lich?'

Dad nodded gravely. 'Yes, I'm afraid so.'

His clammy palms itched as bile rose from his unsettled stomach. '*Shit!* I'm sorry Dad. I had no idea this was why you were so adamant about Lana. Why didn't you tell us?'

'I intended to eventually. I was waiting until you were full magus, Liam. It is not a matter I wanted to burden either of you with before you were mentally and physically ready to handle it. But you were both reckless and now we have the consequences of your actions on our doorstep.'

'What do we do now?' Brendan asked.

Dad sighed. 'For now, I need you both to keep an eye on her. I'm going to bring this issue up with the Council and see what we can do. *Damn it!* Kieran will not be happy with me for letting this happen.' He started pacing. 'Liam and Brendan, until further notice, you're both grounded, along with Alannah. This is both your punishment and for Alannah's safety.'

Liam groaned, but he knew he deserved it. 'Understood, Sir.'

Brendan nodded in silent compliance.

'Also, please refrain from telling Alannah about the Queen. I need to work out how best to broach this very delicate topic with her.'

As soon as Dad left the room, Brendan cursed under his breath. 'I can't believe he kept this from us.'

Liam comprehended his father's reasoning but staying in the dark over something so serious still stung like a bitch. 'I can believe, but I don't like it.' He looked at Austin still standing in the room. At least the grounding meant Alannah would have more time with himself and less with her dubious boyfriend. He could not help but smirk. 'Sorry Austin, I guess this'll be a bit of a dampener on your relationship with Lana for a while.'

Austin returned the smug grin. 'Oh, don't worry about me. I'm sure I'll be fine.'

Brendan snorted. 'I'm sure you will, filthy bastard.' He narrowed his eyes. 'But let this be a warning, friend. If you harm her, I will put you in a world of pain and not the enjoyable sort.'

Liam could not believe Brendan was threatening his best mate. He wondered if something had transpired between the two of them. *Whatever. It's none of my business.* Brendan was clearly on board with protecting Alannah and that was all that mattered.

Turning to Brendan, Austin smiled. 'Don't worry, friend, I love her too. I also know your dirty little secret. It's almost like old times, huh? Almost, but not quite.' He swiftly left the house.

Curiosity piqued; Liam could not help himself. 'What "dirty little secret" was he referring to, Brendan?'

'Why should I tell you?' he huffed.

'Does it involve Lana? If so, spill it or I'll kick your arse. If not, I probably don't want to know.'

Brendan sighed. 'I kinda promised Lana I wouldn't tell you.'

Heat surged through Liam's veins as his temper started to rise. *If Brendan has touched Alannah, so help him Cailleach.* 'You had better tell me.'

'Fine. Don't tell her I told you. And please don't get mad at her or do anything rash.'

He could feel his face turning red. 'Spit. It. Out.'

Backing away from Liam's arm swinging range, he put his hands up in surrender. 'Okay, okay. Lana has been letting Austin feed on her when they have sex.'

Liam was utterly gobsmacked. *That stupid, stupid girl!* 'How are you okay with this?'

'I'm not and I told her as much. I warned her she was playing a dangerous game. I guess that's why she only does it at home.'

'Wait, what? How have I not noticed Austin coming here all this time? And how is it any safer here? Austin could lose control and drain her regardless of where she is.'

Brendan hesitated to answer. 'Lana lets him in through her window, which he can levitate to. They usually meet in the middle of the night when the rest of us are asleep. Well mostly asleep… I usually wake up when….' He started squirming.

'When what, Brendan?' Liam's tone was firm.

'When I feel her, uh, intense emotions.'

All the blood that had been boiling in Liam's face drained away, and he imagined his complexion was as white as Alannah's. 'You felt her orgasm?'

Brendan laughed a little. 'Yup. It's almost as good as being inside her myself. Almost, but not quite.'

Liam glared at him. 'By the Gods, Brendan! Have you no shame? You've got to tell Lana. If you don't, I will.'

'She knows. I told her after the first time it happened. Doesn't seem to stop her wanting to share her most personal experiences with me,' he grinned.

Liam tried to ignore how much his brother enjoyed provoking his jealousy. 'Do you at least switch off the channelling as soon as possible?'

'That's the thing. If you were in my shoes and knew there was a risk the vampire feeding on her might take too much blood, would you turn it off, or would you pay closer attention to make sure she's safe?'

Fuck! This is so sick and twisted! 'If it were me, I'd storm in there and kick the shit out of said vampire.' Liam sighed. 'But I know he's your friend and I get your point. Thank you for watching her back. I can't say I like your methods. In fact, I detest them. But at least you have her safety in mind.' Yawning, Liam left the room and made his way to bed.

Chapter Thirteen

Alannah's grounding had continued for four weeks and counting. As she scuffed her feet in the dirt and bark chips beneath her swinging legs, she wondered how long this punishment would drag on. It was a Friday and most of her friends were partying. Even Austin would be out. He never stuck around to study in the library on Fridays, which was why she decided to wait for her cousins in the empty playground next to the school's parking lot once she had finished her own workout.

'Hello Alannah.'

She looked up and gasped at her mother's likeness. All except for the white hair and red gown. Aileen Winters never wore red. 'Do I know you?' she asked cautiously. The woman had a very powerful aura, so she was probably magical.

'Not formally. But I know you, dear child. My name is Tara Winters and I'm the Queen of the Cursed.'

Alannah's blood turned to ice. She remembered reading the name Tara on her family tree, but the woman before her did not look a day over thirty. 'That means you're…'

'Immortal, yes. And I would like to spend some time getting to know you better. Once you join the ranks of the cursed, that is.'

Frozen by her fear of this woman, Alannah barely whispered, 'What do you mean?'

'Alannah, you are a Winters mage of the first-born line. The shackles of mage society are stunting your potential. If you broke free of those constraints and embraced your true nature, you'd be much better off.' She advanced forward.

Alannah jumped off the swing and backed away. *Shit!*

'Choose your curse and join me. Return to your real family.'

Brendan was up to his last repetition of the bench press when a sudden sense of intense fear struck him. *Oh Gods! Alannah.* Caught off guard and distracted by his concern for her, Brendan didn't even notice the bar dropping across his chest.

'That's gotta hurt.' Ben's voice broke his trance.

Awareness returning, the pain set in. 'Ah, fuck!' *It feels like I've cracked a couple of ribs.*

'Here, let me help you.' Thankfully, Ben was spotting him and removed the weights. He tugged Brendan's shirt up to inspect the damage, wincing at the massive bruises already forming. 'Should I get Connor?'

'No time. Alannah's in trouble. I'll get Dad to look at it later.' He shot up from the bench and ran from the school gym. Using her fear as a beacon, he tracked Alannah's whereabouts to the primary school's playground. He sent Liam a quick SOS text, before approaching the two figures standing alone among the children's play equipment.

Once he was able to make out the conversation and get a closer glimpse of the woman in red, he understood exactly why Alannah was afraid.

'Choose your curse and join me. Return to your real family.'

Brendan shot out from behind a tree and stood next to Alannah. 'I am her real family. Leave us the hell alone, *Grandmother*.' He almost retched as he used her familial title. The thought of a relative wanting to harm Alannah turned his stomach.

'Oh Brendan. How noble of you to jump to your cousin's aid. Why do you bother trying to be the hero after all the years you have spent in your brother's shadow? You always made a better rogue, did you not?' Tara's grin was vicious.

He glared at the evil woman. 'I told you to leave us alone.'

'I heard you, but I have not quite finished talking to my granddaughter.' She turned back to Alannah. 'You have two options, dear child. Become one of the cursed or face my wrath. You have until Beltane to decide.' Tara magiported away.

As soon as the Queen of the Cursed left, Brendan turned his attention to Alannah as she fainted. He grabbed her before she hit the ground. He cried out in pain as she collapsed against his cracked ribs.

'*Brendan!*' Liam came running from the seniors' block. As soon as he found Alannah unconscious in Brendan's arms, his visage paled. 'By the Gods! What happened?'

'Our grandmother gave her quite a fright. Oh, and something about joining the ranks of the cursed or facing the bitch's wrath, which I assume means death.'

'So, she's finally shown her hand. Poor Lana. We should get her home immediately. Are you okay? It looks like you're grimacing in pain?'

'I'll live. I think I busted a couple of ribs when Alannah's fear overwhelmed me in the gym.' He tried to carry Alannah's weight towards the carpark, but almost crumpled from the added weight against his chest.

'Christ, Brendan. Please, let me carry Lana.'

Brendan handed her over hesitantly. He would have tried supporting Alannah with all his ribs broken, but Liam insisted.

Once Dad had checked on Alannah, concluding that aside from some shock, she was fine, he put her to bed. He examined Brendan's injuries. 'How much were you pressing?'

'One hundred and thirty-two kilos.' He squirmed as Dad's fingers probed around the damaged area.

Liam whistled through his teeth. 'That's the same as me. You shouldn't be doing that much at your weight.'

'Elites of my weight can do one forty-five. I normally handle it fine; Lana's predicament distracted me.'

'I'll fix you up, then you'd better rest in bed until dinner.'

Alannah woke in a dark room with visions of her grandmother haunting her fleeting dreams. She sat up startled, relaxing when the familiarity of her own room sank in. A cursory glance at the clock told her it was nearly midnight. She noticed a couple of sandwiches on her bedside table, along with a note:

> *Dear Lana,*
>
> *Didn't have the heart to wake you for dinner. You looked so peaceful sleeping. I'm sorry the evil witch gave my princess such a fright. Rest well. I'll talk with you about things when you've had some time to recover.*
>
> *Love from Liam.*

Alannah scoffed the food and reread the note. She might have considered it romantic if she did not know better. Thoughts of Tara filled her mind, and she recalled her ultimatum: 'Become one of the cursed or face my wrath.' The memory of her icy tone sent shivers down Alannah's back. There was no way she would survive a fight with the Queen of the Cursed this early in her training. She needed to explore her options.

There was one cursed person she knew and trusted. She sent him a quick message: **Just met my grandmother, Queen of the Cursed. Need to talk. Please meet me at my window ASAP.**

Austin's prompt reply made her smile. **On my way. Love you.**

He arrived fifteen minutes later and pulled her into a firm embrace. 'Are you okay?'

'Physically, I'm fine. But I'm pretty freaked out.'

'I can imagine.' He pulled back slightly to look into her eyes. 'What did she do?'

'Only talked. Brendan found us together and told her to leave. I don't know what would have happened if he hadn't arrived.'

Pulling her back into his arms, he exhaled sharply. 'I'm so glad you're okay.'

'Austin…what's it like being a vampire? Do you like it?' With their proximity, Alannah could feel his heart begin to race.

'It's… complicated. Why do you ask?'

'Tara wants me to become cursed. I don't much fancy becoming undead like her and the

232

thought of feeding on people's flesh puts me off the idea of becoming a ghoul, but vampirism… Maybe I'm biased, but it seems kind of… exciting… and sexy.'

'I'm not going to lie to you, Alannah. There's a big difference between starting life a vampire and becoming one. I've grown up learning the ropes and I'm part of a noble family. But a mage who chooses to become a vampire… they'll exile you from your current family.'

Shit! She had not considered that aspect.

Squeezing her even tighter, Austin continued, 'That said, my family would welcome you with open arms and I would absolutely love to share my world with you. And I'm sure Brendan would still hang out with you.'

'Yeah, Brendan's good like that.' *But Liam? Then again, it's not like I can be with him anyway.* 'I have time to think about it. Tara gave me two full months to decide. Right now, I just want to make out with my sexy vampire boyfriend.'

Austin groaned pleasurably, picking her up and carrying her to the bed. They kissed passionately for a while before the clothes started coming off. Alannah stripped his shirt off first. Her own t-shirt and bra followed, falling in a pile beside the bed.

The pressure of Austin's mouth sucking on her nipples made Alannah moan audibly. Perhaps too loudly because her door flung open a minute later and Liam entered her room. 'Right, Austin, I want you gone. I need a word with Alannah.'

Remaining atop Alannah, Austin merely turned to face the intruder. 'Screw you, arsehole! Can't you see we're busy here?'

Liam continued to advance toward the bed. 'I don't care. I have important family business to discuss. Now go before I hurt you.'

Austin moved after a moment's hesitation, grabbing his t-shirt from the floor. After snarling at Liam, he climbed out the window, letting it slam shut behind him; the glass pane rattling in its wake.

Alannah sat up as Liam perched on the edge of her bed. 'This better be good.' It took a moment for Alannah to realise Liam was staring at her naked breasts.

'Would you uh... mind covering up?' he asked, still mesmerised by the view of her firm C-Cups.

A smile started to tug at the corner of Alannah's lips. 'Why? Do you find my bare body distracting?'

'Yes, Lana, I do.'

Alannah's grin widened. Knowing Liam found her attractive was a huge turn-on, even if she knew she could not have him. Leaning across his lap, Alannah stretched out her arm to grab her top from the floor. He let out an audible gasp as she did so. After sitting up again, she pulled the garment down over her chest and Liam's eyes locked with hers.

There was an uncomfortable silence between them for a few seconds. Liam cleared his throat. 'Brendan told me about your meeting with our grandmother earlier. I was planning on letting you rest before having this talk, but apparently you have recovered well enough.' He paused a moment to look at the window. His gorgeous blue eyes turned to her with a fierce intensity she had never seen before. 'I hope you weren't about to make any rash decisions.'

Did he think… 'What? Gods no! You thought I was gonna get myself cursed tonight?' She waited for his nod to confirm what his fears had been. *So that's why he barged in.* 'Liam, even I'm not that impulsive! Yeah, I talked about it with Austin, but I'm going to take my time with such a life-changing decision.'

Pain filled Liam's eyes. 'But you are considering it? Christ, Lana! How could you think vampirism is even an option? You ought to know you will have the entire mage community of Gaeilge Shores to back you up if our grandmother attacks you. Given who this woman is, they might even mobilise an entire army to remove her from the face of the earth once and for all.' He pressed his forehead against hers. 'Please don't become cursed. If not for your own sake, then for mine.'

Alannah froze. 'Okay, I won't.'

'Are we training today?' Alannah asked the guys as she walked into the living room. 'I'm keen to step things up to daily sessions in light of yesterday's events.' *And not so big on dying*, she added silently.

Liam looked up from his book on magic theory. 'Sounds like a good plan, although my schoolwork will make it hard to attend every day. But I will come as often as possible.'

'I'm in,' Brendan replied simply.

'Great, let's get to it.' She started walking toward the cellar.

'Give me a sec,' Liam called after her. 'I need to finish this chapter first.'

Alannah sighed as she turned back to face her cousins and leaned against the doorframe. 'Don't take too long. I know what you're like with reading. One chapter becomes five, ten minutes becomes an hour, et cetera, et cetera.'

Brendan snorted. 'Impatient much, Lana?'

'Always. Also, I have a date tonight, so I'd like to finish at a reasonable time.'

Slamming his book shut, Liam's brow creased as he narrowed his eyes on her. 'Austin's coming again? Tonight? He was here last night.'

'Yeah, he is. I want to apologise for last night because *you* rudely interrupted us.' She stood upright and crossed her arms.

Liam scowled. 'Oh, I'm so-o sorry for showing concern about your wellbeing, Lana.' He paused a moment to drop the sarcasm from his tone. 'I don't like how much time you spend with Austin and I hate seeing the two of you together.'

'That's too bad, because you don't get any say when it comes to my love life, Liam.' Alannah noticed Brendan had abandoned his own reading and was watching her and Liam intently.

Liam shot up abruptly and crossed half the distance between them. 'What if I want to be part of your love life? Do I get a say then?'

Dumbfounded, Alannah needed to lean against the doorframe for support. 'What are you saying, Liam?'

'Do I have to spell it out for you? I'm. In. Love. With you, Lana. I always have been.'

Gasping for much needed air, Alannah closed her eyes. When she opened them a moment later, a single tear escaped before the steam poured out from her ears. *'Why the hell couldn't you have told me this four months ago? Like before I fell for Austin. And what's the fucking point of telling me now when you know you can't have me and my tainted blood?'*

'I don't give a shit how pure your blood is, Lana. I might have told you that earlier had you not spent a week avoiding me as soon as you found out about your father. And just because I haven't said it in so many words, I've been trying to express my feelings ever since you returned home.'

'Sorry I'm not a mind reader. Maybe I should try to become an enchanter instead. Your timing really sucks, Liam. I'm with Austin now.'

'So you keep reminding me,' Liam spat with bitter contempt. 'But it's not like you're married to the guy.'

'No, but I am in love with him.'

Liam blanched, pushing past her. 'I'll meet you both in the ritual room when you're ready.'

Alannah turned on Brendan, closing in on him. *'You!* You've known how Liam felt all along, right?'

Shaking his head rapidly, he threw his hands up in a protective gesture. 'Nuh, uh. Don't put this on me, Lana. You know I have a code. How would you like it if I told other people how you felt about them?'

'But you must have known the feelings were mutual in the beginning. Surely it's not so bad in that case?'

He sighed. 'Don't twist things to suit yourself. I don't *ever* get involved in other people's relationships. It's my rule.'

She slumped down on the couch next to Brendan, tapping her foot as she ran her fingers through her hair. 'I'm so damn confused. Why didn't he tell me in the first place?'

'He did try, Lana. Men aren't good at talking about emotions. When it comes to love, we prefer to show, not tell how we feel.' He placed a comforting arm over her shoulders.

Alannah glared at him. 'Wait, so you're siding with Liam on this?'

He shook his head. 'No, I'm merely suggesting you might need to pay more attention to what guys do rather than what they say.'

Alannah scoffed. 'And what would a slut like you know about love?'

'You might be surprised… Oh, and have you forgotten about the whole emotion channelling thing I do? Speaking of which, we should get on with our training.' Brendan stood and left the room.

Exhaling heavily, Alannah braced herself for the awkward magic session ahead.

If it was possible to call sitting around feeling sorry for oneself work, Alannah was having a very productive Sunday. Whenever she attempted any study, whether it be for school or magic, her mind wandered to her two huge predicaments. Tara wanted her cursed or dead and Liam was in love with her.

Knowing how Liam felt made her heart rate quicken and her girly parts tingle, but other thoughts nagged at her. She had spent years fantasising about him, practically placing him on a pedestal like some hot celebrity. For most of her life they had lived in separate states, where their only real connection had been through social media. But everything had changed, and she did not know how to reconcile her dreams with the reality of being with him. There was also the fact that Uncle Ross would never allow it to happen.

And what about Austin? I love him, sure, but do I love him and want him more than Liam? So many questions cycled through her thoughts that she wound up grinding her teeth.

The knocking on her door was almost a reprieve. Brendan stood on her threshold when she answered it. 'Hey Lana. Dad's called a family meeting. Wants us all in the dining room pronto.'

'Okay, give me a sec to change.'

Brendan's gaze travelled down to her black satin negligee. 'I don't see what's wrong with what you're wearing.' When his eyes returned to hers there was an impish gleam to them.

Alannah scowled as she berated him, 'You are such a pervert!' She slammed the door on his laughter.

Having dressed more appropriately, she found the rest of the household waiting for her at the dinner-table. Alannah could smell Nora's Sunday roast baking in the oven, and it was driving her empty stomach crazy.

Ross smiled at her as she took her seat. 'Thank you for joining us, Alannah.'

She briefly glanced at Liam but found his expression blank and unreadable.

'Right, well to start with, I have decided to lift the grounding from all of you,' said Ross.

'Halle-fucking-lujah!' Brendan exclaimed.

Nora frowned. 'Language, Brendan!'

'Sorry, Mum.'

'As I was saying,' Ross continued, 'the grounding is over, however...' He paused, focusing his intense gaze on her. 'Alannah, your safety is still at risk, which is why I am going to impose a strict curfew and place some conditions on your outings.'

Pushing her chair back, she rose abruptly. 'What? That's so not fair! I've never had a curfew in my life!'

'Lana, please sit down and listen to him,' Liam pleaded.

With a sigh, she sank back in her chair. 'Sorry, Uncle Ross.'

'Please understand, this is for your safety, Alannah. Your grandmother is a very dangerous woman. I don't think any of you realise how much of a threat she poses. Her powers rival those of the Arch Mage himself. I would go so far as to say they exceed his powers because she is attuned to every single mana source.'

'I thought the Arch Mage was fully attuned,' queried Alannah.

'Not quite. There is one source the council forbids entirely,' Ross replied.

'Holy shi—' Brendan paused mid curse as Ross glared at him. '—ishkabob. You mean she's attuned to nether as well?'

'I'm afraid so. And the implications of such power are that she can summon and command demons. The Council has suspected the Queen of the Cursed had been biding her time and waiting for an opportunity to launch an outright assault on the Arch Mage, to take his seat by force. I know she feared the possibility Aileen might have challenged her because while she was not fully attuned, she was able to channel all other sources competently, something she kept a secret even from the Council. Alannah, your mother was probably the only mage who had any chance of defeating Tara outright. That was, until your initiation.'

'So why didn't Mum initiate me earlier? And why didn't she try to take on Tara?'

Closing his eyes, Ross exhaled heavily. He looked at Alannah again with his head hung low. 'Aileen did confront our mother, and she died trying.'

Alannah and the boys all gasped at the revelation. 'But I thought Mum died of—'

Ross cut her off. 'Of an aneurysm, yes. That's what her injuries looked like to the forensic pathologist. Regular humans don't know how to diagnose magic overload. Aileen pushed herself too hard and the surge of power she drew into herself destroyed her brain before she could direct her killing blow.'

The room fell quiet for a moment.

Ross sighed. 'Alannah, your mother didn't want you to become a mage and end up like her; or worse, like your grandmother. You weren't so much as a blip on Tara's radar before your initiation, but now she knows you have become a mage, she sees you as the only real threat to her power.'

She shook her head in disbelief. 'But I can't even do much with my magic.'

'Not yet but given time your power could outgrow hers. She wants to prevent that possibility from arising.'

'Dad, if Tara is such a threat to the Arch Mage, why hasn't he coordinated an attack on her?'

'Two reasons. Firstly, Tara hasn't done anything to warrant an outright assault. Her only real crimes thus far have been the use of forbidden magic. Curse and exile from mage society are punishment enough for this. And the second reason: she is impossible to ambush. Without the element of surprise, the Arch Mage's army won't stand a chance.'

'So, what do we do?' Liam asked.

'I want the three of you to continue with your daily training to prepare yourselves for the inevitable battle ahead. In the meantime, Alannah, I want to restrict your outings to reduce Tara's access to you. On school nights, I want you home before sunset and on weekends and during the school holidays, your curfew is 1AM.'

'Okay, but what happens if I break curfew?'

'I'll ground you again. I don't want to be unfair, Alannah, but I need to know you are safe. If unforeseen circumstances mean you might be home late, I want you to ring me before your deadline. But imposing time limits won't be enough. Except for classroom time at school, I don't want you leaving this house without Liam guarding you.'

'What?' Alannah shot Liam a look. He wore a smug grin. *What the hell? Was this his suggestion?*

She wondered if Ross knew about Liam's ulterior motives. There was no way she was going to enlighten her Uncle. 'What about getting to school in the morning? Can I still take the bus?'

'No, Alannah. Liam will drive you. Now, there are two other matters of business to discuss before dinner, so I'm not going to argue with you Alannah. My terms are final. Do you understand?'

'Yeah, I understand. Curfew times are sunset on school nights, 1AM otherwise, and Liam is now my shadow.'

Brendan laughed until Alannah's death-stare shut him up.

'Good. Next order of business is the Spring Equinox gala. This year the High Magus is inviting all active mages from across the state to attend and he insists on our presence. It is a cocktail reception tomorrow night, and you will all dress accordingly.'

Brendan groaned. 'I hate wearing suits.'

Alannah sympathised. 'Um, I don't really have any fancy dresses.'

'Don't worry, sweetheart, you can borrow one of mine.' Nora smiled.

'What's the final thing you wanted to talk about?' Liam prompted.

'Your mother and I have planned a family camping trip for the October long weekend. We will join several other mage families for a magic retreat at Deep Creek.'

'Sounds good. We haven't been camping in ages,' Liam beamed.

Brendan nodded. 'Camping is much more my style. Finally, something fun to look forward to. Can we eat now? I'm starving.'

Eating her meal in silence, Alannah paid little attention while the others reminisced about previous camping trips. She had not been on any of them anyway. Her thoughts were elsewhere and the intense looks Liam gave her on a few occasions did not help.

As Alannah made her way along the upstairs hallway that night, Liam stepped out of his room and stopped her, halting only a hair's breadth away. 'Better reset your alarm, Lana. I want to leave by seven in the morning.'

'So now I have to fit in with your schedule? What happens when you're off surfing or something? Do I have to stay home?'

A glimmer of amusement appeared in his eyes. 'Or you could come with me and learn how to surf. Seriously though, what's so bad about spending time with me? Your lack of enthusiasm cuts me to the bone.' His tone was light and humorous, but Alannah heard the truth in his words.

'It's not that I don't want to spend time with you, Liam. We lead very different lives. You have your friends and I have mine. You play water sports and I… well I like to party.'

'I go to most of the same parties as you, Lana.'

'That's not exactly what I meant.'

'Oh…. Well, I think more time together is a good thing.' He leaned in closer to whisper in her ear, 'Imagine that we're dating.'

'But we're not dating, and I have a boyfriend. How the hell am I supposed to get time alone with Austin now?'

Liam grinned. 'Who's Austin?'

Alannah whacked his bicep with the back of her hand. 'Not funny.'

'You know how I feel about you, Lana, and I know you want me too. When are you going to stop messing around with that vampire git and give us a chance?'

She stood agape and speechless. Deciding it was safer to go to bed than reply with some snide remark, she pushed past him.

He caught her hand before she was out of his reach, forcing her to turn and face him. 'Good night, Lana.' Liam's thumb caressed the back of her knuckles as he gazed into her eyes for several seconds. He released her and returned to his room.

After running into her room, Alannah leaned against her closed door and released a huge lung full of air. *What am I going to do about Liam?*

'Liam, was it your idea to shadow me?' Alannah asked, having decided to break the uncomfortable silence in the car. She was still half asleep and already regretted her decision to hold out until after her workout for breakfast.

'Not entirely. Dad was adamant you should have a warlock bodyguard before lifting your grounding. I simply volunteered for the job.'

'Why not let Uncle Ross hire someone with more experience? Were you looking for an excuse to get closer to me?'

Liam sighed. 'Believe it or not, Lana, Dad has faith in my abilities as a mage and he thinks I stand as much chance of protecting you as any other warlock in the state. I'll admit, the opportunity to spend more time with you is a huge bonus, but I genuinely care about your wellbeing. I intend to take my duties seriously.'

Knowing that helped Alannah relax. 'Thank you, Liam.'

He glanced at her briefly and smiled. 'You're welcome.' When his eyes returned to the road, they were pulling into the school driveway.

It was odd how the knowledge of Liam watching her made Alannah self-conscious in the gym. Being such a confident woman, she rarely felt embarrassed. Brendan was the only guy who had ever made her blush before, because of their game. But that morning, as Alannah used the machine weights, it felt like Liam's eyes were boring a hole through to her soul and her cheeks flushed.

'Did you want me to spot for you?' Liam asked as she approached the bench press.

'You may as well since you have to watch me anyway.' She adjusted the weights down to twenty kilos. She knew both her cousins could manage over six times her limit, but she wasn't trying to get ripped.

Liam observed her first lift intently. 'Your strength building is progressing well, and you've got some good muscle tone, Lana.'

'Um… thanks.' Her increased heart rate was not due to the exercise alone.

'We should start your combat training soon. It looks like you're ready.'

She gave up after her second set of reps. It was less than her usual four, but she could not deal with Liam's scrutiny. As soon as she was on her feet, she felt her breathing settle.

'My turn.' Liam set the weights up to one-thirty-two.

'What sort of combat?' Alannah asked.

'A mix of martial arts and weapon fighting.' Liam straddled the bench. 'As a mage, you will learn to use enchanted blades. They will give you a real edge in combat.' He flashed her a wicked grin before laying back to commence his exercises.

Alannah groaned at the pun. But she found her eyes drawn to the sight of Liam's muscles as they tensed and quivered. The tight shirt he wore left little to the imagination and she could not help but speculate what sex would be like with such a well-built man. Austin's figure was slim and toned, but he owed much of his strength to his vampire heritage and lacked the definition apparent in Liam's abs. *Shit!* She was already betraying Austin with her mind. Pushing such thoughts aside, she tried to refocus on their conversation. 'Training with swords sounds rather deadly.'

Liam took a few deep breaths between sets before replying. 'Don't worry. We'll start with blunt practice weapons.'

'What about guns?'

'Mages don't use guns or other explosives. Too risky when an opponent could use magic to set them off and injure the person holding them.'

After their gym session and a quick breakfast, Liam walked Alannah to her locker. When they reached her stretch of corridor, she spied Austin waiting for her and her stomach churned. 'I don't suppose you could leave me here?' she asked Liam.

'Not a chance.'

She sighed and advanced toward inevitable awkwardness.

Austin pulled her into his arms the moment she was in his reach. 'Hey beautiful.' As he leaned in for a kiss, the sound of Liam clearing his throat interrupted them. 'Beat it, Winters,' Austin growled.

'Sorry, I can't. Would you like to explain, Lana, or should I?'

Alannah felt Austin tense and his grip on her tighten. 'Explain what?' His tone was apprehensive.

'Liam is now my bodyguard. He will follow me everywhere except around the home and into classes. I'm sorry, Austin. I know this is a serious buzzkill for us. I don't fancy having a chaperone on our dates.' She leaned in to whisper so softly that only Austin's vampire ears had any chance of hearing her: 'But you can still meet me at my window.' She pecked him on the lips and pulled out of his hold.

Austin's expression was a closed book and Alannah feared what he thought of the situation. For once, she wished she could turn her aura reading powers back on. 'I can't say I like the idea of hanging out with Liam, but protecting you is of the utmost importance. I will work around whatever you need.'

'Thank you, Austin. Will I see you at lunch?'

'Unlikely. Too much sun today.'

Alannah's heart sank. If it was only her, she would have joined him in the vamp's common room, but Austin clearly didn't want Liam to see his secret tunnels. 'Damn. Tomorrow then, I guess?'

'I guess so. Bye for now.' He stole one last kiss from her before heading to class.

Liam was waiting outside her English lesson at recess.

Alannah's treacherous eyes could get used to seeing the hottest guy in school this much and they were not the only part of her body feeling that way.

Brendan huffed as he walked out of the room with her. 'Seriously, bro. What trouble do you think Lana could get in within fifteen minutes?'

'If she's spending the time with you? A hell of a lot, I'm sure.'

Brendan laughed. 'Not the sort of trouble I was referring to, but I'll pay that.'

'So how are we going to do this?' Alannah asked. 'Will you join our group, or do I have to hang with your friends?'

'I thought we could alternate. Recess with your friends today, mine tomorrow. Lunch with mine today, yours tomorrow. How does that sound?'

'I guess that's fair. Try to play nice, okay?'

He grinned. 'Don't worry, Lana. I'll be on my best behaviour.'

After dumping their books in their lockers, they made their way to Alannah and Brendan's usual table outside. A few of her friends gave Alannah sidelong glances when they observed Liam standing close beside her and even a few surprised gasps when he sat next to her.

'What are you doing here?' Caleb asked Liam. As an endarkened fae, he had a strong dislike for purists like Liam, and with good reason. The endarkened were the offspring of elves and dark mages and usually practised illegal magic like their dark mage parents.

Alannah sensed Liam tensing, so she shot him a warning look.

'I'm spending time with my favourite cousin,' he replied, still facing Alannah.

Locky, the goth goblin in the group, scoffed. 'What, you don't get enough time with her at home? You have to come and spoil our fun?'

'I'm not here to spoil anything—unless someone tries to hurt Lana.'

Everyone glanced at Alannah with wide eyes and arched brows. Cara, who was sitting on her left side, leaned in close to whisper, 'Are you guys, you know…?'

Alannah turned to her best friend and replied in a hushed voice. 'No. I'll fill you in later.'

A few people tried to carry on with their conversations and Jacob even attempted some small talk with Alannah and Cara, but a nervous energy filled the rest of their morning.

Lunch was not much better, except this time Alannah was the unwelcome party crasher. Liam led her into a private dining hall and rest area that struck her with awe.

'This is the Founding Families' Lounge,' Liam explained.

Yet another common room for the exclusive use of magicals. Alannah wondered how many other such areas existed around campus. This room was much more elaborate than the underground hideout which Austin used. Dark timber tables filled the centre of the room, with matching desks and shelves lining one wall and dark red sofas along another. There was even a kitchenette with a fridge, microwave, kettle, and small sink.

While Liam went about reheating some leftovers, Alannah sat at one of the empty tables to avoid a confrontation with the girls who had been glaring at her since she entered. But she was out of luck. After they giggled and whispered amongst themselves for a minute, Monique made her way over to Alannah.

The queen bee sat next to Alannah and leaned in close. 'Rumour has it that you're cheating on your vampire boyfriend with Liam. One guy not enough for you? But why stop at two when you could so easily jump into your other cousin's bed too? Or have you already been there?'

Alannah narrowed her gaze on Monique. 'You shouldn't believe everything you hear. You might earn a reputation for being dumb and gullible.'

'Everything okay, Lana?' Liam asked as he moved close and placed a protective hand on her shoulder.

Observing the way Liam touched Alannah, Monique's prying eyes searched her blank expression. It made Alannah thankful the bitch was not an enchanter.

'Everything's fine. Monique, you were just catching me up on some school gossip, right? Thanks for the intel, by the way.'

Monique smirked. 'Of course.' She rose and returned to her friends.

Most of Liam's other mates had joined the girls by this point.

'Come on, Lana. Let's sit with them. Don't worry, they won't mind.'

Doubting the truth in that, Alannah followed Liam hesitantly. It was not that she was afraid of them or lacked the nerve to approach the popular kids. Alannah simply disliked conflict.

When they reached the table, more wide-eyed looks greeted Alannah and Liam. At least this time Liam offered an explanation, 'Listen guys, we have a situation. I know you're all wondering why I am following Alannah everywhere.' A few of them nodded. 'There's no easy way to say this, so I'm gonna be blunt…' he paused a moment. 'Tara Winters is back in town and she has threatened Alannah's life.' All of Liam's friends gasped. 'I've taken on the role of Alannah's bodyguard and I expect the rest of you will help me watch out for her.'

Liam's best mate, Blake, clapped him on the shoulder. 'No worries, man. Welcome, Alannah. Sorry about the whole death-threat thing, but don't worry, we've got your back.'

Smiling, Alannah decided she liked Blake, thinking that perhaps sitting with this group would not be so bad, even if the rest of Liam's friends were arseholes.

'Here sweetheart, I picked up a little something from the shops on my way home. I hope I got your size right.' Nora gave Alannah a dress bag as she entered the kitchen.

'Oh, wow, you didn't have to do that. I could have borrowed one of yours—' she began to protest.

But her aunt put her hand up to silence her. 'You ought to have at least one of your own. It was no trouble, really.'

'Um, thanks.' Alannah whistled as she pulled the garment out of the bag. 'It's stunning.' She was holding a short, emerald green A-line dress with a low plunging V-neck. Elaborate beading covered the bodice, while a lace design started halfway down the top layer of the lined skirt.

'I figured it would bring out your eye colour. Oh, and here are some matching heels. Now you'd better go get ready.' She handed Alannah a pair of black strappy shoes.

After hugging Nora, she made her way to her room. The dress was a perfect fit and as Alannah looked in the mirror, she barely recognised herself. She rarely wore anything that was not black and certainly nothing so fancy. *But hey, I look pretty damn good!* When she contemplated what to do about jewellery, she remembered the set she had inherited from her mother. She retrieved the emerald pendant on its silver chain, along with the matching teardrop earrings. The colour was a perfect match. *Must be fate*, she decided as she adorned her neck and ears with the precious gems.

As she stepped out into the hall, she found Brendan emerging from his own room, still struggling with his tie. Looking up at her, he stopped dead, eyes almost popping out of their sockets. '*Wowsers, Lana!* You are smokin' hot.'

'Thanks. You've scrubbed up pretty well too. Here, let me help you with that. I used to fix Dad's ties after Mum…' she left the rest hanging. It was not a night for mournful reminiscing. Taking Brendan's black satin tie in hand, she redid the botched double Windsor. 'There, much better.'

Brendan's eyes stared at her. 'Thanks, Lana.'

For a moment, electricity charged the air between them and Alannah's grip lingered on the tie. As much as Brendan hated dressing in suits, he pulled the look off superbly and it was easy to forget he was not the Winters man she had the hots for.

A closing door at the other end of the hallway broke the spell between them. When Alannah turned toward the noise, she spied Nora heading towards the stairs. She joined her aunt.

'Oh my gosh!' Nora clamped a hand over her mouth. 'You look gorgeous, sweetie.' She touched the emerald pendant. 'Was this your mum's? It's beautiful.'

'Yeah. She liked wearing green.'

'Yes, I remember that now. You look so much like her, Alannah. She would be proud of you. Come on, let's go knock the socks off the rest of the mage community.'

After taking a moment to wipe away a rogue tear, Alannah followed Nora and Brendan downstairs. Liam was waiting with Ross on the ground floor landing and as soon as he spotted her, his eyes lit up. She thought of all those cliché stairway scenes in American teen movies. At least he was not about to present her with a corsage and take her to prom.

Liam in a suit was a breathtaking sight. As they made their way to the car, he grabbed Alannah's arm to hold her back and whispered, 'I think I've just fallen in love with you all over again. You look incredible.'

She smiled back at him. 'Thanks.'

They all travelled together in Ross' Land Rover, with Alannah sandwiched in the back between her cousins. She was conscious of two sets of eyes on her for the duration of the journey. *Liam, I understand; but what is up with Brendan?* She shrugged it off, putting it down to his hormones responding to her attire.

Alannah discovered Cara at the buffet. She was sporting a striking red chiffon maxi dress, with a thigh high split, matching the colour of her hair. Grinning from the relief of finding a friendly face, she hugged Cara. 'Looking good.'

'Speak for yourself, Alannah. That outfit is amazing on you.' She leaned in closer and gestured towards a group of guys. 'Liam can't keep his eyes off you, and he's not the only one.'

A cursory glance told her Cara was right. All of Liam's mates were checking her out too. She spotted Brendan standing with his friends. Three of them were looking her way, but she noticed one set of eyes on Cara. 'Liam has to watch me. He's my bodyguard now and he also ordered his friends to help protect me.'

'Watch you, sure; but that's more than a look of concern for his charge. You've got every guy in this place drooling over you, girl.'

'Not quite. Bailey's got his eyes on you.'

'Yeah, well he's had a crush on me for years, poor guy. He knows I'm not interested. I've got my heart set on someone else.'

'Oh? Who?'

'Promise not to tell?'

'My lips are sealed.' Alannah zipped her mouth shut with a gesture.

Cara took a deep breath. 'Jacob. I love that impish smile of his and he always makes me laugh.'

Alannah giggled. 'You guys would make the cutest little redhead babies.'

'Would if we could!' Cara grinned.

Recollections from her reading on fae came to mind. *Hybrid races can only breed with their own kind or those of their precursor races.* For boggarts that meant elves or gorgons. 'Oh right, I forgot boggarts can't breed with mages.' She offered an apologetic smile.

'Honestly, it doesn't bother me at all. I'm not looking to breed, at least not yet. But seriously, getting back to Liam: you've got to tell me what's going on with you two.'

She sighed. 'He confessed his undying love to me on Saturday, admitting he doesn't care about my tainted blood. Problem is, I'm still in love with Austin. Plus, I know Uncle Ross would never approve of the relationship, despite what Liam says.'

'Well shit! That's huge. For Liam to be willing to break tradition and ignore his father's wishes… he's got it for you bad, Alannah. What are you going to do?'

'I dunno. I'm so damn confused!'

The High Magus called everyone to attention, ending Alannah's conversation as he summoned them into the ballroom. He stood in front of a band who had set up on the stage. After tapping on his microphone, he began his speech: 'I'd like to start by thanking you all for coming tonight. I know some of you have travelled across the state to get here. Thank the Gods for ley lines.'

A few people in the crowd chuckled, but Alannah did not find his attempt at humour very funny.

'The Spring Equinox is a special time of year, marking a season of rebirth and fertility in nature. This is especially important for the shamans among us. But today also represents the struggle between light and dark within all of us. As much as I hate to put a dampener on our celebration, it is crucial that I remind you all of this and the consequences of slipping into the left-hand path. Some of you may have heard an old threat has returned to Gaeilge

Shores and I'm afraid I must confirm the rumours. Tara Winters, Queen of the Cursed, walks among us once again and she has already threatened a member of our community.'

Alannah heard gasps and murmurs among the audience. She scanned the crowd and saw the pale, aghast faces of the people surrounding her. *If my grandmother incites such terror among so many full-fledged mages, what hope do I have?* Her shoulders hunched and it felt as though someone had replaced her stomach with rocks.

Liam stepped closer to put his arm around her shoulders and whispered in her ear. 'Don't worry, Lana. I won't let anything happen to you.'

Kieran continued addressing them. 'This woman is very dangerous, and I advise against approaching or engaging her in direct combat without backup. If any of you have information on her whereabouts, please contact me directly.' He paused for several seconds to let everyone process his words. 'Now, with that unpleasant news out of the way, I invite you all to enjoy the festivities here tonight. Thank you.' The High Magus left the stage and the band started up with some classic rock covers.

'Wanna dance?' Liam asked her.

'No. I don't dance. Not to this music anyway.'

Liam arched his brow. 'What sort of music will you dance to?'

'Anything that's good and heavy. Even then, I only get into it if there's a decent mosh pit.'

'Fair enough. Come on, let's get a drink.' Liam led her outside, swiping a couple of beers from the bar on the way and handed her one. 'Don't let my folks see you drinking.'

Alannah smiled. 'Were you always this rebellious, or is it my bad influence?'

'Hey, I'm eighteen now, I'm allowed to drink. But I'd have to say some of your defiance has rubbed off on me.'

She snorted. 'Right. So, you never partook in underage drinking?'

'Sure, I did. But only with Dad's permission and supervision.' Liam stopped beside the bonfire and took a seat.

Alannah rolled her eyes as she perched beside him. 'So, what's the naughtiest thing you've ever done?'

'Well getting you initiated behind Dad's back is definitely right up there.'

'Yeah, I guess it would be. But come on, was there anything from before my return?'

Liam took several minutes to ponder his answer, leaving Alannah to watch a pair of fire dancers who had started performing nearby. The magic they cast was impressive in its own right, but the way their bodies whirled about was a fascinating sight to behold.

'There is one thing I can think of.'

'Huh, what?' The dancers still mesmerised Alannah and she was only vaguely aware of Liam talking.

He laughed. 'That's Claudia and Clayton, twin fire channellers. They're good, aren't they?'

'Brilliant. Sorry, what were you saying?'

'I can think of something I did that was technically naughty, and I certainly didn't tell my parents about it.'

'Well now you have my attention.' She eyed him expectantly.

'Underage sex.'

That made her grin. 'I had wondered about that. How old were you?'

'You wondered about my sex life, huh?' His eyes sparkled with a hint of mischief. 'I lost my virginity at fifteen. I'd planned to wait longer, but Monique was eager, and Brendan kept bragging about having sex. I guess I let my competitive nature get the better of me.'

'Of course Brendan started young.' She cast her eyes in her other cousin's direction. He was sitting on the opposite side of the fire, laughing, and drinking shots poured from a hipflask with Connor, Bailey, and Cara. Brendan turned to face her, tilting his head, and looking at her from beneath arched brows. She lifted her cup in a toast and he smiled, returning the gesture.

'How old were you, Lana?'

'Eleven,' she replied casually, her gaze still locked with Brendan's.

'So, you started young too.'

She turned back to Liam. 'Does that bother you?'

'Not really. Your previous relationships are not my concern. It's the current one I don't like.'

Alannah sighed as she stared into her drink before sculling a large mouthful. 'What do you have against Austin? I mean aside from jealousy over me.'

'Well to begin with, there's the fact that he's a vampire and owes his loyalty to a Queen who wants to curse or kill you. But it's mostly his past behaviour that worries me. I don't know all the details, but Austin and Brendan used to have a rep for tag-teaming girls. I suspect they employed hypnotic coercion in some cases, but Brendan never admitted that much and there was no proof. What I do know is Austin became addicted to feeding on the girls and took it too far on a couple of occasions.'

Alannah's jaw kept dropping as Liam shed light on her boyfriend's past. She did not want to believe it, but Brendan had already alluded to his dark times. 'What do you mean "too far?"'

'Two of the girls went to hospital on the brink of death and needed blood transfusions. Austin's dad covered it up with all his money and powerful connections, so it never got out to the wider mage community, but Brendan confessed to me. The whole mess distressed him. A lot.'

'Shit. I guess that's why Austin was so reluctant to bite me when I first asked. He was afraid of putting me in hospital.'

Liam frowned. 'I can't believe you asked him to feed on you, Lana. Why the hell would you do that?'

'I figured it would be hot. I didn't know there was such a risk, at least not at first. If I'm honest, I had a bit of a vampire fetish even before I knew they were real. I'm a big fan of Anne Rice and Joss Whedon. When I learned what bites could feel like—'

'So what? You ignored the warnings in the training books?' He shook his head in bewilderment.

'I don't need to justify my actions to you, Liam. I'm a pleasure seeker and I refuse to feel ashamed about it. Some risks are worth the reward.'

'You've changed a lot in the last nine years. You were such a sweet girl back then.' There was no bitterness in his tone, merely resigned acceptance.

'No, Liam. I've always had these tendencies. Obviously, they flourished more when I hit puberty, but your princess was never all that innocent. You simply refused to see me for what I was.' Alannah looked over at Brendan as she cast her mind back to their childhood. They were only five when the two of them discovered her mum's copy of the *Kama Sutra*. They had giggled a lot on their first read through, but it soon became their mission to learn as much as they could about sex. A year later, their game of Sleazy Chicken began.

'What's that supposed to mean?' Liam asked.

'Let's just say, my sex education started about five years before my hymen broke.'

'Christ!' Liam must have followed her line of sight because when Alannah returned her attention to Liam, she saw his blanched face glaring at Brendan.

Chapter Fourteen

The rest of the week passed with little incident, mostly thanks to the amount of schoolwork everyone needed to finish before the end of term. Even Liam seemed content to sit back and supervise Alannah without getting pushy or personal and she began to wonder if he had given up on the idea of dating her. Deciding to test the waters during the first week of the mid-semester break, she walked into the living room and addressed Liam: 'Austin and I are going to the movies tonight.'

Shifting his focus away from the television, he glared at her. 'Not happening.'

'What, why? Do you have other plans, because you were meant to tell me what nights you were busy?'

'I refuse to be the third wheel on one of your dates, Lana. Sorry, but I can't deal with the sight of you making out with him, or anyone else for that matter. If you must see him, keep it to the bedroom.' He turned back to the TV. 'And try to keep his teeth out of your neck, for the love of the Gods.'

'What the hell is your problem, Liam?'

He grabbed the remote to pause his crime show. Tossing it aside, he gave her a penetrating stare. 'I've already told you how I feel about you. What do *you* think my problem is?'

'You've been distant for the last week, so I thought you'd gotten over me.'

Liam shot up from the couch in a flash and pulled her into his arms, pressing her head against his hard chest. His heart was racing. 'Is this a better proximity for you? Because I wish I could keep you this close all day, every day. What I feel for you is not a passing crush, Lana. I've been in love with you for as long as I can remember. Not something I can "get over" that easily.' After loosening his grip on her, he gently lifted her chin to look into her eyes. 'Now tell me how you feel.'

She gazed up into his big blues and years of feelings came crashing into her heart. *Shit!* It would have been all too easy to give in to him there, but she knew it would not be fair on either him or Austin. 'I do want you and I don't even have to dig that deep to find those feelings, but things are complicated now.'

'Because of Austin? Or is there someone else too?'

'Yes, because of Austin. Who else would there be?'

'I don't know Lana, you tell me.' This time his tone was bitter.

'Is this about my relationship history? You said that didn't bother you. Look, I've only ever been in love with three guys in my life and I assure you I've moved on from my ex.'

There was a flicker of emotion in his eyes. 'And the other two?'

'Are you and Austin.' She heard the slightest gasp slip through his teeth. 'Please give me time to sort my head out.'

Liam released his hold on her and slumped back onto the sofa. 'I can give you time, but don't expect me to chaperone any dates.'

When the first week of October ended, Alannah was chomping at the bit to get out of the house. After her heart to heart with Liam, she did not feel like dragging him out of the house much.

The night before their camping trip, Alannah tossed and turned in bed. Sleep was eluding her overactive mind as she thought back to the previous night:

> *It was her only date-night with Austin that week, and they had spent it in her room. Austin scrutinised her with narrow, unwavering eyes. 'You're unusually quiet, Alannah. What's wrong?'*
>
> *She did not want to worry him when she was still working through her feelings, so she told a partial lie. 'I'm annoyed we can't go out on proper dates because Liam has to shadow me.'*
>
> *'I know how you feel. This is trying, but I know a good way to channel our frustrations.' He grinned as he pulled her onto the bed.*
>
> *Even their lovemaking lacked the usual passion.* Is that because I put a stop to his attempt to bite me? He didn't even hide his disappointment when I told him I was not feeling well.

It was early the next morning when Liam drove Alannah and Brendan to the camping grounds in his blue Audi Q7. Brendan had chosen to travel with them, claiming the music on his brother's radio was more tolerable than his mother's Enya CDs. His presence was a welcome buffer for the tension between her and Liam and she suspected he knew as much.

As soon as 'Wonderful Life' by Bring Me the Horizon started playing on the radio, Alannah cranked the volume.

'Fuck yeah!' Brendan cried from the backseat. He joined her in screaming along with the song.

The sight of Alannah's head banging and 'singing' to rock music kept drawing Liam's attention as well as a few laughs and smiles. It did wonders for thawing the ice between them.

The next song was one of those Aussie hip hop tunes none of them liked, so Alannah connected a streaming service on her smartphone to the stereo. Something heavy and progressive started playing.

'Who's this?' Liam asked.

'A band known as TOOL. Apparently, they were big in the nineties.'

After driving through some scrubland, they arrived at their destination: sixteen campsites nestled among tall gum trees that Alannah figured were stringybarks from the signage. The mages had booked the whole place.

'Wow!' she exclaimed. 'It feels like we're in the middle of nowhere.'

'That's the point,' Liam explained. 'Gives us the privacy we need for ritual magic and training exercises. Can't have regular humans seeing what we do.'

The remoteness of Gaeilge Shores made sense. Supposedly, their small country town was the magic capital of the state because it was the seat of the High Magus. She had once thought it odd that the mages chose not to live in the city.

'I've only ever camped in caravan parks before. Are there toilets here?' She started to look around.

'City girl!' Brendan mocked with jest. 'The toilets are over there. Hot showers too.' He pointed to a rustic wooden shack in the centre of the ring road providing access to each campsite. The facilities were about one hundred metres from their site.

Ross approached Alannah and the guys. 'Liam and Brendan, I want you to keep a close eye on Alannah all weekend.' He dumped a large blue canvas bag in front of Liam. 'The three of you are sharing this tent. Your mum's filling up the airbeds at the car.' He returned to his own camp site on the other side of his four-wheel drive.

A huge grin appeared on Brendan's face as he helped position the tent base. 'Looks like I get to sleep with you again, Lana.'

She laughed. 'Just don't poke me in the arse when spooning.'

Brendan let out a pantomime sigh. 'Fine. I guess I can make do with *poking* your front.' He added emphasis to the word by inserting one of the poles into the tent.

Alannah leaned a little closer to lower the volume of her voice. 'Am I to gather you prefer anal?'

Dropping the bag of pegs, Brendan stepped up to her and whispered, 'I would happily take you every which way, Lana.'

That won him a bright flush of red in Alannah's cheeks.

He slapped her left butt cheek. 'Looks like I'm back at the top of my game.' Backing away slowly, he added, 'The champ returns.' Spinning on his heels, he strode away.

Liam called out after him, 'Where are you going, Brendan? We haven't finished here.'

Brendan shouted his reply as he continued walking, 'Gotta see a man about a horse.'

Alannah silently helped Liam stake the tent into the ground for several minutes.

As she caught the rain fly Liam threw across the top, he stopped what he was doing to look at her. 'Lana?'

'Yes, Liam?'

'That night after we found your family tree…' He seemed apprehensive.

'What about it?'

'Did you, uh… sleep with Brendan that night?'

'Yeah, I did.' She tried to hide her amusement as Liam's face turned crimson.

'I'm gonna kill that pipsqueak….' He started towards the toilet block.

The laugh finally escaped her. 'We only slept though.'

Liam spun back around. 'Wait, so you didn't have sex? What about on other occasions?'

'No, I haven't done *that* with him.' She was still struggling to contain her hysterics.

'It's not funny, Lana. The thought of you with Brendan pains me far more than what you have going with Austin. And you know how much it kills me to see you with that vampire.'

She calmed herself with a few deep breaths. 'Sorry, but the two of you really do take sibling rivalry to the extreme. Didn't your parents ever teach you to share?' She winked at him and when he blushed, she considered introducing him to Sleazy Chicken. It might be the only way to get any wins. But it was probably too cruel, considering his feelings for her. 'You don't need to worry about Brendan and me. We enjoy flirting, but it means nothing.'

He gave her a sidelong glance but dropped the subject.

Focus, Brendan! The silent mantra did little to help shift Brendan's concentration back to the ritual High Magus Kieran was leading them in. Alannah was standing next to him and awareness of her presence was all-consuming. Looking that good in ceremonial robes should be a crime. *Shit! This isn't good.* His hormones had never interfered with his magic before. Alannah was going to be his undoing.

The circle had been cast and the High Magus was inviting them to join. The man stepped in front of Brendan. 'How do you enter the circle?'

After stumbling at first, he got the words out. 'W… with love and peace.'

Kieran eyed him with concern before responding, 'Blessed be.'

With the first stage of the ritual complete, Kieran blessed some oil. He approached each member of the circle to anoint them. 'May the Gods watch over you and keep you safe from harm.'

The smear of oil applied to Brendan's forehead pulsed, and warmth spread from it throughout his body. He knew the effect would be temporary, but it was still a welcome shield from the threat his grandmother posed.

Once the protective ritual had concluded, the campers settled in for a relaxed night around a few fires. The Council members convened at one end of the campgrounds, while the initiates were at the other end.

Brendan sat with Connor and Bailey across from Alannah, who sat with Liam and Cara. But it was not long before Bailey moved to the other side of the fire to join Cara. Brendan shook his head. 'That man's a lost cause. Cara will never yield to his advances.'

'Pessimism doesn't suit you, Brendo,' Connor observed.

He laughed. 'Just calling it as I see it. That girl's in love with someone else.'

'Are we still talking about Cara?'

When he looked at Connor, his friend was smirking. 'Come on man, out with it,' Brendan demanded.

'Why do you sit back and let your best mate and brother do all the chasing?'

'Because I've read enough of her feelings to know she's not receptive to me.'

'Bah! You haven't tried hard enough to open her eyes.' He rose in his seat. 'I'm grabbing another drink. Be right back.' Connor left Brendan alone with his thoughts for a moment.

If there was one thing he understood about Alannah: aggression was not the right approach with her. But it was possible Brendan's attempts had been too subtle. He had caught the occasional glimpse of desire on her part, but she was always so quick to shut herself off from those thoughts and emotions.

A set of female hands gripped his shoulders. 'Hey there, little brother. Why the glum face?' Monique appeared beside him.

He intensified his frown. Brendan always hated it when she faked familiarity with him. 'I'm not your brother, Monique.'

'No, but you were practically my brother-in-law for years.' She sighed as she sat next to him. 'I think I made a big mistake and went after the wrong brother.' Her hand began rubbing his thigh.

Trying to ignore the insane girl's flirting, he kept his gaze fixed on Alannah and Liam as he sipped his beer. The two of them were sitting much closer than necessary and Alannah was laughing at something Liam told her. *What the hell? She never laughed at Liam*. His lame attempts at humour usually fell flat with her.

'You know, I've always wondered what sex would be like with an enchanter,' Monique continued her attempt at seduction. It was almost laughable. She was attractive, sure, but Brendan detested everything else about the girl.

He looked at her. 'What are you doing, Monique? If you're hoping to get laid, I'm sure Blake would be obliging.'

'But he's only an illusionist and you're the best enchanter around.' She was giving him the lewdest bedroom eyes he had ever seen on a girl.

Brendan sighed and returned his attention to Alannah, who was leaning in to whisper something in Liam's ear. Whatever she said made him smile.

'You want her too, don't you?' A quick glance at Monique told him her eyes had followed Brendan's. 'Apparently all the guys do. Personally, I don't see what's so good about her.'

'You don't even know her!' Brendan snapped.

Monique laughed. 'Yep, you've got it bad. I could help you forget about her for a while. We could have some real fun.'

Forget? What would I give to forget the pain of envy and unrequited love, even for a few hours? He realised he had not had sex in months; not since his feelings for Alannah had rekindled. Brendan looked at Monique and saw the flicker of flames reflected in her eyes. 'Screw it.' He jumped up and dragged Monique beyond the tree line.

She giggled as they made their mad dash for the cover of the forest.

Once among the dense foliage, Brendan pushed Monique up against a large tree and savagely kissed her. He switched to full channelling mode, reading her every thought and feeling as he heightened her senses. This was how he had become so good at what he did. He focussed on what the girl really wanted and pressed every single button that sent her into a fit of ecstasy.

Monique's triggers were all quite vanilla, which meant he did not need much magic to please her. *Easy, yes—but not exciting.* Brendan much preferred the girls who had at least some inclination for kink.

Having rocked Monique's world, he dressed in silence and walked back to camp without a word.

Liam noticed Alannah yawning. As much as he hated the idea of their night ending, he was getting tired too. Talking to her about anything and everything had felt so good, so right. But there was always the chance they would get some time alone in their tent. The idea made him smile. 'I think it's bedtime.'

'I think you might be right,' Alannah agreed as she stood. She turned to Cara and Bailey. 'Night guys.'

Liam followed her back to their tent, glancing around the place as they walked. Even with the protection spell in place, he would not shake the habit of remaining alert of their surroundings.

As soon as they reached their little dome shelter, Alannah slid into her sleeping bag and started removing her clothes.

Liam fought the impulse to avert his eyes. She covered herself anyway, so he should not feel so damn modest.

Brendan stepped into the tent as Alannah removed her bra and dropped it on her backpack. He whistled and clapped Liam on the shoulder. 'I wouldn't normally include my brother in a threesome, but I guess these are extenuating circumstances.'

Alannah laughed.

But Liam glared at him. 'You are truly disgusting, Brendan.'

'Why thank you, Liam. I aim to please… or offend. Either works for me.'

He pulled Brendan outside the tent. 'By the way, I saw you disappear with Monique tonight.'

'And what of it? Don't tell me you're jealous?' Brendan grinned.

'Hardly. I dumped her, remember? But I know how her mind works. She's probably using you to get back at me.'

'I'm not an idiot, bro. You may be the superior mage, but when it comes to girls, I'm leagues ahead of you. I know the game she's playing, and I don't really care.' Brendan shrugged himself out of Liam's hold and moved back into the tent. 'Nice bra by the way, Lana. Black lace and satin lingerie will never go out of style.'

Liam sighed, stepping back inside.

Alannah had slipped into a black satin nightgown and the cover of her sleeping-bag dropped into her lap. 'Just as well since it's all I ever wear.'

Overcome with some strong urges, Liam ducked for the cover of his own sleeping-bag. After stripping down to his boxer shorts, he lay back to look at the blue canvas ceiling.

Brendan sniggered. 'Hey Lana, I think you made Liam blush.'

'Well that makes one of you.'

'Don't worry, Lana, you turn me red too, just not in the face.'

Alannah laughed. 'Doesn't count if I can't see it.'

Brendan's voice lowered. 'Are you saying you wanna see my cock, Lana?'

Liam groaned as he covered his ears. 'Christ, would you two give it a rest!'

They both burst into a fit of laughter, but when Alannah calmed down, she placed a hand on Liam's arm. 'I'm sorry.'

He turned and locked her eyes with his. Her gaze was unwavering as she chewed on her bottom lip. Liam took a deep breath and relaxed. Alannah's hand was still on his bicep, so he grabbed it and pressed his lips to the soft skin on the inside of her wrist. 'Good night, Lana.'

She gasped, but did not pull her hand back, not even when she settled down for sleep. 'Good night, Liam.'

Having her fingers intertwined with his, Liam fell into the 'sweetest' of dreams.

Wildflowers and grass trees lined the track Alannah hiked along with her fellow mages. It was a sunny spring day, too sunny for her liking. Alannah hoped the sunblock she had applied that morning held out long enough.

Liam was certainly in his element and even Brendan was enjoying himself. They both kept behind her, watching out for danger.

Alannah tried to keep a little distance in front of the guys as she walked alongside Cara. Starting out at a casual pace allowed for some chatting.

Leaning closer, Cara spoke in a hushed voice. 'It looked like you were getting pretty close to Liam last night. Anything you wanna share? Like what happened when the two of you went to bed together?'

'Nothing happened. Brendan joined us soon after we got to our tent.'

'Oh? I thought he spent the night with Monique?'

Alannah screwed up her face. 'Where'd you get that impression?'

'Didn't you hear, the two of them hooked up last night? Brendan as good as confirmed the rumour this morning.'

Shaking her head, Alannah dismissed the odd pang of jealousy she felt. She figured it was probably more disgust at Brendan's poor taste in sexual partner. 'Of all girls, why the hell would he go for her?'

'Probably because she was all over him last night. Monique was easy prey. I doubt he cares for her if that's what you're worried about.'

'I'm not worried, just surprised and grossed out.'

Cara stopped walking for a moment and drew Alannah's attention to her face. 'If you're not worried, I'll eat my hat. I know you care about Brendan and don't want to see him get hurt any more than I do.'

They resumed their stroll before the guys were able to catch up with them. 'Brendan's a big boy, I'm sure he can handle Monique. I thought he had better standards though.'

'Oh my God! You're jealous!' Cara cried.

'No, I'm not! I told you I don't like him that way.'

'Sure, whatever. It's a pity Liam and Brendan don't get along well, because that'd be a pretty hot threesome otherwise.' Cara giggled.

Alannah entertained the idea a moment before punching Cara in the arm for putting the thought in her head.

'Ouch! Gods, Alannah. What was that for?'

'I didn't need that mental image.'

The Council members at the front of the group began to pick up the pace and talking became too difficult. Alannah needed to focus on her breathing and where she was treading.

About three hours into the hike, the group stopped in a clearing where they set up a picnic lunch. After their meal, High Magus Kieran instructed the initiates to sit in a circle and provide a demonstration of their current powers.

Monique was up first. After a minute of meditation, she started with a simple summoning spell from which an old Cabbage Patch Kid appeared. The doll had blonde hair and a purple dress and as Monique worked her magic, the doll began to walk. It was the stuff of nightmares and Don Mancini movies. Directing the doll to return to her, she placed a letter opener in its hands. She sent it walking across the circle to her friend Jessica who handed the doll an envelope. The little plastic construct deftly sliced open the envelope and handed it back to Jessica. Monique clicked her fingers and the doll disappeared, along with the small blade it carried.

A few people gasped and most joined in a round of applause. Alannah remained silent, in awe of the girl's powers.

Brendan, who had chosen to sit next to Monique, was next. The sight of them together was infuriating.

The High Magus scoffed. 'Brendan Winters. Do you have any useful powers to show us yet?'

Monique giggled, along with her friends. 'The demonstration he gave me last night was *quite* useful.'

'*Monique!*' Kieran chided her.

The girls grew quiet.

Unfazed by Monique's behaviour, Brendan grinned at Kieran. 'Sure, I do, Your Honour.' He closed his eyes and commenced meditating.

A few minutes later, Alannah heard Brendan's voice in her head, a power he had mastered in their last training session. *'Hi Lana. You wanna tell me why you're feeling jealous?'*

She felt her cheeks flush.

'I can sense you blushing. I'll take that as your answer.' Opening his eyes, Brendan puffed his chest

out at all the wide eyes and gaping mouths staring at him.

Alannah wondered what he had said to everyone else.

Several other mages displayed their abilities, such as Connor healing Bailey who intentionally electrocuted himself with a lightning bolt, and Cara making a nearby sapling grow at an accelerated pace.

Alannah's turn followed. She took a few deep breaths to calm her nerves, but they did not seem to help.

Brendan's voice was in her mind again. *'It's okay, Lana. Treat it like one of our training sessions. Here, I'll help.'*

A sudden sense of calm washed through her. Closing her eyes, she cleared her mind and began to channel the mana in her matter ring. She focussed the energy on conjuring up the practice sword she had commenced training with. When she opened her eyes, the wooden weapon was firmly in her grip. She smiled with relief. *It worked!* Closing her eyes again, she visualised the shelf the sword belonged on and willed it to return there. A second later it vanished.

The group clapped their praise.

As she looked up, she found Liam staring at her. He was sitting with Ross and Nora and all three of them were beaming with their heads held high. But Liam's gaze was different: focused and intense. It sent a rush of blood through Alannah's body. When she averted her gaze, she caught Brendan's eyes, but he was not betraying any of his thoughts or feelings. She smiled and mouthed 'thank you' to him.

'You're welcome, Lana. Oh, and don't look now, but your display of power gave every straight guy here a hard-on.'

She narrowed her eyes on him, sensing exaggeration in his words. What she had done was hardly impressive. It did not compare to Monique's demonstration.

'I speak the truth. You were only initiated a couple of months ago and you've achieved more than any other mage could in that time. Plus, you're a Winters babe.' He grinned lasciviously at her.

Thanks to the telepathic exchange with Brendan, Alannah was only vaguely aware that the magical show and tell had continued. Once concluded, they packed up and hiked back to camp.

Following dinner, Alannah dragged her aching legs over to the campfire.

The moment she yawned; Liam gave her a reassuring smile. 'It's okay, I can see the tent from here. Go get some rest.'

'Thanks.' Not having him follow her straight away was a little disappointing. She was secretly hoping for some alone time with Liam. When Alannah reached the tent, she was surprised to find Brendan already in bed, reading by lamplight. 'Hey.'

Peeking over his novel, he grinned. 'Hi, Lana. Calling it a night already, huh?'

'Yeah. That walk almost killed me.' Glancing at his reading material, she recognised Stephen King's *It*. 'Good book, that one, although a bit slow to start. I loved the movies too.' Sitting on her mattress, she removed her shoes and slipped into her sleeping bag.

'I haven't watched them yet. I prefer to start with the books.' Brendan closed his novel and put it aside.

'Me too, actually.'

The moment he turned back to face her; Brendan's bare chest came into full view. His abs reminded her of Liam. When her eyes ventured back to his, they gave her a smirk.

'Don't you get cold sleeping out here without a shirt?' she asked.

'Not at all. If anything, I overheat in this sleeping-bag.'

Her eyes wandered back to his muscles and lingered there a moment.

'Lana, you wanna tell me why you're fucking me with your eyes right now?'

Alannah almost blushed but clamped down on her emotions. She was not letting him get to her that easily. 'It occurred to me, I've haven't ever touched a guy's six pack. I've never dated guys with that sort of muscle tone.'

Brendan's visage began to smoulder. 'Well, go on.'

Letting curiosity get the better of her, she pressed her right hand against his pecs and let it slide down over the ridges and valleys forming the terrain of his well-sculpted body. 'Christ, your abdominal muscles feel rock hard.'

'They're not alone. I dare you to keep travelling south and find out how hard I can get.' His unblinking eyes leered at her.

Not one to back down from a challenge like that, Alannah slowly moved her hand lower, keeping her gaze locked with Brendan's. He did not falter once as she inched closer to his waist. Brendan did not even flinch as her fingertips lightly brushed over the soft skin beneath his belly button.

Reaching the top of his boxer shorts, she paused. She took a deep breath and continued, choosing to stay above the silky fabric to avoid getting tangled in his hairs. Her fingers walked hesitantly onto the top of his pubic region, yet he kept a straight face. *By the Gods, how far is he willing to let me go?* Another step and he licked his lips. *Shit!* Losing her nerve at the last, she pulled her hand back.

'Yet another win for me.'

'Hey, that doesn't count. I didn't blush,' she protested.

'No, but you did chicken out, and that, my dear, is the name of the game.'

She sighed and settled back into bed. 'Fine, whatever.'

'So, now you've mastered summoning, what's next on your magic agenda?'

'Constructs, I suppose. Although I think I'll stick to golems rather than Chucky dolls.'

He laughed. 'That was pretty freaky.'

'What's next for you?' Alannah turned to face him.

Brendan was staring at the ceiling as he replied, 'The big one.' He looked at her. 'Mental manipulation.'

The implications sent a shiver down Alannah's spine.

They spent much of Sunday on combat training. Alannah felt a flutter in her stomach when Liam insisted on being her partner for the whole day.

Kieran frowned. 'Alannah would benefit from facing more opponents to learn how other combatants fight differently.'

'With all due respect, Your Honour, Alannah has only started her weapon training. She's not ready to face other opponents.'

'Very well. But don't let your own skills slip. Be sure to get in some practice with at least one experienced fighter this afternoon.'

'Yes, sir.' Liam grabbed a couple of wooden swords and led Alannah to a clear spot. He handed her one and dropped the other on the ground. 'Do you remember the grip and stance I showed you?'

'I think so.' She held the sword in front of her.

'Close.' Liam stepped behind her, encircling her in his arms to correct her grip and posture. 'Try to relax your arms and legs more.' His breath tickled her ear as he spoke.

Intoxicated by his presence, Alannah melted into his hold.

She heard his sharp intake of breath. 'Not that I'm complaining, but that's not exactly what I meant.'

'I know. I guess I got a little caught up in the moment.'

Pressing his body hard against her back, Liam's fingers stroked her left arm as he whispered, 'Save that thought for later.'

Alannah laughed. 'If you insist.' Flirting with Liam was almost as fun as it was with Brendan and it had the added element of meaning.

'I must insist, otherwise neither of us will get any sword practice in today.' His voice was an even deeper pitch than normal. 'Now try that starting stance again.' Liam stepped back enough to give her the room she needed.

She adjusted her weight and kept her limbs relaxed.

'Good.' Liam released his hold and grabbed his own sword. After stepping her through various positions slowly a few times, he taught her how to parry.

Alannah was thankful for the much-needed lunch break when it finally arrived. Every part of her body was aching, and she was perspiring profusely. When she saw that none of the other mages showed any signs of tiring, she wanted to crawl under a rock and hide.

Liam sat on the ground beside her with his own sandwich and smiled sympathetically. 'I guess we'll have to work on your endurance.'

'And how do you suggest we do that?' Her voice came out gruffer than usual, likely due to the warm tingles developing between her thighs.

His eyes darkened. 'Increasing the duration of our combat training sessions, of course. Or did you have something else in mind?'

'Ha! When did you become such a shameless flirt?'

'I dunno. You must be rubbing off on me.' He grinned.

Taking a bite from her salad roll, Alannah tried to hide the extent of her amusement at his choice of words.

'I was thinking you should sit out and watch for the rest of the afternoon. I don't want to break you; plus, I need to duel some of the others.'

'Suits me fine.'

Alannah settled into one of the deckchairs and enjoyed the show. Liam faced off against Blake to start with. It was a good fight, if a little one sided, with Liam clearly more skilled.

After a few more duels in which Liam wiped the floor with his opponents, Brendan approached him. 'Bring it bro. First to draw blood wins.'

'Fine, but it's your funeral.'

Brendan grinned. 'We'll see about that.'

They both tossed their wooden weapons aside and reached for real blades.

Alannah watched intently. She had no idea what Brendan's fighting skills were like, at least not these days. She only ever trained with Liam and the last time she had seen them fight was nine years ago.

The sound of metal clinging against metal filled the air and before long, the Winters boys had drawn a decent crowd. They were both excellent swordsmen and from what Alannah could tell, equally matched.

'Impressive, ain't it?' Cara commented as she pulled up a chair next to Alannah, offering some chips from the bag she had opened.

'Very,' Alannah agreed. She grabbed a handful of the potato crisps. *Ooh, barbecue flavour, nice.*

'Brendan once told me Ross started training them when the boys were five and six. Most of us don't start combat training until after we're initiated.'

Riveted by the display of speed and skill, among other things, she kept her eyes glued on the fight. 'I guess he predicted the need for it.'

The guys were finally starting to break a sweat and showing the first signs of fatigue. Neither of them had struck the other when they both stepped back for a quick breather. Brendan took the opportunity to tear his shirt off and wipe his brow with it. Cheers and wolf whistles coming from Monique's direction rewarded him. As if not wanting to disappoint his own captive audience, Liam followed suit. The cheers continued.

Moving to the edge of her seat, Alannah had become enthralled and aroused by the spectacle. She noticed Brendan was gaining the upper hand as he pushed Liam back. *Shit! Didn't see that coming.* A moment later, he nicked Liam's right arm.

Liam jumped back. His left hand clamped over his bleeding gash as he scowled at the scene before him. Brendan's cheer squad were surrounding him, and Monique showered him in kisses as he revelled in his victory.

Alannah flew to Liam and wrapped her arms around him. 'Are you okay?'

He tore his eyes away from Brendan and looked down at her with a slight smile. 'Yeah. My pride's hurting more than my arm.' Pulling his hand away, he inspected the wound.

Chancing a glance herself, Alannah almost fainted. *So much blood!* 'You better get your dad to fix that, pronto.'

He sighed. 'I guess.' Liam grinned at her. 'One problem with that plan though.'

'What?'

'You'd have to let go of me first and I think I'd rather bleed to death.'

Frowning, she released him. 'Please don't joke about that right now.'

'Seriously Lana, it's not that bad. But I'll get it seen to now, if it makes you feel better.'

'Please do.' After watching Liam walk over to Ross, Alannah directed her gaze toward Brendan.

His fan club continued fawning over him, but his attention was on Alannah. When their eyes met, he shrugged his way out of the hands that were groping him and joined her. 'Is Liam okay? I didn't think I cut him that deep.'

'He claims to be fine, but there was a lot of blood. I insisted on having your dad patch him up.'

'Sorry, Lana, I didn't mean to scare you.'

'It's okay.' She smiled. 'I enjoyed the show.'

He gave her an impish grin. 'Really? Was it the sight of me, or Liam shirtless? Or the fact that I put Liam in his place?'

'All of the above. But shh, don't tell your brother.' She winked at him. Spinning on her heels, she walked over to Liam, the sound of Brendan's laughter trailing away behind her. Looking at Liam's arm again, she found the wound had healed over completely.

Liam smiled at her. 'See, nothing to worry about. Right Dad?'

'Right. It looked worse than it was,' Ross agreed as he packed away his first aid kit. 'That said, you did lose a bit of blood, so you'd better take it easy and get an early night.'

They were walking back to their campsite when Alannah turned to Liam and spoke seriously. 'Will you follow your doctor's orders and rest tonight?'

'Will you be my nurse if I do?' His tone was incredibly suggestive.

'If that's what it takes to make you behave.'

'Who said anything about behaving?' There was a mischievous glint in his eye.

Pausing at the entrance to their tent, Alannah narrowed her eyes and chided him firmly. 'Liam.'

His hands went up in surrender. 'Okay, fine. I'll be good.' They moved inside so Liam could lie down before dinner. 'I'm gonna change my trackies.'

Sitting on her bed, Alannah tried and failed to avert her eyes while he changed out of his blood-stained, sweaty trackpants. The lack of t-shirt did not help matters either. There was also the fact that Liam's boy-leg shorts gave her a perfect view of his shapely backside.

The whistle slipping through Alannah's teeth alerted Liam to her watchful eye. Glancing over his shoulder, Liam smirked. 'And you call *me* shameless!'

'Well, you're the one changing in full view of me.'

'You didn't have to watch.' He finished getting into a pair of clean, grey pants that hung a short distance below the line of his boxers. Still no shirt.

'How could I look away when you gave me such a good show?'

Liam unzipped his sleeping bag to recline on it rather than in it. He shifted onto his side to face Alannah.

She decided to settle down next to him. 'Shove over.'

His face lit up as he made room for her on his mattress. After enfolding her in his arms and staring into her eyes a moment, he whispered, 'Lana? What's going through that beautiful head of yours right now?'

'I'm thinking about how much I want to kiss you.'

Liam gasped. 'Does that mean you've made your choice? You're done with Austin?'

She smiled. 'Yeah. I'll break it off with him as soon as we get home.'

Sliding his hand behind her neck, he pulled her closer. His lips devoured hers with a fierce hunger.

Alannah responded with equal fervour. *By the Gods!* Her lips locked with Liam's and it was every bit as wonderful as she had imagined, if not better. His fresh scent and salty lips filled her olfactory senses.

Rolling Alannah onto her back, he deepened the kiss from above. With his body against hers, the extent of his arousal became evident. His lips travelled along her neck and back to her mouth.

She noticed he was still supporting some of his own weight. *Probably just as well.* Liam was ninety kilos of solid muscle and could easily crush her. It was a passing thought, lasting all of one second before she lost herself to the passion. At some point, her top and bra came off and Alannah moaned in response to the feel of skin-to-skin contact.

'*Shit!*'

Alannah and Liam both turned toward the entrance of their tent.

Brendan stood frozen in place, mouth aghast, and eyes popping from their sockets. 'I thought Liam was supposed to be resting.' He spat bitterly before taking off, leaving the tent flap slightly open.

Letting out an exasperated sigh, Alannah tried to free herself of Liam's hold, but he still had her pinned down.

Liam narrowed his eyes. 'Lana? What's wrong?'

'Brendan's right. You're meant to be resting. We shouldn't let things go any further yet.' She fixed her stern, unwavering eyes upon him. 'You promised to behave, remember?'

He laughed, shifting onto his back. 'Sorry, Nurse Winters.'

After throwing her top back on, Alannah glanced at the time. 'Dinner's probably ready by now. I'll get some and bring it back for us to eat here.'

'Thanks. One last kiss before you go?'

She yielded to his request by pressing her lips chastely to his.

But Liam grabbed a chunk of her hair and gazed upon her intensely. 'I love you, Lana.'

'I love you too, Liam.'

Chapter Fifteen

Alannah needed to act. For all the bliss she felt with Liam, a great big chasm had opened between herself and Brendan and she hated it. The guy had avoided her for the remainder of their camping trip and even chose to ride with Ross and Nora for the drive home. Apparently, Enya is preferable to 'being Liam's third wheel'. He did not even come down to dinner that night.

She barged through his bedroom door. 'Talk to me, Brendan! What the fuck is wrong?'

'Christ, Lana! Ever heard of knocking?' He had emerged from his bathroom, wearing nothing but a towel around his waist, wet hair still dripping water down his face and torso.

A multitude of emotions inundated Alannah in that moment. Initially, her core grew moist and tingled. A racing pulse and burning cheeks followed. Finally, she found herself wishing she had knocked. Yet she stood firm. 'As if you would have answered.'

'Right. And I have my reasons for that.'

'Which is why I'm here. Why are you avoiding me?'

'I'm surprised you even noticed.' His bitter tone, full of vitriol, staggered her. 'I figured the two of you would want some privacy.'

She narrowed her eyes. 'Cut the bullshit. It doesn't take aura reading skills to know you're upset. I want to know why.'

'When did you break up with Austin?'

Taken aback by his question, she stumbled with her answer. 'I… I haven't yet. I plan to do that tomorrow.'

'So, not only are you about to dump my best mate, but you're cheating on him too.'

'Is that what this is all about?' She rubbed the side of her face with her palm. 'I had only sorted through the mess in my heart. I wasn't even sure I'd choose Liam over Austin until last night. You knew I was trying to work through these feelings.'

'I didn't think things would progress so quickly. You should have ended things with Austin first.'

'All we did was kiss, geez. Since when do *you* take the moral high ground over shit like this?'

'Since it involves the people I love. And that was a pretty heated kiss.' Brendan sat on the edge of his bed.

'But still just a kiss.' She perched beside him. 'Sorry about Austin. This hasn't been easy for me either. I'm not looking forward to breaking his heart.'

Brendan sighed. 'Austin's not the only best friend I'm worried about. More time spent with Liam means less time with me.'

Alannah fixed upon his gaze. 'So that's what this is *really* about, huh? We can still hang. You'll probably need to become more tolerant of Liam, though.'

'Bah! He's the intolerant one. The rest of our friends will freak out though.'

'They already did when Liam became my bodyguard.'

'That was nothing. When they see the two of you together, you're looking at social murder. Just warning you.' Humour had returned to his eyes, much to Alannah's relief. 'There are two things I'll miss when you're with Liam.'

'Oh?'

He gave her a wicked grin. 'No more waking up in the middle of the night when you're having kinky vampire sex.'

She blushed and thumped his solid bicep with her fist.

He laughed. 'But this is what I'll miss most of all.'

'This?'

'Our games of Sleazy Chicken.'

'Who said that has to end?' Alannah felt a pang of grief at the thought of no more Sleazy Chicken.

'Are you kidding? Liam would kick my arse!'

'I saw the way you handled yourself in that fight. I don't think you have anything to worry about. Besides, I'll make him aware it's part of how we relate. He will learn that Alannah and Brendan are a package deal.' She smiled at him.

'Damn straight we are.' He stretched out his arms, inviting a hug. 'Bring it, Cuz.'

'But you're wet and naked!' she complained.

'So? Get over here before I make *you* wet and naked.'

Alannah laughed. 'I'd like to see you try!'

His eyes flashed with evil intent. A moment later, Brendan had Alannah pinned down on his bed.

She squealed at first, an automatic response to the sudden movement. As she took stock of her situation, Alannah realised he was straddling her.

Brendan's face was mere inches away from hers, water dripping from his hair. Her cheeks burned.

'Be careful what you wish for, Lana.' He remained still a moment, searching her eyes for something. Pulling back, he stood, the towel dropping to the floor as he did so.

Eyes bulging at the sight of what he was packing, Alannah swore under her breath at first. 'By the Gods.'

Even when limp, Brendan was obviously hung like a horse. He tittered. 'See something you like?' When she met his eyes, he gave her an impish grin. He reached for a pair of black satin boxers and turned around to slip them on. After drying his hair briefly, he threw his towel in the bathroom. 'Now bring it!' His arms opened wide for her again.

Alannah rose from the bed and stepped into Brendan's arms. 'You know I love you right?'

He squeezed her tighter. 'Yup, but it doesn't hurt to hear you say it every so often.'

'I love you, Brendan.'

He drew a deep breath, and exhaled the words, 'I love you, Lana.'

Austin was waiting for Alannah at her locker. She spotted him first and took the opportunity to whisper her warning to Liam. 'Remember I haven't spoken to him yet. He doesn't know what's going on.'

Liam grumbled his response. 'I know. The sooner you talk to him, the better. This waiting is torture.'

It had taken Alannah a week to find the courage to face Austin and break the news to him. When he asked to meet during the second week of school holidays, she gave him the excuse training had exhausted her. It was not a complete lie.

Austin's eyes lit up the hallway when he saw her. As soon as she reached him, he had her pinned up against her locker. 'Gods, I've missed you.' His mouth was on hers in a flash.

Alannah hesitated at first. She did not want to upset Liam, but she did not have time to talk to Austin before classes started.

As she began to yield to Austin's demanding lips, Liam pulled Austin away by his shirt collar. 'That's quite enough of a show for now, thank you.'

Austin growled at him. 'What's your problem, man?'

'You are. I don't like you and I hate seeing your filthy claws and fangs on Lana.'

'You're just jealous. I've seen the way you look at her. Pity she's not pure, huh?'

Liam pushed Austin against the lockers, pinning him by the throat as he raised his fist.

'Liam! Stop it!' Alannah cried. Glancing through the assembled audience, she could see a couple of teachers headed their way.

He lowered his fist but maintained his hold on Austin's throat. 'Don't push me, Pearce.' A second later he released his grip.

'Everything okay here?' asked Mr. Dougherty.

'Just fine,' Austin replied as he glared at Liam.

'Liam?' the teacher asked doubtfully.

'It's okay, Mr. Dougherty. Austin and I were simply voicing our difference of opinion. I'll be going to class now.' He smiled at Alannah. 'See you later.'

'Yeah. See ya.' After watching Liam walk away, she turned to Austin. 'Will you come to my window tonight?'

'Gods, yes.'

'Great. I'll see you then.' She forced a smile, but Austin's goodbye kiss engulfed her lips before she finished the attempt.

Most of Alannah's first day back at school passed with little further incident. That was until final period when her Ancient Studies class spent their lesson on research in the library.

She was sitting next to Cara at one of the group tables, when an unwelcome face appeared. An icy chill seized Alannah as she watched the woman take the seat across from her.

'Grandmother?' Her question was barely more than a whisper.

'Hello, dear child.'

'Alannah? What's wrong?' Cara's voice seemed a distant echo.

Glancing around, she noticed that no one paid any heed to the strange woman in her red cape. Even Cara was looking at Alannah rather than the evil Queen. She returned her attention to Tara.

'They cannot see or hear me. Handy illusion spell, that one. They can, of course, hear you; so, if you continue talking to me, they will assume you are talking to yourself. I suggest keeping your words in your head. I can read your thoughts anyway.'

What a terrifying thought.

'Exactly.' She gave Alannah a wicked grin.

What do you want?

'You know what I want, Alannah. The clock is ticking. If you do not have that handsome vampire man of yours turn you soon, I will send one of my less desirable cursed subjects to do the job.'

Why curse me? I don't understand.

'To put it simply, your very existence as a mage is a threat to my power. I have dominion over all the cursed. When you become one of us, you will swear your loyalty to me.'

Alannah laughed. *I don't see how I'm such a threat. I'm not even a pure a mage.*

Tara's eyes narrowed. 'Has no one told you that your mother conceived you at Beltane?'

What's that supposed to mean?

'I am sure one of your cousins would be happy to explain. Dennis was not your real father. Sorry about his death, by the way. An unfortunate case of collateral.'

That was you? You broke into my house?

'Technically one of my ghouls. I have many cursed servants willing to do my bidding, dear child.' Tara vanished, speaking her final words in Alannah's mind as she left. '*Tick, tick, tick.*'

Trembling with fear, Alannah stood up abruptly. *Gotta find Liam.*

'*Alannah Winters!*' Cara screamed at her. That got Alannah's attention. 'What's wrong?'

314

Everyone in the library was staring at them. Alannah replied in a hushed voice, 'I need to find Liam.' She started to run out of the library.

Cara hurried to keep up with her. 'We're in the middle of class, Alannah. Now's not the time for a make-out session.'

Stopping dead in her tracks, Alannah realised she had no idea where to look for Liam. She turned to Cara. 'This isn't about that. Tara showed up and threatened me again. I need to tell him.'

Cara gave her a sidelong glance. 'Have you finally lost the plot? I was sitting with you. There was no sign of Tara.'

Alannah decided to head for her locker so she could retrieve her phone. 'That's because she used illusion magic to hide herself from everyone else's view.'

Cara walked beside her. 'Seriously?'

'Honest to the Gods.'

'*Shit!* That must be some powerful magic if she could hide from another mage.'

'That's not even the scariest thing she did. She read my mind, Cara. She was in my fucking head.'

Cara shivered. 'That's so creepy.'

When they reached her locker, Alannah grabbed her phone and wrote a quick text: **Tara**

confronted me at school. I'm kinda freaked and wanna go home. She knew Liam would not have his phone with him, so she sent the SOS to her Uncle and Aunt.

Nora sent a prompt reply: **Oh Gods! Are you okay? I'll be there shortly.**

Alannah typed a quick response: **I'm fine, just scared.** She proceeded toward the front office. 'Hi Miss O'Leary. I'm not feeling well. I've contacted my Aunt and she's gonna pick me up soon. Can I wait here with Cara?'

Miss O'Leary smiled warmly. 'Of course, dear.'

They both sat in the waiting area.

At first sight of Alannah, Nora rushed to embrace her. 'Oh sweetheart, you're still shaking.' She pulled Alannah up to the front desk. 'Hi Patsy. There's been a family emergency, can you please call my sons over the PA?'

Miss O'Leary's visage filled with concern. 'Of course.' She spoke into the microphone: '*Liam Winters and Brendan Winters, please come to the front office. Liam Winters and Brendan Winters, to the front office, please.*'

Panic and dread shook Brendan to the core. Two names, not three. Two members of the Winters family, not three. Brendan jumped up and hot footed it to the front office.

Every metre he covered on the approach was one too many and he cursed his legs for not moving faster. He ignored the teachers yelling out to him to stop running in the hall. Consequences be damned. *If anything has happened*…. He could not even finish the thought: that train was too fucking painful. Rounding a corner, he fled the Maths and Science building and dashed across the yard toward the 'Administration' sign.

As soon as he entered the office, he released the breath he had been holding. Alannah was there and she was still standing. 'Oh, thank fuck! You're okay, Lana.'

Mum, who was holding Alannah's trembling form, looked up and frowned.

Alannah turned her head to him. The tears in her eyes combined with her trembling lip floored him.

'Gods, what happened?' He pulled Alannah into his arms.

She whispered two words in his ear, 'Tara happened.'

That was enough to make the blood drain from his face. Icicles stabbed at his spine. A flash of movement in the corner of his eye drew Brendan's attention.

Cara rose from one of the chairs. 'I should go. I'll talk to you guys later.' She placed a hand on Alannah's shoulder. 'Take care, okay?'

She nodded. 'Thanks, Cara.'

Brendan heard a commotion outside which sounded like Cara and Liam arguing. His brother burst through the doors a moment later. *'Lana?'*

She shifted out of Brendan's hold and rushed into Liam's embrace. It felt like she had ripped away another chunk of his heart in the process.

'Come on, get your stuff. We'll talk in the car,' Mum declared.

'Right. Come on Lana, let's get my bag.' Liam led her away towards the Seniors building.

'Brendan?' Mum's voice brought his attention back from the sight of Alannah walking away with Liam holding her hand.

'Sorry, Mum. Just a sec.' He sprinted to his locker and grabbed his bag.

The rest of them were waiting in the carpark. Alannah and Liam took the back seat, so Brendan jumped in the front. 'What happened, Lana?' he asked as soon as they were all strapped in.

He heard her take a deep breath. 'Tara showed up in the library during my Ancient Studies

318

research lesson. She cloaked herself with some form of illusion magic, so not even Cara could see or hear her.'

Brendan let a whistle escape through his teeth. 'Damn, that's hard core.'

'She reminded me time is running out. If I don't choose to become cursed soon, she will send one of her subjects to do the job.'

'Don't worry, I won't let anyone hurt you Lana,' Liam reassured her.

'There's more,' Alannah's voice shook. 'I think she had my dad killed.' She paused as Liam comforted her. 'And she wants Austin to curse me. She said something about getting my vampire boyfriend to turn me.'

Liam released her. 'Christ! I told you he's trouble. When are you going to dump his arse?' His tone was one of bitter hatred.

Even Brendan had to admit Liam was right. If Austin were not already acting under direct orders, Tara could still compel him to hurt Alannah. The cursed were physically incapable of disobeying their sovereign.

'Tonight. I planned to talk to him alone, but now I'm afraid of how he'll react.'

'No way am I letting you spend any more time alone with that creep. I'll be there when you talk to him.'

'Thanks, Liam.' Alannah fell quiet for the rest of the drive.

A cursory glance told Brendan she was silently sobbing against Liam's chest. He sat back in his seat and sighed. As much as he hated seeing them together, Alannah needed both her cousins if she was going to get through this.

'Just a minute, Brendan.' His mum's voice stopped him from following Alannah and Liam into the house as soon as they got home.

He turned back to see her leaning against the side of the car, so he stepped up to her. 'What is it, Mum?'

'I know you're hurting, but remember, all good things come to those who wait.'

'What's that supposed to mean?'

She pushed the hair aside from his right eye. 'It means you shouldn't give up on love. I remember what it felt like at your age. All matters of the heart were urgent, and unrequited love was the end of the world. Alannah may not be receptive to you now, but that doesn't mean her feelings won't change. And even if they don't, the odds of finding love elsewhere are stacked highly in your favour.'

It was easy to forget his mother could read people's emotions when she spent most of her days caring for animals. 'Thanks, Mum.' He hugged her before heading inside.

Sitting on the edge of her bed, Alannah waited anxiously for her midnight visitor. With her tendency to avoid conflict wherever possible, breakups were not something she was fond of instigating. Cole was the only guy she had dumped, and the circumstances that had driven her to end that relationship had been beyond her control.

Knowing Liam was hiding in her wardrobe was some comfort, but only as far as her fear extended to the possibility of Austin attacking her. Oddly, that was the least of her worries. He may be a vampire, but she was confident he genuinely cared about her and that was what had her stomach doing somersaults.

Tap, tap, tap. Tap, tap, tap.

Crap! It was time. She took a deep breath and made her way to the window.

'Hey, beautiful.' Austin gracefully climbed through and landed with ease on the floor. He swept her up into his arms and kissed her fervently.

Gods, she was gonna miss these kisses, among other things. Drawing on her newfound courage and the knowledge of Liam watching, she pushed him back gently. 'We need to talk.'

'Oh-oh. That's never a good precursor to a conversation.' Stern eyes bore down on her.

Tugging on his hand, she led him across the room to sit on her bed. 'Were you ever planning to tell me about your past?'

Austin exhaled sharply. 'So, Brendan finally told you, huh?'

'Brendan only hinted at it, but I learned more from another source.'

His eyes popped. 'Who?'

'Does it matter? I want to know why I didn't hear it from you.'

Dropping his head into his hands, he ran his fingers through his long, black hair. A minute later he frowned at her. 'I'm sorry, Alannah. I would have told you eventually, but those were dark times for me. I find it hard to talk about them. I almost killed two girls.'

'Don't you think that's exactly why you should have told me?' She rose and paced the room. 'Christ, Austin! I let you feed on me. You could've killed me!'

Tears pooled in his eyes. 'I tried to warn you in the beginning. It's also why I've only ever done so with Brendan nearby.'

She blinked at him, trying to make sense of his words.

'If you ever started to feel faint or scared, he would have felt your emotional state and come to your aid.'

Alannah shook her head. 'He would have to be actively reading me at the time.' She remembered what Brendan had told her. Her eyes widened on him. '*Shit!* You knew he was reading me the whole time?'

'Of course. It was the only way I felt safe doing what we did.'

'Didn't help those other girls though, did it?'

He hung his head low. 'Things were different then.'

'Different how?'

'Brendan was… preoccupied. Safety wasn't our first concern.'

Closing her eyes, she braced herself for the difficult question. She held his gaze a moment before asking, 'Did you ever use hypnotic coercion on those girls?'

Austin winced. 'A few times, yes.'

Sprinting into her bathroom, Alannah barely reached the toilet in time to bring up her dinner.

She felt a hand on her shoulder. 'Alannah?'

'Get the fuck away from me!'

Austin recoiled. 'Alannah, please. I told you they were dark times. I'm not proud of what I did. I hated who I was back then.'

Leaning back against the cold, hard tiles on the wall, she squinted up at him with pursed lips. 'Have you tried hypnotism on me at all?'

'Gods, no! I love you, Alannah, I would never...' kneeling in front of her, he attempted to reach out and comfort her.

But Alannah put up a hand in protest. 'Have you been working under direct orders from my grandmother or one of her representatives?'

He was gobsmacked. 'What? No! Alannah, please trust that I would never want to hurt you.'

'It matters little now. Tara knows about us. She can use you against me.'

Sinking back against the shower screen, Austin blanched, an impressive feat for someone so pale. 'What are you saying?'

'I'm saying we're done. You and I are finished, Austin.'

His eyes teared up again. 'Alannah, please don't do this. Surely we can find a way to work things out. I won't let Tara use me.'

'From what I understand, you might not have a choice.'

'What if we spoke to your Uncle? He's a very skilled abjurer. He could craft protective charms for me.'

Damn it! He is not making this easy for me. She was hoping to avoid letting the cat out the bag. 'Austin, please don't fight this.'

'Why not? I'll fight the world for a chance to be with you. I swear to the Gods, I'll find a way to block the Queen's—'

'*Austin!*' she screamed. When he fell quiet, Alannah whispered, 'There's someone else.'

His face shifted into a grotesque grimace. 'Who?'

She remained silent.

'Is he one of your cousins?'

Alannah slowly nodded.

'*Fuck!*' Austin rose and punched a fist into the wall beside the basin, shattering one of the tiles. He turned back toward her with a wicked grin. 'You know if it's Brendan…'

Horrified, she shook her head. 'No, Austin. It's Liam.'

He left a second later.

Reclining against the wall, she closed her eyes and tried to settle her heart rate with some deep breathing.

'Hey.' Her eyes opened to find Liam in front of her, one hand resting on her knee, the other offering her a breath mint.

'Thanks.' Taking the mint, she relished the shock of the strong peppermint burst in her mouth. She took the hand he extended to help her up.

As they walked back into her room, Brendan burst through the door. 'Well that was quite the rollercoaster. You okay now, Lana?'

She perched on her bed and leaned against Liam before replying. 'I think so. What sort of a read did you get on Austin?'

'Let's see, from the top, there was love, lust, anxiety, fear, remorse, sorrow, guilt, anxiety, fear, desperation, envy, anger, anguish, and sorrow. I should spend more time around couples breaking up: they'd give me an endless mana source.'

Alannah narrowed her eyes at Brendan. 'But was he lying about hypnotising me or working for Tara?'

He sighed. 'No. As far as I could tell, he was completely honest with you.'

'Right. Thanks, Brendan. Now get the fuck out of my sight.' She pierced him with a frown.

Frozen at first, Brendan took a moment to register what she meant. With hunched shoulders and moist eyes, he nodded his resignation before leaving the room.

Austin sprinted through the scrub at supernatural speed, swearing to himself the whole time. When he reached the roadside, he collapsed against his car and screamed. 'Curse you, Winters!' He slammed his fist into the roof of his Lexus.

'I am already cursed, but I assume you mean one of my descendants.'

Spinning around on his heels, Austin found himself face-to-face with his Queen. He quickly knelt before her. 'I'm sorry, Your Majesty, but I have failed you. Alannah wants nothing more to do with me.' He made no attempt to hide the anguish in his tone, or the tears in his eyes when she commanded him to rise.

'This is grave news indeed. What reason did she give you?'

'She's with Liam now… and she doesn't trust me anymore.'

Tara's eyes widened as her head jerked back. 'My mental and emotional barrier spells are first rate. No one should be able to sense your deception.'

Austin frowned. 'It's not that, Your Majesty. She knows you are aware of our relationship and fears you will use me against her despite my best intentions.'

A rictus grin formed on the Queen's face. 'She is a smart girl.'

He sighed. 'Intelligence runs in the family, Your Majesty.'

'Flattery gets you everywhere, my pet. Come along. You can sink your teeth into some pretty young thing at my haven. Then we will formulate a new plan.'

Fuck! The news announcer on the radio alarm told Brendan it was already seven in the morning and he still had not caught a wink of sleep. Insomnia had never been a problem for him before. Even during his more stressful times, Brendan usually slept like a log. But that look on Alannah's face haunted him all night. He needed to find a way to apologise for his past sins. Being on Alannah's shit-list was worse than losing her heart to Liam.

Slamming his fist on the 'Off' button silenced the alarm. *Oops! That was a little permanent.* He needed to calm his shit, so he dragged his sorry arse out of bed and jumped under the shower. With the water set to scorching, he closed his eyes and began to meditate. The process grounded him and he felt ready to face the day. At least that was what he told himself.

After completing the rest of his morning routine in a daze, Brendan joined his mates on the bus, bumping fists on his way to the back seat.

'Hey man.' Jacob slapped his palm and bumped his fist before their fingers shimmied away. 'Is Alannah okay?'

Cara inched forward in the seat beside him with her ears pricking up.

He sighed as he slumped down next to Jacob. 'She's safe for now, but not in the best emotional state. She broke up with Austin last night.'

Jacob shook his head. 'Shit! She won't be the only one in a foul mood today.'

Closing his eyes, Brendan recalled the turmoil his best mate had felt when Alannah broke the news to him. He wondered if Austin would even show up to school that day. 'No kidding, especially since she told him she's with Liam now.' When his eyes shot open, he found everyone on the bus gawping at him. Ignoring the rest of the crowd, he focussed on his friends. 'Come on, as if you didn't all see it coming.'

When everyone else turned away, Jacob spoke to him in a hushed voice. 'So, are you hurting for Austin or yourself?'

Brendan glared at him. 'Don't even go there, *friend.*'

Jacob threw his hands up defensively. 'Woah there, easy tiger.' He laughed nervously. When they alighted on campus, Jacob hung back with Brendan and watched as Bailey chased after Cara. 'Gods, that man is relentless.'

Tired and fed up, Brendan threw morality to the wind and turned to Jacob. 'Listen, man, you should go for her. She wants to bang your brains anyway. To hell with Bailey.' He slapped Jacob hard on the shoulder and stormed off toward his locker.

Dread started to fill the pit of his stomach as he approached homeroom. *What sort of reception is Alannah going to give me this morning?* When he reached the door, his heart stopped at the sight of her. Head face down, she was resting on her table, cushioned by her folded arms. She appeared to be sleeping. Cautiously, Brendan approached his seat, which was right next to hers. He stared at her, desperately wanting to say something, but afraid of the response she would give him. So, he sat and waited like a coward.

The bell rang and their teacher commenced the roll call commenced, yet all the while Alannah kept her forehead glued to her arms. When her name breached the chasm, she lifted her face briefly, responding with a simple 'Here' before dropping her head again. This was how she sat through the morning's announcements. As the bell sounded for first period, she stood and left the room without even acknowledging Brendan's presence. *Shit! Not good.* He rose from his chair and started for the door.

Connor stepped beside Brendan, clapping a hand on his shoulder. 'You weren't kidding about her mood. I can still see the icicles around her table. Why do I get the feeling there's more to this than her breakup with Pearce?'

He looked into Connor's unwavering eyes. 'Because Austin confessed the full truth of our past antics.'

'Shit! No wonder she's pissed at you.' Connor was the only person who had known the extent of Brendan and Austin's shared past. He was the one to pull them out of their dark times, after all. He shook his head as they walked along the hall. 'Sorry, Brendo. Maybe give her some time. I'm sure she'll come 'round.'

'I hope you're right.' After a quick fist bump, Brendan parted ways with Connor and headed towards his Maths class. A flash of red in the corner of his eye drew Brendan's attention to the fence surrounding the school. A woman in a red-hooded raincoat and long black dress was walking along the outer perimeter. Her face was not visible, but instinctively he knew who she was. He froze as his heart beat quickened. An idea took hold. *If I can save Lana…*

Resolute in his decision, Brendan put up his mental and emotional walls. He cast a quick glance around the yard to ensure no one was watching before jumping the fence. Ducking behind trees and building corners, he shadowed the woman along Rafferty Street and on to High Gate.

She walked north a few more metres and stopped to allow a figure in a long, black-hooded coat to open the door of a limousine for her. The man in black, presumably a ghoul or vampire, sat in the driver's seat.

Crap! I can't lose her now. Looking around quickly for options, Brendan spotted a young woman stepping out of her car, so he seized the opportunity. He put on all his charms and used his powers to manipulate her. 'Excuse me miss, may I please borrow your car?'

The anxious blonde—who was probably about twenty—hesitated at first, so he placed his hand on her arm and poured all his powers of seduction into it. 'If you tell me your address, I promise to return it tonight.' He gave her a mischievous grin. 'And I'll even pay you a visit if you like.' He had no intention of doing any such thing, especially since this qualified as coercion, but he desperately needed wheels.

'O-of course.' She dropped the key in his hands.

'Do you have a pen and paper?' he asked, cursing himself for the habit of leaving his phone in his locker 'I still need your address.'

'Oh, right.' She smiled. Reaching into her bag, she produced a small notepad and pen which she scrawled on.

As soon as the note was in his hand, Brendan pushed past her into the driver's seat and took off without another word. Thankfully, he could make out the black Bentley ahead. It took all his self-control not to floor it, but he was still in the middle of town and drawing any unwanted attention, especially from the cops, would mess with his plans. The limo turned right at the end of the road. When Brendan followed, he saw them heading up the hill and out of the populated area.

Thirty minutes and a few dirt tracks later, Brendan pulled into the driveway of an old, ruined farmstead. He parked the car behind a copse of trees and walked the rest of the way down the gravel path. Once the main house was in view, he found a sturdy old plum tree promising a good vantage point. Reaching the upper branches was simple enough for a master tree climber like Brendan. Finding a relatively comfortable nook, he settled in for the stakeout.

'Hi, Lana.' Liam drew her into his arms the moment she stepped out of English. He gestured with a nod over her shoulder toward the classroom. 'Did Brendan wag?'

She frowned, still distressed by Brendan's past behaviour. 'Yeah, seems he's up to his old tricks.'

Liam stiffened.

'What?' she asked, studying his narrow eyes.

'Austin skipped class too.'

Alannah shook her head disapprovingly. 'Come on, let's get some lunch.' She took his hand and they walked along the corridor toward her locker. It felt good to show the rest of the school they were a couple, but she still feared what would happen when Uncle Ross found out. When they reached her locker, she dumped her books inside and grabbed her purse.

The moment she locked the door, Liam pressed her against it and kissed her deeply. When they came up for air, he was smiling. 'Gods, I've wanted to do that for so long.'

'What, kiss me? I recall doing that several times throughout the night and this morning.'

'I meant pushing you up against your locker to kiss you.'

'Mm. Anywhere else on campus you want to make out?'

Pressing against her, Liam twirled a strand of her hair between his fingers. 'The list is so long I don't even know where to start.'

She gave him a wicked grin. 'Why don't we find one of those more isolated spots and hide out there for our lunch break?'

Apparently, she did not need to ask twice since Liam grabbed her hand and pulled her towards the building's exit.

'Just a sec though.' Alannah stopped him. 'I need the bathroom first.'

He sighed. 'Fine, but hurry. I'm hungry, but not for food.' Liam winked at her as she disappeared into the ladies' room.

Having completed her business, Alannah was washing her hands when she became aware of the unnatural silence. Not even the sound of footsteps and chatter from the hall permeated the space. *What the hell?* She looked up at the mirror, but did not see anything, so she glanced over her shoulder. Still nothing. The back of her neck prickled. *Is someone watching me?* Shrugging it off as paranoia, she grabbed a handful of paper towels.

Suddenly, a pair of arms pulled her up into the ceiling space. Alannah tried to scream, but a strong male hand shoved a gag in her mouth. She kicked and struggled to free herself, but it was no use: her attacker's grip was too strong. She could not see him, but the smell of rotting flesh suggested he was a ghoul. The cursed man dragged her through the ceiling briefly before dropping her into a dark, empty classroom.

Disoriented, she attempted to run in the direction she hoped was the exit, but another set of arms grabbed her before she got far. This man was taller and stronger, with a less abhorrent odour. As soon as he carried her into a tunnel that had opened in the brick wall, Alannah knew she was in serious trouble.

Several minutes later, someone removed her gag and threw her onto the floor of the vampire common room. Glancing around, she noticed flickering and she was lying inside a pentagram of blood on the floor.

A handsome vampire with short blond hair and glowing blue eyes stood above her, grinning. 'Hello Miss Winters. My name is Anthony. It is such a pleasure to meet you at last.' His accent sounded British, with a gravity suggesting he was much older than his apparent age of twenty.

'The pleasure's all yours, I'm sure.'

Kneeling, he straddled her. 'Not for long.' Pinning her arms, he bared his fangs.

A second later a sharp pain pierced her jugular and Alannah screamed, but it was not long before a familiar ecstasy turned her protests into more pleasant groans. *Christ! I didn't know a vampire's bite could still feel this good without involving sex.* In the back of her mind, she knew she should try to fight back, but it was difficult to find the motivation, so she resigned herself to whatever fate awaited her.

She started to feel faint and a moment of panic seized her mind. It was enough to break the spell and Alannah drew on the mana in her matter ring. *Stupid vampire didn't think to remove my ring first!* She concentrated on a summoning more advanced than any she had attempted and prayed to the Gods it would work.

'Lana! Oh Gods!' Liam's voice filled the room a moment before everything went black.

Chapter Sixteen

Liam sat propped up against the headboard of
Alannah's bed with her sleeping deeply beside him.
Dad had already performed her blood transfusion
in the hospital and arranged for her immediate
release so he could monitor her at home. He had
promised she would be okay after some rest.

But Liam would not believe his father until
he saw her eyes open. So, he sat alone with his
Lana, waiting anxiously for some reassurance she
would be okay. It was terrifying to think how close
he had come to losing her. *If she hadn't….*

Alannah's eyes fluttered and opened. 'Thank
you for rescuing me, Sir Liam.' She strained her
voice.

He smiled. 'You're welcome, Princess. You
did well to summon me in time.'

She coughed, so he handed her some water.
After draining the glass, she lay back. 'I

remembered something. What does it mean to be conceived at Beltane?' she asked.

Liam thought that was an odd question, given the circumstances. 'Why do you ask?'

'Because apparently Mum conceived me at Beltane. That was the other thing Tara mentioned.'

Liam's heart jumped at the news. 'Seriously? If that's true, you would have to be a pure mage. Not only that; it means you are blessed by the Gods.'

'But how?' Alannah's blinking eyes searched his own for several seconds. With a yawn, her lids began to droop.

'Shh, it's okay, we can discuss it later. You need to rest more.' He gently stroked her face to reassure her. Pressing his lips to hers, he kissed her chastely. Her eyes beamed with love for a second before fatigue pulled their lids shut and she drifted off.

Reassured she would be okay; Liam took the opportunity to grab a bite of food. It was almost midnight and he realised he had not eaten since recess. After raiding the fridge for some leftovers, he threw a plate of curry in the microwave.

When he sat down to eat, he heard the front door slam, followed by footsteps in the hall.

Brendan appeared in the kitchen a few seconds later, looking dishevelled with his messy hair, wrinkled clothes, and rotten stench.

'Where have you been?' Liam demanded.

'Out.'

Liam rolled his eyes, assuming his brother had been sleeping around again, or worse. 'Well while you were "out," I was busy saving Lana's arse. One of the cursed attacked her at school today.'

Brendan's brows shot up from his bulging eyes. '*Shit!* Is she okay?'

'It was a vampire attack, so she needed a blood transfusion. She's resting now. Still a little sore, but she's fine. Oh, and apparently she's a pure mage.'

'Hm.'

He eyed Brendan suspiciously. 'What's that supposed to mean? This is good news, right?'

'For you, maybe. But it would give Grandmother dearest more cause for concern.' His voice trailed off as he appeared lost in thought.

'Come on man… if you know something, spill it,' Liam demanded.

Brendan sighed as he collapsed on a chair across from Liam. 'I spent the day tracking Tara. I found one of her hideouts at an old farmstead up in the hills and a horde of vampires live or work there.'

'So, you think Tara sent this vampire to attack Lana?' Liam asked. Brendan's initiative impressed and surprised him.

'That's what I'm worried about. I know it's not Beltane yet, but she may have grown impatient, especially since Alannah broke up with Austin,' Brendan replied, struggling to keep his eyes open.

Liam knew he should let Brendan go to bed, but he needed to know more. 'Was Austin at Tara's?'

'No.' He yawned. 'I still don't have any evidence to suggest he's been working for her directly.'

'I guess I'll have to find out for myself. I'm going to do some of my own digging. Can you give me the directions to Tara's hideout?'

'Fine.' Brendan rose and grabbed a pen from the cup by the phone and wrote instructions on the message pad. Tearing off the page, he handed it to Liam. 'I'm going to bed now.' He started for the door.

'Hold up.'

Brendan spun around and glared at him. 'What?'

'I might be gone a few days. Watch over Lana for me, would you?'

'Liam, dear brother, I will keep an eye on Lana for her sake and my own, but not for yours.' The brief hint of a wicked grin crossed his face before he turned back and walked upstairs.

Sighing, Liam finished his meal, dropped his plate in the sink, and dashed to his room to pack some supplies. On his way out, he decided to check on Alannah once more, so he doubled back to her room. At first, he was startled to find Brendan curled up beside her, but Liam had asked Brendan to watch her. He stepped closer to the bed and looked down at the two of them. Their sleeping faces were angelic, and it took him back to their childhood when the three of them would often share the one bed. They were so innocent back then, or so he thought. But he remembered what Alannah had told him about her sex education and he shuddered. Dismissing the thought as quickly as possible, Liam pressed a kiss to her forehead and whispered softly, 'Goodbye my love. See you again soon.'

Stirring in bed, Alannah snuggled up against the back of the warm body beside her. She slipped a hand across his side and pressed it against his hard stomach muscles. *Gods I love those abs!* But as she became more conscious, she took in the scent of her bed companion and realised she was not holding Liam. She bolted upright. *'What the fuck?'*

Brendan rolled over and grinned at her. 'Morning, Lana. Good to see you're feeling better.'

'Why are you in my bed?'

'Have you forgotten last night?' He feigned offence. 'I'm so hurt. Girls never forget a night with Brendan Winters.'

Alannah glared at him.

But her evil eye did not deter him. 'It must be denial. You couldn't believe how good it was. How else could you go back to Liam otherwise?'

Losing control of her rage, Alannah slapped him hard across the face, leaving a bright red handprint on his cheek.

Grinning wickedly, his own hand covered the mark. 'Damn Lana, that was hot. I didn't think you would be in the mood for foreplay again already.'

Clenching her fists, she screamed, *'you're infuriating, Brendan.* Quit the act and tell me why the hell you are here.'

He sighed. 'Fine. Liam made me your temporary bodyguard. And after yesterday—I'm not taking any chances.'

Alannah shook her head to clear the fog from her mind. 'So, where's Liam?'

'Had some business to take care of out of town. He'll probably be a few days.'

Liam's lack of communication hurt Alannah. He did not even say goodbye.

'He didn't have time for a proper farewell, but he did give you a kiss while you were sleeping.' It was uncanny how Brendan knew what she needed to hear.

She narrowed her eyes on him. 'Are you reading me?'

'Sorry, Lana. I have to while I'm your bodyguard.'

'I'm still really pissed at you. What you did back then…' Closing her eyes, she tried to search for the right words. 'It was so wrong.'

Brendan's forehead creased as his head hung low. 'I know.'

'Do you know how serious a crime you committed? I know the human legal system would have a hard time proving supernatural coercion, but don't mage laws prohibit rape too?'

He cringed at her use of the 'R' word. 'The Council forbid enchanters from using powers of manipulation for such purposes, but it's a lot harder to police vampires. I never used my own powers…'

'It doesn't matter, Brendan! I dunno, but it might be worse. You took the coward's way out by using your best friend to get what you wanted.'

'No, Lana! It wasn't like that. Austin used his hypnotic powers when he was desperate for a feed. I never asked him to do it. Yes, I was party to the act—and I feel like shit for my part in it all—but you've gotta believe I was never the instigator.'

'But you knew you would get laid.'

Brendan's gaze was downcast for several long seconds. Looking up, he replied, 'Not the first time.'

'What happened? How did you get caught up in Austin's mess?'

Brendan hated thinking about those times, let alone talking about them. But if anyone had a right to draw this story out of him, it was Alannah. Closing his eyes and taking a deep breath, he travelled two years back in time. 'Austin and I had been best mates since… well since you left in Year Two. Dad tried to warn me to stay away from him, but I was hurting from losing you, so began my rebellious phase. But at that age, we didn't do much. We were just defiant brats, really.'

Alannah sat with her hands and chin resting on her knees, watching him intently.

'I knew Austin was a vampire back then. A mage normally starts learning about the magic world at a very young age, but Mum and Dad warned us not to talk to you about it. They didn't explain why. But I digress. Following my initiation at the age of twelve, my attunements came to me easily. I kept Austin updated with my progress, and when it was obvious I would become an enchanter, he joked about using my powers to score chicks together. At least, I thought he was joking.'

'Your voice broke at twelve?' she asked.

'Eleven, actually, but the folks thought I was too young for initiation, so they put it off until Liam was also ready.'

Her eyes bulged briefly. 'Go on.'

Brendan nodded and continued his story. 'I was nearly fifteen when it started, and I already had a rep for sleeping around.

> I had been wandering around town
> with Austin for the better part of two
> hours since eating dinner at the pub. It
> was a warm summer night, and we
> were getting bored. The human bouncer
> had kicked our underage arses out of the
> bar, but not before I charmed that
> lovely bartender enough to score a few

drinks. She even slipped us a bottle on our way out.

We started along the esplanade when I peered into the neck of the whiskey bottle. 'Damn.'

Austin spun around to face me. 'What?'

'Empty.' I threw the bottle towards the beach and heard it smash against the rocks. 'What da ya wanna do now?'

A wicked grin took over Austin's pale visage. 'I'm feeling thirsty for something warmer than Jameson's.'

'Hells no! You're on your own there, man. The sight of blood turns my stomach.'

'You're such a pussy, Brendo. Come on, it'll be fun. We'll find a couple of pretty girls. One for me, one for you.'

Come to think of it, I was in the mood for some action. 'Fine. But keep the feeding out of my face.'

Austin laughed. 'You'll be too balls deep in vag to even notice me.'

The thought alone had my cock stirring. We continued walking along the shoreline. Most of the hotties hung around this area on summer nights. We spotted one solitary girl sitting on a bench in the park across the road. It looked like she was texting or something on her phone. 'Forget it, Austin. Only one babe there. I'm not fighting you for her.'

The vampire was sniffing the air. 'But she smells so sweet. We could talk her into calling a friend.' Austin began to cross the road.

I rolled my eyes. Once the guy set his mind to something, there was no stopping him. I trailed slowly behind.

Austin waited for me on the opposite footpath before stepping onto the lush green lawn. 'Let me do the talking,' he insisted in a hushed tone.

I shrugged, not about to argue. Austin had plenty of experience with hunting, although he usually did so alone. When we were a mere three metres away, the girl looked up at them. I had switched on my active reading

*powers, but even my passive abilities
would have picked up the fear
emanating from this girl.*

*Austin's nose twitched. He must
have smelled it too. But he wasn't
concerned. His eyes began to glow
brighter as he approached her. 'Hey
there, beautiful.'*

'Leave me alone!' *she cried. 'My
boyfriend will arrive any minute.'*

*'Boyfriend, huh? I bet we can
show you a better time.'*

*The nervous brunette—who
appeared to be about sixteen—was
shaking her head frantically.*

*'Come on, bro, she's clearly not
interested.' The intensity of her fear
was overwhelming me and a huge turn-
off.*

*But the bright red aura
surrounding Austin suggested it had
the opposite effect on him. Austin
glared at me. 'Shut up, man.' He sat
beside the girl and smiled at her. He
motioned for me to take a seat on her
other side.*

I hesitated at first, but Austin pouted and fluttered his lashes. With a sigh, I slumped down beside the girl.

Austin's arm enclosed her shoulders, and he pulled her eyes into his gaze as he began to sweet-talk her. Slowly, the trepidation in the girl's aura dissolved into lust. 'You wanna get out of here? I live close by.'

The girl giggled. 'Yes, please.'

The pair of them rose and started walking toward Austin's house. When he realised I wasn't following, he turned and yelled to me. 'Don't wimp out on me now, bro.'

After sending a silent prayer to the Gods, I stood up and followed them. The walk took longer than usual because we kept stopping for the frisky couple to pash. When we finally reached the door to Austin's house, I moved close behind the girl and tapped her on the shoulder. 'Hey, you gotta friend you can invite to join us?'

She shook her head. 'I'm new in town, so I don't really have any friends here yet.'

Crap! *No way was I gonna sit around and watch Austin feed. I turned to leave.*

'Don't worry, Brendan. I'm sure Bethany here would be happy to have fun with both of us, wouldn't you beautiful?' Austin's glowing eyes fixed her own.

She giggled. 'Oh yes.' Her hand gripped my arm, and she fluttered her eyelids. 'Please stay, Brendan.'

Those big brown eyes, with thick lashes that went forever, did me in. There was something in the depths of that look suggesting she wasn't asking me to stay for sex. Even her aura showed me she was still afraid. 'Of course.' I trod across the threshold to Austin's home and before long we were in his room.

Sinking into the desk chair, I turned away from the sight of them undressing. The mood hadn't struck me, even with waves of the girl's own desire lapping at my senses, so I turned off my active reading, closed my eyes and tried to relax.

The girl's shock pierced my passive awareness, and the most intense orgasm I'd ever known a girl to have promptly followed. The sensation was enough to make my dick hard in an instant. When I looked toward the bed, Austin was feeding from the girl's neck as he fucked her. In that moment, I was surprised to learn the sight of blood trickling down the girl's neck did not disgust me.

Mesmerised by the strangely erotic scene, I drew closer to the bed.

The movement must have caught Austin's attention because he glanced up, blood dripping from his fangs. He grinned. 'You wanna go?'

I couldn't speak, so I nodded as I stripped out of my clothes. I chose to lie on my back so Bethany could straddle me. A moment later, I was slipping inside the girl, loving every minute of her riding me, as Austin took her from behind and continued to feed on her.

'I'm feeling a little faint,' Bethany said a moment after another amazing orgasm.

*'Sorry, beautiful,' Austin replied.
'I'll stop biting you. Have you had
enough sex?'*

*She giggled and smiled sweetly at
me. 'No way. God it feels so good.'*

*I grinned up at her. 'You ain't
seen nothing yet.' I switched my active
powers back on at that point and gave
Bethany a night to remember.*

Opening his eyes, Brendan looked at Alannah. 'It wasn't until I sobered up the next morning, that I realised what I'd done... what Austin had done. I felt like shit, but at the same time, I wanted to feel those sensations again. Joining Austin on his hunts became an addiction for me, just as blood straight from the vein became Austin's. On most occasions, we found willing girls at parties, but there were a couple of other nights like the first, when we approached strangers on the street.'

Alannah stared at him with wide eyes but remained silent.

'After the second girl went to hospital... I sank into a pretty deep depression. I hated myself for my part in the whole sordid affair. I was skipping a lot of school and drinking myself into oblivion: anything to wipe away the memories of those girls lying on the bed unconscious and pale as corpses. I stopped going out with Austin, ceased going to parties. Connor was the one to pull me out of my funk. He also put Austin on the straight and narrow.'

'I'm sorry, Brendan.' Alannah leaned back against the headboard and placed her hand gently on his shoulder. 'I can see that was a painful memory to relive but thank you for explaining everything.'

He rested his own hand on hers and looked into her eyes. 'Does that mean I'm forgiven?'

'Have you ever used your own powers of coercion to get sex?'

'Gods no!'

She smiled. 'Then yeah, I forgive you. I'm curious about something though.'

'Oh?'

'How old were you when you had sex for the first time?'

Brendan let out a sigh of relief. The interrogation was over, and things were back to normal with Alannah. 'Eleven.'

Her mouth curved into a big grin.

It was enough to give him stirrings. 'What?'

Alannah slapped him on the thigh before getting out of bed. She was at the bathroom door before she turned back to him. 'Yet another thing we have in common.'

Brendan laughed as she vanished behind the door.

The Queen perched herself on the edge of the large four-poster bed taking up most of the guestroom she had given Austin. She ran a long fingernail along the spine of the naked succubus corpse lying face down beside him. 'Tsk, tsk, tsk. Did you have to drain this one too? You are wasting some of my best girls. I will have to teach you a thing or two about restraint.'

Austin grinned as he tugged on the ropes binding the dead girl's limbs to the bed posts. 'I know plenty about restraint.' He still felt drunk on the succubus' blood. It was almost as magically potent as Alannah's.

Tara smiled. 'Yes, I suppose you do. You may well be my new favourite pet. Especially since Anthony failed me.' She rose and strode over to Austin's side of the bed. Her hand slipped over his shoulder and began to caress his bare chest. 'How would you like to become my new paramour?'

'I'm flattered, Your Majesty, but surely I don't deserve such a privileged position.' Austin knew most vampires would literally kill for such an honour and many had. There was no denying the Queen's beauty. She was a Winters, after all. Hair and eye colour aside, he could see the strong resemblance to Alannah. Tara often wore green contact lenses when in public, but never bothered hiding her true self from her subjects.

'True, you have not yet earned access to my bed, but I am going to give you the chance to do so.'

'I will do anything, Your Majesty.'

She sniggered. 'Of course you will. I would like you to convince Alannah to become a vampire.'

Austin sighed. 'You forget she doesn't want me anymore. She's in love with Liam.'

'You have given up too easily. I think you should be more persistent. Here—' she handed him a red potion— 'a few drops of this in her drink will turn her to putty in your hands.'

Austin shook his head. 'She's a mage; surely she'll have active resistance spells.'

The Queen grinned. 'You forget she is still a novice. I doubt she has even learned enchantment resistance yet.'

'Okay. I'll give it a go, but no promises.'

Having called in sick for the rest of the week, Alannah and Brendan spent a few days on magic training with renewed vigour. Alannah strove to master as many powers as possible before confronting her grandmother. She had finally succeeded in constructing and animating a clay golem the day before and was biting at the bit to try something new.

But Brendan was the focus of today's session. As much as she hated the idea of letting anyone into her head, she trusted Brendan and there were few volunteers lining up and offering to become his puppets. So, she agreed to help him.

They sat in the ritual circle facing each other and holding hands. His touch and the fact she was about to let him inside her mind felt strangely intimate and Alannah's skin became hot as her heartbeat increased.

'Relax, Lana.' Brendan spoke with a calm, soothing voice.

She obeyed him even though he was not in her head yet. After a few deep breaths, she whispered to him, 'I'm ready.'

He replied telepathically, '*Good, I'm in and I have control of the mainframe.*' His eyes flicked open and he smiled.

Alannah laughed. 'Now what?'

'*A simple test to start with. Touch your nose with the tip of your right hand.*'

Her hand moved as instructed, even without her giving any thought to the action. It was an odd sensation.

'*A good start. Now pat your head and rub your tummy.*'

Alannah groaned. She sucked at doing this, but her hands complied. It was uncanny. Seeing Brendan succeed made her smile. 'You're doing it, Brendan,' she whispered.

'*Yup. But this is child's play. It's not like I'm making you do anything you don't really want to do. You're not going to like my next order… at least not entirely.*' He winked at her.

She stiffened. *Gods, what is he planning?*

'*Do you trust me, Lana?*' His thumb was gently caressing her hand.

After gulping, she pushed away her fears and nodded. 'Yeah, I trust you.'

'*Good, now take off your robe.*'

'What?' Surely, he knew she had nothing but underwear on beneath her robe.

He grinned. '*Would you rather remove* my robe?'

Alannah blushed. 'Ah, no. I don't want to remove either garment. I'm not wearing much beneath mine.'

'That's the point, Lana. I'm not going to do anything to you. But I won't know if I have the hang of this power unless I can get you to do something you don't want to do. Do you still trust me?'

She nodded.

'You know you want to remove your robe for me, Lana.'

The voice in her head sounded so convincing. Reluctantly, she released Brendan's hands and stood. Lifting the hem of her robe, she brought it up her thighs, past her belly button, above her breasts. Once it was over her head, she looked at Brendan, breathing easier when she saw his closed eyes. 'My robe is off.'

'Good. Now, you know you want to throw it to me.'

Almost without a second thought, she obeyed him.

Brendan caught it with one hand and smiled, still with his eyes shut. 'I'm not gonna lie to you Lana. I would love to see what you look like right now, but I'm not going to peek without your permission.' He was talking aloud again.

And she no longer felt his presence in her head. 'Thanks for being honourable.' Standing there in front of Brendan wearing nothing but her bra and panties, she wondered what the big deal was. She was not naked. Maybe she could have fun with this too. 'You can look at me if you *really* want to.'

He laughed. 'You don't think I want to see your *almost* naked body?'

'Well, you *are* keeping your eyes closed even though I gave you permission to open them.'

A second later, Brendan's gaze was upon her, scanning her up and down. He whistled through his teeth. 'Hot damn! Liam's one lucky bastard.'

She tried not to blush as she kneeled on the floor in front of Brendan. A twinkling of light on the altar caught her attention. Bringing her hand to rest on one of the mana rings in the open case, a cold shiver ran through her body. She took the sparkling opal ring and put it on her left hand.

'Lana?' Brendan's voice was distant.

But she was not afraid. Not even as the white mist in front of her shifted and resolved into an apparition of her mother. 'Mum?'

The ghost's voice was in her mind. '*Hello darling child. I'm so proud of you.*'

'Mum, is it really you?' She wanted to hug the woman, but the ghostly apparition appeared too insubstantial.

'Yes, Alannah, it's me. I've been keeping an eye on you ever since I ascended.'

A tear came to Alannah's eye. The ethereal glow surrounding her mother made her even more beautiful in spirit form.

'You have accomplished so much in so little time. It has been a joy to watch you train. Your grandmother is a formidable opponent and I'm sorry I didn't prepare you for this world, but I have faith you can defeat her.'

'But how?'

Her mother smiled warmly. *'Keep this ring with you at all times. It was mine once and it will connect you to the spirit world. You have many friends on this plane and in your own mage community. And at the end of the day, do not be afraid to seek help from unlikely allies.'* Her mother turned to mist.

Alannah blinked and the room was normal again. She turned to Brendan who was utterly gobsmacked. 'Are you okay, Brendan?'

'W… what happened?'

'Mum's spirit paid me a visit.'

'Wait, what? Aunt Aileen was here?' Trepidation struck his features.

'Yeah, she's been watching all of my training apparently.'

'*Fuck!*'

'What's wrong?'

Brendan held up her robe and gestured to her nearly naked body. 'I'm in for such a spiritual arse-whooping.'

She laughed. 'I don't think Mum worried about that. She had some encouraging words for me regarding Tara.'

He breathed out heavily. 'I hope you're right.' Brendan appeared to relax. '*Shit!* Lana, do you realise what you did?'

'What?'

'You channelled Aether, the celestial element. It could be your third attunement and I'm impressed! There are only three other mages in town who can do that.'

'Really?'

'Really,' Brendan beamed. 'This is fucking awesome!' He drew her up into a strong embrace. 'We're totally gonna kick Grandma's arse! This calls for a celebration.'

'Damn straight! And you pulled off the mind tricks. That's a pretty big deal.' Realising Brendan was wrapping his arms around her barely clad body, she blushed. 'Speaking of which, can I have my robe back now?'

'I dunno. This…' he held it up in one hand, still gripping her with his other arm, 'is proof of my success. I'm tempted to keep it as a trophy.'

'But I will need to consecrate a new practice robe,' she complained.

'Worth it, though.' His hand came down and held the robe behind his back.

Alannah reached around Brendan's waist, but he lifted it high in the air again.

'Please, Lana?' His eyes pleaded with her.

'Are you for real?'

'Yup.'

'You are so weird. But fine, if you really want to keep it.'

He grinned widely and threw his other arm around her to pull her tight against him. 'Thanks, Lana. You know, I have an idea for how we could celebrate,' he whispered seductively into her ear.

She decided to play along for a bit. 'Oh? What did you have in mind?'

'Well, after three days without Liam, I figure you must be feeling… restless. I could show you a good time. You know I got mad skills, right?'

Alannah rolled her eyes and snorted. 'You don't believe in modesty, do you?'

Brendan still held her close but pulled back enough to look into her eyes. ''Course not. Modesty is for chumps.' He grabbed her hips, the fingers of his right hand started to trail up from her left hip along her side. As he reached her bra strap, Alannah felt herself blush, but he did not stop. His fingertips started to trace the outline of her bra towards her breast, all the while keeping his gaze locked with hers.

'Why aren't you stopping? I'm sure my face is bright red already.'

'Because you haven't told me to stop.' His eyes remained steady.

She gulped. 'Since when was that part of the rules?'

'Since now,' Brendan grinned. 'Don't you want to see how far I'll go?'

'I'm beginning to think you have no shame.' Alannah suspected he might not even be playing. It was a scary thought. Arousing, but still scary. Liam would never forgive her. 'Let's stick to the original rules. Game ends as soon as one of us blushes.'

He pouted as he released her from his grip. 'Fine, but if you won't have a private party with me, let's go to Connor's.'

Alannah shook her head. 'I don't know about leaving the house without Liam.'

He tapped her forehead lightly. 'Excuse me, who are you and what have you done with my Lana?'

She laughed.

'Seriously, since when do you obey all orders? I'm your bodyguard now. I'll keep an eye on you and there'll be a bunch of other mages there to watch your back.'

Alannah sighed. *A party sounds grand*. She smiled. 'Okay, let's do it.'

Chapter Seventeen

Liam had spent the better part of three days camping out in the Adelaide Hills where he would frequently spy on Tara's hideout. He had seen plenty of vampires and ghouls come and go, and the evil woman herself made the occasional appearance, but still no sign of Austin.

He perched atop a plum tree out the front of the house on a Friday evening. His legs hurt, his back ached, and he was growing weary of the whole mission. Perhaps he was wrong about Alannah's ex. Giving up on the idea, he dropped down from the tree and began to move back towards the road when he heard the front door open. Ducking for cover behind the tree, he glimpsed the creep he had been looking for.

Austin walked across the yard to a black sportscar. Liam could not see what make it was, but judging by the shape, he suspected a Porsche. When

Austin took off in the vehicle, Liam raced back to his own car and followed. Thirty minutes later, they were in the outskirts of their hometown and from a distance, he observed Austin turning into Connor's driveway.

Several more cars followed the Porsche, and as Liam entered the driveway, it became obvious Connor was hosting the Friday night party.

'Wait here,' Brendan instructed. 'I'm gonna make sure the coast is clear.' He left her standing in the hallway. Alannah saw him talking to Bailey before disappearing outside.

She sighed as she leaned against the wall.

'Hi Alannah.' Turning her head to the right, she found Austin approaching her from inside the house. 'Can we talk?'

'What's there to talk about, Austin?'

'I was hoping we could still be friends. Will you at least come and have a drink with me?' Those luminescent blue eyes were pleading with her.

'I s'pose.' She followed him into the living room.

'Grab a seat. I'll get us some beers.'

Alannah chose one of the armchairs rather than a sofa.

A cup appeared in front of her face a minute later. 'I wanted to apologise.' Austin sat down. 'For not being upfront about my past.'

'It's okay, Austin. I understand why you didn't want to divulge those details. If I'm completely honest, what you did back then hasn't really changed my opinion of you. Both you and Brendan tried to warn me about your feeding addiction early on and I didn't care.' Alannah sipped her beer. *By the Gods it tastes so good!* She sculled the rest of it down in one mouthful.

Leaning forward, he placed a hand on her knee. 'So why did you break up with me?'

Looking into his gorgeous eyes, Alannah realised how much she still loved Austin. 'I… I'm not really sure. I guess I overreacted. I'm sorry, Austin.' She smiled sheepishly. 'Will you have me back?'

Scooping her up into his arms with supernatural speed, Austin whispered, 'Absolutely.' He kissed Alannah passionately as they moved through the house.

Next thing she knew, Alannah was making out with Austin in one of the spare bedrooms.

Stepping out of his car, Liam hit the lock button on the remote as he walked through the crowds of arriving guests. He could no longer see Austin. 'Damn it.' Pushing past a group of smokers, he moved closer to the house. He spotted Brendan and began to feel anxious. Rushing forward, he grabbed Brendan's t-shirt and spun the guy around to face him. 'Hey, where's Lana?'

Brendan gave him a stunned expression. 'Chill bro! She's safe inside. I asked Bailey to watch her while I did a sweep of the perimeter.'

Liam shook his head. '*You* were supposed to watch her.'

'I am. I've only been out here for a few minutes. What's got you in such a tizzy?'

'I tracked Austin here. I followed him from Tara's hideout, but lost him outside of this place somewhere.'

'*Shit!*' Brendan rushed inside. '*Fuck!* She's gone.' Liam detected panic in Brendan's tone. 'Okay, you try upstairs, I'll look around down here.'

Liam took off with bullet speed, not caring what normal humans saw. When he reached the second floor, he searched each room, ignoring the protests from irate couples. His heart was pounding as he began to fear the worst. *What if Austin has already killed her?*

But the sight he beheld behind door number five sent his blood boiling.

Alannah sat on the bed giggling as Austin began to light candles around the room. 'Why are you being so romantic? We didn't even do this for our first time together.'

'I want things to be just right for our reunion.'

'Oh, but they are. There's you and me and a big-ass bed. What more could we want? I mean, aside from the obvious.' She grinned at him as he approached her.

But he did not come to her; he stepped up to another candle beside the bed, which he was whispering to as he lit it. She could not understand him, but it sounded like Gaelic.

'Are you doing some kind of magic?'

He turned to her and smiled. 'I'm sending a prayer of thanks to the Gods for bringing you back to me.' A moment later he was kissing her amidst a frenzy of flying clothes. Pinning her to the bed with his strong arms, Austin gave her a wicked grin. 'Did you miss me?'

Alannah gasped as he entered her. 'Hell yeah.' She began moaning as Austin moved inside her. On the verge of climax, she heard a familiar voice.

'What the fuck?'

Looking over Austin's shoulder, Alannah saw Liam standing in the doorway, mouth agape. His visage reddened as it transformed into a grimace.

When Austin turned his head, he growled at Liam, pressing his weight possessively against Alannah.

The force of him thrusting took her over the edge. The orgasm rippled through her and a deep, guttural sound escaped her throat. She heard the door slam, but Liam's intrusion and sudden exodus did not bother her in that moment.

The next sensation that had her attention was a sharp, piercing pain in her neck, but it was fleeting as a new wave of pleasure started crashing through her.

Brendan was about to step outside to continue his search for Alannah, when a familiar sensation struck him. *Shit! That can't be good!* As he approached the stairs, he spotted Liam running down them. 'Don't tell me you left her up there?'

Startled, Liam spun to face Brendan. The emotions erupting from him almost knocked Brendan to the floor. 'If she wants him that bad, she can have him. I'm done!' Liam bolted through the front door.

Shit! Brendan leaped up the stairs, taking them two at a time. Stalking along the wood-panelled floor, he tried the first bedroom.

Jacob gaped at him. 'What the hell?'

'Sorry, man. I'm looking for Bailey or Connor.'

Cara stuck her head around Jacob's shoulders, her face flushed, and hair ruffled. 'Why, what's wrong?'

Brendan stifled the smile he felt creeping onto his face when he discovered Jacob's companion. The congratulations would have to wait. 'Austin's got Alannah, and he's gone rogue again.'

Jacob threw his legs over the edge of the bed and ran his hand through his hair. 'Crappers.' He stood up and gave Brendan an eyeful. 'You want backup?'

'Sure, but put some pants on first, man.' Brendan left the room and made his way down the hall. Flinging open the fifth door, he gaped at the erotic scene unfolding before him. It was enough to stir his dick. But it did not. Concern for Alannah took priority. He understood Liam's reaction. From this angle their heaving bodies worked together in perfect synchronisation and her moaning was the hottest sound he had ever heard. One could easily assume she was consenting.

But the hairs prickled on the back of Brendan's neck. Stepping closer, he tuned into what the couple before him were feeling. Austin was salivating as the metallic taste of blood washed over his tongue and a surge of power was rushing through his own blood stream. *Shit! Austin's blood lust is more prominent than his sexual appetite.* Focusing on Alannah, he could feel her growing faint. *The arsehole is sucking her dry.* He drew closer. 'Get away from her!'

Blood trickled down Austin's chin when he looked up, his fangs still extended. The sick bastard grinned at him. 'Hey man, why don't you join us. You can fuck her while I feed. Just like old times.'

Something snapped in Brendan. *No one treats Lana with such contempt!* He rushed forward and slogged the vampire in the side of the head. The blow knocked Austin back, leaving him unconscious. Brendan pulled Austin's limp form away from Alannah and threw the guy to the floor.

By the Gods, she looks divine! The sight of her naked body sprawled out on the bed made his blood surge. He smacked himself in the face to regain his composure before shaking her shoulder. 'Lana?'

Her eyes opened slightly, and she gazed at him from beneath heavy eyelids. 'Hey, sexy. Have you come to rock my world?'

Brendan was still empathically aware of Alannah's emotions and he could feel hot, liquid lust gushing from her like torrential rain. *Fuck! It is going to take all my willpower to resist her. Austin must have drugged her or given her a potion to bring on such intense levels of desire.* He scanned the floor and found her clothes. Returning to the bed, he started dressing her.

Alannah giggled. 'You've got it all wrong. You should be taking your clothes off, not putting mine back on.'

Oh hell. Just keep focused. Brendan kept chanting the mantra to himself.

She began pouting. 'Don't you want to fuck me?' Her hand slid between his thighs and groped him. His semi-stiff cock hardened completely at her touch. 'It feels like you want me.'

He kept reminding himself that her feelings were not real. 'Not here, gorgeous. Come on, let's get you home.'

'Christ!' Jacob's voice came from the doorway.

Brendan wrapped himself around Alannah to shield her from Jacob's eyes. 'Can you get Austin out of here?'

Jacob moved in and inspected Austin's unmoving body. 'You got him good.' He dragged Austin out of the room.

Cara shut the door and came forward. 'Did you need help dressing Alannah?' A lopsided grin was tugging at her lips.

The spectacle Alannah was making was probably hilarious to onlookers. Her hands were all over him and she was desperately begging him to fuck her.

'I'll manage,' he insisted. 'Can you find someone sober enough to drive?'

'Sure.' Cara's brow arched. 'You're relishing this too much. Don't do anything stupid.'

Brendan laughed. *I am definitely enjoying this more than I should.* 'Don't worry about me.'

She hesitated a moment before leaving the room.

He continued dressing Alannah despite her verbal protests. Her weakness made the task easier because she was too weak to fight him physically. Brendan wondered how much blood she had lost, especially when he lifted her to her feet, and she fainted on him. His pulse quickened and it took considerable effort to maintain his grip with such clammy hands.

Rushing downstairs, he found Connor. 'Hey man, I need your help. She's lost a lot of blood.'

'What happened to her?'

'*Austin* got carried away feeding.' He practically spat the vampire's name.

Connor frowned. 'You're a terrible liar. This was intentional, wasn't it? Put her on the couch.'

'Yes. Austin was either trying to kill her, or…' *Shit!* Brendan had not thought about it at the time, but in hindsight he realised Austin had filled the room with ritual candles. Brendan gently placed Alannah on the sofa.

His friend started working his healing spells. Relief washed over him when he heard Alannah's breathing deepen and even out. 'Can you detect the effects of any potions or drugs in her system?'

'Yeah. She's taken a strong love potion. It'd take a more skilled mage than me to remove it from her system though.'

Brendan sighed. *Figures. Why else would she come on to me?* 'I'll get Dad to do it. Thanks for your help, man.' Lifting her back up, he carried her as he went in search of Cara.

'There you are.' Cara rushed forward. 'Shit. Is she okay?'

'Yup. Connor healed her. Did you find us a driver?'

Cara nodded. 'Nick's still sober. He's waiting out the front for you.'

'Thanks, Cars.' He moved to the door, pausing to turn and smile at her. 'Congrats to you and Jacob, by the way.'

She beamed. 'Thanks, Brendan.'

He hurried outside to find Nick. The drive home was torturous. Even in her sleep, Alannah was all over him and her hand would not leave his dick alone.

Nick kept laughing every time he caught a glimpse of them in his rear-view mirror. 'You're a better man than me for resisting those moves.'

'Yeah, but you don't have to live with the consequences. *Ah, Christ.*' Alannah had managed to unzip his fly and slipped her hand inside to get a proper grip. Having reached the limits of his self-control, he resolved to let her have her fun as he sat back to enjoy the ride. At least she remained dressed and too out of it to jump him.

When Alannah stirred the next morning, her head throbbed, and she felt foggy. Groaning as she rolled over, she found Brendan sleeping next to her. This was no cause for alarm. He had been doing this every night since Liam left. But something felt wrong. She tried to piece together her memories of the previous night but kept drawing a blank. *How did I get to bed and*—she glanced at herself under the quilt—*how did I end up wearing only panties and a singlet?* And Brendan was only wearing boxers. *Surely not?*

Sitting back, Alannah tried some deep breathing and mindfulness. As she did so, a few images flashed through her mind. The training session, Sleazy Chicken, arriving at the party, drinking a beer with Austin. But then nothing. *Did I really drink that much?*

As soon as Brendan woke, he sat upright and focused his unblinking eyes on her. 'Are you feeling okay, Lana?'

'Um, I think so. I've got a killer hangover, but otherwise okay. How much did I drink last night? I can't remember anything.'

Brendan frowned. 'Dad warned me this might happen.'

'What might happen?'

'A side effect of the treatment he gave you. Probably just as well. I don't think you want to recall what you did last night.'

She clapped her hands to her mouth. A moment later, she curled her fingers down enough to talk. 'Oh Gods! Did we?'

'Have sex? No, *we* didn't. But you did. I had to drag you out of a dangerous situation.'

Alannah's eyes widened as dread set in. 'W-what did I do?'

A grimace took over Brendan's visage. 'It wasn't your fault, Lana. You gotta believe me. Someone drugged you with a powerful potion. It took all Dad's strength to cleanse it from your system.'

Dread turned to fear. 'Who drugged me?'

'Austin.'

'*Shit!* Then what?'

'Then… he took advantage of you.' Brendan closed his eyes. 'He… he was about to turn you, Lana. I'm sorry, I never should have taken my eyes off you.'

'Wait. So, he…' Alannah couldn't bring herself to use the 'R' word. It was too painful to fathom. 'Did Austin drug me and have sex with me?'

When Brendan's eyes opened, they were full of sorrow. 'Yes.'

She began to shiver, so Brendan pulled her into his arms. 'Why didn't the other guys notice Austin dragging my drugged body upstairs?'

He spoke softly against her ear. 'Because you appeared to be enjoying yourself. They thought you got back together with him. It was a love potion, Lana. It made you believe you wanted whoever was touching you.'

Alannah pressed her head against Brendan's chest and began to sob. Something dawned on her. 'Oh Gods! Did you say I believed I wanted whoever was touching me? So, when you pulled me out of that mess?'

'Shoosh, Lana. Please don't go there'

She flushed, but she had to know. Her voice became firm. 'What did I do?'

'It wasn't you—not really. And I didn't let you take things too far.'

Sitting back, Alannah narrowed her eyes on him. 'Brendan, what did I do?'

He sighed. 'You mostly just said stuff. Very provocative stuff.'

'Mostly, huh? What else?'

He squeezed his eye lids closed. The memory was clearly painful for him. 'You also groped me… like a lot.'

She sprung out of the bed. '*Fuck!* I'm so sorry, Brendan.'

Brendan rose from the bed and drew her back into his embrace, despite her protests. '*Shoosh, Lana!* It's okay, seriously. I knew it was the potion, not you. It wasn't that bad. Not for me. I mean, what guy wouldn't want a hot girl grabbing him, right? I'm more worried about you right now. What Austin did to you was inexcusable.'

'What happened to him in the end?'

'I knocked him out cold. Jacob and Connor sent him packing.'

'Good. That creep better not show his face in town again. Any word from Liam yet? When will he get home?'

Alannah felt the muscles in his arms and torso tighten, but he didn't reply.

'Oh Gods! Don't tell me Liam got hurt!' She stepped back to look him in the eyes.

'No, Liam is unharmed. Physically anyway. Not that I've seen him since he took off last night.'

'What? Liam was there last night? Why didn't he…' A horrible realisation hit. 'He saw me fucking Austin, didn't he?'

Brendan nodded.

'Did he know about the potion?'

Brendan shook his head.

'*Fuuuuck!*' She stormed across the room and grabbed her phone. The call rang out at first, so she dialled him again.

This time, a spiteful female voice answered. 'Liam doesn't want to talk to you, *Alannah*.'

'Monique?'

'Yes, that's right. Liam came crawling back to my arms after the stunt you pulled. You screwed up, as I predicted. Have fun with your vampire lover, bitch!' The phone line went dead.

Alannah threw her phone at the wall. She collapsed to the floor in hysterics.

Brendan did not say anything. He simply picked her up and put her back in bed. Sitting beside her, he wrapped her in his arms.

The last of the sun's rays peeked through the bottom slits of the blinds in a last-ditch effort to illuminate Alannah's room. They scattered among the dust particles dancing around the window. As they disappeared, she decided it was okay to move again, because the gloomy ambience matched what she felt in her heart. She shifted her weight and looked at the plate of sandwiches Aunt Nora had left on the desk for her and Brendan. 'I think I'm ready to eat.'

Brendan grinned. 'Thank the Gods! I'm starving.' He reached across to her bedside table and turned on the lamp. Retrieving the food platter and two bottles of water, he brought them back to Alannah's bed.

After eating in silence, Alannah found her legs and stood for the first time in hours. She grabbed a pair of yoga pants from her wardrobe and slipped into them. Thankfully, Brendan had had the decency to put his jeans and t-shirt back on before tucking her into bed earlier that day. She turned to face him and noticed his attentive gaze. She blushed a little before shrugging it off as concern. 'You know what I really need right now?'

'I'm guessing it's not ice-cream or chocolate.'

A slight grin pulled at her lips. 'You know me too well.'

Brendan laughed. 'Well enough to know we're probably going to get shit faced tonight.'

'Can you smuggle a couple of bottles in here?'

'Is my name Brendan Winters?'

The smile was complete. 'Thanks.'

'Anything for my Lana.' He winked a moment before vanishing beyond the door.

In the meantime, she walked into the bathroom to freshen up. A glimpse of herself in the mirror was terrifying. Her eyes were red and swollen, skin blotchy, hair messy. Attempting to tame her locks with a brush achieved partial success. Not much she could do about her face though.

'I got us some snacks too,' Brendan declared as he walked back into her room.

When she returned from the bathroom, Alannah laughed at the mountain of chips and biscuits in the middle of her floor, surrounding two bottles of whiskey and two glasses. 'All my favourite treats. Good work.'

'You know me. I aim to please.' He gave her a wicked grin before dropping a couple of large cushions next to the drinks and collapsing onto one of them.

'Or offend,' Alannah finished for him. 'But in this case, I am pleased.' She locked her door and joined him on the floor. After cracking the seal on the first bottle, she poured them each a shot. They clinked their glasses and drank up. She savoured the burn in her throat for a full minute before pouring the second round. After the third drink, she began to feel the blanket of numbing comfort settle into place. Sighing, she leaned against Brendan. 'At least you didn't give up on me.'

He placed an arm across her shoulder. 'Lana, I will never give up on you.'

She looked into his eyes. 'Promise?'

Holding her gaze, he tucked a strand of hair behind her ear. 'I promise.'

Alannah smiled. 'Thanks. Next round?'

'Sure.' He grabbed the bottle and served the shots.

Several rounds later, Alannah's thoughts shifted from the whole Liam and Austin drama to her success with magic. She smiled to herself and started laughing.

Brendan's eyes squinted. 'What's so funny?'

'I realised I'm a kick-arse mage.'

'Of course you are. But how did you only just realise? I've been telling you all along.'

She shrugged. 'It only just sank in.' Stuffing her mouth with a handful of chips, she revelled in the salty goodness. 'So, what's the big deal with channelling Aether?'

'Are you kidding me? It's like a direct link to the Gods. Only three types of mages attune to the celestial element.'

'Tell me Brendan, what type of mages attune to the cest… celest…ial element?'

He laughed. 'You're drunk.'

Grinning, she bumped his shoulder with her own. 'Kinda the point. Now pour me another drink and answer my querest… quest*ion*.'

Brendan refilled the glasses and drank his before clearing his throat. 'Right, so as I was saying, three types of mages channel Aether. Council leaders, spiritual leaders, and necromancers. Leaders use it to connect to the spirit world and communicate with the Gods. Necromancers use it to talk to *dead people*.' He emphasised the last two words with his best Cole Sear voice.

Alannah shivered. 'Does that mean I may end up becoming a necromancer?' *Talking to Mum was one thing, but other ghosts? No thanks.*

'It's possible, but I wouldn't worry about it. While your attunements choose you to some extent, you do have some agency of choice when it comes to selecting your magus path.'

An analogy occurred to Alannah. 'Kinda like the sorting hat at Hogwarts?'

Brendan laughed loudly. 'Yup, or like how the penis—I mean wand—chooses the wizard.'

She glared at him. 'You spend too much time in the cesspools of social media.'

'But they're the best parts of the internet. Very entertaining.'

Alannah shook her head as she held her glass out for another shot. He happily obliged.

After slamming his own glass back on the floor, Brendan grinned. 'The fact that you can channel Aether also confirms something Liam mentioned.'

'Oh?'

'Only pure magic races can access the celestial element. It's one of the reasons our ancestors were so particular about our bloodline.' He leaned in closer. 'Is there something you're not telling me, Lana?'

'Oh right. I'd almost forgotten about that. Tara mentioned something when she confronted me at school. She said Mum conceived me at Beltane.'

His eyes widened. 'That's fucking awesome, Lana! Do you realise what that means?'

She sighed. 'That Dad wasn't really my dad?'

He curbed his enthusiasm a little. 'Well aside from that. The courtship and fertility rites of Beltane are sacred, so any children conceived at the festival are a literal blessing. They are generally also more powerful than other mages.'

'So how does it… how does that mean Dad wasn't my bio father?'

'Because the High Magus hosts the official Beltane festivals and he only allows pure mages to attend. There are other unsanctioned events in the wider mage community, but Grandmother dearest wouldn't make a big deal about your conception if Aunt Aileen got knocked up at one of those.'

'So how do I find my biological father?'

Laughing, he handed her another shot. 'Here, I don't think you're drunk enough. You can still pronounce bio…logical. Short answer, you can't.'

She arched her brows, waiting for his explanation.

'Thing is, Beltane is a little like Vegas.' He paused for effect. 'For those who participate in the official rites, the Gods choose their partner or *partners* (plural). It's One. Big. Sacred. Orgy.' After flashing a smouldering grin, he downed another shot before continuing. 'No one talks about it after. If a married woman conceives during the official rites of Beltane, it's accepted that the child is a blessing and her husband accepts the child as his own, even if there's a good chance he's not the daddy. I can't wait for my first Beltane.'

Alannah laughed. 'Sounds like your sorta party.'

Those bedroom eyes returned. 'Come on, Lana—as if it doesn't sound like fun to you.'

'Maybe. I'm not sure about the whole blind-date aspect though.'

'All part of the charm really. It's not like you have to fuck everyone you're paired with.'

'Well in that case, sign me up.'

'Would if I could. We gotta wait 'til we're eighteen. For obvious legal reasons, they can't have minors attend.'

Alannah sank into quiet contemplation for a moment. 'Hey, Brendan?'

'Yes, Lana?'

'What if we hosted our own unsanctioned event for the young magic population?'

The widest grin she had ever seen spread across Brendan's face. 'Genius. Pure genius. See, this… is why *you* are a woman after my own heart.' Slapping his chest with force; he fell backwards.

Alannah burst out laughing and collapsed next to him. Before long they were both rolling around on the floor, laughing together. She carried on until her ribs hurt too much to continue and even then, she needed to take several deep breaths to calm down. By this point, Brendan had settled, and he lay on his back with his eyes closed. Sidling up next to him, she peered down into his face. 'Brendan?'

His eyes shot open to lock with hers. 'Lana?'

'Thanks for today.' She reclined her head against his armpit and threw an arm across his chest.

Brendan's arm pulled her in tight and he exhaled sharply. 'You're welcome.'

They remained in this position for the rest of the night, or at least until Alannah fell asleep.

Chapter Eighteen

Alannah was alone in her bed when she awoke and hurried to the bathroom, to rid herself of the toxins she had imbibed the night before. When the urge to retch subsided, she slowly ventured downstairs. The house was unusually quiet for a Sunday morning, and her pulse quickened as she drew closer to the kitchen.

Normally the bustling sounds of crockery clanking, and the aroma of fried food filled the air. But she remembered it was usually Liam who cooked breakfast, or occasionally Aunt Nora. She knew her Aunt and Uncle were busy with the Council all day, and a quick glance of the clock told her midday neared.

Upon entering the kitchen, she was relieved to see Brendan at the table. But she took note of how rugged his appearance was. Slumped over the table, he was nursing a coffee mug, not even looking up as she approached. He simply pushed the green bottle of hangover begone towards her.

She downed a shot of the goop and put the potion back in the fridge before turning on the coffee machine. Taking the seat across from her cousin, she studied him for a minute. 'You're unusually quiet, even with a hangover. Something on your mind?'

He looked up into her eyes and held her gaze for several seconds before returning his attention to the cup in his hands. 'Just a bit.'

'You wanna talk about it?'

After sculling the last of his brew, he pushed his chair back and left his dishes on the sink. 'No, Lana. I don't want to talk about it. For one thing, you need to focus on your magic training right now. I'm gonna shower. I'll meet you in the cellar.' He turned and left the room.

What was up with him? Oh well, there is no use speculating. He is right: I need to concentrate on training if I am going to beat Tara. She went for another mouthful of her drink and cursed, realising her cup was empty. A glimpse of the bench reminded her of the effort required to work the coffee machine. So, Alannah gazed longingly into her empty coffee mug, hoping it would refill itself. Maybe if she focused hard enough, she could summon a cup of the divine drink. It was probably wrong, but she was desperate for more and really did not feel up to the effort of grinding more beans, et cetera. Visualising the coffee machine at her favourite café, she imagined it dispensing a shot of espresso, willing the substance to appear in her cup. When she opened her eyes, she was pleasantly surprised to find it had worked. 'Damn, I'm good.'

With the second shot of caffeine coursing through her body and a sense of accomplishment, she was able to stomach some breakfast and face the day.

As steaming hot water cascaded over him, Brendan thought about his predicament. He had a huge fucking dilemma on his hands. *What the hell am I going to do about Lana?* Even without intentionally reading her, he had caught a glimpse of those feelings last night, yet he could not bring himself to take advantage of the situation. If he played his cards right, he knew he could have her in weeks, if not days. But he also knew it was only a matter of time before Liam discovered the truth about Austin. And as much as he hated to admit it, Alannah needed Liam's protection. She needed as many damn allies as she could get for the impending war.

Shit! The honourable thing would be to kick his brother up the arse and make him face the truth. Of course, that meant Liam would take Alannah back in a heartbeat. But Brendan's inner rogue was telling him to say *'Fuck that! Get the girl, consequences be damned.'* Nothing would piss Liam off more than learning the truth about Austin, only to find Alannah had moved on to his little brother. *Will he still fight alongside us in that case? Will he still protect Lana?*

'Fuuuck!' He punched the tiled wall of the shower, shattering one of the ceramic squares and sending several hairline fractures radiating from the epicentre. When he drew his fist back, Brendan observed rather than felt the cuts on his knuckles. Placing his hand under the stream of the shower, he watched the water wash away his blood in a state of catharsis. With that momentary distraction, he knew what he would do.

Finishing in the shower, Brendan dressed for training. As he pulled out one of his practice robes, he caught sight of the one he had won from Alannah and smiled. But as he finished getting ready, he adopted a more solemn expression. Shit was getting serious.

He found Alannah in the ritual circle, consecrating a new practice robe, so he sat back and watched her.

Once finished, she turned to him and smiled. 'I finally replaced the one you absconded with.'

'Hey, I won that fair and square.' Brendan waggled his brows.

'That was anything but fair. Even so, I conceded willingly, and I'd give up all my robes and train in my underwear if it helps us win this fight.'

'Christ, Lana. You're killing me here.'

She gave him a smouldering grin. 'Sorry Brendan, you're the last person I want to be dealing lethal force to right now.'

Fuck! He could feel his resolve crumbling away and needed to change the subject, pronto. 'So, what's next on your magic agenda?'

'Well, I was thinking about what you told me last night. About channelling Aether. I want to see if I can attune to other mana sources.'

'What? Already? You haven't even mastered all the powers of conjuration yet. You've only imbued one item and that was a fluke. And what about learning to travel by ley lines? That could prove very handy.'

Alannah sighed. 'Call me overconfident, but I feel as though I could probably do those things in a pinch if I needed to. I never told you this, but when that vampire attacked me at school, I was able to summon Liam to help me. I'd never summoned a living being before, but somehow, I knew how to do it.'

He stared at her in amazement. There were few conjurers in the world who could do that. 'Right, well you know the drill. Did you want my help?'

'I'm feeling a little anxious, so I could use some of your calming magic.'

So could I, to be quite frank. 'Great. Let's get to it.'

Alannah recast the circle to bring Brendan into it. They knelt side by side.

He placed a hand on Alannah's shoulder, and channelled the sensation of touch, giving him the power to will her into a state of calm. As her nerves settled, he tapped into her serenity and let it wash over him.

She picked up the silver band with the green peridot crystal and eased it onto her right index finger. Closing her eyes, she began the arduous process of connecting to a new mana source.

Brendan kept his hand on her shoulder, continuing to soothe her and create the feedback loop he so desperately needed.

Finally, after what felt like hours, she opened her eyes and sighed. 'Nothing.' Her shoulders slumped.

'I'm sorry, Lana. Maybe next time?'

'Maybe. Right now, though, I'm famished. Let's get something to eat.' After dropping the ring back in the box on the altar, she rose and broke the circle.

Following her upstairs, Brendan watched as she slipped into her room. He stepped into his own bedroom and changed out of his robe. With this setback in mind, he collapsed on his bed and picked up his phone. He hesitated a moment before dialling.

'Hi Brendan. Is everything okay?'

'Hi Dad. I need you to contact Liam for me.'

Liam was on the phone. A moment after answering the call, he looked up at Monique and told her, 'It's Dad with Council business, might take a while. Can I use your study?'

She simply nodded. Knowing he would be occupied for some time, she wandered out into the garden. The sun was out and only a few white, wispy clouds were in the otherwise perfectly coloured sky. With the weather this good, she decided to go for a run.

Turning onto the gravel driveway, she increased her pace from brisk walking to jogging. As soon as she reached the road, her feet pounded the bitumen at a sprint. She was only a few kilometres down the road when she observed the limousine parked on the verge. *Odd spot for a limo. Is the occupant lost?* Slowing down to a jog, she approached the vehicle cautiously, rubbing her thumbs against her mana rings.

When she reached the driver's door, she knocked, but the passenger window behind the driver lowered. 'Can I help you?' she asked as she approached the back. But when the woman's face came into view, she froze as instant recognition filled her with fear.

'Yes, Monique Lane, I am hoping you can help me. I have a business proposition for you. Something of mutual benefit to the two of us.'

'Why would I help you?' she spat with bitter contempt.

'Because I know how much you despise my granddaughter.'

'Almost as much as you, which brings me back to my question.'

The Queen of the Cursed smiled viciously. 'If you help me, both Alannah and I will leave you and this town alone.'

'A tempting prospect, but what's the cost?'

'A simple favour is all I ask. Alannah and her cousins have something of mine in their possession and I want it back. Will you retrieve it for me?'

'You have the powers of a conjurer, why can't you summon it yourself?'

'Oh, I have tried, believe me. But my daughter kept it sealed away and hidden from me for years. Even now, my son has placed magical wards around his property, blocking all my magic. I even sent one of my pets to obtain it from Alannah's Melbourne home, but that ended badly. I lost one of my favourite ghouls and my daughter's husband wound up dead.'

Monique shook her head in disgust. 'Ross is a smart man and a skilful mage. What do you expect me to do if *you* can't bypass his wards?'

'You have Liam's trust and confidence, do you not?'

'Yes, but—'

'Use that to your advantage. Find out where they have it hidden and take it. Simple. Will you do it?'

'On one condition.'

'Name it.'

'I don't just want you to leave town. I want you out of Australia, permanently.'

Tara grinned. 'Shall not be a problem. I was planning to return to my husband in Romania anyway.'

'It's a deal.'

Returning to Monique's bedroom, Liam spotted her phone, but did not see her, so he searched the house. Considering the enormity of the Lane family manor, it was no easy task. On the verge of giving up, he left the library when the front door slammed shut. He hurried up the hallway. 'There you are!' His voice was breathless.

She lowered her gaze and looked at him from beneath long lashes with a demure smile. 'Sorry babe, I went for a run.'

'I need to get home. Turns out I made a complete arse of myself over the business with Alannah and Austin. He drugged her with a powerful love potion.' Running his fingers through his hair, Liam braced himself as he processed the news. '*Shit!* That creep raped her, and I walked away from the situation. I let him do it.' He collapsed against the wall, sliding down to the floor. It felt like tears were threatening to break the dam.

Monique knelt beside him and placed a comforting hand on his arm. 'It's not like you knew about the potion. You can't blame yourself.'

He shook his head. 'No. I should have known. I should have trusted her. I knew Austin had come from Tara's. I swear to the Gods if I see that bastard again, I will kill him on sight.' As he said the words, he felt his phone vibrate with a text message.

By order of The Council of Mages, I wish to advise all magi that the vampire Austin Pearce is a public enemy. You are permitted to kill or capture him on sight. Anyone harbouring this fugitive will be charged with treason. It was from High Magus Kieran.

Laughing drily, Liam showed Monique the message. 'Looks like your dad shares my sentiments.' It was one thing to target a bunch of human nobodies, but Austin harmed a pure mage this time and no amount of money or influence on his father's part would help him. 'I should go.' Liam rose, but as he moved toward the front door Monique pressed up against him.

'Wait. I want to come with you.'

'I don't think that's a good idea, Monique. Lana will freak out.'

She stood her ground. 'Alannah's gonna need all the assistance she can get. I will help protect her.'

Liam was gobsmacked. 'You would do that?'

Monique smiled. 'Of course. But I need to shower first. Give me a sec.' She sprinted up the stairs.

Leaning back against the wall, Liam thought about how Alannah must have felt when he abandoned her at such a critical time. *Christ! If Brendan hadn't gotten her out of there when he did…* The implications were too painful to consider. Liam had fucked up big time, and he prayed Alannah would forgive him.

'Okay, let's go.' Monique came racing down the hall in one of her brightly coloured spring dresses: one that had been a favourite of his, and he had told her as much when they were a couple. She wrapped her arms around him, planting a kiss on his cheek. Grabbing his hand, she pulled him out the door.

Everyone was talking in the living room when he got home. Alannah diverted her attention from the discussion to take in the sight of Liam and Monique arriving together. Tears instantly brimmed in her eyes and she quickly turned away. He noticed how close she was sitting to Brendan. Their legs were touching, and he had an arm stretched out behind her, across the back of the couch. Liam's eyes narrowed, meeting at the creased bridge of his nose. Brendan was not paying Liam any attention, however.

Dad was talking about the Council's orders to treat all cursed with suspicion. 'After the reports Liam and Brendan gave me concerning Tara's hideout, it is fair to assume she is exercising her powers as puppet master. You should alert all your friends.'

'What direct actions are the Council taking against Grandmother dearest?' Brendan asked.

Their father visibly cringed at Brendan's use of Tara's familial title, even though the tone was bitter and sarcastic. 'A number of soldiers are investigating the hideout, and Austin's family are under house arrest. Kieran issued every magus in the state with a kill or capture on sight command for Austin.'

Alannah's eyes widened. 'That seems pretty extreme. What if he was acting under the Queen's influence rather than his own accord?'

Liam could not believe what he was hearing. 'Are you seriously gonna defend that arsehole after what he did to you?'

She glared at him. 'Why not? He might not have had free will, unlike you when you chose to leave me there.' The venom in her voice pierced his heart, causing it to constrict painfully.

So that's it—Alannah hates me. Liam's eyes darted around the room as he hung his head low. 'I'm sorry, Lana. I didn't know.'

When his gaze rose, her eyes penetrated him with burning intensity. 'You ought to know me better.'

'He apologised already. What else do you want?' Monique piped up.

Alannah placed her hands on her hips as she scowled at Monique. 'What the fuck are you doing here anyway?'

'I came to offer you my help and to provide my boyfriend with emotional support.' Monique drew close to Liam and placed her hand on the small of his back.

Fuck! This was not going well.

'So, it's official again, huh?' Alannah narrowed her eyes on Liam.

Liam wanted to correct Monique and clear up the whole misunderstanding, but his dad stepped in first. 'Girls, please. This is not the time for bickering. We need to be a united front against the Queen and her army of cursed. Now go and call all your mage friends. It's time to muster the troops. We have plenty of spare rooms in the house, plus there's the guesthouse. The rest of the district Council agree that with my wards up, this is the safest house for initiates to take refuge in, while the rest of us prepare for battle.' He turned to leave the room but paused at the door. 'Liam, as soon as you've made your phone calls, please join me in my office.'

'Yes, sir.'

The assembled group began to disband. Monique kissed his cheek before stepping outside to make her round of calls. Alannah gave him a scowl before leaving the room.

Brendan remained seated and Liam observed the way his brother's eyes trailed Alannah intently.

Clenching his fists, his blood was boiling when he returned his attention to Brendan. 'You wanna tell me what's going on between you and Lana?'

The twerp gave him a smug grin. 'No, not really.'

Liam stepped closer. 'So, something happened?'

'It was bound to, leaving her with me for so long, abandoning her in her hour of need.'

He could feel a fireball forming in his hand. 'What did you do, Brendan? Did you touch her?'

'It's none of your business, bro. You're the one who ran into Monique's loving arms. Alannah's really fucking pissed with you. You can't blame her for seeking comfort elsewhere.'

Opening his fist, he let Brendan see the fire blazing in his palm. 'I don't blame her for anything. But I warned *you* to keep your filthy hands off her. Now tell me, little brother... Did. You. Touch. Her?'

With wide eyes focused on Liam's hand, Brendan shook his head. 'No. Despite what you may think of me, I wasn't prepared to take advantage of her vulnerability. This is Lana we're talking about. I don't want to hurt her.' As Liam lowered his hand and extinguished the flame, Brendan stood up and confronted him. 'You're not the only one in love with her. I also happen to have her best interests in mind, which is why I conceded to you this time. But the next time you fuck up... let's just say I won't hesitate again.' Brendan turned and stormed out the room.

Slumping onto the sofa, Liam heaved a huge sigh. He pulled his phone out of his pocket and dialled Blake's number.

'What are you doing?' Alannah asked when she found Monique snooping about in the cellar.

The girl did not even bother facing her to reply. 'Taking stock of your tools and weapons. We need to arm everyone, which means imbuing a bunch of gear.' Monique looked up at her. 'How many weapons have you imbued since the Solstice?'

Alannah bit her lip.

Monique was holding one of the ancient swords Alannah had found in her mother's collection. 'As I figured. Most of these will prove useless against an army of ghouls and vampires. Only blessed weapons will kill them.' She dropped the sword down onto its display stand. 'Face it Winters, you need my help. For all the guys harping on about your immense power and gift with magic, they seem to overlook your faults.'

'Why do you want to help me when you clearly dislike me?' she asked warily.

'You're right. I don't like you. I'm willing to help you yes; but I'm doing it for the street cred and because it helps Liam. The benefits you reap are of no consequence to me—unless of course you try to worm your way back into Liam's bed.' She began walking alongside a shelf covered in crystals, running her fingers along them as she went. 'But if

I'm reading things right, it looks like that won't be a problem. You appear to have moved on to your next victim already.'

Alannah furrowed her brow. 'What are you talking about?'

Monique stopped and looked at her. 'Don't play stupid with me, Alannah. I saw how close you and Brendan have become.'

'That's how we are. You're reading too much into it.'

She raised an eyebrow. 'Am I? Are you sure that's how Brendan sees it? You should ask him how he feels about you.'

Is she for real? Alannah began to reflect on recent time spent with Brendan and things began to add up. '*Shit!*'

Monique grinned. 'Has it only just occurred to you? Maybe I gave you too much credit for your smarts.'

Alannah flew from the room, Monique's laughter behind her. She found Brendan sitting on his bed, talking on the phone. She closed the door and marched up to him, challenging him with her stare.

He cocked his pierced brow as he finished his conversation: 'I gotta go, man. See you tonight, yeah?' Brendan dropped his phone on the bed covers. 'Lana?'

'Is it true?'

'Is what true?' His visage became an expressionless mask, completely unreadable.

'Are you in love with me?'

His eyes grew wide for a split-second before the wall went back up. 'Who the hell told you that?'

'Monique suggested it, so I got to thinking about your recent behaviour. Is it true?'

He gave her an impish smile. 'Do you want it to be true?'

Oh hell, I hadn't even thought about it. Do I? 'Honestly, I don't know. Maybe. But you haven't answered my question.'

'Maybe, huh?' His eyes narrowed. 'Have you considered Monique is trying to stir trouble for you and Liam?'

'Right now, there is no me and Liam.'

Brendan leaned back on his bed, propped up by his elbows. 'But there could be. If you forgave him, I mean. He isn't really back with Monique.'

This was news to her. She stood at the foot of the bed, towering over Brendan's prone body. It was almost as if he was inviting her to join him, which reminded her she was still waiting for an answer. 'You're deflecting, Brendan.'

He sighed. 'Sit down, Lana.'

She perched on the edge of his bed, stretched out beside him, and lay on her side to face him.

'Or you could do that too. It seems like that maybe's leaning toward a yes.' He winked at her.

She glared at him.

He rolled onto his side to face her properly, his nose a hair's breadth from her own. Brendan's eyes searched hers during an incredibly tense moment of silence. 'You know I love you, Lana, but am I *in* love with you? I don't know, but I don't think we should entertain the idea.'

'Why not?'

'You're still in love with Liam, for one thing. And he'd kick my arse if I so much as touch you.'

She studied him for a few seconds, but he was not betraying any of his feelings. 'Is Liam the only reason?'

'No. He'd be right to kick my arse if I touched you, because he knows what I'm like. I don't want to hurt you, Lana. Even you know what I'm like with girls: I'm not boyfriend material.'

'Why is that?'

He shrugged. 'I dunno. I guess I like variety.'

'Either that, or you've never really found someone you want to settle down with.'

'The thought of me wifed up is like trying to imagine an Oscar nomination for a porno.'

'It's a shame.'

'Yup. There are some damn good pornos out there that deserve better recognition.'

Alannah laughed. 'I was talking about you not wanting to commit to someone.'

His expression began to smoulder. 'Why is that a shame, Lana?'

'Oh, you know, for all those girls out there who happen to fall in love with you.'

'Right. I'm such a heartbreaker and all. But are you really concerned about those nameless girls you don't even know?'

'No.' She tried reading him again, but still got nothing from his intensely focused eyes as they studied her. Their gazes locked together, and Alannah wondered if she really did want Brendan to be in love with her. *If so, does that mean I'm in love with him?*

There was a knock on the door. Brendan rose and answered it.

'Dinner's ready. Is Lana in here?' It was Liam's voice.

'Yeah, I'm here.'

Popping his head around the corner, he saw her on the bed and frowned. *Great! Now he probably thinks something is happening with me and Brendan.*

Alannah stood up and followed the guys downstairs.

Chapter Nineteen

The town's initiates assembled in the living-room as they arrived after dinner. Alannah was anxious to see Cara and ran to her the moment she appeared.

Cara embraced her. 'How are you holding up?'

'I'm surprised I'm standing to be honest. I feel like shit.'

'I can imagine.' Cara pulled her aside, out of earshot from Liam and his friends. She continued in a hushed voice, 'I can't believe Liam dumped you over this! At least Austin's gonna get what's coming to him.'

Alannah sighed. 'I think the Council is overreacting. Yeah, I'm pissed with Austin, but I don't want people killing him for what he did. What if he wasn't acting with free will?'

'Alannah, honey, you're the one who told me he used to rape girls with his powers of hypnotism.

414

Even if he drugged you against his will, don't those other girls deserve some justice?'

'I s'pose. But the death sentence without a trial? It's so barbaric.'

'The magic legal system may seem archaic, but it's necessary and it works. Austin had his trial; we just weren't there. The Gods judged and sentenced him.'

'Oh.' Alannah recalled some of her recent reading on mage law, how Council leaders can communicate directly with the Gods to seek advice where a case is not black and white.

Uncle Ross entered the room and cleared his throat. The din ceased, and all eyes focussed on him. 'Right, now that everyone's here, I have a few housekeeping matters to discuss. Firstly, I'd like to thank Brock Sheridan and Charlotte Rowan for volunteering your services. Since you've both recently graduated to full magus status, you don't have to be here, but I appreciate your help.'

The pair simply nodded their acknowledgement.

'Now, there ought to be enough beds, but some of you will need to share rooms. While it should go without saying, I will have to insist on no gender mixing in shared rooms.' An audible groan of disappointment travelled through the group. He turned to Alannah. 'With that in mind, Alannah, I am going to insist you choose a roommate for added protection.'

'Cara can share with me.'

Her uncle nodded his approval. 'I will arrange a foldup bed for her. Now, on to kitchen and dining matters…'

Alannah tuned out as he harped on about the chores roster and cleanliness expectations. Her attention was on Liam, who was looking at her. Aura reading would have been useful in that moment because his expression was blank. *Am I prepared to forgive him?* Seeing Liam again brought a lot of suppressed feelings to the surface. *Brendan was right: I am still in love with Liam.*

'Alannah?' Ross' voice drew her back to the present issue.

'Sorry?'

He sighed angrily. 'I asked if you could imbue the weapons in our armoury?'

'Um, I can try.'

'Get Monique to help you. I want everyone armed with a blessed weapon. While I can guarantee that my wards will keep you safe from Tara and her spells, there is a chance her cursed minions could attack. Guards are stationed around the perimeter, but it is best to prepare. As for school hours, I don't want any of you to travel alone. Even when going to the bathroom, always have a friend with you. Well, that's it. You may get yourselves settled now.' Ross left and the noisy chatter returned.

Alannah looked at Cara. 'Come on, grab your gear and follow me.' She headed for her room, where they found a spare bed.

'This'll be fun. It reminds me of having slumber parties,' Cara said.

Rolling her eyes, Alannah snorted. 'Yeah, only this time instead of watching the horror movies, we are in lead roles of our own.'

'Hey, I'm sure everything will be fine.' Cara began unpacking her bags. She put her toiletries away in Alannah's bathroom. Looking around the room, she beelined for the wardrobe. 'Is it okay if I hang some stuff in here?'

'Knock yourself out.'

Cara opened the closet and her jaw dropped. 'By the Gods, don't you own anything that isn't black?'

'I have that green dress I wore to the spring equinox.'

'Is that it? Geez woman. I gotta take you shopping for some more threads. Being Goth doesn't preclude other colours, you know. You'd look hot in reds and purples too.' She began hanging up her own clothing. 'So… what's up with you and Liam now?'

Alannah sank onto her bed. 'I dunno. I'm confused about my feelings.'

'Confused how?'

'On one hand I'm pissed at him for leaving me and running back to Monique. But I still love him and want him.'

'Are you able to forgive him?'

'Yeah, I think so.'

Cara sat beside her. 'What's the problem?'

'Something Monique said earlier today got me thinking.'

Cara groaned. 'You're not gonna listen to a word outta that bitch's mouth, are you? She's a troublemaker.'

'Brendan said as much too, but that's beside the point. What she said got me thinking about my own feelings. This is what has me perplexed.'

'Go on.'

'In addition to Liam, I think I might be in love with someone else.'

Her eyes lit up. 'Who?'

Alannah felt herself blushing. 'Brendan.'

Cara smiled. 'Called it. Remember what I said on that camping trip? So, what are you going to do?'

'I don't know. As I said, I'm confused. I might be mistaking my strong familial affections for him as something more than they are. Or it could be lust. It's not like this is the first time I've thought about jumping his bones, but I don't know if I could see myself in a relationship with him.'

'Wow, the two Winters brothers,' Cara chuckled. 'Could make for a hot threesome.'

She punched Cara lightly in the arm. 'What's with the Liam and Brendan threesome obsession?'

'Just think about it a moment and tell me you don't agree. Objectively speaking, they are the two sexiest guys in school for one thing.'

Alannah closed her eyes and visualised it. Cara was right. The thought of both guys pleasuring her at the same time... *fuck!* 'Gods damn you, Cara. I'm gonna start having wet dreams about it now.'

She giggled. 'I told you. Do you know how Brendan feels about you?'

'Yes and no. I asked him outright if he was in love with me, but he wouldn't give me a straight answer. He told me he didn't know, but he wasn't prepared to go there.'

'Hm.'

'What?'

'It's probably for the best. If you are still in love with Liam, he is the more sensible choice. Brendan's love could be dangerous. He does break a lot of hearts. That's why I made a point of resisting his charms.'

'You're probably right, and he said as much himself, but that adds to his appeal. I'm not afraid to admit I have a bad-boy complex.'

Cara shook her head. 'If your relationship with Austin was anything to go by, I can believe that. Just be careful, okay? And please try to keep your head in the game. This is a very dangerous time for distractions.'

'I know.' She took a deep breath to clear her mind before changing the subject. 'So, you and Jacob, huh?'

The biggest grin Alannah had ever seen spread across Cara's face. 'Yeah. He is amazing!'

There was a knock at the door and Brendan peered into the room. 'You girls wanna join us for Kelly Pool in the games room?'

'Sure.' Alannah stood and made her way to the door.

'Sounds great,' Cara agreed.

As soon as Blake knocked Alannah out of the game, she stood back against the wall beside Connor. 'Is this the misery wall where we losers come to lick our wounds?'

Connor smiled. 'Not so miserable now that you're here.'

'Right, 'cause I'm such a ray of sunshine.'

'That's exactly what you are. Your smile lights up any room you are in.' He winked at her.

Alannah laughed. 'Is that your best pickup line? No wonder you're still single.'

He clasped his chest above the location of his heart. 'Ouch, woman. You have shattered me.' A sly, lopsided grin graced his features. 'We don't all have the looks and charms of the Winters clan, but I get by.'

She was mid eyeroll when a hand slipped into hers and Liam's voice whispered in her ear, 'Can we talk?'

Alannah turned to see Liam standing in the doorway. She nodded and followed him upstairs.

Liam pulled her into his room and closed the door. 'I'm really fucking sorry, Lana. I know I should have trusted you, but it was like a short-circuit in my brain when I saw you with him. It did not occur to me he could have drugged or even hypnotised you.' His expression was full of shame and remorse as he closed in on her and pressed her against his door. 'I hate myself almost as much as that creep and I know I don't deserve your absolution, but I'm begging you to forgive me.'

His plea for mercy softened her heart and left her skin tingling. 'I forgive you, Liam.' With those words out, Liam's mouth covered her lips. She hesitated a moment before yielding to him. The kiss was even more passionate than their first, filled with a hunger brought on by days of separation. When Alannah came up for air, she pressed her hands to his chest and challenged him with a furrowed brow. 'What about Monique?'

'There's nothing there. I spent one night seeking comfort in her bed.'

'She seems to think you are back together.'

Liam shook his head. 'I never promised her anything. I'm in love with you, Lana.'

She replied with another kiss. Within a few minutes, Liam carried her across the room and laid her down on his bed. Their tops came off, followed by everything else Alannah was wearing. Only Liam's boxer shorts remained as they explored each other's bodies. The moment his fingers plunged inside her, she arched her back and moaned loudly.

Liam attempted to muffle the sound she made by kissing her again. 'Shh, my dear. We don't want anyone else to hear us.'

She grinned at him wickedly. 'You'll have to gag me if you keep this up. Oh Gods. Mm.' He added a third finger and began rubbing her clit with his thumb. Intense pleasure surged through her.

But he covered her mouth with his again and continued thrusting his fingers, bringing her to a strong climax and shaking her to the core.

Alannah could feel Liam's arousal pressing into her leg. Gripping his erection firmly in her hand, she whispered, 'I want you, Liam. All of you.'

Smiling, he tried to stifle a groan. 'Are you sure?' It was not only a question of sex. She knew Liam was asking if she was ready to take the next step in their relationship.

She nodded. 'Yes, I'm sure.'

Sucking in an audible breath, his eyes lit up. Liam stood and walked across to his chest of drawers to retrieve a condom. Their eyes remained locked in a searing gaze as he began to tear the packet open with his teeth.

A sudden movement at the door drew their attention. Monique burst through, jabbering as she entered the room. 'There you are. Surely your dad's rules don't really…' Pausing, she took in the sight of him standing there in his underwear. The foil packet must have caught her attention because she shot a look toward the bed. When her eyes fell upon Alannah, she screamed. '*You fucking bitch! How dare you!*' She charged.

Alannah sat up and promptly covered her breasts with her hands.

Liam acted quickly, grabbing Monique before she could do any damage. 'What the hell, Monique.'

The Queen Bee squirmed in his arms. She turned to face Liam, tears streaming down her cheeks. 'You don't really want to sleep with that whore, do you? Not when you've got me. What about us?'

'Monique, I'm sorry if you got the wrong idea, but there is no us. I'm in love with Lana.'

She flipped, flailing about and beating her fists against his chest. '*What? You can't be serious?* You slept with me. You never have meaningless sex.'

Alannah sat there gobsmacked by Monique's display.

'Look at me, Monique.' Liam tugged her chin, raising her eyes to his. 'I'm sorry. I came to you for solace and I was weak. I never should have let things go that far.'

Monique went rigid. 'Screw you all.' Her tone became ice cold. 'You can fight this damn war without me.' She broke free of Liam's hold and fled through the open door.

'*Christ!* Monique, where are you going?' he shouted from the doorway.

'*Anywhere but here!* It's not like you care.' It sounded as though she was on the stairs.

Shit! I can't afford to lose Monique's help. Alannah brought her knees to her chest and sighed as she dropped her head to rest on them.

Liam dashed after Monique. 'You can't leave the house. It's not safe.'

'What's all the commotion, bro?' Brendan's voice came from down the hall. 'Lover's spat?'

'*Shut up, Brendan*.' Liam's voice trailed off.

'Lana?'

Looking up, she found Brendan standing in front of her. Her nudity did not escape his attentive eye as it scanned her up and down. She flushed.

'What's going on, Lana?'

'Monique walked in on Liam with me. It tipped her over the edge.'

He nodded.

'Can you, uh, pass me my clothes?'

Letting out an exaggerated sigh, he bent down and scooped up the clothing pile on the floor. 'I suppose.' He dumped them on the bed beside her.

She plucked her black lace panties out of the pile and looked at Brendan again. 'You gonna turn around so I can dress?'

Leaning casually against the bedpost, he grinned at her. 'No. You've seen me naked, so it's only fair.'

Alannah glared at him. 'I'm not in the mood for games right now.'

'Who said I was playing?'

'Brendan, please.'

'Fine.' He turned, crossing the room to pick up the half-open condom wrapper from the floor. 'I guess she caught you guys at an inopportune moment.'

'Yeah. Talk about cockblocking. It would have been the first time with Liam.'

Brendan spun around as she retrieved her bra. 'Seriously? You guys haven't done it yet?' His eyes dropped to her breasts.

Blushing, she attempted to cover them with her bra, but fumbled and dropped it.

He exhaled sharply; his eyes pinned on her chest.

'Brendan! I told you to turn around.'

426

'Sorry,' he whispered, unwilling or unable not avert his eyes.

Giving up, Alannah threw her clothes on in front of his heated gaze. She advanced toward the door.

As she reached him, Brendan blinked a couple of times, and grabbed her arm. 'Shit. I'm sorry, Lana. I forgot myself for a moment there.'

She looked from where his hand gripped her wrist to his eyes. His unwavering gaze focused on her. She smiled. 'It's okay. I guess we're even now.'

Releasing her, Brendan grinned. He continued talking as he followed her out of Liam's room. 'So, you guys really haven't had sex yet?'

Alannah strode toward her own room. 'Not yet. He wanted me to be sure I was ready for a serious relationship.'

Seizing her hand, Brendan stopped her. He stepped closer and stared. 'It's the real deal with Liam, isn't it?'

'Yeah.'

There was a flicker of emotion in his eyes before Brendan's expression went blank.

'Does that bother you?' Alannah tried to read him, but his wall was too high.

'Of course not. Why would it?' His visage gave nothing away, but his thumb was gently stroking her knuckles.

'Because of what we discussed earlier today.'

Dropping her hand, he sighed. 'I don't feel that way about you, Lana. I'm sorry if I gave you the wrong impression.'

'So, you're not in love with me?'

'No.'

His admission stabbed her in the gut and knocked the air from her lungs. It was a ludicrous reaction, considering she had Liam, and was not even sure of her feelings for Brendan. *Does that mean…?* She dismissed the idea before letting it surface. 'Well, if you're sure. You had me wondering back there when you kept staring at my boobs.'

He laughed. 'I'm still a hot-blooded guy, Lana. Those amazing tits on anyone would captivate me.'

She smirked at him. 'So, you liked what you saw?'

Brendan pinned her against the wall with his hands pressed against her wrists. 'You're lucky I value our friendship and my own life so much. If I didn't, I would have shown you how much I liked what I saw right there on my brother's bed.'

The thought gave her a mental image that sent sparks shooting through every nerve in her body. Alannah looked to his lips and wanted to kiss him. *I'm done denying Brendan's sex appeal.*

He gave her a devilish grin and stepped closer.

Fuck! Every part of her body was humming, and her core was throbbing. She should have pushed him away, but instead she looked at him with lidded bedroom eyes.

A step closer and Brendan pressed his body against hers. He probably thought they were playing. 'Nice aura, Lana.'

'I told you not to read me.' She spoke with a hushed voice.

'I can't help it when your emotions are this strong. Be careful what you wish for, Lana. I only have so much self-control.'

'I thought you said you didn't want me.'

His eyes narrowed on hers. 'I didn't say that. I'm not in love with you, but that doesn't mean I don't want to fuck you.' Brendan's hands travelled up her arms and down her sides, pausing on her hips.

Alannah breathed in deeply as she revelled in the sensation of his hands on her body.

He pressed his forehead to hers and clenched his eyes shut.

Just kiss me, damn it!

His eyes shot open, penetrating her with their ferocity.

'*Get away from her!*' Liam growled as he pulled Brendan back and flung him into the opposite wall. He followed up by punching Brendan in the eye, knocking his face sideways.

Brendan turned back to look Liam square on with a smug grin. 'Sorry, bro, I didn't realise Lana was off-limits when you went running after Monique.'

Liam—still in only boxers—clasped the collar of Brendan's t-shirt. 'You promised you wouldn't touch her.' He raised his fist again.

Alannah screamed in panic. '*Stop it, Liam! Nothing happened.*'

He turned to stare at her, releasing Brendan. 'That didn't look like nothing.' Liam stepped closer to her. 'The two of you were about to kiss, weren't you?'

Tears began to trickle down her face.

'Weren't you?'

What can I say? It's probably true. She wanted it to happen and that alone made her feel guilty. She bit her lower lip and lowered her gaze.

'*Christ!* I need some air.' He stormed off to his room and slammed the door.

Alannah felt stunned. *What have I done?* Liam emerged from his room several minutes later, fully dressed. She ran after him as he darted down the stairs and out the front door. 'Listen to me, Liam.'

Reaching the carport, Liam pulled a set of keys from his pocket. 'I don't want to hear it. Not right now. I have to find Monique before she gets herself killed.' He was in his car and gone in a flash.

She turned back to the house, freezing as Brendan stepped outside.

'I'm so fucking sorry, Lana. I never meant to hurt your chances with Liam.'

'It's not your fault. I should've stopped things progressing that far. I don't know what came over me.'

'I do. It starts with L and makes your aura bright red.' Brendan smiled.

She rolled her eyes. 'I didn't—'

A pair of strong arms pulled Alannah off the ground, hoisting her onto the roof of the carport. A man held her back against his body and a knife at her throat. 'This has been a very entertaining piece of family drama to watch, but all good shows must come to an end.'

'Austin?' Alannah croaked the name, overwhelmed by the rising terror she felt with the cold steel against her skin.

'Hello again, beautiful.' His tone was full of bitterness. 'Looks like you've got yourself mixed up in an interesting love triangle. Let me see if I have this right. Liam and Alannah are in love, but that's not enough for our kinky Alannah is it? She's gotta have more, so she seduces Brendan, who is fed up with holding back from months of pent-up sexual frustration… and bam! It happens, but Liam finds out and loses his shit. This leaves Alannah without the man she loves and wishing she had behaved herself because she knows it'll never be more than sex with Brendan. Or will it? Does that sum it up?'

'What the fuck do you want, Austin?' Brendan roared from the ground.

'The same as you and Liam: I want Alannah. Only I'm not afraid to take her. Here's how this is going to work. I'm going to leave with Alannah, and nobody will get hurt. But if anyone tries to stop me, I will use this knife.' He pressed the tip of the blade into her throat, producing a droplet of blood.

'Please, Austin, this isn't you. Tara must be pulling your puppet strings,' Alannah pleaded.

'That's where you are wrong, my dear. I serve my Queen freely.'

'Then kill me already. I'd rather die than become a vampire.'

'*No, Lana!* Don't!' Brendan cried.

'His love for you is touching, really. But I feared you might say something like that. Thing is, my Queen really wants me to bring you back alive; so, I brought a backup plan. *Advance!*' he called out. A large mob of vampires and ghouls stepped out of the trees and slowly moved towards Brendan. 'I wonder if you love Brendan as much as he loves you. Give yourself over to me and my friends will back down. Otherwise, we will stand here and watch them tear your cousin limb from limb and feast on his flesh and blood.'

Alannah swallowed a lump in her throat. 'Fine. You win. Just don't hurt him.'

'*Lana, no!*' Brendan screamed as he moved closer to them.

'Naw, so sweet. Makes me speculate on how much the two of you really feel for each other. I guess you'll never know. Men, stand down and return to base.' Austin pulled Alannah into a firm hold and rose into the air.

She could no longer see Brendan, but she heard him crying after her as Austin floated down towards the road.

'*Lana!*' Brendan screamed as though at a lost limb, anguished and real as death.

Chapter Twenty

Liam pulled into his driveway and killed the engine. He threw his head back against the seat and closed his eyes. *Could my love-life get any more twisted and complicated?* After driving around for about an hour to check Monique's usual haunts two or three times, he had returned unsuccessful. He hoped she had found somewhere safe to hide out.

It was time to confront Alannah and Brendan. *Why can't my douchebag brother keep his hands to himself?* Liam got out of the car and stormed into the house. Feeling parched, he beelined for the kitchen to grab a bottle of water.

'You can't simply waltz into her hideout, Brendan. It would be suicide.' Dad's stern voice drifted in from the direction of the dining room. 'I know you're hurting, but you need to think rationally. Let the Council handle this.'

Curiosity got the better of him, so Liam popped his head around the corner and saw Brendan and his friends sitting at the table with Dad. No sign of Alannah though. This was probably his chance to catch her alone before kicking his brother's arse again. He was about to make his way upstairs when Brendan looked up and caught his eye. *Shit! Had he been crying*? His eyes were red and puffy in addition to the bruising around his left eye from Liam's punch.

Ducking out of view, Liam headed to the stairs. He was not ready to deal with Brendan's drama. But he only made it up the first three steps before a voice stopped him.

'Where are you going?'

Turning, he met the scowl on Brendan's face. 'To talk to Lana. She is *my* girlfriend, after all.'

'She won't be *yours* much longer.'

'Fuck you, arsehole.' Liam resumed his climb.

'You won't find her up there.'

Liam sighed. He was not in the mood for Brendan's games. 'Where, pray tell, is she?'

'I don't know for certain, but if I were to hazard a guess, I'd say Tara's hideout in the Hills.'

His heart stopped for a moment as he spun around to face Brendan again. 'What the fuck?'

'Austin took her after you left. Sound familiar? Liam abandons Lana, leaving her at Austin's mercy.'

It felt as though he was flying when he charged at Brendan and knocked him back into the wall. 'I left her with *you*, you little shit! Don't pin this on me.'

'Why not? If you hadn't run away like a pansy, she wouldn't have gone after you and Austin wouldn't have grabbed her.'

'And if you weren't about to shove your tongue down her throat and Gods know what else, I wouldn't have left in such a fury.' Liam practically spat his retort in Brendan's face.

Brendan cast his gaze downward. 'I was trying really fucking hard to resist her.' His voice had dropped to a whisper.

'What was really going on with you and Lana?'

'In short? Nothing.'

Liam shook his head. 'Bullshit. I saw what almost transpired between you. I want the truth.'

'I'm telling you the truth, bro. Nothing like that has ever happened before. Monique's intrusion probably left her frustrated. Her aura was flashing "come fuck me signals" all over the place and she was literally begging me to kiss her.'

'She asked you to kiss her?' *How could Lana betray me like that? And so soon after being intimate with me.*

'Well, not verbally. I read it in her thoughts.'

Liam felt his jaw drop. 'You can read minds now?'

Brendan nodded. 'Surprise! Just keep that little detail between us though, hey?'

'Since when?'

'A few months now. Whatever almost happened, it was nothing. She's in love with you Liam, not me.'

'You must take me for a fool because I saw the way she was looking at you. That wasn't nothing.' Sick of his brother's face, Liam marched away and shut himself in his room. Collapsing on his bed, he kicked off his shoes and stripped back to his boxers. He felt a wave of nausea when he thought of how close he had come to making love to a girl who would happily jump from his bed into Brendan's. Thinking back, he realised he had been an idiot to believe Alannah when she told him the flirting with Brendan meant nothing. He should have seen this coming, especially after what he had overhead Alannah telling her friend Emma all those years ago.

'You wanna tell me what's going on with Liam?' Dad's voice startled Brendan as he watched Liam walking off in another huff.

'Not really.'

'That wasn't a question, son. I'm guessing that shiner was his doing?'

Brendan sighed. 'Fine. But you'd better sit down.' They walked into the living room and took their usual seats. 'Firstly, did you know Liam and Alannah were a couple?'

Dad's wide eyes answered even before he spoke. 'Ah, no. I assume this must be a recent development since she recently ended her relationship with Austin.'

'Officially, they hooked up on the second day of term. Alannah dumped Austin because of Liam. But it's been a long time coming. They have always been in love with each other.'

'I see. Is that why Monique left abruptly? She was jealous?' It was almost possible to see the gears turning in his father's brain as he put the pieces together.

'Yup. But there's more.' He took a deep breath. 'I also happen to have some strong feelings for Alannah and Liam knows this. He warned me to keep my hands off her.' Brendan paused to gather his courage. His old man was not going to like the next part.

Dad narrowed his eyes. 'You didn't heed his warning, did you?'

'I tried, believe me I tried. Technically I didn't do anything. But there was an incident earlier tonight…'

'Go on,' Dad prompted him after a moment of silence.

'After Liam ran off after Monique, Lana and I had a… uh… heated moment in the hallway. We were on the verge of kissing when Liam caught us. Hence the black eye.'

Dad was shaking his head in disbelief. 'You couldn't leave well enough alone, could you? You were always jealous and coveted what your brother had.'

His words cut deep. 'We're not kids anymore. This isn't like fighting over toys.'

'I know that, Brendan. This is much more serious. You made a move on his girl. You're lucky to have escaped with one black eye.'

'You sound so misogynistic. We are talking about Alannah here. She is not just "Liam's girl."'

'Watch your tone, young man. I'm perfectly aware of whom we are speaking and frankly, I'm appalled by both of you for betraying Liam.'

Brendan was furious. He rose from his chair and towered over his dad. 'Don't my feelings count for anything here? Wait—no—of course they wouldn't! Not when compared with those of your fucking golden boy. *Well, fuck you Dad!*' He was fed up with the lot of them. Had they all forgotten what happened to Alannah? It was time for someone to act. He raced into the cellar and grabbed Alannah's athame.

'What are you doing?' Dad called from the doorway.

'I'm getting her back.'

'You will do no such thing. It's too dangerous.'

After collecting a few other weapons and crystals, Brendan stood face to face with his father. Sometime in the last couple of years he had managed to outgrow the man in height and muscle tone. 'Get out of my way.'

'Don't be stupid, Brendan. You'll get yourself killed.'

'Why do you care? I've only ever been one huge disappointment in your eyes.' He used his superior strength to push past. Bolting up the stairs, he burst into Liam's room.

Liam sat up in bed and glared at him. 'What the—'

441

'*Shut up!* I'm only gonna say this once, so you'd better listen carefully. I don't give a shit what you think of me or how you feel about that almost-kiss. Austin kidnapped the woman we love tonight and here you are moping about like a sad-sack. I, for one, am not gonna sit back and wait for the Council's members to get off their lazy arses and do something. I'm gonna get her out of there, even if it kills me, which it probably will. But I'd stand a higher chance of success with your help. So, why don't you stop being a pussy! Lana needs you now more than ever. What do ya say?'

Liam's outer aura resembled the Aurora Australis as waves of different emotions washed over him while Brendan spoke. When he concluded his tirade, the colours surrounding Liam settled to a courageous orange. 'Fine. Let me get dressed.'

He leaned against the doorframe and waited with his arms crossed.

Black jeans, black t-shirt, black hoodie. It was the same outfit Brendan had changed into. Liam was a dolt in many respects, but when it came to matters of war, he knew exactly what he was doing. They both made their way out to Liam's Audi in silence.

Brendan had not banked on the farewell party waiting for them by the car. As much as he loved his friends, he was not keen for any more delays.

'We're going with you,' Connor announced.

He raised his brow in surprise. 'You guys know this is certain death, right?'

'Yeah, but this is Alannah we're talking about. You guys aren't the only ones who love her.'

Brendan looked around at the assembled group. Bailey and Cara were there of course, but they had also recruited the help of Locky, Ben, Nick, and Caleb. Even a few of Liam's mates joined the party. 'I guess she has that effect on people. Come on, time's a-wasting.' They all loaded into various vehicles. To avoid the tension with Liam, Brendan chose to ride with Nick. It was heartening to see how many mages and other magical folk rallied around him and Liam.

Grandmother dearest is in for one hell of a rude shock.

After opening her eyes, Monique gasped as she realised she was chained up against some dusty old stone wall. The last thing she remembered was running down Liam's driveway, then nothing but blackness. *Someone must have knocked me unconscious, but why?*

Shivering, Monique looked down and found all but her bra and panties missing. When she noticed her fingers were bare, she panicked. *They took my channelling rings!* Whoever captured her either thought they held some monetary value or knew what they were really for. The latter prospect terrified her.

She took in her surroundings. Judging by the old barrels, the room must have been a wine-cellar at some point. But the various anchor points bolted into the walls, along with the stainless-steel tray of surgical tools sitting beyond her reach, suggested the space had been repurposed for more nefarious use. It was a dimly lit area, with one small filament globe in the stone ceiling.

The sound of a bolt shifting out of its lock drew her attention to the door. 'Ah, I see you are awake at last.' Tara Winters stepped into the room.

Her blood froze. 'Wha… what do you want from me? I th… thought we had a deal?'

'That is right, we had a deal. But you are yet to fulfil your end of the bargain despite having the time and opportunity to do so. Where is it, Monique?'

'I… I don't know. I tried looking, b… but couldn't find it.'

'You are lying. I know, because I can still read your surface thoughts and I sense you are trying to hide something. Now tell me, where is it?'

Shit! Her mental block was not strong enough. Closing her eyes, she took a deep breath and focused more. She visualised the tendrils of Tara's power creeping into her mind and pushed them out. One by one, she pried them away and warded herself. 'There's a mystic chest in their ritual room. It was the only place I didn't look, so I assume it was in there. I couldn't get the chest open.'

Tara picked up a scalpel and stepped closer. 'Couldn't… or wouldn't?'

Her eyes widened at the sight of the blade.

'You have two options, Monique. You can either let me into that precious little head of yours, or you can slowly bleed out from the hundreds—or possibly thousands—of tiny cuts I will inflict upon you. What will it be?'

'Your Majesty, sorry to interrupt, but we have her.' The familiar man's voice came from upstairs.

The distraction was a welcome relief. At least she would not have to endure any torture yet. But her heart sank when she watched Austin enter the cellar and chain Alannah's unconscious body to the

445

opposite wall. *The war is as good as over before it has really begun.*

'You have done well, my pet. Come, let me reward you a little. My granddaughter will not wake for a while.' Tara pulled Austin out of the room.

They bolted the door shut, leaving Monique alone with her thoughts and Liam's unconscious cousin.

Chapter Twenty-One

When Alannah came to, the first thing she noticed was an intense, throbbing headache. She was afraid to open her eyes and accept defeat. Perhaps if she went back to sleep, she thought, her dreams could become her reality. Her subconscious returned to that moment in Liam's bedroom, only this time there was no intrusion. *After pulling on the rubber, he mounted her gently. He penetrated her, driving himself deep inside and bringing her to climax over and over, all while telling her how much he loved her.*

A strange rattling noise brought her back to the real world and her eyes flicked open.

'About time you woke up. I was starting to get bored.'

'Monique? What are you doing here?' *And why is she only wearing underwear?* That was when Alannah noticed her own state of undress matched the girl on the opposite wall. *Did my dreams take a turn for the worse?*

'Waiting to be tortured. Apparently, it doesn't pay to get on your grandmother's bad side. But you probably knew that, huh?'

Fuck! So, this was it. She was Tara's prisoner and would soon become another of her vampire servants. 'What did you do to piss her off?'

'It's what I didn't do. She wanted me to steal a trinket from you. But there was no way in hell I was doing anything to help that bitch. I lied and told her I'd do it so she would leave me alone. Probably not my brightest moment.'

Who would have thought Monique Lane would ever earn my respect? Alannah laughed. 'I bet she was furious.'

Monique smiled. 'Yeah, that's putting it mildly. Look, I'm sorry for how I acted with Liam. I know how much he loves you. I couldn't handle losing him again. But if I'm honest with myself, I never really had him in the first place. Even during the years I dated him, I knew his heart belonged to you.'

Alannah's chest tightened. It hurt to think about what she had lost. Even if by some miracle she escaped this hellhole, Liam would never forgive her. 'Thanks. Not that it matters now, but I think I blew it with Liam.'

'What? How?' Monique perked up and spoke with more volume.

She sighed. 'It happened after you left. What started out as some innocent flirting with Brendan rapidly escalated into a heated moment. Liam caught us in what felt like an almost-kiss. That's what it looked like to him, anyway. I don't know what Brendan's intentions were.'

'I knew it! You totally want Brendan too. Did you ask him about his feelings?'

'Yeah. He said he's not in love with me.'

Monique shook her head and laughed. 'And you believed him? That guy has had a boner for you since you returned.'

'If anything, it's probably only physical attraction. To be honest, I don't really know how I feel about Brendan, but I know I love Liam, and the thought of losing him is heart-breaking.'

'That's something I can relate to.' Monique gave her a wicked grin. 'But come on, you can't tell me you're not at least curious about what it would feel like to have sex with Brendan.'

'Maybe a little.'

Monique arched an eyebrow and gazed at her sceptically.

'Okay, fine. More than a little. You know, you're probably the only girl who's slept with both those guys. If either of us should be jealous, it's me.'

A satisfied grin took over Monique's visage. 'I never thought of it that way, but you're right.'

'So… who was better?'

Monique giggled. 'You aren't serious! You don't really want to know, do you?'

'Sure, I do. It's not like I'm gonna get a chance to find out for myself.'

Frowning, Monique's tone turned serious. 'Have you resigned already?'

Have I? 'I dunno. I guess so. Aren't you?'

'No. There's gotta be some way out of here. What if we both try to channel the surrounding matter together?'

'I s'pose that might work, but then what?'

'We could summon a pair of big ass bolt-cutters. I know my dad has a pair in his shed that could break these chains.'

'I never thought I'd say this, but you're a fucking genius Monique. Let's give it a try.' They both closed their eyes and Alannah began to slow her breathing down. After a few minutes of meditation, she pressed her hands against the stone wall and drew on the mana within the atoms making up the rocks. As she felt the buzz of power collect in her hands, she directed the flow of energy in Monique's direction.

'You can stop now.'

When Alannah opened her eyes, Monique was holding the bolt-cutters. She could almost taste her freedom.

After cutting her own chains, Monique stepped forward and got to work on Alannah's. As soon as Monique finished, Alannah stretched her limbs and basked in their moment of victory.

'That was the easy part. Now to get out of wherever the hell we are. Any ideas?'

'What about magiportation?' Alannah suggested.

Monique sighed. 'I already thought of that, but I can't sense any ley lines within range.'

'If you can lend me your powers, I could create a golem from the clay beneath the cellar floor. We could imbue it with the strength to break down the door and smash a few vampire heads.'

'Sounds like a plan.'

Everything was dark and quiet on the approach to Tara's hideout. Brendan looked across to Liam and waited. He was listening to his brother's thoughts for the signal he needed.

'Okay, Brendan. Go.'

As soon as his brother gave him the command, he stealthily led his taskforce around the back of the house.

Their strategy was simple enough. Liam's team would create a diversion with an outright assault, while Brendan located Alannah and got her out. He brought Connor with him in case any healing became necessary, and Bailey could provide covering fire. But if things went according to plan, he would not need either of them.

He found a hiding spot in the back garden and waited. Liam's next signal should be obvious enough. But the sudden tremor beneath his feet, followed by shouting inside the house, were not what Brendan expected. Connor and Bailey both shot him concerned glances. *Is that magic, or an earthquake?*

The ground shook more violently, and the guards posted at the back door ran inside. Liam must have taken advantage of the confusion within to make his move, because the sky lit up with the biggest fork of lightning Brendan had ever seen, and it appeared to strike somewhere in the front yard.

Brendan's heart was racing, and he was eager to move, but he forced himself to wait and count a full minute before doing so. Stepping up to the windows, he peered inside, but it was too dark to make out any details. He closed his eyes and tried to get a read on Alannah.

A few minutes later, he breathed a sigh of relief. She was still a mage, and by the feel of it, she was performing some powerful magic. He waved the guys over and stepped inside. It was necessary to heighten his vision to see, so he spoke telepathically, *'Stick behind me and stay close.'*

The minute Brendan stepped inside, a strong arm grabbed him around his throat and reeled him up against a man's body. A hand clasped his mouth, so he could not even cry out a warning to his friends.

'I should kill you now,' a familiar voice hissed in his ear in a hushed tone.

Brendan felt a chill down his spine as the guy who had once been his best friend showed his true colours. Some part of him had been holding on to the hope Tara had been pulling Austin's puppet strings all this time.

'But I think I'll have too much fun hurting you.' Austin ran a sharp blade along Brendan's cheek, causing him to flinch from the sting of the shallow cut.

Their physical contact allowed Brendan to get a solid read on Austin and his heart sank at the realisation there was no cloud of mental compulsion in the traitor's mind. Oddly, there were no surface thoughts available for him to read either, but that was not surprising. The Lich Bitch had probably provided all her goons with protection charms, which would have been how Austin slipped through Brendan's radar in the beginning.

All attempts to wriggle free of Austin's grip were futile. The jerk was unnaturally strong, too powerful even for a mage well-trained in the art of combat. As Austin dragged him further into the house, he heard a couple of muffled cries behind him.

Austin sniggered as Brendan tried to turn his head back to see what was happening. 'Looks like the ghoul guards have caught our other mates. I guess it's just us for now.'

Austin freed Brendan's mouth, allowing his bitter retort to spring forth: 'You will pay for raping Lana, you fucking arsehole.'

Stopping before a solid wood door, Austin laughed. 'Such a pity you turned into a pussy-whipped coward. Tell you what, I'll give you a chance to redeem yourself. Help me with Alannah's transformation ritual and I'll let you live. Not only that, but I'll even share her with you.'

The implications of Austin's offer hit him straight away. Involvement in such a ritual would send him down the path of a dark mage, if not result in an outright curse of his own. *Is it worth it for a chance to save my own life and be with Alannah?*

They both staggered as the ground shook violently beneath them. 'Fuck,' Austin cussed. The hint of fear in his voice suggested whatever was happening was not part of Tara's plan. 'Hurry up and decide, bro. I'm growing impatient.'

The heavily bolted door across the hall collapsed in front of them, forcing Austin to jump back, but his reflexes were not quick enough to avoid a blow to the head which sent him flying and losing his grip of Brendan.

As he dropped to the floor, Brendan rolled out through the doorway in time to see two figures step through it, followed by a big fuck-off golem. Once the dust had settled, he copped an eyeful of Alannah and Monique's scantily clad bodies, complete with manacles around their wrists and ankles.

Jumping up, he brushed himself off and grinned. 'Hot damn, I feel like I've walked onto the set of an award-winning porno.' He kept his voice hushed as he directed his comment toward Alannah.

She grinned. 'But not an Oscar award.'

'No, that would be inconceivable.' A glance in Austin's direction told him the vampire was out cold. He sent off a quick mental message to Liam: '*I found Alannah and Monique.*'

'*Good, get them out of here.*'

He gestured for the girls to follow. 'Come on. I know a quick way outta here.'

'Wait, what about Fluffy?'

'Fluffy?'

'My golem. I named him after my first cat.'

Brendan laughed. 'You are full of surprises. I don't think he should come with us though. He'd draw too much attention. Can you instruct him to move through to the front of the house, crushing all the vampires and ghouls he encounters? Could be a helpful distraction.'

Alannah nodded. 'Right.' She placed a hand on the golem's arm, closed her eyes and softly chanted a new set of instructions.

Fluffy took off a moment later and the girls followed Brendan outside.

Connor's eyes practically bulged from their sockets when he saw Alannah. 'Um, hi. Are you hurting anywhere?'

'Nah, I'm good.' Alannah slapped Connor on the shoulder. 'But thanks for asking.'

With a sigh, Connor slumped his shoulders and averted his gaze.

It had not ever occurred to Brendan before that night how much his mates also fancied Alannah. *I wonder if Liam has noticed the extent of his competition.*

'Ahem.' Monique grabbed everyone's attention. 'Can we go now, please?'

Brendan retrieved a couple of citrine crystals from his backpack and handed them to Alannah and Monique. 'Did you girls wanna summon some clothing first? Not that I'm complaining, but it's pretty cold out here and I don't want you dying of exposure.'

'Ah, thanks.' Alannah took the crystal and promptly produced an outfit much like Brendan's. He kept his eyes glued to her. *It's amazing how she even makes getting dressed look erotic.* As she tied the last of her boot laces, she looked up at him and held his gaze for a few seconds, searching his expression. She stood, breaking their eye contact. 'Well, I'm ready.'

'Me too,' Monique chimed in. 'Let's go.'

Brendan was scanning the grounds. 'Where's Bailey?'

'He took off after a couple of ghouls through those trees. You go, I'll wait here for him.'

'But…' Brendan began to protest. He hated the idea of leaving his friends behind.

Connor cut him off. 'We all signed up for this. Get the girls to safety.'

Nodding silently, Brendan gave Connor a sideways hug and pat on the back before leading Alannah and Monique around to the front yard. He made a point of keeping behind the cover of trees along the fence-line.

Brendan caught his first glimpse of Nick's car when he heard Alannah gasp behind him. Spinning around, he saw her frozen in place by something catching her attention. When he followed her sightline, he cursed under his breath. Tara was advancing on Liam. She had him suspended in the air by some invisible hand that was choking him. 'No Lana, don't!' Brendan hissed as he grabbed her arm. He had come this far—he could not lose her now.

Ignoring him, she shrugged free of his grasp and charged into the fray. '*Liam!*'

The moment the ground began to rumble, several vampire guards burst forth from the front door to join their comrades on the front porch. Their clustered formation was too good for Liam to resist, so without any further ado, he brought a shitload of lightning strikes down on their cursed arses. Their bodies crumpled to the ground, sending the distinct odour of burnt flesh wafting in his direction.

That was too easy, Liam thought.

A cliché evil laugh emerged through the front door, followed by a cloaked figure. 'Do you honestly think I would station so few guards out here? That I was unaware of you breaching my perimeter tonight, or on those previous occasions?'

Liam had little patience for discourse with his horrid grandmother. Without hesitation, he sent a lightning bolt in her direction.

But Tara was one step ahead of him, deflecting the attack and redirecting it at Blake's real form, not one of his many illusory images. His best mate screamed in agony as he dropped to the ground.

Shit! This woman is powerful and brutal.

She laughed. 'Have you only come to realise that now, dear boy? Your father has not told you much about me, clearly.'

And an expert mind reader who can bypass our mental defence spells! Great.

'Let me introduce you to my pets.' Tara's arm extended in a sweeping gesture.

A second later, a swarm of ghouls and vampires stepped out from behind the trees and shrubs surrounding the large front lawn area.

'I'm going to give you a choice, Liam. Send your friends home and join me or die here tonight.'

'That is no choice. I'd rather die than further your sickening cause.'

She grinned viciously. 'So, you would not even consider it to save your brother?'

'Are you okay Brendan?' He frowned at the radio silence.

'I guess Brendan is a little preoccupied with my new favourite. I do wonder how long Austin will keep up that torture.'

Shit! So much for that plan.

'Sorry, Liam dear, but no one gets the better of me, not even my own family.' There was no hint of remorse in her tone, only pure malice. 'This is your last chance. Stand down and join me and I will spare your brother from further harm. Just think — following your precious Lana's path will make life much easier.'

'I still refuse to sink to your level,' Liam spat.

The tremor he had felt earlier intensified and Tara's smile vanished. 'That troublesome girl,' she hissed. 'I thought Austin used cold iron to restrain them. You lot,' she pointed to a group of ghouls, 'get in there and stop my granddaughter. The rest of you, engage the enemy, but leave my grandson to me.' She returned her attention to Liam. 'I am going to enjoy watching the life drain from your worthless body, you piece of Council scum.'

The sounds of blades clashing, teeth gnashing, and claws slashing filled the night air. Drawing his sword, Liam charged Tara, but she pushed him back with a strong gust of wind, knocking him to the ground.

'*I found Alannah and Monique.*' Brendan's thoughts pierced Liam's mind.

He let out a quick sigh of relief. At least this fight would not be for naught. *'Good, get them out of here.'* The moment he replied to his brother, Tara's lips curved upward again, and he reprimanded himself for forgetting she could read his mind. *We are all fucked!* There was no way to outwit or overpower this woman. Well, he would still die trying. Rising to his feet, he attempted to move toward her.

But Tara's arms jutted forward and lifted as Liam felt his feet leaving the ground. Her hands appeared to grip something as an invisible force tightened around his throat. He struggled at first, but there was no use fighting anymore. The vice around his neck was crushing his windpipe, depriving him of air. His vision began to blur as his imminent death approached.

Chapter Twenty-Two

When Tara spied Alannah approaching, she dropped Liam and laughed maniacally. 'It never ceases to amaze me how stupid people will act for the sake of love. You could have been well on your way by now, dear child.'

Clutching the citrine tightly, Alannah raced forward, empowered by her love for Liam and hatred for Tara. With a mere thought, she summoned a sword from the family armoury. Gripping the hilt as she continued to advance, she prayed in a whisper, 'I call upon The Dagda. Please bless this weapon with your strength and magic.'

'*Lana, no! Get out of here!*' Liam's strained voice shouted.

The sword began to glow when she reached him. 'I'm not leaving you. Here, take my sword and give me yours.'

After rising to his feet, he swapped swords with her in time to run the blade into a vampire who ran at them.

She blessed the sword she took from him and struck out at a ghoul who tried to sneak up on her. Power was surging through her and it felt incredible. Movement in her peripheral vision caught her attention and she grinned as Brendan closed ranks with her on the left. She noticed he held a small dagger. 'Give me your weapon to bless.'

'Nah, I'm good. You did this one already.' Opening his hand more, he revealed her athame.

'Oh, what a lovely surprise.' Tara's bitter voice drew their gazes. 'A family reunion. Such a pity Ross couldn't join us too.'

Alannah's heart began to sink as she observed the swarm of cursed encircling them, shuffling slowly forward with teeth and claws bared. But something sparkled on Tara's finger, catching her eye. In a flash, Alannah lunged forward and clasped her grandmother's hand. She glared straight into the startled woman's eyes as she spoke. 'If a reunion is what you're after, I can do you one better.' She looked to the sky. 'Come forth Aileen Winters and all spirits who call themselves my ally.'

Hundreds of white, swirling shapes circled above them, slowly descending as each spirit manifested into a recognisable form. Landing, they surrounded the army of cursed and charged them. It was quite a sight to behold, as these beings of pure, heavenly light tore the vampires and ghouls limb from limb.

Alannah spotted a warm, friendly face. Stepping forward, Mum smiled briefly before turning to face Tara with a scowl. 'Hello mother. Up to your old tricks, I see. I thought I told you to leave Alannah alone.'

'That was on the condition she remained uninitiated. She is very much an active initiate now, so no more deal.'

Alannah gasped as realisation dawned. Her hand was still gripping Tara's when the woman whirled on the spot and threw her at Austin, who stepped out of the swarm of cursed.

'Grab her, quick, and disarm her.'

Austin pulled her into his arms, holding her firmly with her back against his chest. He yanked the sword from her hand and slipped it into his belt.

Tara grinned, turning back to face Aileen, Liam and Brendan, who all froze. 'Now if any of you make a move against me, Austin will kill your precious Alannah. I suggest you all drop your weapons and stand down.'

Everyone who held a weapon obeyed her instruction.

Using his bodyweight, Austin pushed Alannah forward slightly. They stood directly behind Tara. He spoke softly in her ear: 'Whatever happens, I want you to know I will always love you and I'm sorry for all the pain I caused you.' His tone was genuine and caring, without any of the bitterness she had come to expect from him of late. A second later, he returned the sword to her hand and released his grip as he whispered, 'Now!'

Alannah did not hesitate to plunge the blade deep into Tara's heart. Her grandmother went rigid and let out a strange gurgling sound before collapsing.

At the sight of their dead Queen sprawled out and bleeding on the ground, most of the cursed fled the scene. The few who remained were either injured or bowing in submission. Austin was the only one who remained standing. He smiled at her, slowly dropping to his knees like the others.

She returned the smile and mouthed a 'thank you' before turning back to face her friends.

Brendan rushed forward and scooped her up into his arms, lifting her off the ground as he swung her around. *'You were fucking amazing!'*

Alannah laughed. 'Put me down, I'm getting dizzy.'

'Oh right. Sorry.' He set her down and grinned widely.

Glancing at Liam, Alannah noticed his beetroot-red visage, and the veins pulsing in his temples. Everything seemed to slip into slow motion as she watched him grab a blessed sword from the ground and charge toward Austin. By the time she realised what he was doing, it was too late. But she still screamed at him: *'Liam, no!'* She sank to her knees as the blade pierced the vampire's heart.

Austin gave her one last look as his life slipped away. Not an expression of surprise or pain, but of love.

Liam glanced back at her briefly to see tears streaming down her face. He picked up Blake's lifeless body and walked away, leaving her at a complete loss.

What the hell happened? One minute, Brendan was revelling in victory with Alannah. The next minute, Liam lost his shit and killed Austin. He drove his thoughts into Liam's brain, *'Seriously, what the fuck, bro? Sure, the guy had it coming; but still, there are ladies present.'*

He watched as Liam turned a cursory glance toward Alannah. There was still battle rage in his expression, but his aura told Brendan something different.

Liam's thoughts filled his mind. *'Tell her I did it to protect her; because I love her.'*

Brendan shook his head. Even though he understood Liam's motives, the guy was a Class A moron who would be lucky if Alannah ever forgave him.

Liam gathered up Blake's scorched body and walked away. *Shit!* Brendan did not even notice Blake had fallen. A quick scan of the battlefield revealed he was not the only one. A few others were sitting up nursing wounds, but the shot of green hair atop the motionless head of a goblin drew his attention.

'Locky!' he cried as he rushed over. 'Oh Christ, dude!' Tears began to trickle down Brendan's face at the sight of his mate's limp body. There were several ghoul bites, including one that had torn a large gash in the side of Lachlan's neck. Judging by the red stain on the grass, the guy must have died from blood loss.

'It's okay, man. I'll take his body home. Go comfort Alannah.' Brendan looked up into Caleb's teary eyes.

Rising to his feet, he nodded and patted Caleb on the shoulder. Approaching Alannah, the tears in her eyes broke his heart. Kneeling beside her, he put his arm across her shoulders. 'Hey, let's get out of here. I don't know about you, but this place gives me the creeps.'

She looked at him and nodded. With Brendan's assistance, she rose to her feet and let him lead her to the car.

When he reached Nick's station wagon, one glimpse of Bailey's unconscious body on the back seat had his heart rate galloping and his palms perspiring.

Holding their friend in his lap, Connor looked at Brendan with an ashen face. 'I'm trying everything I can, but he needs your dad ASAP.'

'What happened to him?' Brendan asked.

'Ghoul bite.' Connor shifted slightly to show him the large chunk of flesh missing from Bailey's side. It was deep enough to see the muscle tissue.

'*Fuck!*' It was depressing how few of them were returning unscathed. Images of Locky's dead body flashed in his mind and clawed at his heart. Losing Blake was a huge blow too. He may have been Liam's best mate, but their older cousin was still a decent bloke.

The sight must have been too much for Alannah because she buried her face against Brendan's chest.

'You guys can ride up front,' Nick called from the driver's seat.

He let Alannah climb in first, pulling her onto his lap to make room for Monique.

When they got home, Nick and Connor carried Bailey inside, where Dad was waiting for them. They placed him on the bed Bailey had been using so Dad could begin his work.

Liam and most of his friends had retired for the night, but Brendan and his mates gathered in the living room and waited anxiously for news on Bailey's condition. Alannah clung to Brendan the whole time.

While the guys were debriefing on the fight, Brendan pressed his mouth to Alannah's ear. 'Hey, Liam still loves you. That's why he did it.'

'He has a funny way of showing it. Was it out of jealousy because he saw Austin as a threat again? Does that mean you're his next target?' Her tone was intensely bitter.

Brendan sighed. 'No, Lana. He did it to protect you. If I were in his shoes, I would have killed Austin too, although I wouldn't have done it in front of you. The guy was a scumbag and the Council had already sentenced him to death.'

She flashed him a glare. 'Do you know what he said to me before I killed Tara?'

Brendan shook his head.

'He told me he was sorry, and that he would always love me. He was the one who enabled me to take Tara down.'

'Christ! You sound like a domestic abuse victim, Lana. That jerk date raped you and almost turned you into a vampire. If I hadn't pulled you out of there, you'd have much sharper teeth by now.'

'I know. You're right. Still, I can't help but wonder if he did all that to win Tara's trust and give me that opportunity.' She had an interesting point.

'I guess we'll never know.' He wondered about that mind shield of his. 'So… you did an amazing job out there tonight. How did it feel to kick arse like that?'

She grinned. 'Yeah, it felt exhilarating.'

It was so good to see her smile in the face of everything. 'You know I got a major hard-on when I saw you go all badass.'

She snorted. 'Trust you to have sex on the brain in the middle of a serious skirmish.'

He gave her his biggest smoulder. 'You ought to know sex is *always* on my mind.'

'No doubt,' she sighed. 'I know we did well to defeat Tara and most of her army, but I can't fight this nagging feeling in my chest that something's wrong.'

'We did lose a couple of friends tonight, and we still don't know if Bailey will survive.'

'True. I guess that must be why.'

As if on cue, Dad entered the room, and everyone stopped talking. 'Bailey is in a stable condition. He will recover well after some rest.' They all let out a chorus of relieved breaths. 'What you did last night was reckless and stupid. All of you could have been maimed or killed. You should have let the Council handle Alannah's rescue.'

The other guys lowered their heads submissively, but Brendan glared defiantly at his father.

'That said, I want to thank you all for saving my niece.'

Their heads rose.

'What you kids did took strength and courage. It proves your loyalty to this family. Which is why you are always welcome in my house from this day forth.' There were a few murmurs in the group. He smiled. 'Yes, even those of you who are not mages. But only you lot. I don't want…'

The din of chatter in the group made it impossible to hear him continue. Brendan rose and clapped his dad on the shoulder. 'I hope you realise you essentially declared this house party central. You should probably stock up on ingredients for that hangover cure.'

Dad shook his head walking away mumbling something about being a masochist.

Alannah felt exhausted, so she turned in despite her friends protests and Locky's vigil. She was making her way to the stairs when Monique stopped her in the kitchen.

'You got a minute?'

'I guess. What's up?'

Monique fidgeted uncomfortably with her head lowered. 'I uh… I wanted to apologise for the trouble I've caused you.'

Alannah's eyes widened. Even after their bonding session in Tara's cellar, she found it hard to fathom such remorse from Monique. 'Um, thanks.'

Raising her head, Monique focused on Alannah with serious, unblinking eyes. 'I promise I won't try anything more with Liam. I know things are well and truly over for us, and I respect that the two of you are in love with each other.'

'I appreciate that. Thank you.'

Monique walked across the room. Pausing at the door, she turned back and grinned. 'It was Brendan, by the way.'

Alannah squinted. 'What was Brendan?'

'Remember that question you asked me in the cellar?'

Casting her mind back, Alannah recalled their discussion and snorted. 'Figures.'

'I don't know if that knowledge will influence your decision concerning which brother you want to be with, but in either case, I'm still done with Liam. I can't promise to stay away from Brendan though.' She winked and left the room.

Alannah sighed and headed upstairs. As she passed Brendan's room, she noticed his light illuminating the gap beneath the door. Pressing her forehead to the wood panelling, she took a few deep breaths before knocking.

'Come in, Lana.'

After closing the door behind her, she took in the sight of Brendan, who sat above the covers of his bed. He wore a pair of grey trackpants, but no shirt. *It's fortunate he's holding his legs to his chest.* 'How did you know it was me?'

He shrugged without looking at her. 'Call it a hunch.' Lifting a glass Alannah only noticed in that moment, he took a sip of the amber liquid within.

She took a seat beside him and placed a comforting arm around his waist. 'How're you holding up?'

'I've been better.' After grabbing the whiskey bottle beside him, he turned and offered it to her. 'Want some?'

The Jameson's was practically begging for her to drink it, so she took the bottle. 'Thanks. Got a spare glass?'

'No, sorry. If it makes you feel better, I'll stop using mine and we can both slum it.' He downed the rest of his glass and threw the empty vessel aside, where it landed on a pile of dirty laundry.

Alannah took a few swigs from the bottle before returning it to Brendan. 'Wanna talk about it?'

He looked into her eyes for a moment. 'I'm a huge fucking mess of emotions right now. I'd like to focus on my grief for Locky, along with the other guys downstairs; but I'm also conflicted over Austin.' He sighed. 'That dude was my best mate for nine years. How do you turn your back on all those years of friendship? He hurt me, Lana. And I'm not only talking about the cuts he inflicted tonight.' He pointed to the fading scar on his cheek where the five-centimetre gash had almost vanished thanks to Connor's handiwork.

'I get that, Brendan. I really do. He hurt me too. Don't forget I was in love with the guy not so long ago.'

A sardonic laugh slipped from Brendan's lips. 'Trust me, I'll never forget what he did to you. That pain he caused you is what hurts me the most.' He chugged on the whiskey for a bit, piercing her eyes with an intense focus as he handed it to her. 'But it's not as simple as feeling hurt and betrayed, either. Something Austin said got me thinking that if I were in his shoes, I'd likely succumb to temptation too. I'm not angelic like Liam. I am full of darkness, Lana.'

'We all have darkness inside, even Liam. It's what we do to keep it in check that matters.'

'Trust me, gorgeous, my inner demons are much bigger than Liam's.'

Her chest tightened to see him like this. She wished she could reach into him and mend the damage. But she needed to know where she stood first. After drawing on some liquid courage, she gave him the bottle and took a deep breath. 'Brendan?' She gazed directly at him.

'Yessm?'

'About what happened in the hallway earlier…'

His breath hitched. 'I guess I took our game a little far. I'm sorry, Lana. I didn't mean to cause any trouble between you and Liam.'

Alannah's level of disappointment surprised her, but she buried her feelings. 'Apology accepted. It might pay to ease up on the game for a while, especially when Liam's around.'

'Of course.' His face betrayed a hint of a scowl before he gave her an impish grin. 'But not for too long.'

Laughing, she fell back into the bed. 'That's like no time.'

'I told you I'm wicked.' His eyes scanned her body. 'Christ, I need to get laid. Unless you want to do the honours, Lana, I suggest you remove your sexy arse from my bed right now.'

She folded her arms behind her head. 'Is that your way of propositioning me?'

He swiftly moved to straddle her, his face mere inches from her own. 'Is this your way of consenting to my proposition?' The heat between them was sweltering. Brendan did not usually press the weight of his body into her when they played this game, but he was not holding back this time.

Alannah could even feel the growing bulge in his pants.

Is he really playing, or is this for real? The raging fire in her core tugged at her resolve. *I'm done fighting this. If he does want me, he can fucking have me.*

Their eyes remained locked in a contest of wills for several long minutes.

Brendan leaped from the bed, grabbed a box of condoms from his drawers and headed for the door.

The moment Alannah realised he was not sticking around, the disappointment returned tenfold. 'Chicken,' she goaded him, trying to mask the anguish in her tone.

Stopping at the door, he refused to face her as he replied, 'I'll give you this round.'

When he walked out of the room, Alannah decided she would never allow herself to entertain sexual thoughts or feelings for Brendan ever again. *He does not want me, so garnering any hope will only frustrate me. If he only wants to play games, that is exactly what I'll do.*

There must be some truth to the adage 'time heals all wounds,' Alannah thought, because after two weeks she felt she had mourned Austin enough and was ready to forgive Liam. The two of them had been avoiding each other since the night at Tara's hideout and, on those occasions where they needed to be in the same room, the tension between them was palpable.

When he returned home from his morning surf, Alannah ambushed Liam on the back porch. 'We should talk.'

Liam jumped, spinning around to face her. '*Christ, Lana!* You scared the shit outta me.' He still wore his wetsuit through which Alannah could see every ridge and valley of his delicious eight-pack.

She tried to remind herself they still had unresolved issues to discuss. But when he ran a hand through his wet hair to pull the longer strands out of his eyes, she practically melted in a puddle of her own juices.

He hung up his surfboard, slumped into one of the patio chairs and sighed. 'So, talk.'

'Why did you kill Austin only minutes after he helped me defeat Tara?'

'Why did you want my brother to kiss you only minutes after we were about to make love?'

She stared at him intently. 'Answer my question first.'

'He hurt you, Lana. There was no excusing what he did. I could not risk him doing anything to you again. I'm not sorry for what I did, but I am sorry you had to see it.'

'Did you worry I still harboured feelings for him? Did you act out of jealousy at all?'

He frowned. 'No. Should I have worried? You took his death harder than I expected.'

'I was sad because I lost an ally and friend, but I wasn't in love with him anymore.'

Liam shook his head, spraying water about and sending a few drops in her direction. 'I don't understand how you could call that man a friend after what he did to you.'

'I don't expect you to understand. But thank you for your apology.' She breathed deeply. 'As for what happened with Brendan—' Liam stiffened and narrowed his eyes. 'Our encounter left me aroused and frustrated after Monique's interruption. When he instigated a round of our little game... things got carried away.'

'Game? What game?'

'We call it Sleazy Chicken. It's something we've been playing since we were six. We flirt and do sleazy shit. The first one of us to blush or chicken out loses the round. It was usually harmless fun.'

'Usually. Except when you almost kissed?'

She bit her bottom lip as she nodded.

He sat back and crossed his arms. 'Are you in love with Brendan?'

'No.' She did not hesitate. After two weeks of shutting those feelings away, she had almost convinced herself.

'You should be careful playing that game with him. I doubt his intentions are as innocent as yours.'

'We have spoken at length about our feelings and intentions since that night, and I can assure you there is nothing to worry about.'

He eyed her sceptically. 'You should still be careful. Despite what Brendan says, he is a hot-blooded guy, and I wouldn't put it past him to take things too far again. I don't want to see you get hurt.'

'I promise to be more careful.'

'Good. I'm glad that's settled.' He rose from his seat and headed for the door.

Alannah stood quickly. She wasn't finished with him. 'Liam, are you still in love with me?'

Turning back to face her, his expression softened. 'Always. And you?'

'Yes.'

He moved swiftly, pulling her into his arms and pressing his lips to hers. Gods, how she had missed his kisses. His mouth tasted extra tangy as their tongues found each other. Sweet and salty: such an addictive combination. When they finally came up for air, they were both panting.

'We should probably try to take things slow, though. After everything that's happened,' Alannah suggested.

She caught a flicker of disappointment in his eyes, but he smiled. 'Yeah, we should.'

'Why don't you go shower and change, then meet me in the living room and we can hang out.'

'I'd love to, but I've got a biology exam tomorrow, plus two other exams this week. I need to study.'

'Oh right. Sorry.' This time Alannah tried to hide her own disappointment. She had forgotten Year Twelve exams were much earlier than her own.

'But I'm sure I'll need a break tonight. Let's watch a movie after dinner.'

Alannah beamed. 'It's a date.'

Chapter Twenty-Three

Nine Months Later

The sound of the front-door closing had Alannah jumping to her feet and racing through the kitchen, to accost her boyfriend. Anticipation for the night ahead fuelled her, but glimpsing Liam in his work gear sent tingles coursing through her bloodstream. She had never figured herself the type to go weak at the knees for the boys in blue, but Liam in a police cadet uniform definitely did things for her. 'How are you? How was your day?'

Liam laughed as she jumped into his arms and swung her legs around his waist. 'I'm great and I could get used to greetings like this.' His mouth clamped down onto hers, kissing her deeply.

They had been going steady for nine months and Alannah doubted she would ever tire of Liam's strong, passionate kisses, or the feel of his rock-hard body pressing against her.

'Unless you're gonna invite me to join you, would you guys get a room?' Brendan called out as his footfalls approached from the hallway.

Snorting as she lowered herself to the ground, Alannah swung around to look at him. She kept her arm around Liam's waist as she gave Brendan her best attempt at bedroom eyes. 'Well come on.' Liam's body tensed, even though she had told him countless times the flirting was meaningless fun.

Brendan laughed as he drew closer to her. 'You know I would in a heartbeat, Lana, but I'd like to live long enough to see you graduate and Liam's eyes alone are killing me.' He slapped Liam on the shoulder and walked into the kitchen.

Alannah followed him with Liam close behind her. 'So how was school?'

Brendan had plans to finish high school so he could study a bachelor's degree and become a youth counsellor. It was a job he was going to be amazing at, and not only because of his powers as an enchanter. 'Good. How was TAFE?'

'So far so good. I'm especially loving pattern drafting and design work.' After discovering Nora's sewing machine eight months ago, Alannah had fallen in love with sewing and dressmaking. It was her ambition to run her own business as a designer and dressmaker of alternative fashions. She figured it would tie in well for her conjuring work, because she would be able to make robes and battle gear imbued with magic upon request. And her vision had driven her to explore the vocational education system in her senior year of high school.

'Sweet,' Brendan replied. 'Well, I'm gonna get ready for tonight.'

As soon as they had the room to themselves, Liam pulled her back into his arms and pressed his face into her neck. 'Gods, you smell so good. I should go shower. I probably stink after the physical training we had today.'

She inhaled his manly scent mingled with ocean fresh cologne. 'You smell pretty damn hot to me, but I might be biased.'

Liam smiled and shook his head. 'It still amazes me how you could get so turned on by my sweat.' He pressed a kiss to her forehead. 'I'll see you in a few minutes.'

Alannah had spent the last two hours getting ready for her big night, so she returned to the living room and picked up the fashion magazine she had been reading. Life had been relatively peaceful since the showdown with Tara. While there had been the odd run in with the town's ogres and other undesirables, most of the surviving vampires in the state kept to themselves and magic crime was at an all-time low. That was not to say Liam was in for an easy ride with his future career. Mundane crime kept the local police busy, but it was nothing they could not handle.

Even so, Alannah was still unable to shake the doubts that had lodged themselves in her subconscious after the night she had killed Tara Winters. The fact that the Council had been unable to locate the Queen's body during their clean-up operation, did not help to ease her mind either.

But this night was not a time to worry. When she looked up from her magazine at the two handsome men who stood before her, both dressed in tailored suits, she beamed with joy. Having the love and support of them both made her feel like the luckiest woman alive. The brothers stepped forward and linked arms with her as they escorted her from the house, down the garden path, towards the ceremonial grounds in her Uncle's backyard.

It was time to celebrate her eighteenth birthday by becoming a full magus and registered conjurer. The ceremony marked an important milestone on her magic path, possibly more important than her initiation. This ritual was not a secret, unsanctioned event: Alannah was done hiding. This was the night she stepped into the

public eye and joined the wider mage community —
one weighed down by archaic laws. But if she got
her way, that was all about to change. *The Council of
Mages will not know what hit them.*

To be continued...

What's Next?

Thank you for reading *Winter's Maiden 1*. I would be most grateful if you could show your support by leaving a rating or even a review.

Alannah's story will continue in:
Winter's Maiden 2
Pre-order now for November 2021 release.

Bonus Content

What happens when Liam and Alannah take a second chance at love? This bonus chapter will fill in some gaps with all the juicy details of their first official date:

Winter's Maiden 1: Second Chances

You can find this and more exclusive content on the FREEBIES page of my website: www.starlaarts.com

Winter's Maiden 2

The power to protect is also the power to corrupt.

When Alannah joined The Council of Mages, she expected an exciting life of fighting crime and ridding the world of evil. This could not have been further from the truth. Buried by bureaucracy, and bored out of her brains, Alannah is almost grateful when the Council's spotlight shines on her hometown.

An illegal potion hits the Unseelie Market, and the source gets tracked back to Gaeilge Shores. Unfortunately, this case is a little too close to home and when Alannah learns the truth, she becomes trapped within the web of lies surrounding Brendan and herself.

Amidst all the deception, Alannah and Brendan find the path to the ultimate truth. How much are they willing to risk by uncovering the secrets of the magic world? And will working for a common cause be the catalyst that finally brings them together?

AVAILABLE NOVEMBER 2021
Keep reading for a sample…

Chapter One

High Magus Kieran was the epitome of pompous ass. 'Thank you, Councillor Rowan. Councillor Alannah Winters, do you have anything to report?' He stared at her with a stern eye. Her appointment to the Fleurieu District Council of Mages still displeased him, and it continued to show in his open hostility at every meeting.

'There has not been much activity involving the use of Aether, Your Honour, and none of it has caused any negative energy.' As the representative for all mages attuned to Aether in her district, one of Alannah's responsibilities was to remain open to this mana source to detect any misuse and investigate the issue. Given how few mages were even capable of channelling the divine element, she had an easy time of it.

Being one of a handful of mages in the state with this attunement had its benefits. There was no competition when she applied to fill the seat vacated by the late Shaun Ó Máille in August of the previous year, a few days after her twentieth birthday. But even with the community endorsements she received following her epic showdown with Tara all those years ago, the High Magus was not happy about having a Winters woman on the Council.

'Are you certain of this?' Kieran did not second guess the other Council members.

He is such a chauvinistic bastard. Clenching her fists in her lap beneath the table, she bit back the sarcastic retort on the tip of her tongue. 'Yes, Your Honour.'

'Very well. On to our next matter of business…'

Most mages regarded the seat of Aether with reverence because the mage in that role has a direct link to the Gods. Alannah recently learned the High Magus treated her predecessor with far more respect. Kieran had always insisted Shaun Ó Máille present his report first rather than last. Still seething, she tuned out while Kieran harped on about some bureaucratic nonsense, catching the odd buzzword here and there like commendation, sanctioning, and authority. Using mindfulness meditation, she calmed herself.

This is so damn boring. Alannah had expected more focus on hunting magic criminals when she signed up for the Mages Council. It made her mourn the days of fighting her grandmother's threats. Gaeilge Shores may have been a dangerous place with Tara Winters around, but it was a hell of a lot more exciting.

A sudden nudge in her side brought Alannah's attention back to the room. She looked at Liam, the owner of the offending elbow, and met his frown as he gestured in Kieran's direction.

'Huh?'

The High Magus gave her a death glare. 'I asked, if you had an opinion on the matter, Councillor.'

'Oh. Sorry Your Honour. No, I have nothing to add.'

'I look forward to the day when you have anything at all to contribute to these meetings, Miss *Winters.*' His fellow cronies sniggered.

Aunt Nora, representative for emotions, smiled at her with pursed lips. As one of three women on the Council, along with Monique Lane, she understood the difficulties Alannah faced in such a patriarchal system.

Kieran glanced at his watch, and turned to face his daughter, Monique, who took the minutes. 'I would like to call the meeting closed at seven fifty.' He stood up and the room filled with the sound of chairs scraping against wooden floorboards as everyone else rose. Standing whenever the High Magus was on his feet in the Council Chambers was important etiquette.

They all waited for him to exit the room before collecting their belongings and leaving.

After saying goodbye to Ross and Nora, Liam spoke in a hushed tone as he followed Alannah outside. 'You shouldn't take your place for granted Lana. Kieran could easily step down into your seat if you keep pissing him off.'

She huffed. 'I doubt he'd be willing to give up his position of power. That said, it's not like I'm actively trying for top spot on his shit list. He's never liked me and my being on the Council is enough to make him hate me. Besides, it's not my fault that bugger-all mages practice necromancy in this area.'

Pausing when they reached the car, Liam sighed. 'I know. But you could at least try to pay attention to the rest of the business.' He unlocked the car but waited for her.

'Why? It's pointless paper pushing. Where's the real action?' She slumped into the passenger seat.

He dropped into the driver's side and shook his head. 'I warned you it wouldn't be all fun and games. I get as much admin work as a police officer, if not more sometimes.'

'The whole bloody system needs reforming. When I become High Magus, my first order of business will be to liven up those damn meetings.'

'I hate to burst your bubble, yet again, but you know that'll never happen. They would never allow a woman to head up the Council.'

'Never say never, sweetheart. I will get there or die trying. Once I get my fourth and fifth attunements, it's game on.'

They rode the remaining two blocks from the Town Hall to their seaside terrace house in silence. Council meetings were long and draining, and neither of them felt up to walking on such nights. Getting home to eat and sleep were the priority.

Being in a solid relationship for years made the decision to purchase their own home together easy. While Alannah had an extensive list of requirements, Liam only had two criteria: a place in town close to work and easy access to the ocean. Even with all his responsibilities to the Council and the police force, her boyfriend lived and breathed the surf. It took them a while to find somewhere suitable, so it was like a dream come true when this place became available almost a year ago.
Liam groaned at the sight of his brother's Jag as they pulled into the driveway. She could not blame

him. Alannah understood Liam's moods and anyone's company, other than her own, was the last thing he wanted to deal with when exhausted. But she did not mind. Spending time with her best friend and cousin, Brendan, was exactly what she needed to lift her spirits.

'Dagnammit!' Brendan jumped at the sound of the front door slamming, cursing as he dropped a serving spoon on his foot. He had almost finished laying everything out on the dining table for dinner. *At least I wasn't holding a plate!*

Liam stormed into the open-plan living area and threw his keys at the kitchen bench. 'Don't you have a home of your own?'

'Well hello to you too, bro.' Brendan still lived with his parents on their country estate, and while the privacy of the guest house was great for taking chicks home, on school nights he much preferred the convenience of a place to crash in town, especially one Alannah lived in. Pushing past the grumpy sack, he placed the rogue piece of cutlery in the dishwasher and grabbed a replacement from the drawer. 'And is that any way to talk to your chef?'

After casting a cursory glance at the plastic containers on the table, Liam turned his scowling face back to Brendan. 'Unless you're now moonlighting as a Chinese chef at the local take-away, I doubt you can claim any credit.'

He smacked Liam hard on the shoulder blade. 'Well, you're welcome.' Turning aside from his ungrateful brother, he grinned at Alannah and drew her into a hug. 'Hey, gorgeous, how's life?'

When they stepped out of the embrace, she gave him one of her award-winning smiles. 'Mostly good. Although I came close to dying of boredom and frustration in that meeting. I need a drink. You guys want one?' She approached the bar fridge.

'I can't. I have an early start tomorrow,' Liam complained.

Brendan returned to the table and took a seat. 'I'll have a pale ale, thanks, Lana.' He also had work the next day, but a couple of beers wouldn't be a problem for his job as school counsellor.

Alannah handed Brendan the drink in a stubby holder and sat across from him. Reaching forward, she clinked the tip of her own bottle with his. 'Cheers.' She took a huge swig of her drink. *Damn, that woman makes drinking beer look sexy.* Returning her gaze to him, she smiled again. 'So, how's work and stuff treating you?'

'Same old, same old. Work's not bad, but the ol' social life could use some more excitement.' He took the opportunity to check her out while she filled her plate. He liked Alannah's new habit of wearing her long black hair in a half ponytail. It reminded him of Katie McGrath as Morgana.

Sitting back, she gave him an impish grin. 'Social life, or sex life?'

'Both, but you're right, I do need to get laid soon. How's tomorrow night looking for you?'

She snorted before turning on the smoulder. 'I'll check my calendar.'

Liam growled as he pointed his chopsticks at Brendan. 'I know the flirting is part of your stupid game, but please spare me. I'm not in the mood to put up with your bullshit.'

Brendan had gone to serious lengths to assure his brother there was nothing going on with him and Alannah, after messing up and almost kissing her five years ago. He even managed to convince Alannah he was not interested in a relationship with her. As much as it pained him, especially when Alannah first expressed interest, it was for the best. He reasoned he would end up hurting her. Not to mention getting a major arse whooping from Liam—almost one-hundred kilos of pure muscle with perfect aim when rapid firing lightning bolts—not someone whose bad books you wanted to be in.

He narrowed his eyes at Liam. 'Right, 'cause your mood is the only one that matters. I was trying to cheer up Lana.' As an enchanter attuned to emotions, Brendan could tell Alannah felt miserable. He could sense it through his empathic link.

Rising from his chair, Liam grabbed his plate and glanced at Alannah. 'I'm taking this to bed. I'll see you there later.'

'Okay, night.'

He leaned in and pecked her on her cheek. 'Night.'

The tension in the room lifted and Alannah heaved a huge sigh as though breathing freely for the first time in hours.

'What got up his arse and died?' Brendan asked.

'Well aside from his mundane work being relentless, High Magus Kieran got snarky with me tonight. I know that gets to him. And I didn't help matters when I zoned out again.'

He laughed. 'I don't envy you, Lana. Those meetings sound like a big waste of time.'

She went quiet for a few minutes and toyed with her food. Biting her lip, she gazed up at him. 'Maybe you should look at renting a place in town. As much as I love having you here, the frequency of your visits is wearing at Liam's patience. He can't relax when you're here this often.'

'That man can't relax properly full stop.' He sucked a noodle into his mouth and sighed. 'But you're right. I'll start searching this weekend.'

Stretching her arm across the table, she placed a hand over his. The warmth of her touch sent a jolt of pleasure through his nerves. 'Hey, you are still welcome here and I'll drop in to see you. If you have your own place, we could both escape Liam's moods.'

'I know. I guess it's time I grew up and cut the apron strings.'

Humour returned to Alannah's visage. 'Just don't grow up too much. I love your carefree attitude.'

A hearty laugh escaped his throat. 'Trust me, that'll never happen. I'm a playboy for life, remember?'

'Right.' Her fingers were still resting on the back of his hand and he perceived their rough pads brushing against his skin. Hours of sewing every week for years had produced callouses on the tips of her otherwise soft hands. The sensation was strangely erotic.

Flipping his wrist, he grabbed her hand as he stared into her eyes and probed her mind. Brendan knew he should not invade her private thoughts, not only for the immorality of it, but because knowing the truth would be futile either way. But he could not help himself.

She grinned, but there were no thoughts suggesting she wanted him. Only the usual '*I'm not gonna let him win.*' Over the past few years Alannah had become a lot better at Sleazy Chicken, a flirtatious game they started playing at the age of six, although he still won most times.

Rising to his feet, Brendan pulled her up against his chest and planted soft kisses along her arm, running from her hand towards her neck. He watched her face for signs of blushing. There was no hint of colour in her cheeks as she gave him bedroom eyes that made his blood rush. It was just as well he was able to magically control his erections; else he might give away his true feelings.

Closing in on her shoulder, he could no longer see her face when she drew an audible breath. 'Stop. You win.'

A wicked grin formed on his face when he stepped back to look at her. 'The reigning champion keeps his crown.'

'You will have to give it up to me one day.'

'Oh, I promise I'll give it to you one day, Lana. I'll give it to you real hard.' He winked at her, seized his beer, and chugged down the rest of the bottle.

After tiptoeing across the bedroom floor, avoiding the squeaky floorboards, Alannah slipped into bed alongside Liam's sleeping form. He looked handsome beyond compare when asleep, the stress and fatigue gone from around his eyes.

Liam must have sensed her presence, despite her best efforts to avoid disturbing his sleep, because he snuggled in closer to her. The moment their bodies connected, he groaned and his eyes flittered open. The bright moon peeking through a slit in the curtains was the only light illuminating the room, but it was enough to reveal the features of his face. He smiled. 'Hey gorgeous.'

'Sorry for waking you.' Although Alannah was secretly glad she did, still feeling horny after the game of Sleazy Chicken.

'You're the one person who doesn't ever need to apologise for that.' His deep voice was raspy from sleep and it heightened her arousal. 'I love you, Lana. You are the most incredible woman to walk this earth and I feel blessed to call you mine.'

Her heart melted at his words. Rendered speechless, she inhaled sharply and claimed his mouth with a heated kiss. Before long she straddled Liam's naked body, grinding against his pelvis. Her hands skated along his muscular arms as she immersed herself in the addictive sweet and salty taste of his mouth.

After making out for ten minutes, Liam rolled them sideways and fell back asleep. Alannah sighed, another typical weeknight, with Liam exhausted after work and mage commitments. She would be calling on her rabbit again soon.

Brendan beelined through the front bar of Doyle Dougherty's, the only pub in Gaeilge Shores, and found his mates in a booth. It was Friday, the night following his dinner at Alannah's. Ben and Nick were arm wrestling, giving the girls around them a show of bulging tatted muscles. Connor had an arm wrapped around Amy, whispering sweet nothings in her ear. Bailey and Caleb were showing each other memes and sharing metalcore music on their smart phones. And Cara sat in Jacob's lap, sucking his face off. *Yup, business as usual. Except someone was missing.*

Bailey looked up as Brendan approached. 'Hey, Brendo. How ya doin', man?' He extended his hand out for a fist bump.

'Okay, I guess. What's up with you all? And where's Bianca?' He slid down next to Caleb, an endarkened fae and the only member of their group to have more piercings than Brendan. Caleb gave him a silent nod before vaping some sweet-smelling herbal stuff.

Jacob came up for air a moment later, giving Brendan an impish grin. 'Didn't you hear? Bianca has a dark cabaret band now. They're rehearsing tonight.' The red-headed boggart had become his best mate in the years following the death of Lachlan Munroe. The goofy goblin had been Jacob's closest friend at school and losing him in their battle with Tara Winters had been heartbreaking for all his crew. The passing of Austin Pearce, Brendan's previous bestie, also contributed their growing bond. Although Austin was dead to Brendan when he date raped Alannah.

'Yeah, they are gearing up for a regular spot at some cabaret lounge in Adelaide,' added Bailey.

'Oh? This is all news to me.' *How am I the last to hear about all this?*

Nick, the punkish orc, tittered. 'I guess you guys are always too busy boning to talk about her side hustle.'

While true to some extent, it was not like they *never* talked. But it had been a few months since he had invited Bianca to his bed. He did not want to give her the wrong impression, even if she was the best lay he could get in town. Commitment was a dirty word to Brendan in most cases. Leaning back into the seat, he sighed. 'I guess I'll have to hook up with a human tonight.' Brendan did not mind human girls, but they did lack the magical talents of a nymph like Bianca.

'Well Chelsea's had her eye on you since you arrived.' Ben directed his head of long, caramel coloured hair towards the table of girls a few metres away. The weredingo's attention shifting to that group of girls did not surprise Brendan. Ben's reputation as a man-whore was almost as notorious as Brendan's.

Brendan shook his head. 'Been there, done that too many times. I need a challenge. I want more excitement in my life.'

'What about her?' Ben's gaze travelled to the door where a stunning woman with long black hair entered. Legs reaching the sky were on display beneath a short black skirt. She completed her outfit with a purple brocade corset and silver necklace. Her curvaceous figure alone took Brendan's breath away. The moment he looked up at her face, he found himself drawn into her eyes. As dark as night and outlined with purple makeup, they scanned the room. Peering through the veil of her glamour, he glimpsed pointy ears lined with silver studs from lobe to tip. *Most likely fae and her dark colouring suggests unseelie.*

'Son of a gun!' Caleb's eyes widened, as though he had seen a ghost.

As if hearing Caleb's muttered curse, the woman turned her attention to their group and grinned, eyes darting to each of them before settling on Caleb. She advanced and Brendan felt Caleb trembling beside him. Reaching the booth, she scrutinised Caleb as she spoke in a deep, rich voice, 'Hello, Brother dearest.'

Also By L. Starla

The Phoebe Braddock Books
(Taboo romance)
I Heart Mr. Collins
From Prying Eyes
Crystal's Crucible
Undeniably Wrong

Winter's Magic Series
(Urban fantasy / paranormal romance)
Winter's Maiden 1
Winter's Maiden 2
Winter's Thrall
Winter's Mother 1
Winter's Mother 2
Winter's Bride (TBA)
Winter's Crone 1 (TBA)
Winter's Crone 2 (TBA)

Acknowledgements

Many thanks to my editors Jason and Felix for your tireless efforts.

A special thanks to my beta readers for providing such helpful feedback on this book: Ariel Mareroa, Amanda Mashburn, Breen Rodriguez, Elli Morgan, Hayley McKenna, and Maria Varley.

And a huge shout out to all my launch team and ARC readers for your reviews and for sharing this book with the world.

About the Author

Laelia Starla is an Australian author who was often found raiding her mother's shelves for any form of fiction she could get her hands on. Her first love was the horror genre, but she owes her love affair with the romance novel to her high-school English teacher, who got her hooked on the classics. Given her earlier reading, urban fantasy and paranormal romance seemed like a natural progression. Along with erotic romance, these have become her favourite genres to write.

Laelia also loves spending her spare time playing tabletop and video games, paper crafting, singing, dancing, and watching anime.

Access Exclusive Content

Join my newsletter to access free stuff like short stories, deleted scenes, fan art, and invitations to future launch events.

Newsletter: www.starlaarts.com>freebies

Follow me Online:
Website & Blog: www.starlaarts.com
Goodreads: 19660804.L_Starla
BookBub: www.bookbub.com/profile/l-starla
Amazon Author Profile: author/l.starla
Instagram: lstarlaauthor
Facebook: StarlaArts